CAUGHT IN THE HORIZON

EVERY NEW BEGINNING MEANS SOMETHING MUST END

J.L. Schaffer

First edition August 2024
Second edition June 2025 by Get It Write Publishing Company

Printed in the United States of America
ISBN: 979-8-9993421-0-2

TABLE OF CONTENTS

CHAPTER 1

"When everything is wrong, nothing seems right."
– Kannon

"Two years wasted, every dime I had spent, but I'll be famous tomorrow when everyone picks up their newspapers. I might even make the front page. Imagine me on the front page," the young man remarks to himself while sitting on the hood of the car with his head buried in his hands. His little car sits in the middle of a small clearing on top of a knoll overlooking the small town of Hidden Bridge. The darkness begins to approach as the sun slowly creeps out of sight. Crickets begin to awake with the sounds of chirping. The streetlights from the little town below begin to turn on one after the other. They are joined by random fireflies and a sky full of stars. It's quite a peaceful sight. A limb from a small tree beside the car hangs just overhead, blocking some of the night sky. A slight breeze rustles the leaves of the tree as if they are trying to speak to the young man. He seems as if he isn't listening to the sounds around him. He is lost in thought as the night begins to surround him.

He pulls his phone out of his hoodie pocket and stares at it. With the phone not on, he can somewhat see his reflection in the screen.

The young man speaks to his phone, talking to his reflection. "Well, Kannon, here we are, alone still." He clicks the power button and the phone turns on, revealing a picture of Kannon standing in a tuxedo with a beautiful girl in a wedding gown. Kannon speaks to the picture. "Awe, my beautiful Dayne. Today marks our third anniversary." Kannon slowly wipes a tear from his eye and continues. "We were high school sweethearts. We agreed this would last forever. Where are you?"

The picture does not respond. Kannon reaches into the other pocket of his hoodie and pulls out an old newspaper clipping. He opens it, revealing a picture of Dayne dimly lit by his cell phone. The article written beneath the picture states, "Girl gone missing December 4, 2020, from a small town of Hidden Bridge. Last seen around 11 a.m. on Niles Road. If anyone has any information, please contact the Hidden Bridge sheriff."

Kannon just stares at the picture, even after the light from the phone turns off. "We were only married for two months, and you vanished. You were supposed to start college in the spring. I just got my dream job at the newspaper. We were on our way to having it all." Once again, Kannon wipes a tear from the same eye as before. He begins to explain to the picture, "We've lost the house. I've exhausted all our savings, even the wedding money. The bank wants me to drop the car off tomorrow morning. I've used everything we had to find you. I have nothing left."

Kannon sits on the car hood, a broken man, exhausted, with no answer in sight. He only has the darkness and the stars above. He lays back and stares at the sky, watching the millions of stars. Kannon speaks softly while staring at the night sky.

"You'll never leave. I always know you'll be there every night."

A breeze begins to pick up as if it's answering Kannon. The crickets now sing louder, and, in the distance, a lone owl joins them. Every few seconds, Kannon holds his phone up as if, at any second, he will get an important call. Finally, Kannon speaks out into nothing and interrupts the cricket's song.

"I remember the first time I saw you in that wedding dress—your big smile from under that veil. I knew any second I was going to see the most beautiful girl I'd ever laid eyes on. The only thought that raced in my mind was, 'There's no possible way any man could be as lucky as me.' I had won in life; nothing could ever destroy this moment."

Kannon stops talking and flips through all the pictures on his phone. Every flick he makes brings a bigger smile to his face. "I know you're out there. You'd never leave me here all alone. I will find you, and once again, we'll be forever." But, after a few more pictures, his happiness turns back to sadness as his voice begins to crack a little. "The only thing I have is you. I need nothing else. Please come back to me. . . Please?" Tears now roll down his face from both eyes.

Slowly, the crickets begin to sing once again to him. Kannon's face changes from sadness to anger as he speaks to the darkness again. "If I don't have you, I've lost everything. Nothing else matters. I need you, Dayne."

Kannon covers his eyes with both arms and collapses onto the car's windshield. After a few more tears, Kannon wipes his eyes with his hoodie sleeves and stares at the stars with part of the tree limb swaying in his view. Then, out of nowhere, he begins to yell at the stars as if addressing the entire universe.

"Why? Why don't you want me to be happy? Why take my everything from me?" He pauses for just a second. "What have I ever done to you?" Kannon's voice breaks back to a low tone. "You're supposed to love us…and watch over us."

Tears are now running down his face at a much quicker pace. With blurred sight, all the stars seem to become one. Kannon folds his arms over his stomach as if his stomach hurts.

He softly murmurs, "Why don't you love me? Why would you take Dayne? You're supposed to love us." Kannon rolls to his side as if he didn't want stars to look at him.

The breeze of the night air rustles the leaves above him as if they are trying to console Kannon. He taps his phone, and a picture of Dayne appears again. "It's been almost three years since you left me here. Why didn't you take me with you? I'd travel this world and the next with you." Kannon sighs for a moment. "I love you; I miss you; I need you. Please help me find you. I can't do this on my own anymore." Kannon stops as if he expects Dayne to answer his question. He places the phone on the hood next to him and says, "I will not live here anymore without you."

His hands shake as he moves his head from side to side. "I will not give up on you. If I can't find you in this life, I'll look in the next. And then the next one after that until I find you and hold you once again."

Kannon slides down off the car hood and punches the hood in a fit of anger, leaving a crimson stain on his knuckles. He shakes the pain from his hand and walks around to the passenger door. Kannon presses his head against the passenger window, and the coolness of the window feels good for just a second. He reaches slowly and grabs the door handle, and you hear the click from the door opening. Kannon stares at the empty seat; he can almost picture Dayne sitting there. The image quickly vanishes as he sits down in the seat. Leaving the door open, Kannon reaches for the glove compartment and opens it. The small light inside emits enough light to see the contents.

Kannon reaches into the compartment and pulls out a small black box. He holds it between his thumb and finger, spinning it with his other fingers. Kannon shuts the glove box, leaving him in darkness once again. He sits for a few minutes, spinning the small box in his hand and looking at it as if it is going to speak to him.

Then Kannon exits the car, leaving the door open, and walks back to the front of the car, still twirling the box.

"Is this what you want?!" he cries. "Is this more important to you than I am?"

Tears once again begin running down his face, this time uncontrollably. The wind picks up and rustles the leaves, trying to answer Kannon. He holds the box up as if he wants the wind to take it from him. As he holds the box high enough for the moonlight to show its silhouette, it reveals itself as a ring box.

Kannon yells to the stars once again. "You want this? You've taken everything else from me." A crazed look comes across Kannon's face. "Well, sorry, but you won't be getting this until you can take it from my cold dead hands." Anger replaces crazy. "This is Dayne's! When we meet again, I will put it back on her finger. You will not take this from me today; I guarantee it." Kannon squeezes the small box as he falls to his knees in front of the car, looking and feeling completely defeated. Slowly, he begins to whisper as if running out of breath. "Please, please, please give her back to me. She's mine, not yours."

Kannon squeezes the box even harder, causing the box to pop open and reveal an empty box. Kannon's face drops as he desperately begins frantically feeling around on the ground. "No, no, no, no. I told you that you couldn't have it. It's not yours! It's hers."

He is sobbing to the point where he can no longer see through the tears and pulling gobs of grass and dirt. "It's hers! You can't have it! You can't have it! It's not yours!" Kannon frantically searches until he's so exhausted he lies in a pile of pulled grass and dirt, broken, beaten, and speechless, still clenching onto the small box. The ring is lost in this world, just as his Dayne is.

Kannon drops the empty ring box to the ground beside him. He reaches up to the hood, grabs his phone, and sits back beside the ring box. Flicking through his phone, he gets back to their wedding photo.

"I'm sorry. I'm so sorry. I did everything I possibly could do in this world, but I still couldn't find you." He pauses for a moment. "Maybe in the next one, I will find you, my love." Kannon reaches down into his hoodie pocket and pulls out an object that fits his hand. He points it to the stars. "You win in this world, but I'll find her. Don't think for one minute that I'll stop looking for her. Even you can't stop something this powerful."

Wind now shakes the tree as if it's trying to stop Kannon.

Kannon brings the object down to his chest, right to the location of his heart. With no emotion on his face, he looks to the stars. "This story is not ending; it's just beginning."

"Click."

One sound that could be heard. No crickets, no wind, and an eerie feeling fill this hillside. Kannon looks down at the object pointing at his heart. "Click" rings through the air once again. He raises the object to inspect it. In the moonlight, it makes the silhouette of a pistol. Kannon checks to see if it's loaded. It is full, so why didn't it work? Kannon points the pistol to the stars, and one of the stars begins to fall, followed by another and another. One by one, they continue to drop out of the sky. Kannon, now puzzled, points the pistol to his chest and pulls the trigger again.

"Click." Nothing happens.

Kannon is confused. The stars continue to fall as Kannon

yells to the few that are left. "You can't even give me this?!" Kannon turns and throws the pistol into the darkness. He begins punching the car hood with both fists. He can feel them getting wet with blood, but even the pain can't stop him.

Then, out of the corner of his eye, Kannon catches a light off into the distance. His curiosity gets to him as he walks towards the little light. As he approaches the light, he notices a door in the middle of nowhere. Kannon looks the door over and walks around it, but there is nothing. It is just an old door standing in the middle of a field.

He grabs the doorknob, and the light turns off, which startles Kannon, causing him to let go of the doorknob. As he does, the light comes back on. Now, Kannon is more intrigued with the door. He grabs the doorknob and cracks the door open a little, and the light turns off again. Kannon looks up to the stars to see if ropes are holding the door up, but there is nothing.

He also notices there are no more stars in the sky. How curious. Looking back at the door, Kannon pushes it, and it opens, but he can't see anything on the other side. It is totally black. Kannon turns the flashlight on his phone and slowly steps into the doorway. It is dark even with the light from the phone.

As Kannon crosses the threshold, he feels a change rush through him, which gives him cold chills down his arms. Something doesn't feel right. Kannon turns to leave, but the door slams shut, leaving him trapped, the darkness beginning to overwhelm him.

CHAPTER 2

"Every new beginning means something has ended."
– Kannon

Kannon wakes to bright, warm sun rays hitting him in the face. He squints his eyes until they adjust to the warm light. Kannon stands and brushes off the grass and dirt from his backside. He stretches and tries to shake the sleep off. Nothing looks familiar. He has no idea where he is. But it is gorgeous out. Kannon wonders how it can be this beautiful out and not a bird or animal in sight, as it seems to be too peaceful. Kannon's first thought is he is in heaven. Just then, he notices a park bench in the middle of a freshly mowed hay field. Kannon makes his way towards the bench as the smell of freshly cut grass fills the air, bringing him back to when he was a kid on his grandpa's farm. As he reaches the bench, it seems to be nothing but an old bench that desperately needs a painting job. Kannon sits down, thinking to himself, *Why is there a park bench in the middle of a country field? It makes no sense.* He takes in the view of the incredible landscape surrounding him.

Now sitting on the bench, Kannon lays back with his arms crossed over his face, just basking in the sun's warmth. Peacefully, Kannon lays there, contemplating his next move.

Suddenly, out of nowhere, a kind voice speaks. "Hello. Is this seat available?"

Kannon jumps back, startled, as he almost goes over the arm of the bench. "Who are you? Where did you even come from?" Kannon yells with disbelief on his face.

"Oh, hey there. Let me introduce myself. I'm Jim with a J," the little old grinning man replies.

"Well, Jim with a J, where the hell did you come from?" Kannon asks, still puzzled.

Jim chuckles. "I'm from here."

"You're from here? Where is *here?*"

Jim happily states, "Well, this is the great Horizon, of course; where else would it be?"

"So, we're in the great Horizon?" Kannon states, very confused.

"The great Horizon is the most beautiful place. Have you ever just stood on a hill and stared off as far as the eye can see? That is the Horizon. The Horizon is where the land meets the sky," Jim replies, snickering. After a little back and forth with Kannon, Jim begins to explain. "This bench is here for you whenever you need a safe place or need help with your objective. You come here and I would love to talk to you and assist as much as I possibly can. I love having guests."

"So, this is a safe place?" Kannon points at the bench.

"Why yes, Sir Kannon. This is your safe place. As a matter of fact, every park bench you see is your safe place." Jim smiles then continues. "No one but me can see you or hear you when you're on a park bench."

Kannon is so confused; he just looks at Jim with a puzzled expression. Jim slides back on the bench, dangling his feet. "Maybe I should start from the beginning."

"I really think you should," Kannon states.

"It all started in a place called Hidden Bridge. In this world of Hidden Bridge, there were four mighty kings who ruled and protected this realm. They are the deciders. They are kind, caring and generous. They had quite an important job. Maybe one of the most important jobs ever. For it is up to them to decide whether you become a star or remain here in the Horizon until your time is up and you earned the right to become a star."

Kannon butts in. "A star? What do you mean you become a star?"

"Well yeah, when you're done with that life, barring any circumstances, you become a star, and the kings place you in the sky to watch over your friends and family."

"So, this is where people go. When they pass from my world, they are sent in front of the kings," Kannon pretty much repeats Jim.

"Not just people, but all living things. When they arrive at the Horizon, they must first meet the kings. If they've lived their life to the fullest, they become a star. If they arrive here before their time due to an accident, premature or by their own hands, they must finish their time out here."

"So, it's like heaven?" Kannon asks.

"No, nothing of the sort. To some, heaven is your final stop, but it can be difficult; not everyone refers to it as heaven. This is the Horizon, as I said before," Jim adamantly explains. "This is a beautiful, tranquil place until the Jokers showed up. The Jokers schemed a plan to capture every star and imprison them as a penumbra figure to do their bidding."

"What's a penumbra?"

Jim rolls his eyes. "A penumbra is a shadow you cannot see through."

"So why didn't you just say Shadows?"

Jim clears his throat and continues. "When the Jokers collected the stars, they turned them into soldiers and marched against the kings. The Jokers' forces were too much, and they overthrew the kings, imprisoning them." Jim stands and stretches, walking around the bench.

"Well? Then what?" Kannon prods.

Jim jumps back up on the bench to finish his story. "Well, the Jokers knew that as long as there were four kings, they'd continue to be strong enough to eventually beat the Jokers' army. So, they had their shadow minions attack the King of Saints and vanquish him to render the other kings powerless, for the kings only have strength if all four are present. The battle lasted three days, but as the kings were almost depleted of power, they mustered up enough power to pick the next king. When this new king is of age and strong enough, they will be able to try and regain their realm. But until then, they would also send five warriors. These warriors are the Horizon's last hope as the kings have been toppled."

"So, you think I'm one of these warriors."

Jim replies, "Why yes, that's why you were brought here before your time."

Kannon holds his hand out towards Jim, gesturing to him to stop. "Look, I'm no Warrior. Trust me, I'm far from a Warrior."

"Well, I'm sorry pal, but you were chosen, whether you like it or not." Jim states reluctantly.

Neither one knows what to say next. The conversation had gone from nice to awkward really fast.

Finally, Kannon asks, "What happened to the remaining three kings?"

Jim quickly replies, "Well, as the story would have it, the three kings were thrown into a deep hole to live out the rest of their days, guarded by elite penumbra."

"Really?"

The two men sit there, not knowing what to say to each other. Kannon thinks, *is this guy for real?*

After a few minutes, Kannon says, "How do I defeat these Jokers and the legion of penumbra under their control?"

Jim begins to pace back and forth. "Well, you must release the light that lies trapped inside each shadow so they can rise to the sky and fill the night sky with stars once again. These Shadows are starring the Jokers ripped from the night sky. All Shadows hold a star; when defeated, their bodies vanish, and their light returns as a star. The star itself will return to its rightful spot in the empty night sky." Jim puts his right hand above his face on his forehead. "As far as the Jokers, I truly have no idea how to defeat them."

"If the kings couldn't do it, then how am I supposed to?" Kannon asks loudly.

With a puzzled look on his face, Jim says, "You must use a light source on the Shadows."

"Light source?"

"Yeah, if the Shadows encounter a decently bright light source, it will harden. They then can be attacked, and the light will be freed."

"So, I can't beat the Shadows unless they've hardened first?" Kannon is more confused than before.

"Well, if you don't harden them, you can't hurt them. Have you ever tried to step on or hit a shadow before? Doesn't work very well, does it?" Jim sarcastically replies. Then, without a breath, Jim continues. "When you defeat a hardened shadow, you will release their light within, and it will rise to the sky as the shadow vanishes into thin air."

"So, they are totally not there anymore?"

"Nope, there's nothing left. Just gone." Jim throws his hands in the air as if he had just finished a magic trick.

Kannon thinks for a bit and finally says, "Ok, then I should be taking off if I'm to rescue this world and the stars." Kannon stands up, not believing he's doing this. "It's been a pleasure speaking with you."

Jim puts his hand out to Kannon. "While you remove trapped souls, please keep an eye out for the whereabouts of the remaining kings. Look high and low; leave no stone unturned. We need the three kings so they can join the fourth and train him to right this wrong and return the Horizon to what it once is."

Kannon extends his hand and shakes Jim's. "So, I have no choice. You're sure I'm one of the warriors?"

Jim, shaking Kannon's hand, says, "Sorry, you have no choice."

Kannon turns away from Jim and begins to walk away. Jim yells suddenly like Kannon is far away. "Oh, one more thing. Be nice to the town folks and passersby you meet. It's not easy for them either!"

Kannon doesn't turn around but instead puts his thumb in the air in an "ok" signal, while reaching the end of the field. Still holding his thumb up, he turns to look at Jim, but he and the bench are gone. Kannon is standing in an empty field with his thumb up in the air.

Kannon lowers his thumb and stands at the edge of a freshly mowed field. He looks to his left and then his right, but there is nothing and no one. Just an empty field. Finally, Kannon resorts to his old videogame strategy—always going right first.

After walking through field after field for what seems like hours and feeling the whole time he is being watched, he decides to stop and rest for a few minutes to catch his breath. But with the day coming to an end in a few hours, he doesn't rest long and continues toward the right. The sun slowly descends. Dusk now setting in, Kannon finally stumbles onto an old dirt road. Knowing that it's probably not good to be out in the dark when you're hunting for Shadows, he decides he needs to find shelter sooner rather than later.

Kannon, now with the choice of left or right facing him again, notices what looks like another park bench off in the distance that resembles Jim's bench. As Kannon stumbles towards the bench, really needing a rest, an old lady carrying a basket of apples comes walking down the road towards him.

Kannon reaches the bench before the lady but remains standing as the lady approaches. Politely, Kannon asks, "Ma'am, would you like some help carrying those apples? They look heavy." Though he isn't sure he has the strength to carry them very far.

The lady stops and looks Kannon up and down. "No, thank you, Warrior. You must save your strength for what's to come." She then smiles and tosses a couple of apples to Kannon before continuing down the road. She suddenly stops and turns around. "If we don't meet again, Warrior, I thank you for what sacrifices you'll be making in the coming days."

Kannon doesn't answer; he just gives a wave back. Then he sits on the bench, feeling drained and hungry. He eats both apples as he watches the lady walk out of sight. With not much rest and the sky getting close to darkness, Kannon thinks he should probably find some shelter. He wonders if he should've followed the old lady, but it is too late now. Kannon thinks if the park bench is a safe place, maybe he should stay here for the night. Then he thinks better of it.

What am I, crazy? I'll be a sitting duck for Shadows out in the open like this.

As he begins to stand, he hears the old man's voice come again. "Well, well… That certainly took you a long enough. We aren't selling sunshine, and we aren't getting anything done with that dilly-dallying!"

Kannon, now tired and a little temperamental, replies, "Well, it would've been nice if I had any clue or inkling of where I was going or even what I was supposed to do."

Jim polishes the arm of the bench and says, "I need to catch you up to speed, sunshine." Kannon is not amused. "I know it's dark, and you're hungry and exhausted," Jim hurries to continue, "but if you would, I'm going to have you take a look over your back right shoulder."

A hedgerow appears right behind the bench as Kannon turns and almost sticks his face into the large bush.

"Use your hands to make an opening," Jim instructs, making a motion like he's pulling apart curtains. He quickly adds, "But please don't leave the bench area, and I'll show you why you're here."

Kannon turns and kneels for a better look. He pushes the hedgerow apart, which reveals what the old man had wanted him to see. He pulls the bushes apart enough to see a crowd of penumbra gathering in the middle of a small town square.

Kannon jumps back, quickly closing the bush.

"Don't worry," Jim quickly assures Kannon. "As long as you're on the bench, you're safe from everything. Relax, and please continue to watch." The man gestures over again to the hedgerow.

Reluctantly, Kannon peers through the hedgerow again. In the distance, he spots a small sign stating, "Welcome to our beautiful Town of Hoyle." The crowd of Shadows grows until you can't see anything but Shadows. Then, as if they know Kannon is watching, the shadow spreads apart like a stage curtain to reveal three big older men on their knees in the center of the town, as if they are being judged. The men look as if they have been beaten to within an inch of their lives. Blood trickles down their faces. They are broken and beaten. Three crowns lay on the ground in front of the defeated men. Kannon thinks they must be the three kings Jim had spoken of.

Two slim figures step out from the crowd of Shadows. They are dressed in suits that look as if the two were born in them. The suits seem to be part of them. They begin to dance around the damaged kings as one of them kicks a crown over. Silence fills the air, and the kings act as if they are looking right through the two Jokers and directly at Kannon—so much so that one of the Jokers turns to look behind him to see what the kings ae looking at.

Finally, one of the Jokers says, "*Soo,* this is what's left of the mighty, indestructible kings?"

The other one jumps in. "Don't look so mighty now, do you?"

The two turn and smile at each other before one says, "Sorry, but it seems as if one of you couldn't make it."

The other Joker tosses a crown on the ground in front of the kings. Then both begin dancing and humming once again.

One of the kings speaks up, interrupting the two, stopping them in their tracks. "You are pure evil. Why would you slay one of your kings?"

One of the Jokers leans toward the king. "One of my kings?"

The other Joker jumps in even louder. "One of my kings? You, sir, are not one of my kings. Would a king be kneeling looking all old and broken?"

"If you're a king, then where's your crown?"

The other Joker kicks the crown from in front of the man. "Would a king look this bad?"

One pats the head of the king as if he is petting a dog. The king quickly jerks away, which startles the Joker, as he pulls his hand back. The Jokers lean over, one on each ear of the king, and take turns whispering, "Just be glad it wasn't you who perished." And the other one adds, "Because I really wanted it to be you."

Then, they once again pat the king on the head and begin dancing.

Kannon cannot believe what he has seen; the disrespect is way over the top. But he never takes his eyes off the kings throughout this whole ordeal. As the other Shadows begin dancing as well, as if they are at a celebration, one of the other kings speaks.

"Then why don't you just kill us all and get it over with, cowards?"

The partiers stop dancing, and one of the Jokers approaches the loud king. The Joker then once again leans over to the loud king and whispers, "Kill you? Why would we kill you? And send you up there?" He slowly looks up at the blue sky then back at the king with a smile on his face. "We're thinking more in terms of putting you down there." He points to a big hole in the ground behind the king. "We figure we might as well put our pets in the hole over there. We'll let you kings dispose of each other, and the last one left can be our own personal pet." He pats the king on the head once again.

The Jokers look at each other and begin to hysterically laugh. "Kinda like a memento of this special occasion."

They once again begin to hum and dance. But the celebration soon ends when one of the Jokers picks up the crowns. "I'm bored of this; let's just toss the old crowns in the hole with these old men." He tosses the crowns into the hole and gestures to the Shadows to grab the first king. The Shadows wrestle the king over to the opening of the hole. Then, as the Joker pushes the king into the hole from behind, he shouts, "Don't forget to write!"

The king vanishes with a thud following soon behind.

"Oh no, I hope he didn't damage the crowns," Jokers

snickers, then turns to the next king. "Well, big boy, looks like you're next. Probably wish you had wings."

The Shadows wrestle the second king to the hole and push him in. The third king states, "We will return. You should kill us now before the new king rises and we regain our powers."

The Jokers smile and wave as the Shadows push the third king into the hole. They lean over the hole only to see darkness in the depth of it.

One of the Jokers yells, "When the new king arrives, we'll be sure to introduce you guys to him." The Jokers laugh and begin to walk away.

A voice from behind the Shadows rings out. "The warriors are here, the new king will rise, and a new day will come." Ringing through the crowd, the voice repeats itself. "The warriors are here, the new king will rise, and a new day will come."

The crowd of Shadows part to reveal the old lady who had given Kannon the apples.

A Joker yells, "Turn this hag into a shadow!"

The Shadows proceeds to consume her, and just like that, she is gone—transformed into just another shadow.

The Jokers look at each other. "What warriors?" They turn and look in Kannon's direction.

Kannon quickly jumps back from the bush, not wanting to be seen.

Jim reassures him. "Don't worry, they can't see you while you're on the bench. It's a safe place."

"But they looked right at me. And that poor lady… We should've done something."

"Well, trust me, they didn't see you. What you just watched is what we call a flashback. All this happened over two weeks ago. Like I said, this is a safe place." Jim once again reassures

Kannon.

"I just saw the old lady an hour ago." Kannon's confusion is evident.

Jim replies, "No, you didn't." He continues to clean the bench.

Kannon, confused even more now, says, "I'm no Warrior; you have the wrong guy."

Jim looks at Kannon. "Oh, but you are the Warrior. You have the Warrior's mark." Jim points to Kannon's right hand. Kannon pulls up his hoodie sleeve to reveal a mark on his arm that looks like a 'W' tattoo with a crown above it. "This is the royal seal," Jim explains. "You are one of the five warriors. You must find the other four and destroy the Shadows and the Jokers." Jim points down the dirt road. "Your destination awaits you in the next town."

Kannon stands up from the bench to look in the direction Jim pointed. Then, Jim and the bench are gone, leaving Kannon standing alone on the side of the road.

Kannon begins to walk down the dark road. "You're no hero. What do you know about saving people? You couldn't even save Dayne, or, for that matter, yourself," he mutters softly.

With the darkness surrounding him, and no idea where he's heading, Kannon decides to crash for the night. He hides in a high patch of grass that will hopefully keep him from being detected by the Shadows till daylight. As he begins to doze off, an image of the beaten kings appears.

"You are the one to lead; they will follow you into battle."

Kannon jumps awake only to be alone. "Wow, you might be losing it, ole boy." Then slumber finds him just as quickly.

CHAPTER 3

"First Round's on Me." – Hunter

Once again, Kannon wakes to a sunny, warm morning. "Is this place always beautiful?" he marvels.

The high grass he slept in is not that comfortable, and his neck is killing him. Kannon climbs to his feet and tries his best to stretch his neck pain out. With a big yawn, he wipes sleep from his eyes and tries to compose himself.

I'm definitely not in my Hidden Bridge anymore, he thinks.

Then he stretches once more and is ready to begin the day and whatever the journey brings.

Kannon continues in the direction Jim had insisted he go. While walking, he comes upon the largest blackberry bush he has ever encountered. The blackberries on the bush are the size of a cantaloupe. Kannon picks two berries, one for each hand. Since it is breakfast time, and he is starving, he dives into one face-first. He doesn't know if it is because he is starving, but the berries are the best he's ever tasted. By the time Kannon finishes the second berry, his face is covered in berry juice. Even though the berries were filling, Kannon figures why not just one more, and he reaches up to grab another. Just as he reaches the biggest one on the bush, a young boy comes skipping by him.

Suddenly, he stops and looks at Kannon, who has berry juice on his face. The boy begins to laugh. "Good morning, sir. It's a beautiful day, isn't it?"

Kannon knows he looks ridiculous with berry juice on his

face, but he tries to be courteous. Well, as courteous as you can be with a mouth full of berries. "Good morning to you as well. Would you like a blackberry?" Kannon holds a berry out to the boy.

Without hesitation, the boy snatches the berry out of Kannon's hand. "I thought you'd never ask," the boy giggles. The boy seems to be as hungry as Kannon is and soon devours the offering.

For a few minutes, neither speak as they are too focused on their breakfast. Then, with both faces stained and covered in berry juice, Kannon shoves the last piece of berry into his mouth.

"Names Kannon. What's yours?"

The small boy wipes his mouth with his arm and hand. "My name is Dak." He puts his hand out, which is the same one he just wiped his mouth with.

"Pleased to meet you. You could say I'm new around here." Kannon reaches his hand out and shakes the boy's. After pulling his hand away, Kannon wipes his hand off on his hoodie. As he does, the boy catches a glimpse of the mark on Kannon's hand.

"You have a crown mark on your hand. Are you a Warrior?" Dak excitedly asks.

Reluctantly, Kannon answers, "Well, I guess. But I'm not so sure about that."

Dak clammers back, "Wow, I've never met an actual Warrior before today, and who would've thought I'd meet two in one day."

Kannon quickly grabs the boy's shoulders and looks him in the eyes. "You met another Warrior? Where? You must tell me; I need to speak to him immediately."

"In a town just up ahead, in a small tavern." Dak points in

the direction Kannon is already heading. Kannon continues. "Was it just recently?"

The boy nods his head. "Yeah, probably about an hour ago. But I ran away from town because Shadows were everywhere and they're bad news. Everyone knows that."

"Shadows *are* bad news. You are right about that." Kannon tries to calm Dak down.

Dak's voice gets a little shaky. "Plus, my mom said to stay away from them. Because if they see me, they will hurt me and throw me down the hole with the kings."

Kannon tries to console Dak. "That's why I'm here—to stop them from hurting anyone else." Even though Kannon has no idea what he is going to do, he is just as scared as Dak is, but he can't show it to the boy.

Dak turns to leave. "I better go tell my mom about the Shadows, plus she'll want me home for dinner.

"Yes, get home quickly. This is no place for a kid to be." Kannon stands, waving goodbye to Dak.

Dak runs down the path Kannon just came from. Just before he's out of sight, Dak turns back around and yells to Kannon, "It was awesome to meet you, Kannon—I mean, Warrior. Thanks for breakfast. I'll be sure to tell Mom about you. Be safe." Then he turns back and is soon out of sight.

As Kannon begins walking towards the town that Dak said was full of Shadows, he thinks, *What a nice, proper young boy. His parents must be so proud of him.*

After walking for about twenty minutes or so, Kannon comes to a road sign that reads, 'Welcome to our beautiful Town of Hoyle.' Kannon wonders where he has heard that name before. Then it hits him. It is the town he had seen in Jim's flashback.

"Oh no, I can't go there; it is crawling with Shadows. I'm

not ready for that." He stops in his tracks. Then he paces back and forth, trying to build up enough courage to make himself go. "You have to go help the other Warrior. They won't stand a chance." Finally, Kannon realizes he has no other choice in the matter. He needs the other Warrior as much as that Warrior needs him.

As Kannon approaches the little town, fear takes over, and he freezes. He looks down one street as far as he can, scouring the town. Then he realizes he is just standing out in the open; he is a sitting duck. So, Kannon backs into a hedgerow so he will not be seen so he can plan out his next move. Kannon's mind races: he is not made for this. He isn't a violent guy. He felt bad when he had to scold his puppy. *What am I going to face with a Joker, let alone a shadow? Also, what's with Jim's infatuation with park benches?* Finally, he comes to the conclusion that what's going to happen is going to happen, and there is no sense in prolonging it.

Kannon steps out from the hedge row and scampers to the first building he can reach. With his back against the building, he gently slides along it to the other end of the building. Kannon is surprised to see that the town is so lifeless. No people walking around, as all the businesses look run down and closed. Then he notices a flashing OPEN sign in the window of the tavern. He thinks someone in there might have seen the Warrior. After Kannon builds up some courage, he decides to make a run for the tavern. He crouches into a track starting position and takes off. But abruptly, he stops and dives back behind the building. Voices are coming from around the corner of the building. Praying the voices didn't see or hear him, he peeks around the corner to see if he can see who is talking.

The good thing is they didn't see him; the bad thing is that it is three Shadows, and they are in a heated argument. From what he can hear, it is a one-on-two argument. Kannon creeps around to get a better look and to make out what they are saying. As he gets closer, he can hear the whole conversation clear as a bell. The one shadow is pointing toward the tavern, saying, "I saw the Warrior go in there, and he is alone." Another says, "Let's go in and set his light free; the Jokers will surely reward us for that."

The two Shadows begin to rub their hands together as if they are going to get something. The lone shadow barks back at the two. "Wait, this Warrior is different from the rest."

They bark back, "What makes him so different?"

Lone responds, "This Warrior can release your light in either form, mist, or solid. They don't call him 'Hunter' for nothing."

The two Shadows gasp. "That's Hunter in there? Why didn't you say something? We need backup and fast."

Lone shadow agrees and sends the two off to get more backup while he stands guard to make sure the Warrior doesn't leave.

Kannon ducks back behind the corner and thinks, *I must help this Warrior; they are going to outnumber him and release his light. I must warn him and get him out of here before they get back with more Shadows.* I'm going to have to make a run for it. If I make it to the Warrior before the Shadows do, we'll have this one outnumbered.

Kannon quietly collects some stones to use as a diversion. He figures if he can toss the stones in the opposite direction, it will distract the shadow and get him to move farther away from the tavern. To give himself a bigger start, Kannon tosses the first stone, but the shadow doesn't even flinch since he is too focused on the tavern. Kannon starts to toss another stone but accidentally drops the handful he has. When he bends down to pick them up, he somehow steps on his own hand and tumbles out in the open. Kannon quickly jumps back behind the building, hoping the shadow is still focused on the tavern and has not seen him. But as Kannon's luck had it, the shadow did catch a glimpse of him.

The shadow rounds the corner as Kannon back peddles, searching his hoodie for something to defend himself with.

As the shadow closes in on Kannon, he says, "Looks like hunting season starts sooner than normal."

The only thing Kannon has in his pocket is his cell phone. He pulls it out and points it at the shadow, saying, "Stop, or I'll use my weapon on you."

The shadow laughs. "That's an iPhone 10. What, are you going to take my picture? Make sure you get my good side."

Just as the shadow reaches Kannon, the camera's flash goes off, blinding the shadow. It begins to change to a solid form, its feet change first, and the transformation works its way up its legs as the shadow winces in pain. Within a few seconds, the shadow is completely changed into a solid.

"What have you done to me? I will take your light for this. Say goodbye to this world as well. You'll make a good shadow."

As the shadow raises his hand to strike Kannon, a voice is heard behind him.

"Batter up!"

Then there is a clinking sound like a cheap bat hitting a baseball. The shadow falls in a pile at Kannon's feet, then light rises out of his body and floats up in the air as if a little kid lost his balloon at a fair.

Kannon looks back where the shadow once stood to see a smaller, young guy about eighteen or so standing with a baseball bat. The young guy looks at Kannon. "That dog won't hunt," he says and begins chuckling to himself. Then he reaches a hand down to Kannon to help him up off the ground.

When Kannon gets to his feet and brushes himself off, the kid helps him by brushing off Kannon's backside with his baseball cap. Kannon extends his hand to thank the young man.

"I appreciate the help. Name's Kannon."

Smiling, the young guy reaches out and shakes Kannon's hand. "Name's Bug; pleased to make your acquaintance."

Kannon, still brushing off a little, continues. "Boy, you don't know how happy I am to see you."

Bug laughs. "Yeah, I seem to get that a lot."

"How did you know hitting in the head with a bat is going to free his light?"

"I didn't, but I just figured I might as well get one good shot in before we got our asses beat."

The two begin laughing together before Bug says, "What brings you to this town, Kannon? I know it's not the nightlife."

Kannon smiles. "No, it's definitely not the nightlife. I'm looking for some people. Have you seen any other people by chance?"

"Nope. Just your pretty face." Bug is still joking.

"Well, thanks again for the help. I need to get going. There's a man in the tavern I need to see." Kannon points towards the tavern across the way.

"Well shoot, I'm pretty thirsty myself. Mind if I join you?"

Kannon shrugs his shoulders. "Sure, why not? The more the merrier."

So, the two cautiously venture over to the tavern. As they get to the tavern door, Bug gestures to Kannon to lead the way.

Kannon looks at Bug and says, "Here, let me get the door for you. It's the least I can do."

Bug quickly responds with, "I could never let you do that;

I'll get the door for you."

The two just stand at the tavern door, neither really wanting to go first in case it is full of unfriendliest.

"Well, this kind of crazy. One of us must go first," Bug states.

"True statement; I totally agree. I'll tell you what. You crack the door open and peek inside. If you think it looks good, I'll go in first," Kannon suggests.

"Why me?" Bug whispers.

"Because you have a bat, and I have a cell phone."

"Makes perfect sense. Can't really argue with that."

Bug leans toward the door, and just before he gets to it, he turns back towards Kannon. "Here, hold my bat. So, if I see that it's clear, you're going in first." Bug is just trying to get on the same page as Kannon, who holds the bat up behind Bug. Just as Bug realizes he gave Kannon the bat, Kannon pushes him through the tavern door and out onto the floor and closes the door behind Bug. Bug quickly stands up, hoping no one has seen him on the floor. Bug walks back out and starts yelling at Kannon as the two remain out on the tavern doorstep.

"What was that? Since I have the bat, I am supposed to peek in the door, and if it is clear, you would go in first."

"Correct, sorry for my mistake. Let's try it one more time. This time, you peek inside because you have the bat, and if it's clear, I'll bust through the tavern door," Kannon explains to Bug.

"That sounds more like it. Here, hold my bat." Bug hands Kannon his bat again and crouches down and cracks the tavern door open to see if it's clear for Kannon.

Kannon once again pushes Bug through the door and onto the tavern floor. Bug gets up a bit slower this time and walks back outside to Kannon. The bartender at the bar just shakes his head and continues to wipe the mugs. Bug is now a little upset with Kannon as he uses a louder tone to speak.

"What is that?"

"I am wondering the same thing. You said you wanted me to go first, and both times you barged in. I have an idea since yours didn't work. Why don't we walk in and sit at the bar and survey the place from our seats?"

"That sounds easy enough. I'm in."

The two walk into the tavern together and grab a seat at the bar. The tavern is very dimly lit, and the barkeep stands at the other end of the bar, washing beer mugs. He doesn't even acknowledge the pair at the other end. Tables and chairs are strewn all about, and a small pool table is sitting directly in the middle of the room. A small pool light hangs over it, and one of the bulbs is out. A tall, slender man stands at the pool table, playing all alone. He stops playing for just a second and glances up at the two, then gets right back to playing. Kannon and Bug watch the man shoot three games in a row, never missing a shot. He would run the table, rerack, and then run the table again. The man continues this repeatedly.

Bug turns to Kannon. "Do you think it kind of stinks here?"

Kannon nods. "Kind of like smoke and shattered dreams."

"Yeah, I smell smoke too," Bug agrees.

Kannon turns toward the barkeep and holds up a couple bucks. The barkeep completely ignores him.

Bug then yells to get his attention. "Barkeep, two beers pronto!"

The barkeep still makes no movement.

Bug says to Kannon, "I know he heard me."

Kannon gestures for the two to walk down to the other end by the bartender. As they approach the barkeep and sit down in front of him, he glances up quickly, then right back to his mugs.

"What'll it be, boys?"

Bug replies, "Two mugs of your finest ale, good sir."

Without looking up at the two, the barkeep fills two mugs from the tap and places them on the bar. "That'll be three bucks."

Kannon grabs a mug and walks away. "Pay the man, Bug."

Bug gives Kannon a dirty look and then pays the barkeep. Kannon walks to one of the filthy tables, straightens a chair, and sits down.

Bug joins Kannon, saying, "Oh, you know that shit isn't happening again; you got next round."

Kannon doesn't respond to Bug's bitching. The two men drink their warm beer and watch the slender guy shoot pool. They can't believe that the guy never misses a shot. Game after game, he never misses; he just racks and runs the table.

Finally, Bug shouts to the man, "Hey, buddy, do you ever miss?"

The man makes a slight glance at the two and then continues to shoot. Kannon tries his luck with the man.

"Hey buddy, we just saw a couple Shadows outside. They are discussing you. They sent for reinforcements; I don't think it looks good. Maybe we should all leave before they come back."

The man stops shooting, and Kannon and Bug think he is going to say something. But he doesn't. He just grabs the chalk, cues his stick, and continues to shoot.

Kannon just looks back at Bug, and Bug shrugs his shoulders. The two return to the bar. Bug asks the bartender, "Hey, what's that guy's problem? We're only trying to help him."

But before the bartender can answer, the man says in a very dry voice, "No one needs your help. How can you two possibly help me? Do I look like I need help? I walked into this bar alone. I'm pretty sure I can leave it alone."

The guys are stunned by the man's answer.

Bug leans over and quietly asks Kannon, "Did he even look up from the table?"

Kannon shakes his head. Bug, now in shock, yells at the man. "We're here to help you. Can't you understand you're outnumbered? You need us!"

The man stops playing as the bartender walks to the other end of the bar. The two begin to feel uneasy as the man approaches them. He leans in towards the two so as to not raise his voice.

"One, I'm going to forget you just talked to me that way. Two, no one asked for your help. Three, if anything, they'll need to get more Shadows because you're beginning to piss me off. Finally, if you're not big enough for this ride, get out of line."

The man stares at Bug. Bug swallows hard as the man turns around and picks up where he left off on his game. Kannon and Bug slink back to the other end of the bar.

Kannon questions the barkeep. "What's his deal? We're only trying to help. The Shadows are coming, and he is going to be way outnumbered."

The barkeep finishes with his last mug and then throws his towel onto his shoulder. "Do you two know who you're talking to?" But, before either can speak, the man continues. "That's Hunter. He's one of the king's chosen warriors. Out of all the warriors, he's the only one who can release Shadows in either form. Or, in layman's terms, he's what we call a badass."

The two just sit there staring at Hunter. Then the barkeep adds, "See his hand? It has the royal mark." He points at Hunter's right hand.

Kannon pulls his hoodie sleeve up, revealing his royal mark. "Like this one," he proclaims, as he shows the barkeep.

The barkeep's eyes open wide as a smile forms on his stone face. "Two chosen ones in my little bar. The Shadows are making a huge mistake coming back here."

Now that they have him talking, they can't get the barkeep to shut up. "Hunter arrived here yesterday. He said that he is supposed to meet four warriors here. Since they hadn't shown up by closing time, I tossed Hunter the keys and told him to lock up. The next morning, when I returned, he is still shooting pool. I don't think he sleeps."

Hunter can hear the whole conversation but remains silent. Then the barkeep asks Bug if he is a Warrior.

Bug replies reluctantly, "Not yet, but my mark should be coming any day. Yesterday, it started tingling, so it's coming."

Hunter, with a low voice, says, "If you don't have the mark when you get here, you won't get the mark. Story over. Sorry, little man."

Bug fires back, "Well, once a douche, always a douche."

"It's better to stay out of the road than be run over. Especially if you can't even get up in the truck." Hunter smiles at his own comment.

Bug, now completely fired up, says, "If you think I can't handle myself, then step up or shut up." Then Bug turns and walks out of the bar, but as he walks by Kannon, he adds, "You can stay and help this asshole, but I'm out of here." As Bug leaves, he slams the door behind him.

Kannon is now mad as well because there is no reason for anyone to make enemies at this time. "What did that do to help this situation?"

Hunter replies, "I figured since there's no way he's going to let anything happen to you, it's better if he's mad than scared."

"Why wouldn't he let me get hurt?"

Hunter is quick to answer. "Because he's your watcher; anyone can see that."

"What do you mean, my watcher?"

Hunter puts his hands out in front of him and gives Kannon an "are you serious?" look.

"Your watcher—the one sent here to watch your back. Every Warrior has a watcher, and he's definitely your watcher."

The barkeep agrees. "Yeah, he's your watcher."

"Well, I better go after him." Kannon starts for the door, but Hunter stops him.

"You can't tell him he's your watcher. He's got to figure that out on his own, or you may lose him to the Shadows."

Just then, Bug comes running through the door and dives over the bar.

"They are coming. It must be at least fifty of them!" He points towards the door.

Hunter looks at Kannon. "Get behind the bar. If you're not ready, I'll understand."

"What's a better time to learn than right now? Besides, there isn't any way I'm going to let you have all the fun." Kannon smiles at Hunter.

They could hear many footsteps and mumbling coming from the front and back door. The barkeep thinks, *I'm definitely getting too old for this shit,* as he ducks behind the bar with Bug.

Kannon's mark begins to glow as his right arm gets a shooting pain. "Ow. Something is wrong—my right arm. It hurts really bad."

Hunter pulls out his pool stick, and his mark begins to glow as well. Kannon is awed by Hunter's pool stick broken in half and seized to his arms as they take the form of pistols. The pain in Kannon's arm continues to get worse as he looks down to watch his own arm transform into an actual cannon. The pain vanishes, and Kannon holds up this cannon that looks awesome. He can move it as easily as his actual arm. When Hunter sees it, he pumps his arm. "Yeah baby, now we're cooking with fire—or should I say fire power."

Kannon states, "This is awesome. It's like we just stepped out of a comic book."

"Oh, trust me, that isn't the best part," Hunter blurts out.

Both doors burst open as fifty-plus Shadows storm in and surround the two warriors. One of them takes the lead. "Oh looky—here we get a two-for-one deal. Now that's my kind of shopping."

Another shadow joins him. "Goodie, now we can each give the Jokers a mark."

Hunter stops them. "The only mark you're going to leave is high in the sky when I set your light free." Then Hunter looks at Kannon. "Time to shine."

As the Shadows attack, Kannon fires a massive shot that rolls through the crowd and puts a big hole in the wall. Realizing he has no effect on the Shadows, Kannon dives over the bar to join Bug and the barkeep. Bug is flickering light all around him from his body. Shots are heard, sounds of tables and chairs breaking as blue goo flies everywhere.

Kannon tells Bug, "If you can flash bright enough to turn them solid, I can release a lot of light."

Bug jumps back over the bar and emits one quick large flash, then jumps back over to Kannon. "Done."

Kannon slides over the bar, and with one big shot, the noise stops. Slowly, Bug and the barkeep raise their heads to see the bar trashed, with Hunter and Kannon in the middle of the room shooting pool.

"How about a drink on the house?" Hunter asks.

The barkeep puts his hand to his forehead as he assesses the damage. "There's nothing left," he mumbles. He tosses the keys to Hunter. "Lock up when you're done." He folds up his towel and puts it away, grabs his jacket, and walks out through the hole Kannon made.

The tavern is destroyed, covered in blue goo, and looks like it is made from Swiss cheese. "Well, we definitely can't stay here tonight. C'mon guys. I know a place just up the way," Hunter tells the guys as they walk out through Kannon's hole. Hunter steps back through and shuts off the lights.

As they walk away, Bug points to the sky. "Now that's a pretty sight," he says as they watch the lights float off into the night sky.

CHAPTER 4

"It's hard to be a star that nobody knows." – Hunter

The warriors leave town and head east; they know it will be dark for a few more hours. With both warriors needing some rest, they volunteer Bug to be on the lookout as they crash into a nice, soft, grassy area just off the path. Not happy with the vote, Bug sits, pouting as he keeps a watch out for the warriors.

"Why do I get stuck being lookout? Don't they think I'm tired as well? If I don't get eight good hours of sleep, I'll look like shit," he mumbles.

"Trust me, there's no amount of sleep to save that face," Hunter says while lying on the ground with his eyes closed. Kannon does not open his eyes either; he just smiles.

"Ha, ha, very funny. I'll let you know. I am considered the twenty-fifth best-looking guy in my class," Bug retorts.

Kannon asks, "Out of how many?"

Hunter answers before Bug can. "Fourteen."

"Ha, joke is on you. There were twenty-eight of us," Bug, trying to be smart, replies. The warriors just burst out laughing. Bug ignores them as he mumbles to himself. "Go ahead and laugh. Won't be laughing if I tea bag you in your sleep, Huntress."

"I swear to God, if you touch me while I sleep, you'll be wiping with your elbows from now on," Hunter quips with eyes still closed.

Kannon adds, "Don't do that, Hunter. He's the fourteenth best wiper in class." The two warriors burst out laughing—

mainly because of being overtired.

Bug is angrier now. "Go to sleep, douches. Because I'm not doing this all night. One of you is switching in a couple of hours."

Hunter adds, "Good night, boys and Bug."

Kannon laughs and rolls over. "Night."

Bug still grumbling, "Good night, warriors."

While the guys sleep, Bug just sits there tossing stones at a bigger stone. After a little while, Bug's eyes begin to droop slowly, and he begins to fight sleep. His head begins to slowly go down as he quickly pops back up. This continues multiple times. But eventually, sleep wins, and he joins Hunter and Kannon in slumber.

"Excuse me, sir, excuse me." A little old man stands in front of Bug, gently shaking him. Bug, startled from a dead sleep, jumps up while pulling his bat back.

"Whoa, whoa, whoa, relax," the old man announces while holding his hands out in a calm-down manner.

Bug, with his bat, pulled back and ready to swing, says, "Who are you, and what do you want?"

The old man cautiously tries to explain. "Name's Jim. I'm a friend."

"Really, because I don't know any Jim. One wrong move and I'll wake these two warriors, and you'll be toast."

Jim replies, "No need for that; I won't be long. I just needed to talk to you alone."

"Well, talk. I'm all ears," Bug answers.

Jim laughs. "That's a funny saying. Nobody is all ears. Anyway, I would like to discuss your watcher duties so we're all on the same page."

"What do you mean my watcher duties? I know how to be a lookout. If you see something, you say something. It's really that easy."

"Well, you see me, and yet you haven't said anything," Jim responds.

Bug realizes Jim's right, and he begins to yell to the warriors. "Guys, a little help here. I got a weird little old guy here."

As Hunter and Kannon quickly rise to their feet, Bug points behind himself to show them Jim.

"Are you losing it, Bug? There isn't anyone or anything behind you," Kannon says, rubbing the sleep out of his eyes to get a better look.

"Right here." Bug turns around to see nothing but darkness. "I swear, guys, this little old man named Jim came here to teach me how to lookout." Bug tries to get the guys to believe him.

"Let me guess, you dozed off, didn't you?" Hunter asks Bug.

"Well, maybe for a minute, but definitely not longer than a couple minutes," Bug explains.

"See, he fell asleep! And worse, he is dreaming of old guys," Hunter bitches to Kannon.

Kannon stops Hunter. "Let's all relax; shit happens. Bug didn't mean to fall asleep. We've had quite a couple of crazy days. Let's regroup our thoughts, and since it's almost morning, let's find some grub. I'm starving." This calms down the other two but they refuse to look at each other.

So, they begin their trek to find the remaining warriors, continuing down the path they had started on last night. They are quiet adventurers. No one says a word as the hungry warriors walk down the beaten path.

Kannon is deep in thought. *How do I control this arm? Maybe I'm too dangerous for my own good. I could've really hurt one of the guys last night. Look what I did to the tavern wall.*

Bug, kicking stones just ahead of the other two, is daydreaming of what adventures and battles await them. While Hunter only thinks, *Boy I hope this blue goo washes off my new boots.*

After a few more miles, Bug can't contain himself as he turns and walks up to Hunter. "What the hell is that?" Hunter stops since Bug is directly in front of him. Before Hunter can say anything, Bug blurts, "You go all matrix on that group of Shadows. Where do you get all those pew-pew abilities? That is totally insane."

Hunter just looks at Bug, then steps around him as they begin walking again. So, Bug approaches Kannon. "A bazooka for an arm; it is like you become a real-life videogame."

Kannon just shrugs his shoulders as the three keep walking. Bug, now walking in front of the two warriors, makes a big circle with his hands in the air. "Shit, you put a hole in the tavern wall you can drive a truck through."

As the two warriors stop to listen to the eerie quietness, Bug keeps rambling. Hunter interrupts and whispers, "Quiet; do you hear that?"

Bug looks around. "Hear what?"

Kannon cuts him off. "Shhh, it's way too quiet."

"Oh, now I see what you guys mean. I can't hear anything." Both warriors simultaneously put their fingers to their mouths to gesture to be quiet. Bug whispers, "What is it?"

Hunter, with an angry look on his face, snaps, "Will you shut up for a minute?"

Bug makes a gesture as if he's zipping up his lips, and Kannon says in a really soft voice, "Hunter, are you familiar with this area?"

Hunter shakes his head no. Bug adds in a loud whisper, "Kinda feels like we're being watched."

The two warriors slap Bug in the back of the head at the same time, knocking his baseball cap off his head.

"What the hell, guys?" Bug leans over and picks up his hat.

Hunter angrily says, "Well, when we tell you to be quiet, that pretty much means shut up!"

"Ok, ok, all you had to do is ask. Next time, I won't be so nice," Bug hesitantly answers.

Kannon looks at the sky. "Well, I doubt its Shadows with this midday sun out beating down."

Hunter adds to it. "Well, it isn't solids either. They're too loud when walking."

They stand still, looking around at the environment, but see no one.

"Maybe we're just imagining it. Since we are pretty hungry," says Kannon, trying to lighten the mood.

"I guess you're right. We better get moving. We don't want to be sitting ducks if we are being watched," Hunter suggests.

Kannon points up ahead of them. "Bug, run up ahead of us, but stay in sight. Maybe if we split up a little, we might find our culprit."

Bug takes off running till the two can barely see him. Hunter looks at Kannon. "We should be coming up on something soon."

Kannon questions, "You think maybe Bug's a little too far out there?"

Hunter smiles. "Who's going to take him? After twenty minutes, they'll bring him back."

The two have a good laugh over that. Just then, they see

Bug jumping and waving his arms, and the two warriors take off running. As they approach Bug, Kannon yells, "What's up? Are you all right?"

"Check out what I found, guys," Bug says, standing there and holding up what looks like a little shiny glass heart.

Hunter takes it from Bug and holds it up to inspect it. After a few seconds, Hunter looks straight at Bug and says, "Where did you find this?"

Bug looks extremely nervous. "I just found it here on the road." Bug points towards the ground beside him.

Now staring at Bug like a parent getting ready to ground a kid, Hunter says, "We didn't see you pick up anything. Where did you find it?"

Bug is now even more nervous, as if he has done something wrong, "Really, I found it in the road."

Bug is now pointing at a different section of the road than earlier. Kannon and Hunter can definitely tell Bug is lying to them. The two stand there looking at Bug with disapproval, waiting for him to break.

Hunter calmly says, "I'll tell you what it is if you really tell me where you got this. Because something like that you don't just find in the road."

Bug snatches it from Hunter's hand and squishes it back into his pocket. "You really want to know where I got it from?" Bug looks toward the ground and kicks a small stone. "I'll tell you, but I didn't steal it. I just borrowed it. I'm going to give it back." As Bug looks up towards Kannon for forgiveness, he adds, "I'm no thief. I am really going to return it."

Kannon and Hunter stand patiently waiting for Bug to explain it to them. Bug apologetically begins.

"Before I made it to town and met Kannon, I went to this little camp cabin, which looked lived in, but no one was home.

The owners had to be weird because the little building had all kinds of spices and creepy bones, feathers, and other items strewn all about. While inspecting and looking for food or water, I heard the owners coming back and, by the sound of it, not in a good mood. As the door opened, I dove into what I thought is a broom closet." Bug, shaking his head, continues. "It was not; it was filled with these ugly little wooden dolls. I tried to look out of the crack in the door. But this lady was yelling at two Shadows as they were frantically looking for something. I kind of shit myself because I thought for sure they were going to find me. But whatever they were looking for, they couldn't find. She sent them back outside to search. She followed them out the door, slamming it behind her. So, naturally, I thought that was my chance to sneak out the back door." Bug wipes his forehead off from sweating while telling the story.

"Continue!" the warriors both yell simultaneously.

Bug continues. "I tried to tip-toe out slowly without being heard. But that didn't work as I stepped on a loose board that made a loud creaking sound. It was loud enough for the lady to hear as she yelled, 'Someone's inside my house, get them!' Luckily, the board I stepped on was very loose. So loose that I could pick it up. I noticed the space below the board was big enough for me to fit into. Since there was no way I could make it back to the broom closet, I dove in the space and covered it back up with the board." Bug stopped for a moment and stretched as if done with the story.

"Dude, finish the story," Hunter said, wanting to hear the rest.

Bug sighs. "Oh, all right. While lying there, I could see through the cracks on the floor. The three busted in as if they were going to catch someone. I could see the lady and two

Shadows from my spot on the floor. She was not too pleasant looking, and man, was she just as ugly on the outside as she sounded on the inside. She meanly yelled at the Shadows, 'Find them and find my heart, or you two will pay for it with your lights.' They searched high and low, but luckily for me, not low enough. Since they were mist, they had no weight to creak the board. After what seemed like forever, they all walked out and left. I could hear the lady yell at them, 'If the Jokers don't give up one of their hearts, you two will join the kings.' I laid there for a good twenty minutes before attempting to leave. This little beauty caught my eye when I lifted the floorboard to get out." Bug held up the shiny rock between his thumb and forefinger. He continues once more. "So, you see, it was under the floor. It must have fallen through the cracks in the floor. My feeling about it was 'finder's keepers' as I put it in my pocket. I placed the floorboard back and ran as fast as I could till I came to the town where I met Kannon and you." Then, as if Bug were a lawyer giving his closing arguments, he says, "So you see, I can't be accused of stealing it, due to it may not be theirs. Therefore, I'm not stealing it; I'm holding onto it till I find the owner."

Hunter, in a stern voice, said, "That shiny rock is one of the three hearts. The story is that there are three hearts that were made from the fallen king's crown. Each Joker and a mad witch hold these hearts. When brought together, they are incredibly powerful and give whoever controls them an enormous amount of strength."

Bug begins to jump around and dance. "I'm powerful!"

Hunter stops him. "You're not powerful unless you possess the other two hearts. But that explains why you were lighting up like a Christmas tree with blinking lights. This means your flashing lights can change Shadows to solid, making Kannon very relevant now. Which makes you and Kannon a very powerful team."

Kannon and Bug begin nodding their heads as they fist-bump each other. Hunter breaks in and joins them, fists up, giving knuckles in celebration.

Kannon adds, "Now we need to find this witch and set her light free before she gets her hands on another piece of heart." The other two agree as they head out with their first actual mission.

While walking, all the men can do is think about food as Bug's stomach continues to complain to him. "Man, we have to find food fast. I think I'm wasting away while I'm talking to you," Bug joins his stomach in complaining.

"Relax, there's got to be a town coming up soon." Kannon tries to comfort Bug.

"He isn't lying. I think I could eat a horse right about now." Hunter joins the complaint department.

"Maybe even the saddle," Bug adds. Then Bug changes his complaint. "Maybe Horizon should've had bikes or four-wheelers to get around with. All this walking sucks. By the time we meet up with any Shadows, we'll be too tired to fight or outrun them."

"Amen, brother; you only speak the truth," Hunter agrees.

Kannon can't believe his ears. "Wow, we must be really delirious if Hunter's agreeing with Bug."

As they stagger along, the men finally approach an intersection in the road. Simultaneously, they all look to the left and down the roadway. Then, they look at the road straight ahead. Finally, they look left down that road.

Bug looks at Kannon. "Videogames!"

Kannon nods his head in agreement. "Videogames!"

Hunter gives them a confused look. "What'll you all mean

by videogames?"

Bug places his hand on Hunter's shoulder to explain. "In every video game, when you come to an intersection or a Y in the road, you always go right first. I don't make the rules; it is what it is."

Hunter looks at Kannon as Kannon nods his head, agreeing. "He's right. It's the law of the videogames."

So, our weary warriors head to the right, not wanting to anger the video gods. The farther they walk, the less the path looks traveled, until eventually, it looks like an old cow path. Once they get to the end of the path, Bug stops and looks at the scenery.

"Have we been walking in circles? Because this bush looks familiar."

Hunter jokes and nudges Bug. "Like you've seen a bush before."

"Ha, Ha, funny. I know I've seen this bush before."

"I doubt it; there's a sign over there." As Kannon points to the end of the field, Bug takes off running so he can be the first to read it.

When Bug reaches the sign, he yells back to the two-lagging behind, "Hey guys, it says 'Welcome to Little Creek.' It also says 'Beware' underneath the sign. Wonder what they want us to beware of?"

"Hey, any town is fine with me. With how hungry I am, they better beware of the hunter," Hunter boasts.

Kannon and Hunter take off running, leaving Bug behind with the signs. As Bug realizes this, he takes off after them, yelling, "Hey guys, wait up; I call dibs on any food you see."

The very first building they come to is a little run-down country store. It looks as if it hasn't been open for some time. But it does have a big porch with a couple of tables and chairs.

Hunter wastes no time walking through the front door and a little bell rings. They enter and notice that it is open, and their menu includes real sandwiches and Starletta soda.

The clerk, who really resembles the barkeep, asks, "Can I help you boys?"

Hunter has to ask. "Hey, aren't you the barkeep from the tavern?"

The clerk laughs. "That's my brother, but he just retired a couple days ago, I think."

Kannon looks at Hunter, then begins to order. "I'll have ham and cheese with mayo. Do you use Kings Best Mayo? Because I can't stand anything else."

"Yes, sir. And for you two?"

Hunter orders next. "Mixed with everything, please."

"No problem. And for the little guy?" asks the clerk, looking at Bug.

Bug replies in a low voice, "I got your little guy right here." Then he raises his voice so the clerk can hear him. "I'll have some tuna with onions and just a hint of lettuce, with hot sauce and a smidgeon of peanut butter, please."

All three of the men just stare at Bug. The clerk finishes writing and then turns around to begin making the sandwiches. "You guys can have a seat on the porch. I'll bring them right out. Oh, and don't forget to grab a soda on your way out."

Hunter, with three Starlettas already in his hands, says, "Drinks are on me."

As the three head out on the porch and grab a seat, Bug takes a big breath. "Finally, something good happens to us."

Hunter punches him in the arm. "Don't jinx us, idiot."

Bug rubs his arm. "Someday when you're not ready… *pow*, right in the kisser! I'll knock you out, big boy."

Hunter and Kannon both laugh and put their feet up on

another chair. While the boys wait, Hunter seems like something is on his mind, like he wants to share something with the guys. As Hunter begins to tell the guys what is on his mind, the clerk walks out with the most beautiful sandwiches the men have ever seen. Bug begins to tear up as the clerk places the sandwiches in front of each rightful owner.

"What do we owe you, sir?" Kannon asks.

The clerk just smiles. "On the house, warriors." Then he turns to Bug, saying, "That'll be ten for the sandwich and three for the soda. For a total of thirteen, sir."

Bug looks at the clerk in surprise. "Are you serious?"

"Oh yes, sir, very. You're not a Warrior. Sorry, I don't make the rules," the clerk said as he holds out his hand for money.

As Bug hands him fifteen, Kannon tells the clerk, "Keep the rest."

Bug quickly gives Kannon a dirty look as the clerk walks away and returns to the store. Even though he had to pay, Bug doesn't care because that is the best sandwich he's ever had.

The men are now stuffed and reclining in the chairs with the front legs of the chairs off the ground.

Bug asks, out of the blue, "So Kannon, now that we have to wait for our food to digest, why don't you tell us your story."

Kannon defiantly is not ready to tell his, so he quickly turns to Hunter. "Mine's boring; I'm more interested in Hunter's story."

Hunter takes a big breath. "Really, you guys want to hear my story? No one has ever asked me about my story."

"Really, let's hear it. If you tell us yours, I'll tell you mine," Bug says, trying to coax Hunter into telling his story.

Hunter puts his chair legs back on the ground and stands up as he walks to the end of the porch and sits on the railing.

Hunter begins.

"After high school, I wandered from one dead-end job to the next. On weekends, I'd go out on the streets and sing for the passersby, hoping one would really like me and give me the big break I was looking for. I was an incredible singer-songwriter and was just hoping for that chance to record something. Then, one day, I was late for work, and they fired me immediately on a first offense. I couldn't find a job—no one wanted a wet-behind-the-ears kid. No one was willing to train, and no one wanted to hire someone who had no training. It was a no-win situation. So, down on my luck, no job in sight, I went to the big city, New York, to try and get heard. Day after day I would sing my heart out for strangers, praying for that one person to hear me. Well, believe it or not, that day came. A fine-dressed man approached with a business card, saying, 'Be at my studio at 8 a.m. sharp. I'll make you shine.' The next day, I was there at 6 a.m., patiently waiting. That was all I ever wanted.

"At eight exactly, the man pulled up and got out of his very expensive car, asking, 'Ready to be a star?' 'Oh, yes, sir," I replied as I followed him into this huge studio. It was exactly as I had pictured it; I was finally there. Day after day, we were in the studio. After over a month, I had my first album ready to be released. My new manager and nice contract meant I would be around for quite some time. With some of my newfound money, I went and purchased my first car. It was an old jeep, but it was awesome to me—all jacked up with a new lift kit and crazy lights. Anyway, I'm riding to the studio, and I hear one of my songs play. I pulled over and cranked the radio. They were playing my song on the radio. I jumped out of my jeep and was dancing in the street. Life was good."

Just then, Bug lets out a huge burp as he pounds his chest

with his fist. "Wow, that one came from deep."

Kannon apologizes for Bug's interruption and asks Hunter to continue. Hunter shakes his head, disapproving of Bug's interruption, but continues.

"As the song finished, the DJ announced to the singer that it wasn't *my* name that he had said. My mouth dropped; it must be it was just a mistake on the DJ's part. I figured my manager would clear that up quickly. Then, before I got to the studio, it played again, and once again, the DJ said the wrong name. I thought to myself, *This is crazy.* When I got to the studio, I ran into my manager's office to explain the mix-up on the radio. He told me to sit down as he closed the door behind me. He then abruptly told me, 'Yes, it is your voice. But you don't have the look fans want, so this other guy would fake sing your songs on TV and interviews to your actual voice.' I was not going to stand for that. People had to know I was singing those songs. My manager told me that it was stated in my contract that I had a gag order. If I talked to anyone, I lost everything I had, plus more. That was it. Nothing else I could do. I lost, once again, back to being a guy in the crowd."

"That's it? You did nothing?" Bug was upset for Hunter.

Hunter once again continues. "There was nothing I could do; my hands were tied. Until one day, when I had had enough, I went to the radio station where my song was first played. I sat down and told the DJ everything. He left our discussion and immediately went to air with my story. The phones lit up like a Christmas tree. Fans were mad at *me,* calling me a liar and trying to destroy their favorite singer's career. I was amazed. I got death threats and was treated horribly everywhere I went. Soon, I had to move out of the city, and with what money wasn't stripped from me, I bought a trailer in this backwoods little trailer park upstate. I vanished from the media and hatred.

But it wasn't long before they found me. My manager sent two guys to talk to me, but trust me, they were not the talkative kind of guys. I tried to escape them in my jeep; I took them on some crazy curvy back roads built for my ride. I had the pedal to the metal—pushing that jeep to its limit. Suddenly, I came to an unfamiliar road, and the curve came up to me too fast. I lost control, flipping multiple times in the air as the jeep sent me flying out through the front window due to not having my seatbelt on. When my jeep came to a stop right beside my destroyed body, the two thugs chasing me wrote me off for dead and left me lying there. All bloody and unable to move, I just laid on my broken back, staring at the sky. As I knew my end was near, I noticed stars falling from the sky, one after another like dominoes. I thought, *What an amazing sight it is to be my last.*

"Just as it was about to end, a door appeared just above my head. I couldn't really move my head to look up, but I heard the door open. A pair of hands reached out the door and pulled me back into the darkness inside the door, which closed behind me. Next, I woke up here in the Horizon."

Kannon and Bug just sit there with their mouths gaped open in disbelief. Bug finally asks, "Was that for real, for real?"

Hunter just nods. Then Kannon and Bug stand up and walk over to Hunter. Both hug him as his eyes filled with tears. Bug, without letting go of Hunter, says, "I would've bought tickets to your concert."

Kannon adds, "You'll always be a star to us."

They can hear the clerk crying inside the store as well.

CHAPTER 5

"How'd they fit a giant's ego in a boy's body?" – Hoss

The guys pick up their garbage, and Hunter goes back inside the store to grab a few Starletta's for later.

While Hunter is in the store, Bug asks Kannon, "Should we ask Hunter to sing for us?" Kannon shakes his head. Bug's eyes widen. "Why not? Now, *I'm* a little curious. Aren't you even just a little curious as well?"

"Sure I am, but I don't think Hunter will ever want to sing again. If he does, then let him pick the right time. It's not for us to decide."

Hunter walks out of the store, holding a six-pack of Starletta, and heads down off the porch with Kannon right behind him.

"WHOA, WHOA, WHOA—is that what we're doing?" Bug yells while standing on the porch, holding his arms out from his sides. The two warriors turn back towards Bug. "What?" Bug stands there dumbfounded. "We can listen to Hunter's story. But let's shit on Bug's. I guess I'm not that important to know about my story."

Kannon looks at Hunter. "Really, I guess this is what's happening now." The two take a seat back on the porch to listen to Bug's story.

"Well, go ahead. Enlighten us," Hunter remarks, still with red eyes.

Kannon adds, "We're all ears."

Bug adjusts himself as he mumbles, "Well, that's a little

more like it; it's called respect."

The two wait patiently for Bug's story to begin. Bug clears his throat and then starts.

"It all started on my final day of school when the last class ended. The bell sounded, meaning we were finally free adults. I was even more excited than the other new adults due to the fact that I had finally saved up enough money to pay off and pick up my dream pickup truck. Cherry red with the biggest lift man could make—dual stacks out the back. My truck was a monster."

Hunter butts in. "How'd you get into it? Get a running start and high jump?"

Both men giggle and nudge each other.

"Funny, but men are talking now, so *shhhh.*" Bug put his finger to his mouth to quiet them down. He continues. "I felt like a king in that jacked-up truck. Now, as you both should know, I was an extremely popular guy in our area." Bug points at himself with his thumbs. "So, I stopped by our favorite hangout, Joe's Freeze and Go, where my whole crew was hanging out. As soon as I pulled in, a couple of cheerleaders jumped in the cab with me as the rest of the baseball team climbed on back. This guy called Cougar and I were co-captains of the baseball team. Cougar yells up, 'Today's the day, Babe.' That's what they called me."

"Why, because you're the same size as a baby?" Hunter jokingly adds.

Bug gives him a dirty look but moves on. "*Babe* because I hit the shit out of the ball. Either way, Cougar was talking about my deal, that if we all graduated, I would jump from the top of High Bridge into the pool to nowhere. No one that we know of has ever even attempted it."

Hunter breaks in once again. "Shit, with your size, you

could jump into a cup of water and still not touch the bottom."

Bug scowls at Hunter, mumbling, "I wish someone would punch you in the nuts." Then Bug smiles and once again continues. "One of the cheerleaders told me that Becky Jones was heading up there to go swimming. And believe me, you did not want to miss Becky in a bathing suit. She was the kind of girl whose legs would go all the way up to make an ass out of her." Bug laughs at his own joke, but Hunter and Kannon find no humor in it. Bug is a little angry that they didn't laugh at his joke.

"So, we headed for High Bridge. I rolled my window down and hung my head out like a dog until a bug hit me. The radio was jamming the Applebee's song, "Life is good". On our way there, every mailbox we came to, Cougar would crush with his bat." Bug shakes his head. "Man, he took out a lot of mailboxes. When we approached the bridge, it seemed to be higher than I remembered. I thought maybe it wasn't such a good idea, but they all began to cheer my name. Even Becky was cheering, so I had to do it. A deal was a deal. Trust me, you don't really know if you're scared of heights till you're up on the High Bridge. It is correctly named, believe me.

"As I finally reached the top and looked down, I thought, *Wow, the pool to nowhere looks really small from way up here.* Thoughts raced through my head of chickening out, but there was no way I could do that in front of Becky. As I stood there on top of the world with my arms raised, stars began to fall from the early night sky. Many begin to fall like someone pulled the floor from beneath them. I looked down at the crowd that had now gathered, but they didn't act as if they had seen what I had just seen. Why didn't they see the stars? Were they too fixed on me and my leap to fame? Well, I could wait no longer."

Hunter breaks in. "You didn't really jump, did you? That's crazy."

Bug looks down towards the ground, feeling ashamed. "The crowd began to count down from ten. Ten, nine, eight, seven. . . Then the weirdest thing happened. A door appeared right next to me on top of the bridge. It slowly cracked open and startled me as I lost balance and began to fall. A hand reached out through the door, grabbed *my* hand, and pulled me through as it closed behind me. The next thing I knew, I was here—in the Horizon."

Both men couldn't believe that Bug actually had the balls to even get up on High Bridge, let alone jump. Stunned, the guys gather and begin to head out as the clerk runs out to Bug and hands him back his fifteen bucks.

"You may not be a Warrior, but you are one crazy son of a bitch that I'm glad we have on our side."

The clerk shakes Bug's hand. Bug looks proud as a peacock and glances over to make sure Hunter and Kannon witnessed it.

Hunter is disgusted. "Awe, now we're going to have to hear about this forever. Someone take my ears, please."

Kannon pats Hunter on the back. "Oh, you know it. Come on, let's go find us a witch."

The two walk off, leaving Bug standing there with a huge smile on his face, counting his money. "Hey, wait up," he yells as he runs to catch up.

Bug finally catches up with them, but the town looks deserted, just like the last one.

"This is weird. The first town only had the tavern open, and now this town only has the store open. Kind of strange," Kannon says to Bug and Hunter.

Hunter adds, "Well, maybe we can hear another story about

Becky to lighten the tension."

The warriors both begin to giggle.

"Shut up and walk!" Bug angrily shouts. They continue to walk through the dilapidated old dusty town, not finding any movement whatsoever. Out of nowhere, Hunter suggests to Bug, "Maybe so they don't find the heart, you should put it in a really safe place."

Bug pulls it out of his pocket to look at it again, "Oh yeah, like where?"

Kannon joins in just jokingly, "I'd swallow it, then they could never find it." He nudges Hunter, and they hear 'gulp' from behind them. They stop immediately and look at Bug.

Hunter quickly asks, "You didn't just do what we think you did? Did you?"

"Yup, they ain't finding it now," Bug says as he rubs his stomach.

"Man, you are one simple person, aren't you?" Hunter shakes his head.

Bug is now a little mad because they called him simple. "Yeah, I ate it, and I'll do the same with the other two if I get my hands on them."

Hunter wisely responds, "Well, smart one, what happens if the Shadows release your light, and you vanish? The heart will just fall out on the ground."

Bug thought about that for a moment. "Well, that will never happen."

Hunter sarcastically says, "And why wouldn't it?"

Bug looks at the stone on the ground and kicks it. "Because I got you two here to protect it and me."

Kannon smiles. "Damn, right." Bug and Kannon fist-bump each other.

Just like that, they were through the small town, looking at the final cabin on the street.

"Well, that was an eventful tour," Hunter jokes.

As Hunter finishes speaking, Bug notices something out of the corner of his eye. "What's that?" Bug points to the little cabin.

"What's what?" Hunter boringly asks.

Bug points to the cabin window. "I just saw the curtain in the window move."

Kannon adds, "Bug, it's probably the wind. There isn't anyone here."

Bug points again. "There it goes again; I'm telling you someone's in there."

Since Bug is so adamant about it, they decide to take a closer look. They then walk up to the first step and stop.

"Ok, so go check it out," Hunter says, pushing Bug from behind.

"What? Are you crazy? I'm not going in there alone. There could be some crazed lunatics in there. "Oh, no, count me out," Bug answers, backing away from the steps.

Hunter, still lightly pushing Bug towards the stairs, says, "I bet if Becky asked you, you'd go running in."

"Enough with the Becky shit; this is serious," Bug snaps.

"Ok, let's come up with a plan," Kannon suggests as the three men stand there in thought. Kannon rubs his chin and thinks, *I know since I'm in charge, they're going to want me to go in first. But you don't want something to happen to the leader. So, it should be Bug.*

Hunter, itching his trigger finger, thinks, *Maybe I should bum rush them with guns up in case they're not friendly.*

Bug stands there rubbing his hands together. *I bet they have cake in there. This place definitely has cake. No, wait—pie. Hot apple pie. Maybe chocolate pie with whipped cream.*

Kannon and Hunter are now looking at Bug as he's licking his lips from side to side. "What's seriously wrong with you?" Hunter asks and just watches Bug.

Kannon then arrives at a plan of attack. "Hunter, you take the back, and I'll go in the front. Just don't shoot me, please."

"Don't shoot. Got it." Hunter tips his head and repeats Kannon.

Kannan then turns to Bug. "Bug, you stay here and guard the road."

Bug looks at Kannon as if he wasn't serious. "Guard the road? What the hell is the road going to do?"

"Guard the road. It's that simple." Hunter smiles.

Bug continues his rant but in more of a mumble. "Oh, I'll just be sitting here guarding this evil road. Whoa, road, stay back. Don't make me go off on you, road." Bug pulls his bat over his head as if he is going to hit the road if it tries anything.

Now mad at Bug's childish behavior, Hunter says, "Are you serious? What are you, like, ten? Stop being a bitch and do as your told."

Bug barks back while pointing the bat at Hunter's face, "Shut up, Huntress; the men are talking."

Hunter reaches over and cuffs Bug behind his head. "Watch yourself, little man. Big words could bring big problems."

Bug's face begins to turn red from anger as he realizes what just happened. "Trust me, Huntress, you don't want any of this. Guarantee you don't touch me again."

Hunter is heated up. "Listen here, little bug, talk to me one more time, and I'll roll you up into a ball and punt your bitch ass."

Kannon jumps in, feeling the discussion is taking a turn for the worse, and it probably won't go well in Bugs' favor. Kannon shouts in a whispering voice, "Alright, you two, enough! This isn't helping our situation at all." Kannon steps between the two, but suddenly, they all notice the curtain moving. Kannon, now frustrated himself, says, "There's someone or something in there. Because of you two bumbling idiots, they now know we're out here. So much for the element of surprise."

Bug leans over by Hunter as if Kannon can't hear him, "You're lucky Kannon just saved your ass, pretty boy."

Bug barely gets the words out of his mouth when Hunter grabs him, sending Bug flying through the cabin door as if he were a bowling ball. When Bug comes to a stop, he's lying face down in the middle of the room. When the dust settles, Bug slowly glances up to see the largest man he has ever seen in his life. Bug's first thought is, *How did this guy even get into the tiny cabin?* The man never makes a move as Bug quickly gathers himself back to his feet. While backing towards the broken door, Bug, with a nervous voice, asks, "Who—I mean *what,* I mean. . . Who are you?"

The man doesn't answer. He just stands there ducking under the ceiling, looking at Bug.

Bug continues with a slight stutter, "M-m-my friends are just outside waiting for me to report my findings." Then he tries to sound brave and tough. "They are very dangerous men. If I don't report soon, they'll come in here and destroy every living or non-living thing. They're ruthless."

The giant man turns towards the fireplace and stirs the coals. With a deep voice, he says, "Well, then you better report."

Bug, now realizing the mountain of a man means him no harm, says, "Oh, I will. But first, I need a name."

The giant man takes a step towards Bug and extends his hand. "Name's Hoss. But most people call me Big Man."

Bug gingerly steps towards the behemoth, reaches out, and shakes Hoss' hand.

"I'm known as Bug around these parts." Bug's hand looks as if it were a newborn's hand inside Hoss' hand.

"Well, it's a pleasure to meet you, Bug. You'd better report before they think I ate you," Hoss laughs, even though Bug doesn't think that is funny. As Bug begins to leave the cabin, Hoss adds, "Tell Hunter he still owes me a six-pack of Starletta. From that beating I gave him on the pool table a few months ago."

Bug stops in his tracks. "You know Hunter? Then you know how dangerous he is." Then in a low mumble, Bug adds, "And how big of a dick he is."

Hoss hears him but ignores it. As Bug leaves the cabin, Hoss walks to the window and pushes the corner of the curtain back to see Hunter's expression. He watches as Bug describes what he has seen in the cabin. Bug is very vocal and uses many hand gestures to describe Hoss. So much so that Hoss begins to laugh at the sight. Hoss closes the curtain as the three men approach the cabin. Hunter enters first, followed by Kannon, and then Bug.

Bug slowly closes the broken door as he whispers to Kannon, "See how big he is?"

Hunter takes a step closer to the big man with no words. Hoss takes a step towards Hunter while having to duck the beams of the little cabin. The two men stand face-to-face with each other, but not exactly face-to-face since Hoss has a good foot, taller than Hunter. The room feels awkward as the two just stand there, sizing each other up and down.

Hoss speaks first. "So, this is the big bad Hunter, the fastest hands in the Horizon. I'd thought you would have been taller."

Hunter replies, "Really, who wants to be that tall? I was

always told the bigger they are, the harder they fall."

Kannon and Bug both take a step back. Finally, the tension breaks as both big men smirk and embrace in the manliest hug Kannon and Bug have ever seen.

"My friend, I haven't seen you in over a month," Hunter tells Hoss.

"Brother, it's been more like months," Hoss answers.

The two men release each other as Hunter announces, "Kannon and Bug, let me introduce you two to Hoss, the mountain that moves."

Kannon extends his hand. "Pleased to meet you, sir."

Hoss nods towards Kannon as he shakes hands and he laughs. "He called me sir."

Bug decides that he'll pass on another handshake since the last one almost wrecked him.

Hoss looks at Hunter, saying, "Where's my six-pack? I know you didn't come to see me without payment."

Hunter holds up the six-pack and hands it to Hoss. "You know I pay my debts; a bet is a bet, even though I think you cheated." Hoss chuckles at Hunter's attempt to sound like the better man.

Kannon notices the crown symbol on Hoss's hand. "So, you're a Warrior as well, I see."

Bug interrupts. "You're a Warrior? Awesome; that's one more big man on our side. We are going to shit on these Shadows."

Hoss laughs, "We? What are you going to do, bite off their kneecaps?"

Bug lets his temper get the best of him again. "Listen, Big man, don't think for one minute I won't take you out behind the woodshed."

Stunned, Hoss says, "Ok, let's go; take me out back." Hoss

points to the backdoor.

"You think I won't go. Bring it, mountain. Maybe I'll let you keep your kneecaps," Bug remarks, storming out the backdoor with his bat on his shoulder.

Hoss slams the door behind Bug and locks it. "Little dude, fight the door to get back in."

All three warriors break down laughing. Bug stands at the back door, patiently waiting for them to let him in, refusing to use the front door for pride reasons.

The men sit down at the table to discuss plans and fill Hoss in on the witch situation. After briefing Hoss on everything, Hunter asks, "How's Dillo? He's still with you, I hope."

Hoss chuckles. "Yeah, he's still with me. He's out grabbing some grub and some more wood for the fire."

"That's great to hear! I'm excited to see him," Hunter happily remarks.

Bug, listening through the door, yells, "Is Hunter smiling? Kannon, quick, take a pic of it."

Hoss looks toward the backdoor. "Is he always so wound up like this?"

"Yes!" both men answer at the same time.

Making small talk, Kannon asks Hoss, "Have you been in the Horizon for a long time?"

Hoss thinks about it before he answers, "About eight or nine months, I guess." Hoss slaps Hunter on the back. "I met this S.O.B. about three months ago, trying to take on a handful of Shadows all by himself. Lucky for him, I saved his ass."

The men can hear Bug laughing behind the door. Hunter quickly replies, "You didn't save shit; I had it all under control."

"It's your story, and you're sticking to it, but Dillo knows the truth. We'll ask him when he gets back," Hoss says, smiling back at Hunter. Hoss pulls a Starletta from the six-pack. "Would either one of you like one?"

From behind the door: "I'd like one, please."

Hoss jokes, "Even the doors are thirsty." The guys laugh again at Bug's misfortune. "Don't worry, I'll leave one on the table for you, little man. If you ever get back in," Hoss yells to Bug. Then Hoss leans over to the guys and whispers, "He knows he can just walk around the house and come in, doesn't he?"

"Don't think for one minute I'd give you a chance to better me. I can stand here all night."

Hoss shrugs his eyebrows. "Ok, little buggy, you stay right there. You're showing me."

The men shake their heads in disbelief.

The front door opens as a middle-sized man walks in and drops a handful of wood by the fire as Hoss explains, "We got company, Dillo."

The man turns around. When he sees Hunter, he runs over and hugs him. "Hunter, you're alive."

"Dillo, you old goat, you're not getting rid of me that easily."

Hoss interrupts, "And this young gentleman is Kannon. He's also a Warrior."

"Dillo. Pleased to meet you," he says as he avoids Kannon's extends hand and hugs him instead.

Kannon doesn't know what to do. This strange man he doesn't know is hugging him.

Hoss explains, "Dillo is a hugger. Best, most honest guy you'll ever meet. But his elevator doesn't quite go to the top."

Hunter adds, "Just let him finish."

Still sitting with his arms out straight, Kannon lets him continue until Dillo lets go. Dillo turns back towards Hoss.

"You know you have a strange little man standing at the backdoor?"

"Yeah, he's teaching me a lesson," Hoss tells Dillo.

Dillo walks to the back door to answer the door as Hoss yells at him, "Don't open that door! Let him stay out there all night. As I said, he's teaching me a lesson."

Dillo yells through the door, "Sorry. Hoss said I can't let you in the back door. My name is Dillo; what's yours?"

"Name's Bug, and Hoss won't let me in because I threatened to beat his ass."

All the men laugh except Dillo, who yells back, "Well, Doug, you know you can go to the front door and come in."

"Who's Doug? I said, *Bug,* and I won't use the front door because Hoss wants me to."

"Doug, if you do make it in, you can sleep next to me on the floor; we have extra blankets and space."

The guys are totally amused by these two talking to each other. They can hear Bug mumble to himself, "Did I just get invited to a slumber party? And where the hell did he get Doug from?"

The warriors burst out laughing and Hunter can't hold his soda in, spitting it across the room.

After a nice meal prepared by Dillo, the guys settle in the living room area to relax a bit before bed. Finally, Hoss tells Dillo he can let Bug in because it's getting dark out, and it isn't safe out there alone. Dillo opens the door, and Bug falls to the floor because he is leaning against it and did not anticipate it to open. Bug stands up fast, the imprint of the doorknob on his forehead. He claims victory.

"Finally came to your senses and gave up, Big man."

Hoss questions, "Is that the only way you know how to enter a house?"

They all burst out laughing. Even Dillo, who doesn't understand the joke, laughs.

"Whatever. I still won the argument," Bug states, still feeling victorious.

Hoss hands Bug the ring off his Starletta cap. "Here's your championship belt."

They are all so tired, they laugh again.

Bug sits at the table, eating what the warriors left from dinner. Dillo walks out to join him.

"There's more on the counter if you need more, Doug," Dillo says, still trying to be helpful.

Bug looks up from eating. "No, this is fine. The name's Bug, not Doug."

"Excuse me, I'm so sorry. I thought you said Doug. Actually, Bug fits you better."

"Thanks, I guess," Bug replies, also trying to be nice.

Dillo grabs a chair and sits next to Bug. Kannon walks over to grab the last Starletta by the two new friends as Hunter and Hoss remain in the living room, joking and laughing about everything.

Bug says in a low voice, "Never thought I'd see Hunter smile."

Kannon replies, "Oh, I saw him smile earlier when he punted you through the front door."

Bug gives Kannon a dirty look as Kannon walks back into the living room.

"So, that's how the door got broken," Dillo adds.

Bug and Dillo join the others in the living room as they are getting in position to call it a night.

Bug jokingly says to Hoss, "So Hoss, how'd you get in this little cabin? What'd you do, lift the roof off and step in?"

"Yeah, pretty much," Hoss answers.

Bug sits there dumbfounded, not knowing if Hoss is telling the truth or not. Hunter looks at Bug, making a lifting gesture by pushing his hands up as if he is lifting something. Bug laughs but still wonders how Hoss got in.

Hunter turns to Hoss. "You know, Kannon is named appropriately for a good reason. Earlier, when I first met him, we were surrounded by Shadows, and his arm turned into an actual cannon."

Hoss grabs Kannon's arm and pulls him close. Then he begins tapping on Kannon's arm to see if it sounds like metal. Hoss inspects the arm up and down. "Really, a real cannon?"

Hunter nods. "He blew a hole through the tavern wall big enough to drive a car through."

"Cool. Welcome to the team," Hoss replies as he makes his way over to the big comfy recliner for the night. "Good, now there are four of us; just one more to go." Then Hoss pulls an old cob pipe from his pocket and lights it. In a matter of seconds, the cabin is filled with the smell of Hoss's pipe.

Bug walks over and sits on the arm of the chair. "Sorry, but I'm no Warrior just yet."

"Sorry, small fry, I wasn't talking about you." Hoss takes another drag from his pipe. "Kannon, Hunter, Dayne, and the most beautiful of us four, yours truly."

Kannon's eyes immediately widen, and a lump forms in his throat. "Dayne! Did you say, Dayne? As in, Dayne is a lady?"

"Dayne is not only a lady, but she's one of the most badass ladies I've ever met. Shit, that little lady…Well, let's just say I'm glad she's on our side." Hoss chuckles, then adds, "Shit, she'd probably give me a run for my money."

Kannon begins to fumble through his hoodie pockets as he pulls out his phone. He then begins to flick through pictures on his phone till he gets one of just Dayne alone. Kannon holds the phone up in front of Hoss. "Is this Dayne?"

Hoss adjusts his eyes. "Yup, sure is. But now she has red hair and is always with Dak. I don't think I've ever seen them apart."

"Who's Dak?" Bug blurts out before Kannon can say another word.

"Dak is just some young guy, kind of the same age as you." Hoss points his pipe at Kannon. "Actually, Dak looks almost like Kannon, which is so weird. Dak is quite a Warrior in his own right. They're never apart. Dayne is always at his side. It's crazy because, trust me, she doesn't need anyone's help. It's kind of like she's protecting him," Hoss explains while rubbing his chin.

After hearing all that from Hoss, Kannon's heart jumps into his throat, and he can't speak. Thoughts run through his mind a million miles an hour. Kannon needs to find Dayne and see her for himself. *Can this be true? Might she love another? Has she given up on us? Who is Dak? Is he forcing her to stay with him?* Either way, Kannon knows he has to find Dayne and find the truth. *As soon as she sees me,* Kannon thinks, *we'll be us again.*

While Kannon sits there deep in thought, Hoss packs his pipe away, pulls out a deck of cards, and starts dealing them out.

CHAPTER 6

"Papa's Always Got My Back." – Dillo

Hoss picks up the deck of cards as if he and Hunter are going to finish a previous game that is interrupted. Hoss only deals the cards for him and Hunter, excluding Bug, who is sitting at the coffee table with them.

Bug sarcastically says, "Nah, that's alright. I'm really not a card player anyway. I'll go hang out with Dillo." As Bug approaches Dillo, he raises his hand and waves as if he and Dillo are little kids meeting at a playground for the first time. "Mind if I join you?" Bug asks Dillo.

"Sure, buddy, have a seat," offers Dillo, pulling out a chair for Bug.

Bug sits there watching Dillo polishing this big shell. Finally, Bug has to ask, "What's with the big shell?"

Dillo answers, "My papa gave it to me for the geese."

Bug doesn't know what to do with the answer, so he asks, "What do you mean the geese? What do geese have to do with a big shell?"

"Papa gave me the shell so the geese wouldn't bite me."

Bug is completely confused as he watches Dillo finish cleaning the shell. Dillo walks out the back door and hangs the shell up to dry. When Dillo comes back in, he leaves the door open to keep an eye on his shell. Dillo then goes over to the coffee table and sits down and deals himself a hand to join the game.

Bug walks over to Kannon, "Did you just hear that

conversation I just had with that Dillo guy? I think I'm actually dumber after that."

But Kannon is in his own little world, thinking about Dayne, and he doesn't even act as if he heard Bug at all. Annoyed, Bug goes over and sits at the coffee table as well. After watching three hands go by and not being invited to play, Bug speaks up.

"Yo, can I get some cards here or what?"

Hoss looks at Bug and skips him again. "You don't know how to play."

"How do you know?"

"I don't. You just look like you don't know how to play," Hoss replies.

"Well, what are you playing?"

"Rummy. You know the game?" Hunter puts in.

"Yeah, I know how to play, but I just feel like not playing right now. I'll just watch to see if you guys have different rules than I play," Bug retorts, sounding not too confident. After a couple more hands, he looks at Hoss. "What's with Dillo's shell?"

Hoss doesn't look up since he's studying his cards. "It's for the geese."

"What geese?" Bug asks, now even more confused.

Hoss tosses a card down, "Dillo's geese."

Bug now begins to get mad because he thinks the guys are messing with him. "OK, I'll play your little game. What geese?"

"The geese on Dillo's papa's farm," replies Hoss.

"Can someone please start from the beginning?" Bug is still not understanding.

Hoss leans back and begins to tell the guys Dillo's story. "See, it all started back on Dillo's papa's farm. Dillo was in charge of taking care of the geese, the chickens, and the sheep every day on the farm. He would go out, feed them, and gather up all the eggs they had laid that morning. His papa would sit on the front steps and watch him. After grabbing the eggs, Dillo would run with everything he was worth back to the steps. Those geese would be right on his heels. For some reason, the geese didn't like Dillo. Every time he'd turn his back on them, they'd run up and bite him in the butt. His papa would laugh, but Dillo did not think it was funny at all. So, one day, Dillo decided he'd sneak from tree to bush to the next one so the geese wouldn't see him. His papa found this even more amusing than the geese just chasing him. Dillo bent down behind a tree to avoid the geese. But when he did, a goat caught a glimpse of him bent over and charged Dillo. Before his papa could warn him, the goat knocked his ass over the tea kettle. Now, with Dillo rolling around on the ground holding his backside, it became open season on him with the geese. By the time he made it back to the steps, he was nothing but red pinch marks. For a few days after that, Dillo refused to do his chores, no matter what his papa offered him. So, Papa took Dillo into his trophy room, where Dillo was never allowed to go. Papa reached up and took this big armadillo shell off the wall. The plaque on the wall underneath it said, 'Largest Armadillo ever recorded in Texas.' Papa handed it to Dillo and told him if he wore the shell, nothing could hurt him. The next day, Papa almost died laughing as Dillo came out with the shell tied to his shoulders and waist with baling twine. It was quite a sight to see. Papa had all he could do to keep himself from busting out laughing. But Papa knew if Dillo saw him laughing at him, he wouldn't wear it. Dillo strutted out into the barnyard as if he were wearing a suit of armor. The sight of the shell frightened the farm animals. They would run from Dillo if he got near them; he was invincible in that shell.

"One morning, Dillo got up early and strapped on his shell. He waited two hours past Papa's normal chore time. Dillo thought if Papa didn't come out soon, the rest of the farm animals wouldn't eat. Well, either way, Dillo had a job to do. He headed out and fed his animals, but Papa was still not up yet. So Dillo gathered the eggs, took them in, and put them in the refrigerator. Dillo knocked on Papa's bedroom door, but Papa didn't answer. Dillo cracked his door open and quietly asked, 'Papa, are you going to get up, lazy bum? I already tended to the chickens; we got three more eggs than usual.' Papa didn't make a sound. Dillo knew something wasn't right, so he ran to the neighbors to get help."

Bug asks, "Where were Dillo's parents or grandma?"

Hoss shakes his head. "Dillo's parents left him with his papa because they couldn't care for a boy like him. As far as his grandma, she passed away before Dillo was born. Dillo only had his papa, and his papa only had him."

Kannon asks, because he had joined in to hear Dillo's story, "What do you mean a kid like Dillo?"

"In case you guys didn't pick it up, Dillo is a little slower than the rest of us."

Both Bug and Kannon figured something was off with Dillo, but that didn't mean he should've been abandoned by his parents. Hoss continues. "When the ambulance pulled out with his papa fully covered, the paramedics told Dillo that his papa was covered because he was cold. Dillo just sat on the front steps all alone. The police told the neighbors to keep an eye on Dillo until the State came out to get him. The neighbors let Dillo sit on the steps to be alone with his thoughts and told him if he needed anything to come get them.

"Dillo had no idea what to do. He just sat on the steps with his shell. Dillo thought maybe if Papa had his shell, he wouldn't have gotten hurt. Dillo got up from the steps and went to Papa's garage. He opened the door to view Papa's old truck, which he would never let Dillo drive. Dillo entered the garage and shut the door behind him. He jumped in the driver's seat and pretended he was driving. As he wiggled the steering wheel, the visor flipped down, revealing the keys to the old truck. Dillo knew where the keys went. He'd seen Papa start the truck many times. Dillo put the keys in and started the truck. It started on the first turn. Dillo sat in the running truck. He felt as if he were Papa. He then rolled the window down and turned the radio on. It was playing one of Papa's favorite songs. The garage started to get really smokey, so Dillo rolled the window up so the smoke wouldn't get in. Dillo started to doze off. For some reason, he suddenly got really tired. Then, all he remembered was someone opening the truck door and pulling him out. They walked through the nearest door, and Dillo woke up here in the Horizon."

Both Kannon and Bug sit with their mouths wide open, and Dillo sits fumbling with his cards and not really paying attention to the story. Bug just wants to get up and give Dillo a hug, but he will wait till later when not everyone is watching.

Dillo nods. "Yup, that's what happened. Hoss said maybe Papa was brought to the Horizon. I hope so because my chickens must be so hungry. There are probably a hundred eggs by now."

"I'm sure there are, Dillo," Hoss agrees.

Dillo gets up from the card game and goes out to get his shell since it should be dry by now.

Bug is still amazed as he commends Hoss for taking him under his wing. "That's amazing that you are watching over Dillo. I had you all wrong. I'm glad I didn't kick your ass earlier."

"Watching over Dillo? You have it all wrong, Rumpelstiltskin. Dillo is *my* watcher. He's my bodyguard."

Bug laughs out loud. "He's *your* bodyguard."

Dillo walks in. "Hoss is right. I'm his watcher. Just like you're Kannon's watcher."

Bug, still laughing, stops immediately. "What do you mean I'm Kannon's watcher?"

Hoss explains the watcher situation to Bug as Hunter sits eerily quiet. "Every Warrior has a watcher to guard his back. He helps protect the Warrior's light, even if it means he might lose it. They usually become friends, if not family. And you, Barney Rubble, are Kannon's watcher."

Bug sits back with his arms folded behind his head. "I'm Kannon's bodyguard." Bug looks at Kannon and laughs. "Wow, did you luck out. You could've got some loser. It's like you won the lotto."

Kannon smiles. "Yeah, I'm the big winner."

The guys decide to pick up the cards and get a little shut-eye. Bug quickly grabs the only blanket and picks a spot on the floor to crash. Kannon lays on one side of Bug, and Dillo lies on the other side of him. Hoss takes the sofa, even though you can't tell something is under him. A very quiet Hunter takes the recliner with his hat pulled over his face and his pool stick lying across his midsection.

When the warriors are almost out for the night, Dillo whispers to Bug, "Are you really Kannon's watcher?"

Bug rolls over towards Dillo. "I guess. I just found out about it tonight."

They aren't as quiet as they thought since everyone in the room could hear them. Dillo asks Bug, "Would you give up your light to save Kannon's light?"

Bug thinks about it for a minute, then replies, "Yeah, I guess. I mean, if that's my job, I'm going to have to."

Dillo lightly punches Bug's shoulder. "Well, I hope you never have to. Because I'd really miss you."

Bug chokes up a little. "I'd miss you as well, Dillo." Bug punches Dillo's shoulder back. Then Bug rolls over and nudges Kannon. "Don't worry, Kannon. I'm guarding your body as we speak."

Kannon, almost to sleep, states, "Great, now go to sleep."

Bug rolls back over towards Dillo. "Wow, to think I'm a bodyguard."

Hunter speaks up. "Will you go to sleep? Besides, what body are you going to guard? Maybe you can save Kannon's ankles from bed bugs."

All the guys but Bug snicker at that one. Hoss even reaches over and fist-bumps Hunter.

Bug snaps back after being humiliated. "Yeah, that's a good one, Hunter. Where's your watcher hunter? Did they see they got stuck with you and ended their own light?" Bug laughs at his own joke by himself. The room turns into a somber mood as Hunter stands without saying a word and walks out of the cabin.

Hoss, in a low, sad voice, says, "There is no need for that, Bug!"

"No need for what? It is a joke," Bug says, dumbfounded.

Dillo adds, "No need at all."

Kannon sits up and begins putting his sneakers on to go find Hunter. Hoss explains why Hunter left the cabin.

"Hunter lost his watcher in the great stone bridge battle. It was easily the most Shadows we've ever seen at one time. The Shadows split us in different directions. Dillo and I went towards the woods and Hunter and Lakin towards the stone bridge. Lakin was Hunter's watcher. She was so much like Hunter, you would have thought she was his twin sister. Long, straight black hair and a Warrior's attitude to go along with it. The shadow's numbers were impressive, but they weren't alone. They had brought a Beast with them. He was huge, like someone who just stepped out of a King Kong movie. We gave them everything we had, but they were overpowering us."

Bug interrupts. "I didn't know any of this. I feel so terrible. What an asshole I am!"

Hoss continues. "The Jokers surprised us with the Beast; we've never seen such a shadow. The Beast was definitely giving me all the fight I could handle. I stumbled backward as more Shadows climbed on my back. My foot twisted, and I went down and soon completely covered by Shadows. The Beast must have thought he had defeated me because he turned his sights on Hunter and Lakin. Amazingly, Hunter's daggers and Lakin's whips had no effect on the Beast whatsoever. When the Beast finally got his hands on Hunter, he began throwing Hunter around like a rag doll. I still can't believe Hunter's and Lakin's weapons had no effect on the Beast. It was like it was shielded against our attacks. As Hunter laid on his back, with his guns just out of his reach, the Beast raised his fist to crush Hunter to nonexistence. When the Beast lowered his fist, Lakin dove in front of Hunter, pushing him out of harm's way. She took the entire blow as her whips went flying in opposite directions, and she laid there motionless. Hunter reached for his pool stick, but by the time he pulled out his daggers, he was engulfed by Shadows and disappeared into the darkness."

Bug interrupts, sitting on the edge of his seat. "So, what happened?"

Dillo adds, "We don't know."

"When we came to, we had to squint our eyes from the sun beating down on us. Dillo and I regrouped and gathered our senses as we looked around for our friends. You definitely could tell one hell of a battle took place there. We noticed Hunter lying face down in the sand, not moving. When I leaned down and shook him, he began to move and moan. Hunter opened his eyes and immediately began screaming for Lakin. He stumbled to his feet and frantically started searching for her. The battlefield was covered in blue goo, but Lakin was nowhere to be found. We did find one of her whips, and what we think is a piece of her clothing.

"Hunter lost it as he dropped to his knees and screamed at the stars, 'She did this for you! For you!' Then he tipped his head towards the ground, looking at her whip. 'Now I'm going to do it for her. I will hunt every last light and send them home for her.' Then Hunter looked towards the woods. 'Now you are the hunted; it's time to make you all shine.' He stood and walked into the woods, leaving us just standing there on the battlefield."

Dillo says, "And that is the last we had seen of him, till today."

Kannon pokes Bug. "That must be how Hunter got his name."

Dillo nervously says, "The stories that went around about Hunter is that he destroyed every shadow he came across. He went looking for them with a crazy look on his face. Even the people in the towns avoided him. He is scary."

Hoss nods. "Dude is a one-man wrecking crew. I talked to one of the towns folks, and they said they had watched Hunter personally free seven Shadows. They said he'd yell at the Shadows 'Time to shine' as he dispersed each one." Hoss seems a little shaken as well.

Kannon ties his boots and heads for the door. Bug grabs Kannon, "Let me go talk to him. I'm the reason he left."

Hoss quickly stops him. "That's an unhealthy decision there, little dude. Better let someone who didn't just set him off go talk to him."

Bug fumbles for words. "But, I…"

Kannon, now angry with Bug as well, says, "But nothing! I think you've done enough with your wise-ass remarks. Now sit down and try not to offend anyone else while I'm gone."

Bug sits on the floor and covers himself completely so no one can see him. Dillo wants to hug Bug, but when he leans towards Bug, Hoss shakes his head. So Dillo just turns away from Bug and closes his eyes as if he is going to sleep.

Hoss just has one more thing to really put the dagger in Bug's heart. "Friends just don't do that to friends." Hoss closes his eyes to get some rest.

As Kannon approaches the front steps, he can see Hunter's silhouette sitting on a big rock at the end of the walkway, his back to the cabin. Kannon cautiously walks up to Hunter and places his hand on his shoulder to comfort him.

"Mind if I sit here with you?"

Hunter doesn't answer, but Kannon sits anyway. As the two sit staring out into the darkness, Kannon is trying to figure out what to say. The silence is incredibly awkward.

"You know," he finally says. "Bug didn't mean anything by that. Shit, half the time, I don't think he knows what he says."

"I know, it's not just him. This place is very hard at times. I don't know if I'm the good guy or the bad. Everyone just looks at me weird here."

"We're so sorry; we didn't know about Lakin or even about the watchers till tonight. Shit, if you want, you can have mine."

Hunter doesn't even react to Kannon's attempt at humor. It becomes quiet again and Kannon can see a tear run down Hunter's cheek through the little bit of light coming from the porch. The tear seems to be following a trail made by the ones before it.

Hunter softly says, "I couldn't hurt the Beast. My daggers had no effect on him. They just bounced off him." Hunter begins shaking his head. Kannon can see Hunter is losing the battle inside himself. Hunter, now with a trembling voice, says, "I was helpless. As I looked at the Beast, all I could see was my music manager's face." Hunter places his face in his hands. "It should've been me, not her."

Kannon tries being stern. "Now stop that. You said you did everything you could. At least now you're here, and we can figure out how to take this Beast down together."

Hunter, feeling sorry for himself, says, "If I were you, I wouldn't stay around me. Everyone around me gets hurt. I'm not a good guy."

Kannon places his arm around Hunter's shoulders. "Yeah, I'm not going anywhere. We're figuring out this Beast together so Lakin doesn't lose her light for nothing. All I see in the future is the Beast taking a serious ass beating." Kannon nudges Hunter. "Plus, we have something the Jokers and the Beast don't."

Hunter looks at Kannon, "What's that?"

"One very pissed off Hunter."

Hunter smirks just enough for Kannon to see. Kannon attempts humor one last time as Hunter wipes the remaining tears from his eyes. "Plus, like I said, you can have my watcher."

Hunter giggles a little, "What would I do with a fun-sized watcher?" Both men laugh at that one. They stand and walk back into the cabin.

The rest of the group sit at the table, eating since they can't sleep. At least all of them but Bug, who still sits on the floor, all covered up.

Hoss gives Hunter knuckles as he asks, "Yall good? Nothing like a midnight snack."

Hunter nods his head. All is good. After stuffing their faces once again, it is finally time to crash for the night.

Kannon gestures Hunter towards a quiet Bug on the floor. "You know, he's taking it hard."

Hunter nods. "I'll talk to him first thing in the morning."

One by one, the men settle back in their spots. Hunter turns off the lights, and the group drifts off to sleep.

CHAPTER 7

"Any chance you get to be a friend, be the best friend you can." -Bug

When all the men are fast asleep, and Bug is sure they are all totally out, he opens his eyes. Bug is only pretending to sleep. He quickly gathers his bat and a few leftovers from dinner and creeps out of the cabin. Quietly, he closes the broken front door behind him as he places a note on the door. Bug wrote the note while he was under the blanket. He leaves it on the door so when the guys get up in the morning and open the door, it will fall, and they will see it.

Bug walks down the path to the road. As he approaches the road, he quickly turns back to check if he is being followed. After a minute or two and not seeing anyone, Bug heads down the road. He knows he needs to make amends for his rude comments and his behavior. The only way he can do that is to send the Beast's light home so his friends can't be hurt anymore by it.

As Bug walks off, letting the darkness swallow him up, he holds his bat on his shoulder just in case he runs into anything unfriendly. Bug continues to look behind him because he feels he is being followed. As Bug is making himself feel more and more unsettled, his stomach turns every so often. He begins to talk to himself. "There is no one behind you. You got this, kid. Besides, it's only the normal nighttime sounds. Frogs, birds, and other little woodland creatures. What's so scary about a squirrel, besides their nuts?" Bug made himself giggle.

Even though Bug's eyes adjust to the darkness, he still can't see that far in front of him. Thirty minutes go by as Bug's mind is still playing with him. He is sure he is being followed. With nothing but darkness around him, doubt joins his thoughts as well. *What if I find the Beast but can't defeat him? What if I cross paths with the witch and she wants her heart back? What if the chocolate bar didn't fall in the peanut butter? We wouldn't have had Reese's Peanut Butter Cups.* That thought makes Bug a little hungry, so he sits on the grass just off the road and digs into the leftovers he brought with him. While eating, he has his worst fear ever: What if Hunter and the guys never like him anymore? He's never had friends; he finally gets some, and he screws it up. Maybe it's just him; maybe he's supposed to be alone forever.

As Bug is finishing and putting what is left away for later, he hears footsteps coming down the road towards him. Bug jumps back and hides in the brush. He pulls his bat back because spring training is about to come early.

The footsteps come to a stop right in front of the brush, hiding Bug. Bug sticks the bat out of the brush to show his weapon. "Someone's about to catch an ass whooping."

The voice speaks back. "Put the bat away, Bug."

Bug swings the bat at the voice but misses.

"Strike one!" the voice shouts like an umpire.

Bug's moment causes him to fall out of the brush and into the road. He quickly looks up to see Dillo standing over him, smiling.

"That would've been a homerun for sure if you made contact."

Bug gets up and brushes himself off. "Dillo, what are you doing following me? I could've decapitated you."

"I've followed you since the cabin. Why are you way out here?"

"Well, if you really need to know, I'm going to free the Beast's light and save my friends." Bug begins walking away. "And don't try to stop me. The Beast must pay for what he did to Lakin."

Dillo begins walking beside Bug. "Stop you? Hell, I'm going with you. I really like Lakin; she was very nice to me."

Bug is now very relieved since he doesn't have to be alone anymore as the pair walk down the roadside by side. But he has to ask: "OK, What's with the turtle shell?"

Even though Hoss has already told Bug, Dillo disgustedly answers. "It's not a turtle shell; it's an armadillo shell. It's none of your bee's wax."

Bug put his hands up. "Ok, ok, sorry, armadillo shell. Well, if you won't tell me about the shell, then what about the rubber bands?"

Dillo holds the rubber bands up to show Bug. "These are not rubber bands. They are called slingshots, and they'll hurt you badly if they hit you."

"How can rubber bands be dangerous?" Bug smirks.

Dillo picks up a stone and places it in the slingshot; he then swings it around and shoots the rock at a small tree, shearing a small limb off as the guys watch it fall to the ground.

"That's cool; I want to try," Bug says impatiently.

As Bug reaches for the slingshot, Dillo slaps his hand. "Not so fast. These are very dangerous, so be careful."

"Yeah, yeah, just give it to me. Really, how hard can it be?" Bug loads a stone in and begins swinging. The stone flies out too early and hits Bug in the shin as he falls to the ground.

"You let it go too fast," Dillo explains to Bug.

Bug holds his shin as he gets up, limping around and talking to himself. "Walk it off. It's just a flesh wound."

Eventually, when he stops limping, Bug insists that he wants to try it again. He thinks, *if Dillo can do this, it can't be that hard.*

Dillo hands Bug another stone. "Here, try again."

Bug swings the slingshot with everything he's got as the stone flies out straight up above them. Both guys run with their heads down and their arms over their heads as Bug yells, "Heads up!"

When the stone finally reaches the ground again with a thud, Dillo snatches the slingshot out of Bug's hands and continues to yell, "No!"

Bug tries to calm Dillo down so no one hears him. "Ok, I'll never touch your sling shot again."

Dillo puts his slingshot back in his pocket and storms off down the road. Bug catches up with him, still apologizing. As they walk, Bug tries to get Dillo to swing his bat to make things even. But Dillo isn't having any of it. Bug even offers to train Dillo.

"I can teach you to hit a curve ball and send it flying over the wall."

Dillo stops walking. "OK, I'm not mad anymore. Just stop talking about baseball, please."

Bug smiles. "Now we are cooking with gas." As the two continues walking, Bug asks Dillo, "Do you have a name for your slingshot?"

"No, that'd be stupid."

"Well, I have a name for my bat. You want to know what it is?"

Even though Dillo knows he shouldn't, he asks, "What's the name of your bat?"

"Glad you asked. Its name is Babe," Bug proudly boasts.

Dillo replies once again, even though he knows he shouldn't. "As in Babe Ruth?"

Bug gives Dillo a weird look. "Babe Ruth? Nah. I named it after the greatest Little League player I know: Babe Schmit." Bug grabs Dillo to stop so he can tell him about his friend, Babe Schmit. "You see, Babe Schmit is one of the greatest little power hitters of our generation. Since Babe could crush a baseball, it made him very popular in town. So popular that he opened his own town newspaper called Schmit Happens. Everyone couldn't wait to read about the Schmit family. There is Schmit everywhere in the world. New York Schmit, California Schmit, Hell, there is even Schmit in England. There is one Schmit that is seven feet tall. I don't know about you, but that's one big Schmit. They had a Schmit play in the NFL. He was six foot three inches tall and weighed three hundred and sixty-five pounds. That sounds like a lot of Schmit right there. He even had a one-year-old niece; she was a cute little Schmit. You don't know how lucky that family is. I'd give anything to have a little Schmit in me. But that's only a dream. I'll never be Schmit."

Dillo thinks Bug is just messing with him now, but he doesn't know a lot about Schmit. "Are you messing with me?"

Bug nudges Dillo with his elbow. "Would I Schmit you?"

They both break out laughing as they continue down the path. Then, out of nowhere, a light turns on, revealing a very large barn.

When the light then turns off, Bug says, "That must have one of those sensor lights on it."

Dillo whispers, "Maybe the Beast lives there."

Bug whispers back, "It could be it's definitely big enough for him. Let's sneak up and take a look but be careful; it's almost daylight out and will easily be spotted."

Dillo nods, and the two sneak up to about twenty feet from the barn without being seen. Bug points to a hole in the fence and then to a pile of hay bales against the barn wall. Dillo nods again in agreement as they go through the fence and quickly hide behind the bales, still unseen.

Bug scours the barnyard as he wonders, with such a huge barn, where the farmhouse is. Bug's thoughts conclude that something big must be in that barn. He whispers to Dillo, "I really think the Beast is in there. What else could be that important that they need this big of a barn?"

Dillo shrugs.

The sun is breaking over the hill, and the rays pierce the cracks in the barn, allowing them to see inside the barn. The light reveals the two Shadows and the witch that Bug had a run-in with a few days ago. Bug points to the witch and informs Dillo that's who he borrowed the heart from. He explains to Dillo that she is as mean and nasty as the Jokers, and she shows a worried expression. Bug and Dillo agree that they will wait till the coast is clear before they make a move on the barn.

As the two sit there waiting for the witch and her henchmen to leave, Bug breaks out the rest of the leftovers, and they finish it up. Dillo pulls two Starletta's out from his shell and hands one to Bug. Bug smiles from ear to ear as he takes it and pops it open. As the Starletta makes a loud fizzy sound, it brings the attention of a passing shadow. Bug and Dillo duck, but the shadow is still approaching them to inspect the noise.

Dillo thinks fast, picks up a stone, and flicks it into a sign at the other end of the barn with his slingshot. This catches the shadow's attention, and he heads in the opposite direction to inspect that noise. The two sit back down, trying to stay as hidden as they possibly can be. Once the shadow is out of sight, Bug and Dillo stack the bales as if they are building a kid's fort, hiding them from the world. They decide to just wait till at least the witch leaves before they choose their next move.

Bug whispers, "Relax, we may be here awhile," as the two both lay back and doze off from the food they have just eaten.

CHAPTER 8

"Always tell the truth, even though it may hurt more than a lie." – Hunter

The early morning sunlight pokes its way through the cracks of the old cabin walls. It hits Kannon in the eyes, waking him up. He tries to avoid it by covering his face with his arms. After the annoying ray of the sun refuses to give up, Kannon gives up and sits up. His back is killing him from sleeping on the hardwood floor, so he tries to stretch the pain away. Finally, Kannon completely throws in the towel, stands up, and makes his way to the table. He grabs a seat and checks the crown mark as he rubs the sleep from his eyes. "Yeah, it's still there," he says sarcastically. "Boy, could I go for a cup of strong black coffee right now."

"There's coffee?" Hoss asks with his eyes still closed tightly.

"No, I think I'm still dreaming, but yeah, I want coffee," Kannon moans.

Hoss yells for Dillo. "Dillo food, need it now, stat!"

Nothing.

Hoss yells it once more, then realizes Dillo is not there. "Where is that boy? He knows I need to eat first thing in the morning, or I'm a grouch all day."

Hunter rolls over. "Maybe he's out getting takeout. By any chance, is there a Dunkin around here?"

Hoss smiles. "Ahhhh, Dunkin, I can almost taste that bagel sandwich now."

Kannon tells the guys, "Bug isn't here either."

"Maybe he's helping Dillo carry the food and drinks. They better use a cup carrier, so they don't spill my iced green tea."

Kannon, a little concerned, decides to go on the porch to check and see if they're out there. As he walks out, he doesn't see the note as it falls down and off the side of the porch. Kannon makes a trip around the cabin but has no luck finding the two. So, he takes a seat on the porch and dangles his feet while he waits for them to return. After ten minutes or so, Hunter also comes out, stretching, to keep Kannon company and use the little boy's room.

As Hunter stands at the end of the porch relieving himself, his eyes catch the corner of the note sticking out from under a bush on the side of the porch. When he finishes, he walks down the steps and around to the bush to retrieve the note. Hunter holds it up to examine it as he begins to read it to himself. His eyes get large as he tells Kannon, "You're going to want to see this."

Kannon takes the letter from Hunter and begins to read it; after a few seconds, Kannon folds it up and heads into the cabin to get Hoss. As the three men gather at the table, Kannon looks extremely nervous.

"Where'd you get this?" he asks as he holds the note up towards Hunter.

Hunter explains he found it under the bush at the end of the porch. "It must have blown off the porch during the night."

Kannon unfolds the note and begins to read it aloud.

Dear Kannon and Hunter: Let me first begin by saying I'm sorry. I'm sorry you lost Dayne, and Hunter lost Lakin. Only hope one day I can find love that powerful. I had no idea about Lakin's demise, and as always, I stuck my foot in my mouth. I truly didn't mean to make fun of her. I'm also sorry, Kannon, that with all these awesome

watchers, you drew the short stick and got me. Trust me, you two are much better off without me and my mess-ups. I'd only have been in the way if I had stayed.

Lastly, I'm sorry I lied to you two about my story, but after hearing how Hunter was a big star, I realized mine looked even worse. I wasn't popular. I've never even had a friend till I met you guys. It was one of my best days. It was not that we were really friends, but it was an awesome feeling. Growing up as a very small kid, I was an easy target to pick on; I was bullied on a daily basis. My father left us when I was two—even he didn't want me. My mother turned to drugs and overdosed a year later. From there, I moved from family member to family member, then on to foster parents to foster parents. Each one is worse than the previous one. I was beaten, starved, and even changed up for five days once, but no matter what they did to me, I never gave up. I knew there had to be good somewhere. The world can't be this mean everywhere. I never found that place, though; I would just sit and stare off into the Horizon, knowing out there was where I'd be accepted.

Finally, the day came: my graduation. I'd be free—my own person; no one putting me down. I was going to be someone because I had a diploma, and no one could take that away from me. I got up early and put on my good two-sizes-too-big clothes, grabbed my dilapidated bike, which only had half a pedal on one side, and made my way to school. No one came to watch me, and I wasn't invited to any parties, but that didn't matter to me as I walked across that stage and the superintendent handed me that diploma. It would've been nice, right after the ceremony, to hear congratulations from a teacher or classmate. Or to have been asked to get in a picture. I would've even taken a handshake. But I was proud of myself, and that meant the world to me.

As I got back on my bike, holding that diploma as if it were a bag of gold, I rode to the only store in town. I saved up enough money to buy myself a Starletta and a honey bun by taking cans back all week. I thought I definitely deserved it. I sat on the curb next to my bike, holding my diploma in one hand and the honey bun in the other, thinking nothing could ruin that day. I finished the honey bun and popped open the Starletta. Life was good. A few of my classmates pulled in with their jacked-up trucks, and a couple of cheerleaders jumped on the back of it. They were all hootin' and hollerin', just kids being kids. One of them was the captain of the baseball team; his name was Branton. Branton never really liked me since I was usually the butt of his jokes. Branton yelled over to me, "Hey, Bug Boy, you want to party with us?" He threw an empty beer can towards me. "No, thank you," I said politely as I grabbed my bike because I knew where this was heading. They drove off, leaving me in a loud cloud of smoke. I just covered my diploma and pedaled off.

A couple miles down the road, I could hear the loud truck heading my way again. They pulled up beside me, and I tried to act as if I didn't see them. They raced the truck really loud as they began throwing empty beer cans at me, yelling, "Hey, Bug Boy, here's to your college fund." I tried to pedal faster to get ahead of them, but that didn't work. Branton is standing on the back with a broomstick, acting as if he was getting ready to bat. He swung the broomstick at me, but I ducked, and he missed me and almost fell off the truck. He regrouped and drew the stick back again. So, I ducked again, but he didn't swing. Instead, he stuck the stick in my back spokes, sending me flying into the ditch. They stopped the truck as Branton jumped off, grabbed my diploma, and tossed it to someone on the back of the truck. Then he picked up my bike and threw it in the ditch on top of me. As he jumped back on the truck, he held my diploma out towards me to tease me. I tried to get out of the ditch in time, but they drove off before I could. Branton yelled, "You can find your diploma at the bottom of High Bridge Bug Boy!" Then they drove off in a cloud of smoke.

I sat on the side of the road, bleeding and disgraced. No diploma, no bike, no family or friends, no nothing. For what was supposed to be my best day turned out like all the rest. It took me over an hour to get to High Bridge, just to find my diploma ripped to pieces and scattered all around. I started to pick the pieces up, but they were too scattered. So I threw what I picked up back on the ground. So disgusted. How could everyone I meet be so mean? Was it just me that everyone must hate? As I stood there looking at the water and then the bridge, my mind began to hate me as well. The thoughts that I was thinking should never enter someone's mind. I finally had enough and walked over to the end of the bridge. There was a wooden bat leaning against the base of the bridge; must be some kids were hitting rocks in the water earlier. I picked up the bat and swung it a couple times. It felt good to swing it. I began talking to the bat, telling him what I was about to do. He didn't try to talk me out of it, so we began trying to climb the bridge together. As we made our way to almost the top, the wind picked up a little, so we had to hold on better. But we finally made it. Fearing heights, it didn't seem to bother us much. It was the most amazing view. We could see almost the end of the Horizon. As we stood on the top of the world, the stars began to fall. It was as if they were being poured from the sky.

I was so amazed I accidentally dropped the bat. Knowing how much the bat wanted to join me on this adventure, I climbed down to rescue him. Back on the ground and bat in hand, I turned to climb once again. But something caught my eye. It was a door stuck on the side of the rocky cliff. We had to investigate, so we climbed down to it to see where it led. As we approached the door, it slowly cracked open. We couldn't see in it, so the bat agreed to go first as he jumped in. He didn't come back, so I had to go in and get him. That's what friends do for friends; they never leave them alone. So, I went through the door to find him as it closed behind us, bringing us here. When I awoke, I realized it was just a bat and not a friend. But I'd keep him with me now that we were a team, and we might need to protect each other.

Sincerely, your possible friend, Bug.

PS - Thank you for trying to be my friend. It meant the world to me. Please tell Hunter that I'm truly sorry that he's lost Lakin and that I'm going to free the Beast so he can't hurt any more of you. Truly sorry to everyone. Alone forever, Bug.

Kannon places the letter on the table, stunned. Hunter is still emotional from the night before.

"We need to find him. I lost one friend to the Beast already; I damn sure won't lose another one."

Hunter runs out the door with a crazed look on his face.

Hoss yells to Kannon, "Go get him before he destroys the whole land. When you find Bug, slap him for me for being so stupid and careless."

Kannon heads out the door without shutting it as he runs down the road after Hunter.

Hoss yells louder. "I'll wait here for Dillo, then catch up with you guys!"

Hunter runs at full speed with his daggers already out. Kannon, losing ground on Hunter, screams, "Hunter, wait, we don't even know where they went!"

Hunter answers him but in a low voice that Kannon can't hear. "Then I'll free them all till I find him."

CHAPTER 9

"A beauty of a lady, will make a man do the dumbest
things."-Dillo

Bug peeks through the bales and can see no one. He then
explains the plan to Dillo, who is drowsy and looks as if he has
fallen asleep while they wait. Bug grabs a stick to draw the plan
in the dirt for Dillo.

"Ok, we need to get over here by the barn so we can hear
what's being discussed and get confirmation of what's in such
a large barn in the middle of nowhere. So, we'll crawl to this
spot here." Bug draws a line in the dirt and puts an X next to
the awfully drawn barn. Dillo gives him the thumbs up sign.

When the coast is clear, Bug kicks a bale out of the fort and
they both crawl out. Neither get up as they slowly cross the
barnyard on their stomachs, looking like slow-moving snakes.
As they near the barn, Bug stands up and goes flat against the
barn wall. Dillo does the same as the two slide along the barn
wall till they are close enough to hear what's happening inside
the barn.

Bug looks at Dillo. "*Shhhhh.*"

Dillo nods his head as he pretends to lock his mouth and
throw away the keys. They place their ears against the wall to
hear the witch and her cohorts.

One of the Shadows begins to speak. "I'm sorry, Agoth, but
we can't find the heart."

The other shadow adds, "Someone must have stolen it."

"Who'd be dumb enough to steal from me?" the witch

clamors.

Neither shadow can answer that. As they continue arguing, the barn door slowly opens and two very sharp dress men stroll in, one looking just like the other.

The witch yells, "Why would you give me these two stupid buffoons?"

"You're lucky we gave you anything, *hag*," one of them retorts as the two approach the witch.

Bug and Dillo can't believe their ears. So, they find a crack in the barn wood big enough to see inside. As the two gentlemen step into the light, Bug's mouth drops as the Jokers stand right in front of him.

Bug whispers incredibly low, "That's got to be the Jokers."
Dillo once again gives Bug the thumbs up.

Just then, one of the Jokers looks in their direction, as if he hears them. Bug and Dillo both duck even though they are on the other side of the wall. Bug, relieved, looks at Dillo and wipes his forehead. They place their ears again on the wall.

One of the Jokers tosses something to the witch. "Here, take mine, but this time take care of it."

The other Joker explains, "We only have one more, hag."

The witch barks back at the young gentlemen, "Don't act like you're doing me any favors, clowns."

Both Jokers grab her chin at once. "If we hear that name once more, we'll have your tongue hanging next to our pet." Both Jokers look up at a small cage hanging from the rafters.

Then, as quickly as they came, they leave. One of the Jokers sticks his head back in the door and says, "Lose this heart and it will be your light lost next." He smiles then is gone.

The witch can't leave well enough alone and yells, "Without this heart, your precious Beast would've parish against that sharpshooter and the giant man. You can at least thank me for the shield spell and the victory." Then she softly mumbles, "Clowns."

This brings the two men back into the barn, looking unhappy. One speaks to the witch as the other circles around her. "Just be glad you're useful, you old hag, because if we didn't need you. . ." The Joker pauses as the other Joker finishes. ". . .we wouldn't need you."

The Joker behind the witch grabs her arms and holds them tightly behind her, so she can't fight back. The Joker in front of her grabs her chin and forces her mouth open.

"I'm sure you heard what we said about that word." He then reaches into the witch's mouth and rips her tongue out. The Joker holds it up for the Shadows to see. Screams fill the air from the witch as she runs out of the barn. The Joker smiles as he tosses the witch's tongue to one of the Shadows.

"Do me a favor, young chap. Hang this from the rafters for us, please."

As they exit, the other says, "Clowns. What a hideous word."

They are gone, leaving one of the two Shadows holding the witch's tongue. Before the door completely shuts, one of the Jokers adds, "I hope you got everything you need."

The Shadows responds, "Yes, sir, we understand."

The Joker looks at the two Shadows. "I wasn't talking to you." Then they were gone.

Bug and Dillo fall back on the ground, and Dillo asks, "Was he talking to us?"

Bug's glaze over as if he's seen a ghost. "I believe so, Dillo. I believe so."

When the two come to their senses, they lean against the barn to listen to the Shadows. The first shadow is climbing down from the rafters, as the second one is poking at something above him. Bug can't see through the crack high enough to figure out what it is.

As the shadow reaches the ground, he says, "Will you leave the Joker's pet alone? You know they don't like it when you aggravate it."

The second shadow jumps down once he gets close to the floor. "Can you believe he ripped her tongue out?"

"Maybe they know of her plan to get all three hearts and overthrow them," the other shadow adds.

The second one shakes his head. "Well, she damn sure isn't telling anyone about it now."

As the two exit the building, the first shadow laughs. "One good thing came out of this tonight."

"What's that?"

"We don't have to listen to her bitch anymore."

They both laugh as they leave saying, "Good night, pet."

Once they're alone, Bug tells Dillo, "That's why Hunter and Hoss couldn't affect the Beast. She had a protection spell on him."

"We need to tell them now. Let's go."

Bug grabs Dillo's shoulder. "Hold on. Don't you want to know what's up above? Like what's the Joker's pet?"

"No!"

"Ok, just walk away, but I'm going in to see what it is. It might help in this battle," Bug states, trying to change Dillo's mind.

Dillo turns back towards the barn as he walks past Bug. "Alright, but just one quick peek then we are out of here."

Bug runs in front of him and gets to the door first. "Ok, just one quick peek."

The barn door is open, so the two step through without making a sound. They quickly sneak behind some hay bales to remain unseen. Once they realize they are alone and no one is in the barn, they look up to see a cage hanging from the highest rafter. Right next to that hangs the witch's tongue. The two try their best to maneuver around to see if they can see what is in the cage. It is way too high for them to get a good look. But Bug thinks he sees a small hand hanging out of the cage.

"Is that a girl?" Bug asks.

"I can't tell; it might be."

"Could it be Lakin?"

Dillo shakes his head. "Lakin is bigger than that; the cage is too small."

Bug begins walking around to try and get a better angle to see in the cage. "It's just too high. One of us is going to get higher to see." Bug is hoping Dillo will accept to climb.

Dillo points to the corner of the barn. "There is a barn ladder hooked to that wall. That must be how the Shadows got up to the cage."

Both men stare up the ladder, waiting for the other to start climbing. Bug explains something as if Dillo is going to climb. "Let's see, if we climb the ladder, then get to those rafters, we can shimmy over to the center and then cross the really high beam right to the cage. Easy peasy."

Dillo looks at Bug like he is crazy. "Yeah, I'm not going up there. I'm scared of heights and besides, we haven't even seen any movement from the cage to even know if something is up there. It's a definite no from me."

Bug asks him, "If we can prove someone up there will you go then?"

"Ah, no," Dillo quickly adds.

Bug grabs a stone and throws toward the cage but doesn't even come close. Dillo joking, "I see you weren't a pitcher."

"Shut up!" Bug barks at him.

Dillo grabs his slingshot out of his pocket and fires a stone into the bottom of the cage. A small hand drapes over the edge of the cage.

Bug yells, "See someone is in it! Come on, we need to save them."

Bug runs to the ladder and stands there looking up, trying to gather any bit of courage he has. Dillo says, "What are you doing, you climbed High Bridge like nothing?"

"Oh yeah, High Bridge," Bug says reluctantly. Then, he checks with Dillo one more time but gets the same response. Bug takes a huge breath, then starts up the ladder. After getting up about five rungs on the ladder, Dillo waves and mumbles something. Bug climbs back down to see what it is he is trying to tell him.

"What did you want? Is something wrong?"

Dillo smiles. "No nothing, just telling you good luck."

Bug, with a mean look on his face, begins to climb again. Finally, Bug reaches the top of the ladder as he holds on with every ounce of strength he has.

Dillo yells, "Look how high you are. You'd never catch me up there. Imagine if you fall. Splat—no more bug."

Bug frees up one hand long enough to flip Dillo off then begins to crawl up on the first beam. The only thing running through his mind is *don't look down.* It also doesn't help much when Dillo yells, "Hey, they say if you don't look down it's better for you. Oh, look a pretty stone."

Once Bug is securely on the first beam, he slowly looks up towards the cage and notices that it is actually a young lady. Bug yells, "Dillo, it is a girl!"

Dillo, being a wise ass, yells back, "What's that? You're a girl?"

Bug can hear Dillo laughing at his own stupid joke. Bug

sighs as he continues crawling to the next beam. The next beam is a little tricky because he has to change directions and turn to the left.

Dillo yells to him, "Should've turned right. You know videogames."

Bug now works his way to the middle where there's a big enough base for him to sit and rest for a minute. But he screws up and looks down, bringing back thoughts of the bridge as he grasps the center pole beside him. Bug is frozen; he can't move a muscle. Fear has filled him.

Dillo tries to help as he yells, "Why are you stopping? You're only halfway."

Bug yells with a shaky voice, "I'm stuck; I can't make it. Go get help."

"Go get help! Where the hell am I going to go to get help? What'd want me to go yell outside for some firemen or cops? They aren't coming, so stop being a scaredy cat and get moving. We don't have all day; those Shadows will be back real soon." Dillo kicks an old metal pail lying beside him on the ground.

Just then, Bug thinks he hears the girl try and talk. He feels the fear instantly leave his body and he continues towards the girl. Bug has two beams left till he reaches the cage. Suddenly, the barn door opens and five Shadows walk in having a not too serious conversation.

Dillo dives onto his stomach and crawls behind three bales. Bug tries waving to tell him to put his ass down because they could probably still see him. As for Bug, he lays sideways on the beam so they can't see him at all. They are horsing around, wrestling, until one of them yells, "Hey, let's see who can get a rock to hit the Joker's precious little pet."

They all begin throwing stones at the cage, but barely any

of them have a good enough aim to hit it. Every fourth throw clanks to the bottom of the cage. A few missed throws hit Bug as he tries not to make a sound. Bug can't believe the girl doesn't flinch whatsoever. He wonders if she is alive.

One of the Shadows accidentally hits the witch's tongue and knocks it down right in front of Bug on the beam. Bug cringes as he slowly tries to back away from it without being seen.

The shadow who hit the tongue begins to complain. "Ahh shit. Leave it to me to hit the old nasty tongue. Now I'm going to have to climb up there and rehang it. Just my luck."

The other four laughs and yells, "Not it," as they run out of the barn.

When the shadow gets close enough to Dillo, Dillo jumps up, startling it. The shadow falls backwards as he claws his way away from Dillo and runs out the barn door. Dillo looks at Bug as if to say "hurry" as he takes his hiding spot again.

Bug yells, "Dillo, up here!" and he gestures for Dillo to climb up with him to hide.

Even though Dillo is a hundred percent against it, he climbs his way up to the rafters and lay sideways, his shell sticking out partway and is visible. Bug grabs the slimy tongue, trying not to throw up, and hangs it back in its original place.

The five Shadows come bursting through the door, almost taking it off the hinges. They rush over to where Dillo is spotted, but they find nothing. One of the Shadows complains, "Are you messing with us? Look, the tongue is hanging right there. Come on, guys, he's an idiot getting our hopes up like that for a prank."

The shadow who had seen Dillo tries to explain to the other Shadows, "Guys, I know what I saw."

A third shadow states, "Come on. guys, we're out of here

like a fat guy in dodgeball."

The Shadows left the barn one by one. The last one who saw Dillo stops to look once more, then he shrugs his shoulders and leaves as well. Bug wants to giggle at that remark so badly but instead just exhales and wipes his forehead with his hoodie sleeve.

As Bug turns to tell Dillo the coast is clear, Dillo is already back on solid ground. He yells, "I can't believe you touched the witch's tongue! Although I'm sure you've touched worse."

Bug just ignores his stupid remarks and sets his sights on the task at hand. He finally makes it to the cage, and, once close enough, he can tell the girl is about his age. She has a purple tint in her short hair as well as on her fingernails. She is smaller than Bug, but not by much. Bug almost loses his breath from her beauty; she is the most beautiful girl he's ever seen. He thinks, *Why would anyone want to hurt something so delicate?* Bug shakes the cage to get a response from her, but nothing. He tries pulling on the lock, but that doesn't work. So, he reaches back to grab his bat, but Babe isn't there. Bug immediately begins panicking as he looks all over the barn floor from above. He can't locate Babe. Where could he be? Bug thinks, *I had him when we got to the barn; I used him to prop the fence open. Oh shit, is he still there holding the fence?* Either way, Bug has to focus on one problem at a time. He has to figure out a way to open the cage lock, since he definitely is not going back down to get something. Finally, he comes up with a solution.

"Dillo!" he yells.

Dillo makes his way underneath Bug, as Bug says, "If I hold my hand on the lock and give you a quick flash, can you hit that spot with a rock?"

Dillo yells back, "I can give it a shot."

Bug places his hand on the lock and flashes quickly. Before he can move his hand, the stone clanks off the cage just above his hand. Bug pulls back his hand and counts all five fingers. Bug explains to Dillo that he must wait a second for him to move his hand. Dillo gives him the *ok* sign.

Bug turns to the young girl and says, "Don't worry, we'll get you out of here."

The girl doesn't move or answer him. Bug places his hand once again on the lock. He flashes then quickly removes his hand. The stone grazes the metal lock, making it jump. Bug yells down, "Nice shot! One more like that and we've got it."

Once again, he flashes and quickly removes his hands. The stone hits a direct target, shattering the lock as pieces of it fall to the barn floor. "Bingo!" Bug shouts.

Bug swings the cage door open and quickly checks if she's breathing. He yells to Dillo, "She's breathing. I'll bring her down."

Bug pulls the almost lifeless girl out of the cage right to his side. He takes off his hoodie and puts it on her. He studies the beams, knowing he'll not be able to crawl and hold her. Then, as if he was never scared of heights, he stands up and gains his balance. Bug tells the girl, "I'm going to pick you up over my shoulder, so try to hold on to me. I promise I won't let go of you. I'm going to get you out of here."

The girl opens her eyes barely and gives Bug a half-hearted smile. She tries to squeeze Bug but goes limp and motionless. Bug, without a second to waste, picks the girl up and begins carrying her across the beams, crossing one after another, never taking his eyes off the girl. As he comes to the final right turn with just one beam left, Bug begins to wobble, almost losing his balance. But he catches himself and makes it to the ladder, where Dillo is waiting to help. As the two finally reach the ground with the young lady, they place her on the ground and Dillo slowly tries to pour water into her mouth. She takes a couple minimal sips.

"We need to get her out of here and to somewhere safe, now!" Bug says, trying to rush Dillo to leave the barn.

They pick up the young lady as Bug grabs her upper half and Dillo grabs her feet. They make their way to the broken barn door, and Bug peaks out to check if it is safe to move her out.

"It all looks good, let's go." Bug pushes the broken door open, and they head out across the barnyard following the same path that brought them there.

Dillo has to stop just once for a quick rest, then they move on. When they finally make it back to the fence, there sits Babe, still holding the fence for them.

"Here you are, old friend, you had me a little worried," Bug says as they climb through the fence to the other side. Bug regains Babe and puts him back in his rightful spot the three head off into the woods.

Dillo knows of a good hiding spot that he had seen on the way in, so that's where they take the young lady to rest. They place her on the ground, and Dillo gives her his hoodie to use as a pillow. Dillo then runs off into the woods without saying a word, leaving the two there to rest. Bug just sits there and watches the girl sleep, being he isn't a doctor and has no idea what she needs. Bug is totally spent by rescue and slowly drifts off himself.

CHAPTER 10

"Beauty is in the eye of the beholder, and I'd like to be holding her."-Bug

Dillo awakens to rays of sunlight dancing on his face from the brush above him, gently swaying back and forth in the breeze. He rolls over to see Bug's face almost touching his.

Bug, without opening his eyes, smiles. "Good morning, beautiful." Then Bug continues to hug Dillo.

Dillo gives a rabbit punch to Bug's stomach, then quickly jumps to his feet. Bug, rolling around on the ground, laughing while holding his stomach, says "What's wrong? I said 'beautiful'." Dillo continues to try and wipe Bug's hug off him. In the meantime, Bug regroups and gets to his feet. They stop their little routine as they notice the young lady is awake, laughing at the two clowns while she eats the blackberries Dillo had fetched her in the night.

Simultaneously, they ask the girl, "Are you alright? Do you need more food, maybe a drink?"

The young lady makes a drinking gesture with her hands. "You want a drink; got it." Dillo pulls a Starletta out of his shell and hands it to her.

Bug snatches it and opens it before giving it back to the girl. "Sorry about my friend's rudeness."

She laughs again at the pair, then drinks the Starletta in one attempt. Dillo takes the empty bottle from her, opens another bottle, and hands it to her. Bug gives him a weird look. "What about me? I'm also thirsty."

Dillo looks at him. "Sorry, all out."

The girl drinks a couple of sips from the bottle and then hands it to Bug. "No, I'm just messing with Dillo. You need it more than I do." He pushes it back towards her. Then he puts his hands to his chest. "My name's Bug, and this is Dillo."

Dillo copies him as he mocks Bug. "My name is *Buuuuuuuuug,* and this is Dillo."

Bug punches Dillo in the arm, and Dillo begins instantly rubbing the spot Bug hit. The girl laughs as she makes her hand look like a bug crawling up her arm. Then she turns towards Dillo and tips her head towards him as she knocks on his shell. Dillo asks her what her name is, but she shakes her head back and forth like she doesn't want to tell them.

"Well, if you don't feel like talking right now, we understand. But till you tell us your name, we're calling you Beautiful," Bug says.

Then both gentlemen extend a hand to help Beautiful up. She takes both their hands and stands up. She is almost the same height as Bug. Dillo laughs. Bug gestures towards the direction of the cabin as they all head off down the path with a guy on each arm. While they walk, Bug fills her in on Kannon, Hunter, and Hoss. He explains about the five warriors and how he and Dillo are both watchers. Finally, he tells her how they must find Dayne and some guy named Dak. Dillo also tells of the passing of a watcher named Lakin. It is a lot for her to take in all at once. She likes how excited they talk about their friends.

The three come to a fork in the road. Bug insists they come from the right, while Dillo disagrees and says they come from the left. As the two stand there bickering about which way to go, Beautiful turns and puts her finger to her mouth to tell the boys to be quiet. They immediately stop when they see her. She points up ahead, then pushes both guys in the hedgerow. She follows behind, joining them. Bug and Dillo don't have a clue what is going on but sit still and remain silent. Then, out of nowhere come voices coming towards them. Bug's curiosity gets to him as he tries to get a peek at who owns the voices. But he leans too far out and topples out of the hiding spot. Bug lands right in front of three Shadows.

The Shadows are startled at first but regroup and go on the offensive side. "Well, well, well, looky here, boys. We have ourselves a real one," one of the Shadows points out.

Bug quickly gets to his feet, trying to act tough. "Back up, or I'll free your lights."

Before the Shadows can speak, Beautiful steps out from the hedge row between Bug and the Shadows. The surprised Shadows speak. "Well, if it isn't the Joker's little pet." They laugh as the shadow continues. "How'd you get out of your cage? Bad girl, you know we must take you back. Oh, what a reward we'll get."

Beautiful shakes her head. The three Shadows circle around the two as another shadow speaks.

"We might even get a reward from the witch as well. She is pretty fond of you."

Bug nervously begins to flicker just enough to solidify the Shadows.

"What have you done, you little turd?" the Shadows yell at Bug.

Another shadow says, "You see what your little toad did to us, Spin Doll?"

At that moment, Bug notices Spin Doll's hand lit up like Kannon's and Hunter's. Her hands begin to grow into what looks like oriental hand fans. The shadow in front of her rubs his hands as he steps towards her. Spin Doll splits him right down the middle from head to toe as each side of his body falls to the side and vanishes, leaving a ball of light to just float up in the sky. The other two rush from each side as she decapitates both at once, and their light joins the first one.

Bug's eyes about jump out of his head. "What the hell was that? That was some next-level shit right there. We aren't in Kansas anymore."

Dillo, stuttering from the hedgerow, asks, "Can I come out now, Spin Doll?"

Spin Doll nods as she grabs Dillo's arm and pulls him out onto the path.

Bug asks, "Are you also a Warrior? And if so, can I be your watcher?"

Spin Doll laughs as she brushes his cheek with her changed-back fingers. Bug seems to melt right there on the road. The three regroup and head down the road towards the cabin. Like before, each guy grabs one of Spin Doll's arms as they walk. Bug and Dillo tap knuckles behind Spin Doll's back as if she doesn't know they did it.

Finally, they make it back to where Dillo joined Bug on this outing.

"We should make it there by dark. Should only be another hour or so," Dillo informs them.

Bug stops. "Well, this is where I say goodbye to you two. It's been one of my life's highlights to meet you, Spin Doll, and your beauty shall forever be etched in my mind. As far as you, Dillo, make sure she gets back to the guys safely, douche." Bug walks off the path and begins walking through the field.

Dillo yells, "What are you doing? We need to get back."

Bug just keeps walking as he waves his hands in the air. Spin Doll looks as if she wants to yell at Bug as well but just stands there as puzzled as Dillo is.

Bug suddenly stops. "You make sure she gets to the cabin. Besides, your friends are waiting for you. I set out to release a Beast, and that's what I'm going to do."

Dillo and Spin Doll watch till Bug is no longer visible. Dillo turns towards the cabin. "Come on, Spin Doll, we still have awhile."

The pair begin to walk in the direction back to the cabin. A barely visible tear sneaks down Spin Doll's face in confusion. Dillo and Spin Doll walk for another few minutes as Spin Doll stops. Dillo asks, "What's wrong? Why are we stopping were almost there?"

Spin Doll points across the field, and in the distance there are two figures coming at them. Spin Doll's hand begins to light up as Dillo pulls out his slingshot. As the two images get closer, Dillo recognizes that it's Kannon and Hunter, and he waves to them. He quickly turns to Spin Doll and gestures to stop. "They are good guys; they're with us."

Spin Doll calms down and returns to form. Kannon and Hunter wave back as they continue towards them. Once they make it to Dillo, Kannon, out of breath, explains how they've been searching for Bug all night and wants to know if he's seen him. Dillo tells the two tired warriors how he followed Bug and about their adventure to rescue Spin Doll and also that they saw the Jokers and what they did to the witch.

Kannon questions, "Where is Bug now? Why isn't he with you?"

Dillo responds, "He plans on defeating the Beast for Hunter's and Lakin's revenge. He is with us about thirty minutes ago, but he went that way." Dillo points off behind them.

Kannon tells Hunter, "You take them back to the cabin where it's safe, also so she can meet Hoss. The other part of our dysfunctional family of misfits."

Hunter resistantly says, "They can make it back; it's only over the hill a few fields away. I better come with you in case we run into some uglies."

But Kannon insists that he can handle finding Bug. "Spin Doll needs to get food and rest if she's going to be any good to us. Plus, if something does happen, they both won't perish."

Finally, Hunter agrees as he gestures to Spin Doll and Dillo towards the cabin. As Kannon begins walking away, Hunter yells, "Bring back our friend in one piece!"

Kannon continues walking away, but he doesn't turn back to answer Hunter; he just gives a thumbs up signal.

* * *

Bug so much wants to stay with Spin Doll and Dillo to make sure they safely made it back to the cabin. But he made a commitment, and he has to show the guys that he is a significant part of this group as well. Whether they are his friends or not, he has to help them win this fight. They are not going to lose because of him.

Bug has come to a quick-flowing stream that has the perfect layout to cross it by jumping from rock to rock. Once Bug makes it across without falling in, his confidence grows a little more. He thinks, *See, nothing can stop me. I made it this far without friends. I'll be alright.* But then he thinks, *It would definitely be cool to have Kannon, Hunter, and Hoss as friends, though. I'd love them to meet Branton.*

Bug decides to stop for a minute and rests at a stone wall on the top of the steep hill that overlooks the whole valley. As Bug sits there looking over the valley, he truly can't believe how serene and peaceful the view is. He thinks, *This is what I thought the Horizon would be, only it's even better.*

Bug takes it all in, as he may never see this much beauty

ever again. Because this could be his last day here in the Horizon; tomorrow is never promised. The night begins creeping in as he sits there, leaning up against the stone wall with his hands behind his head, watching the sun say goodbye. Yeah, he should've looked for a safe place to hide, but he is done running and fearing the dark. He closes his eyes to listen to the crickets sing to him. A breeze sends a chill up his spine, and he remembers he forgot to get his hoodie from Spin Doll.

* * *

Kannon makes it to the top of the hill, but on the opposite side of the stone wall is Bug. He also is amazed at the sight of the valley as the darkness slowly erases the sunlight. Where Kannon stops to rest a minute, he is a mere ten feet from Bug. Kannon looks over the valley to see if he can spot Bug. Kannon thinks that there is no way he can be that much further away from him.

Bug hears grass and brush rustling from something on the other side of the stone wall. So, he pushes himself as close to the stone wall as he possibly can while grabbing his bat. Bug then lays there as silent as a church mouse. Kannon knows he can't stop long if he wants to catch up to Bug before it's too dark to see, so he takes off down the hill and soon out of sight. After a few minutes of not hearing anything, Bug slowly peeks over the wall to see only an empty field. Then he returns to his spot against the wall as he thinks, *Whew, that was a close one. I would hate to beat a couple of shadow asses tonight.* He is proud of his never-happened victory. After such a scare, Bug can't sleep. He just sits there looking over the darkened valley, wondering where the Beast could be and how he is going to bring him to his demise.

Suddenly, a tiny light way off in the distance comes on out of nowhere. Bug is hypnotized by it, as his curiosity makes him want to see what it is. Bug figures it won't hurt to check it out since he is too cold to sleep. Bug approaches the light, avoiding it enough to not be seen. It is a light from a little country-style house. The house looks lived in and well taken care of for being in the middle of nowhere. Bug is close enough to the house that he thinks he can smell food cooking on the stove. He has to see if the house is occupied, so he crawls up to a small side window.

Bug slowly raises his head to look inside, when another light turns on inside the house, revealing a kitchen with a real live meal cooking on the stove. A lady walks in, yelling to another room, "I say, leave the lights on. How am I supposed to cook in the dark?" Then she checks the food on the stove before going back into the next room.

Bug's mouth is watering as he can almost taste the food. He can't quite see what is in the pans, but it smells incredible. Bug wonders if he knocks on the door, will they be nice enough to invite him to join them? They have real food cooking, and his eyes can almost taste it.

The lady enters once again, as she checks the food and yells, "Food's done; who wants to eat?"

Bug, standing outside the window, waves his hand. Next, the lady sets the table for two people, which makes Bug wonder who the second person is. As he waits to see the second person, the lady opens the oven and reveals a huge chocolate cake. Bug bumps his head on the window, making a thud sound. He ducks as the lady quickly looks towards the window, then he runs behind the nearest tree and hides. The lady opens the window and looks around to see no one. She then closes the window and goes back to setting the table. Bug sits behind the tree, torn at what to do. Suddenly, Bug is joined by some footsteps as five Shadows stop and stand in front of Bug's tree.

They discuss their plans to take out the lady in the house

without knowing Bug is listening to the discussion the whole time. Bug knows he cannot let them hurt the lady, so somehow, he needs to release their lights. Before Bug can think of a plan, the Shadows begin to talk.

"Just as we were told Dayne is in the house, our only hope is that Dak is in there with her. When the rest of the group gets here, we can storm the house and erase one of the five warriors."

Bug cannot let them end Dayne, especially since he is a watcher. He must do something, and it must be quick. Bug knows he is outnumbered, but soon there will be many more. It is now or never.

Bug jumps out from behind the tree. The Shadows overtake him quickly, with one on each arm.

"Well, look what we have here; a little watcher warm-up," one states.

The shadow draws back to strike Bug, but with his nervousness, Bug flashes and turns them all solid.

"What have you done? Oh well, today's your last day either way." The head shadow laughs.

"Let him go, you clown wannabes. It's me you want; not this little guy." Dayne steps out on the porch to reveal herself.

The head shadow questions, "Why would we let him go? It's the perfect deal. End one Warrior and get a watcher for free."

Thirty to forty Shadows run in and surround the little house as the head shadow grins. "Oh no, looks like the end of the road and on such a beautiful night. Guess who's getting a bonus tonight?"

The Shadows unhand Bug, who then runs over to Dayne.

"My only question for you, Dayne, is do we get the boy as well? Where is little Dakky? Tell him to come out and play.

Besides, you don't want to be rude to your guest, now do you?" the head shadow states, since that he's got the upper hand.

"I'd rather not bother him. He's taking a nap," Dayne sarcastically adds.

Not liking Dayne's response, the five solid Shadows charge. As they get closer, Bug pulls his bat back and swings with everything he has. It sounds like an explosion as all five vanish, and their lights rise to the sky.

CHAPTER 11

"All battles can be won if your friend has your back and a cannon." - Bug

Bug's eyes light up as all five charging Shadows have gone. The Shadows that surround them all take a step back in amazement. Bug looks at his bat but sees no blue goo on it. Confused, he looks around and spots Kannon not far off in the distance.

Kannon's arm is smoking as he remarks, "You don't think I'd let my best friend have all the fun alone, do ya?"

Bug smiles bigger than he ever has before. "I'll light them up."

Kannon nods. "And I'll set them free."

The two begin dispersing Shadows as quickly as they can, but just when they start getting the upper hand, Kannon and Dayne lock eyes as both stop fighting and stand there stunned. Neither have words for the other.

Bug yells, "A little help here would be nice."

The warriors take to the fight once again. Bug looks as if he is a disco ball, sending flashes of light in every direction as Kannon fires repeatedly as quickly as his arm will let him. Dayne, trying to make her way to them, is hacking and slashing with every ounce of strength she can muster up. Being so outnumbered, they just can't keep up with the charging Shadows. Soon, Kannon, Bug, and Dayne find themselves cornered with their backs against the house. The Shadows have them dead to rights as the warriors are completely exhausted, and it shows.

One of the Shadows says, "Looks like this is going to be over before it really begins. I really thought you'd put up a better fight then this, Dayne."

Kannon stares at Dayne. There is so much he wants to say to her.

Dayne notices Kannon looking at her. "Do I know you?"

Kannon whispers, "It's you; it's really you."

The shadow interrupts. "Sorry to break up this little reunion or whatever it is, but it's definitely going to end here." The Shadows close in to end this short but sweet battle. "Any last words?"

Kannon's arm changes back as Bug covers his head with his arms. Dayne pulls her sword back to her chest for her last defense. The Shadows cheer as they draw back for the final blow.

"Time to make you shine," a voice from behind them says.

Surprised, the Shadows turn back to see who said that, to reveal Hunter, Dillo, and Spin Doll standing there, ready to continue the battle. Kannon's arm lights up as Bug yells, "Here comes the cavalry!"

Then, all hell breaks loose as the warriors do what they do best. As light after light rises to the sky, our warriors push full steam ahead till only a few straggling Shadows remain. The final few Shadows flee to fight another day. Exhausted, the winners collapse to the ground, checking to make sure everyone made it safely.

Dayne suddenly jumps up and runs into the house. Seconds later, she returns frantically, yelling, "He's gone. They must have taken him!"

Kannon asks, "Taken who?"

"I have to go get him," she says as she takes off running in the direction the stragglers ran.

"Dayne, what about us? I just found you," Kannon yells back to her.

Dayne turns back just long enough to answer. "Sorry, but Dak needs me more. But I do thank you all for the help." Then she runs into the darkness and out of sight.

Kannon whispers, "But I need you too." He stands there devastated as the others watch like they have just seen his heart fall out on the ground. Kannon collapses as a beaten winner.

Bug rises to his feet to check on Spin Doll. "Are you alright?"

Spin Doll nods but holds Bug's hoodie up to show that it has gotten destroyed in the fight. "Awe that's alright. The only thing that matters is what's inside it didn't get hurt," Bug, blushing, answers.

Spin Doll gives him a big hug for forgiving her about the hoodie. Hunter and Dillo compare new wounds as Bug and Spin Doll approach them.

Bug extends his hand to Hunter. "Sorry for everything. I really would like to be your friend. If not, I understand."

Hunter, in return, gives Bug a blank look and doesn't extend his hand. "Nah, we'll never be friends."

Bug lowers his head and hand as he turns to walk away. Dillo's face is just as shocked as Spin Doll's.

Hunter grabs Bug and hugs him from behind and says, "We can never be friends, because we're family."

Bug looks as if he is going to explode as Dillo and Spin Doll join the hug. Tears of joy run down Bug's face, because not only does he have friends, but he also has a family as well.

Hunter looks at Kannon. "Well, are you part of this family?"

Kannon puts on a fake smile and halfheartedly joins the

hug.

The exhausted group sits in a small circle, tending to their wounds and trying to regroup some energy in case more Shadows want to test their luck.

"Wait a minute. I'll be right back." Bug dashes into the little house. None of the warriors pay him much mind as they finish patching themselves up. A few minutes later, Bug reappears. "Dinner is served." Then he gestures to them all to come on in and eat. One by one, the battle-weary warriors enter the house.

Hunter says, "I'm not turning down a free meal."

"I hear that," Dillo adds.

Bug puts a big pan of stew and bread and butter on the table in front of the crew. "Dig in." Then he goes to the front door to make sure it's clear to chow down. Something shiny on the ground catches his eye. Bug bends down and picks it up. It is a crown symbol like the Warrior's mark. Bug quickly puts it in his pocket and joins the others. The stew hits the spot perfectly, and they still have some leftovers to take to Hoss.

"My compliments to the chef," Hunter announces as he rubs his full stomach. Dillo follows that with an enormous burp. That makes everyone laugh, except Kannon. Kannon doesn't say a word throughout the entire meal, and he just sits there as if no one is there with him. Kannon is only thinking about Dayne choosing Dak over him.

Bug gets up and goes into the kitchen to make Hoss's doggie bag. Once in the kitchen alone, Bug pulls the crown symbol out to examine it. It is a spitting image of Kannon's, Hunter's, and Spin Doll's marks. During the meal, Bug checked all their hands to make sure it wasn't any of theirs; he thinks it must be Dayne's mark. But they just don't fall off. Then Bug thinks that maybe Dayne is fake. Maybe she isn't a

Warrior after all. Either way, Bug decides to keep Dayne's secret till he can figure out what she is up to. Bug places it back into his pocket. Then he opens the oven and pulls out the chocolate cake with vanilla frosting and sprinkles.

Bug enters the dining room. "Whose got room for cake?"

As Bug places the cake in the center of the table, Kannon stands up and leaves the house, not saying a word. Hunter immediately calls dibs on Kannon's piece. Spin Doll holds her plate up, as Dillo points out the piece he wants.

Outside, Kannon begins to walk the perimeter, while looking off into the Horizon for Dayne. Kannon works his way up to the top of the ridge for a better view. Something in the distance looks familiar. Is that a park bench there in the distance? Kannon has to check it out immediately, as he has questions for Jim. As he approaches the bench, Kannon thinks it looks just like Jim's bench. He sits down, but nothing happens.

"Oh, great. There's just something else to let me down today," he says as he lays back and covers his eyes with his arms.

"Anything new?" Jim's voice breaks the silence.

Kannon is ecstatic to see Jim. "Jim! Boy, do I need to talk to you!"

Jim, acting as if he's cleaning the arm of the bench, nonchalantly says, "What's up, bunny? I'm all ears."

"I actually saw my Dayne. But I don't think she's *my* Dayne anymore. At least, she didn't act it."

"Yes, yes, I see, continue." Jim finishes cleaning the arm.

Kannon lays back on the bench as if he is in a psychiatrist's office. "She ignored me. She is only worried about some Dak dude. I tried to speak to her, but she ran after him and just left me standing there alone."

"Have you met this, ah, dude yet?" Jim asks, already knowing the answer.

Kannon shakes his head. "The only reason I'm here is to find her. Now I don't think she wants to be found. She seems only interested in him. We were supposed to grow old together." Kannon slams his foot on Jim's newly cleaned bench arm.

"Well, maybe she needs to be reminded that she needs you," Jim states as he once again wipes off the arm of the bench. "I'm sure this Dak is not going to want to meet me."

Kannon begins rubbing his cannon arm. Jim tries to de-escalate the conversation. "Now, now, let's not get too hasty. Don't put the cart in front of the donkey. Maybe this Dak needed her more than you did at the moment."

Knowing this does not help the situation, Jim tries another approach: "Maybe there's something special about this Dak. You should meet him before you pass judgment."

Kannon is a little puzzled about why Jim doesn't see what he's trying to tell him. Kannon snaps at Jim, "Well, if he's so special, then why was I brought here to save this Dak and everyone else?"

Kannon looks Jim in the eyes. "Maybe I don't want to save this place, just so Dayne and Dak can live happily ever after. No thanks."

Anger now fills Jim's face. "You were brought here to rid this place of the Jokers and help restore the kings to power. That is all, period! Everything else is superficial."

Kannon barks back at Jim, "You wanted me here; I didn't ask for this. This is your mess to clean up, not mine. I'm only here for Dayne and me, end of story."

Jim slaps Kannon's legs off the bench and gets right in Kannon's face. "Without this place, you have nothing—no

Dayne, no Kannon! Nothing here is just yours, you selfish twit. If you want Dayne, find her. I'm sure there's a reason she doesn't want you. Try not to feel sorry for yourself and think of someone else for once. Believe it or not, the Horizon is much bigger than your ego. If you don't want to help, then don't help. Sit your selfish ass on the sidelines and watch your friends do all the work and put their lives on the line for your precious Dayne." Jim is gone, leaving Kannon to sit alone once again.

Kannon sits for quite some time by himself, thinking about how Jim is right. He is ashamed of himself for the way he has behaved. His Dayne would've been ashamed of him as well. "We just won a major battle, and all I can think about is why me. I truly am a piece of shit."

Kannon takes off running down the hill to the tiny house, thinking, *These guys will need me even more now. After defeating the Shadows tonight, they'll come bigger and better next time. I will have to pick my game up and get those kings back.*

As he reaches the door, he yells, "There better be some cake left for me!"

Bug points to the table. "One left just for you."

Hunter adds, "I was about to call dibs on it; you're lucky."

They all laugh as Kannon reaches over and wipes frosting on Bug's face. Bug smiles. "Real funny, Kannon." Bug grabs a small piece of cake left on his plate and fires it at Kannon.

Kannon ducks as the cake hits Hunter in the ear, and the room goes silent. Hunter wipes his ear out, saying, "You may be able to hit, but you suck at throwing." Hunter stands up and smashes his plate in Bug's face. They all arm themselves at that moment as the great cake war begins. Once the battle is over, a truce is called. The entire gang has cake everywhere. Bug is covered from head to toe.

Spin Doll goes into the bathroom and grabs towels for everyone. She gives Bug his last, as she keeps pulling it away when he reaches for it. So, Bug gives her a big hug, covering her once again with frosting. She laughs and runs from him as he runs after her. The two run outside and out on the lawn, where Bug finally catches her and tackles her. The two roll around on the ground until Spin Doll ends up on top, pining Bug. As she gets up, she pushes his head into the ground and laughs. Before pulling his head out of the mud, Kannon, Dillo, and Hunter come running out the door as Kannon yells, "Bug pile!"

The three men dive onto Bug until he can't breathe, making Bug give up. They all lay there with full stomachs, not wanting to move. Kannon suggests they head back to their cabin because, by now, Hoss has not eaten in almost twenty-four hours. So, he might have eaten the couch. They all laugh and brush themselves off as Kannon asks the guys not to tell Hoss about the joke he made about him. The group gather their belongings and Hoss's doggie bag and head towards the cabin.

CHAPTER 12

"When your imaginary friend is real, everything is better."
- Colt

Dayne finally catches up with one of the fleeing survivors as she is led to what looks like an abandoned old factory. She watches as the shadow approaches the only gate she can see in the twelve-foot-high fence surrounding the complex. The gate slowly opens just far enough for the shadow to slip into it, then closes immediately behind him. Dayne knows they'll never let her just waltz through the front gate. So, she frantically searches for an opening in the old rusty fence. There is a small gap at the bottom of the fence. She thinks, with a little digging, she might be able to fit under. So, she begins to dig until it is deep enough then begins to shimmy her way under, but her pant loop catches on a piece of broken wire. Dayne can't move forward or back, which leaves her a sitting duck if any Shadows come by.

She quickly bends the wire back and forth, trying to break it off. But the old wire just won't break. Desperation fills Dayne as she continues to work the wire. When all hope seems lost, the wire finally breaks, freeing Dayne and she quickly shimmies the rest of her body through the fence. She then gathers herself and checks the surroundings to make sure she isn't detected. With no Shadows in sight, she scours the factory to find an old broken window. The window is broken just enough for Dayne to enter the factory unseen.

Once inside, she finds a hiding spot behind some old,

stacked pallets. She scans the layout of the old factory. Feeling a burning sensation, she notices a trickle of blood rolling down the backside of her arm. To ease the slight stinging coming from her arm, she quietly rips the bottom of her shirt and ties it around her arm to stop the bleeding. Once she gets the bleeding under control, she goes back to scanning the factory. Off to her right, she sees what looks like four Shadows standing around a decent-sized hole in the ground. The Shadows are standing like royal guards protecting the hole. She really wants to look in the hole. But, with the guards standing there like statues, there was no way she'd get close enough to look. Next, she looks to the left while keeping the guards in her side-eye. At the other end is a large group of Shadows hooting and hollering, standing as if they are at a concert. The crowd of Shadows cheer as if they are at a sporting event and their team just scored. Dayne just has to see what all the commotion is about. The shadow guards never move or join in, so at the moment, they are not a concern of hers.

Just as Dayne is about to make her way to the crowd of Shadows, two Shadows walk by her, holding a sack with something in it. Dayne quickly dives back behind the pallets without being seen. She peers around slowly to watch the Shadows as they approach the hole guards. One of the Shadows opens the sack to show one of the guards the contents of the sack. The guard nods his head as the two Shadows empty the contents of the sack into the hole. Dayne can hear one of the Shadows saying, "Here you go, eat up." The two completely empty the sack and walk away, laughing at one another. The shadow guards just remain in their original spots while not joining the two in laughing. Dayne once again leans back behind the pallets as the two walk past her. She watches until they join the rest of the crowd of Shadows cheering.

Dayne's only thought is that it must be where the Jokers keep the Beast. Dayne's mind is making her nervous as thoughts fly through her. "What if that is the Beast? She is not strong enough to battle the Beast on her own. Maybe she should've brought Kannon and his friends with her. Why is Kannon here, and when did he get here? How is she going to explain everything to Kannon? This makes the situation worse. How can she protect Dak and Kannon?" Before her next thought, the crowd erupts again, drawing her attention back to them.

Dayne slowly moves from pallet pile to pallet pile until she is behind the crowd of excited Shadows. Dayne still can't see what all the commotion is about. She needs a better view. A tall pile of stacked pallets stands next to her. So, she shakes the pile of pallets slightly to see if they will be strong enough to hold her. As quietly as possible, Dayne climbs to the top of the unsteady pallet pile. Finally, she makes it to the top without being seen. She notices two ladies with their hands and feet bound and their mouths sealed with duct tape. Dayne once again scans the layout of the factory to see what the best way to help the girls escape is. The Shadows below Dayne are pushing and trying to jockey for a better view. Soon, they begin to push one another, and one is pushed into the pile of pallets Dayne is on top of. The pile comes crashing down, bringing Dayne with it. Dayne spills out onto the floor, and her sword falls out of her reach. The Shadows are on her like a pack of wild dogs. Before she knows it, Dayne is bound and taped just like the other two girls. As Dayne wrestles to try and get free, she searches for her sword. She cannot free herself or find her sword. She knows she stands no chance of escaping, with how tightly her hands and feet are tied. Even if she does escape, how would she find her sword? Dayne is trying to fight herself free but to no avail. She notices that the symbol on her right hand has fallen off, revealing that she isn't actually a Warrior. This makes the situation even more dreadful.

The girls stand there awaiting their fate. Fortunately, they do not have to stand there as long as the door behind them opens. Two very sharp-dressed men step out from the door to an eruption from the crowd of Shadows. The two men walk around examining the girls while they let the crowd continue to cheer them on. With smiles on their faces, the two men stop directly in front of Dayne. One of the men leans over to face Dayne, and the crowd instantly goes quiet. The man begins to speak to Dayne in a gentlemanly voice, "Well, what do we have here? Two little watchers and a big bad great Dayne." The other gentleman adds, "What do we owe to the honor of having The Great Dayne in our little abode? Please do tell?" Dayne does not try to respond; she just looks towards the ground. The first gentleman still in Dayne's face whispers, "You don't look that great to me. I thought you'd be taller." Before he can continue, the second gentleman breaks in, "Now, where are our manners? I haven't even introduced us to you. My name is Sinister, but you can call me Sin for short. Here is my brother Ominous; he likes to be called Omin. You might know us better as the Jokers. I feel like we're going to be real good friends." Dayne, once again, does not answer the gentlemen as she continues to look at the ground.

Sin and Omin turn towards the crowd to get more cheers. While doing this, Dayne peers over at the two girls. She notices that neither girl has the mark, making her wonder why they are so important to the Jokers? Quickly she returns her eyes towards the ground as the Jokers approach her once again.

Omin grabs Dayne by the chin and lifts her face to look him in the eyes. He states, "Please since we're friends now. Tell me why they call you The Great Dayne?"

Sin joins his brother in Dayne's face. "Really, what's so great about you?"

Dayne remains silent. The sound of two Shadows dragging Dayne's sword out of the crowd and along the ground stops the questioning for a minute. Dayne quickly looks up as they place the sword on the ground in front of the Jokers. Sin's eyes light up. "Say it isn't so. Is that the famous sword The Releaser!"

Omin claps his hands with glee, "Oh, it is, brother, it is." The Jokers act as if they are kids on Christmas morning. Neither dare to touch it due to the stories told about it, that state if anything touches mist or solid, it perishes to its blade.

Sin immediately turns towards Dayne. "Is this what makes you great?"

Dayne finally answers sternly. "No, it's not a sword; it's Dak."

Omin squawks, "Dak! What the hell is a Dak?"

"Dak is the end of the Shadows and you two clowns." Sin punches Dayne in the stomach, buckling her over and screaming at her, "We are Jokers! Jokers! Jokers! Jokers!"

Omin tries calming Sin down by telling Dayne, "We're going to introduce ourselves to your friends, so don't go anywhere."

Dayne spits blood on the ground as she sarcastically adds, "I can't wait."

Sin steps over to the next girl, able to tell she must've been an athlete. She is well-built with a long black ponytail. He reaches up with the back of his hand and brushes her cheek. "So tell me, who do we have the pleasure of meeting here?"

The young girl looks at Sin directly in his eyes, not showing an ounce of fear. "Name's Colt, and trust me, you won't forget it."

Omin sneers, "Colt? Don't recall any Colt. So, tell me why you are relevant?"

Sin doesn't give her a chance to answer. "Well, Colt, if you're a Watcher, then who are you watching now?"

Colt smiles as if she's in charge of this situation. "My warrior's name is Cam."

Sin scoffs. "Nope, sorry, never heard of a Cam."

Colt smugly responds, "You will soon, trust me."

Omin shakes his head. "Well, where is this Cam? I'd really like to meet him."

Colt smiles as she shakes her head and answers, "He's standing here with us right now," making the Jokers feel a little uneasy. She giggles. "If you really want to meet him. Just say hi. He's standing right beside you."

The Jokers immediately jump back as Shadows surround them for protection. All the Shadows search for Cam in the facilities and come up with nothing. The Jokers recompose themselves, as they kind of giggle to themselves. Dayne thinks this girl has totally lost her mind; there is no way she'll be any help.

A calmer Omin speaks to Colt once more. "So, my Shadows tell me you're extremely fast."

Sin laughs. "Can't be too fast; we caught you now, didn't we."

Colt adds a wise-ass comment. "I'd be quick enough to end your Ronald McDonald lights."

"Now stop that foolish talk, or we might have to slow you down permanently." Omin points at Colt's legs. Colt instantly stops the conversation and looks at the ground.

The Jokers now move on to the third girl, but not before firing up the crowd again. "Finally, last but not least, our favorite, Lakin. Take a bow Lakin," Omin announces while looking over the battered and beaten watcher.

Sin joins in. "Why so quiet? Oh, that's right. I heard you had a Beast of a day."

Both Jokers laugh and high-five the crowd of Shadows.

Lakin stands, slumped over, not able to speak, and acting as if she doesn't know she is even there.

"Well, this one isn't much fun. She's ruining the mood of this party," Sin remarks.

The Jokers grab a couple of Shadows and circle into a huddle, discussing what they're going to do with Lakin. The Jokers take turns popping their heads out of the huddle to look at the girl.

"And break!" The Jokers clap their hands and turn back towards Lakin. "Well, I guess since she is our first contestant out." Omin mimics pulling a mic from his brother's hands. "Well, Bob, tell her what she's won."

Sin grabs the imaginary mic back from his brother and responds, "She's won an all-inclusive trip to the HOLE! Where she'll be able to make new friends with our pets. Transportation will be provided by these three Shadows in the front row."

Sin gestures for the Shadows to come to take Lakin away. The three Shadows pick her up and carry her through the crowd of Shadows. One of the Shadows yells, "Better make some room down there, you've got company."

Dayne only sees the silhouettes of the Shadows and a lifeless Lakin as they drop her into the hole.

The Jokers turn their attention back to the two remaining girls. "So, this Dak and Cam. Sound like a couple of nice guys. When do we get to meet them?"

Before the girls get a chance to answer, Sin remarks to Dayne, "So if you're not a Warrior or even a watcher, why are there all these great tales about you?"

Dayne quickly replies, "Because of Dak!"

The Jokers' faces rapidly turn to anger, as Sin yells, "Dak! Dak! Dak! That's all you can say!"

Omin snaps, "Maybe we'll cut your tongue out so you can never say that meaningless word ever again."

Sin leans in, sneering. "We can easily just release your light." He grabs Dayne's sword and holds sit up. The Releaser.

"That probably won't work out well for you. I'm guessing you didn't plan this idea out too well, you clown," a voice says from behind them.

The startled Jokers jump back as Sin drops the sword. Sin screams as a crowd of Shadows surround him and Omin. "Who said that? Show yourself, coward!"

Colt turns to the Jokers. "Looks like Cam got his invitation to the party."

The now-frighten Jokers yell in unison, "Show yourself, coward!"

The voice responds, "I don't think that would be a good idea at this point in time."

The Jokers look aimlessly around for any sign of the voice.

Cam speaks again after about five minutes of silent torture. "Now this doesn't look like a party." The Jokers don't notice as Colt and Dayne are being untied. "I just dropped in to check on my good friend Colt and make sure she is enjoying herself and wasn't in any trouble. You know kids these days."

The Jokers still can't pinpoint the voice, as Cam continues. "My names Cam. I'd shake your hands, but I don't like getting shame on my hands. Thanks for everything, but I think it's about time for us to be leaving. This party won't do; it's such a drag."

Colt and Dayne's ropes drop simultaneously. A quick acting Colt picks up Dayne and The Releaser, and they are gone instantly, leaving only a trail of lights rising in the sky from Dayne's sword piercing the crowd of Shadows.

The Jokers yell, "Get them! Free them all!"

Instantly, all the Shadows run out of the factory, except the Jokers and the hole guards.

Silence fills the room. Sin turns to his brother. "We must find the witch and get a revealing spell."

Cam cuts in. "Well, that wouldn't be good. How about we discuss this Beast I hear all these rumors about?"

Omin snaps, "Well, if you're going to remain a coward, were done here. I guess we'll call it a night."

"Ok, since we're friends now, I guess it'll be alright to show myself." Cam reveals himself but still remains out of harm's way of the Jokers.

Omin is stunned. "Why, you're just a kid."

"I'm seventeen! I'm very adult for my age."

The Jokers continue talking to Cam, as they try and work close enough to grab him. But he disappears before they can reach him.

Sin angrily says, "Coward! Go ahead, little boy, play hide and seek. Eventually, we'll find you."

"I really would watch how you say things. Someone might take your jokes seriously. Then there would be no more Jokers… Sorry, I meant jokes."

As Cam leaves, he brushes against Sin. "Excuse me, it'll never happen again."

Sin is totally surprised at how easily Cam walks by him without him even knowing Cam is that close. The Jokers stand quietly, looking at each other without saying a word.

Off in the distance, the Jokers watch as one of the guards falls into the pit, and the other three turn to light and rise. They can faintly hear Cam say, "You're relieved, gentlemen."

The factory door opens off in the distance. "Hey guys, I think you have a couple job openings at this end of the factory. Later, Bozo's."

Cam exits, and Omin clenches his fist. He whispers, "We need to end that one brother sooner than later."

Sin answers, "You're so right, brother. Trust me, it'll be sooner."

The Jokers wait till the factory door closes to make sure Cam has left. Sin says, "I can't wait to see their faces when the Beast doesn't come alone."

Omin jests, "Too much info, brother. Too much."

The two Jokers exit the same back door they had entered earlier, leaving the big hole all alone.

CHAPTER 13

"Cheers to the weird places you meet new friends at."
- Dayne

Once Colt knows they are out of harm's way and far enough from the factory, she stops and lets Dayne stand on her own feet again. Colt tries to apologize to Dayne in between breaths. "Sorry if I had gotten too rough, but we had to get out of there as quickly as possible."

Dayne regroups herself while dusting off her clothes. "No, it's me who owes you a thank you. You just saved us; I owe you big time." Dayne reaches out to shake Colt's hand for a proper introduction. Colt, being a hugger, embraces Dayne with a strong hug.

Colt, refusing to let go, excitedly states, "That is amazing how easily you released lights as we ran through the crowd of Shadows."

Dayne, trying to break the hug, avoids telling Colt that it was because everything happened so fast that she didn't have time to put her sword away. "Trust me, it is nothing," Dayne answers. "That is incredible how fast you can run. I bet if you put your hands out, you could probably fly."

Colt giggles. "I love to run; I could run all day. It's what I'm best at."

Colt finally releases the death grip of a hug on Dayne as Dayne places her sword back behind her back where it belongs.

"You rest here for a minute; I'll be right back." Like a light being shut off, she is gone. Dayne smiles as she thinks, "That little girl has more energy than this entire Horizon."

In just a few seconds, Colt returns, holding her arms out in front of her as if she were carrying something. She then makes a gesture of putting something down on the ground. Colt blurts out, "There… now we're all safe and sound. Another successful mission. Thanks to Cam."

Dayne looks at Colt as if she's crazy. "Girl, are you alright there? I'm a little worried about you."

Colt giggles again and responds, "I'm fine, just talking to Cam."

Dayne, not seeing anyone else with the two girls, begins to have doubts. Suddenly, a voice from out of nowhere speaks to Dayne. "I hope to find you well, Dayne. I may have waited a little longer than planned, But I was hoping to find out some info on the Beast. My apologies."

Dayne is a little shaken, thinking that she is possibly losing it as well. "Who said that? Are you a ghost?"

Cam laughs as he reveals himself to Dayne and answers, "There's no such thing as a ghost. Sorry about that; sometimes I forget people can't see me all the time."

Dayne reacts just as the Jokers had. "You're just a kid."

"Yes, ma'am, I'm seventeen. Name's Cam; pleased to meet you. That's short for chameleon, in case you were wondering." Cam removes his hat and bows toward Dayne.

Dayne smiles as she replies, "Pleased to meet you as well, Cam. I see you already know my name is Dayne. Thank you so much for helping me back there."

Cam smiles. "It is my pleasure. Don't let my age fool you. I act and behave much older than I am. My grams always told me I must have been born with an old soul."

"Well, old soul or not, you two kids just saved my hide. I owe you guys huge."

Cam chuckles. "Naw, ma'am, you don't owe us anything. We'd do anything to help out Dak. With you being Dak's mom and all, we would also do anything for you."

"You two are friends with Dak? Do you know where he is? I've been looking for him for quite some time. He was supposed to return home yesterday."

"Sure, we're friends with Dak. But we have no idea about his whereabouts now. When we first met Dak, he was picking blackberries off from this really fat bush. His face showed that he liked them quite a lot. Dak and I have a lot in common due to us being close in age. After some good conversation and way too many berries, we had to part ways. Dak said he had to be on his way because his mother had dinner waiting for him." Cam chuckles. "After all of those berries, I don't know how he could possibly think of dinner."

Colt jumps in to finish the story. "Dak took off down the road, kind of skipping. He stopped for a minute just to wave goodbye to us. Then we watched him as he walked off into the Horizon. I waited a few minutes, then ran out to see if I could still see him, but he had vanished. That was the last time we saw him until he met up with us and told us about the factory."

"He told you about the factory? How did he know about the factory? Was he there?"

Cam shrugs. "Nah, he wasn't there. He had to go talk to a man who was looking for him. But he did ask us to tell you, if we ran into you, that he would meet friends. Let's say he made us promise to tell you and help you if you got in over your head."

"And ta-da, we're here," Colt says with a big finish.

Dayne is surprised at what she just heard from these kids. "Do you have any idea where he is now?"

"Yeah, he went to meet some guy," Colt explains again.

Dayne's is very worried at hearing this. "How did Dak know I'd be at the factory, and how did you know I was Dak's mom?"

Cam places his hand on Dayne's shoulder. "I'm much wiser than I should be. You don't have a Warrior's mark on your hand as I do." Cam shows Dayne the mark on his right hand, and he adds, "You're not a watcher, being this far from your Warrior." Cam points to Colt, and Colt gives a little wave.

"Besides a mom, who else would risk losing their light for just some kid?" Cam takes Dayne's right hand and holds it between his hands. "A mother's love is never ending; they'd walk through hell and back for their babies. I know my mom did." Cam's eyes begin to water up as a tear escapes down Dayne's face. Colt hugs Dayne from behind to help comfort her.

Before the waterworks begin to flow, Cam breaks up the moment by stating, "Well, we aren't going to find Dak by pissing the day away here."

The group regains their composer and heads down the path in the Warrior's direction. Cam sends Colt up ahead to scout out the area. While she's gone, Dayne explains to Cam how she met the other warriors and how they helped with the battle at her house. After a short discussion about her house, Cam agrees that they should go to Dayne's house first and try to figure out which way the warriors went from there or to see if Dak returned home. Colt returns empty-handed, seeing nothing but goat trails and trees, so Cam sends her off again. But this time towards Dayne's house. Dayne and Cam change direction also and head towards Dayne's house.

After only five minutes, Colt runs over the hill towards the pair. She tries to explain while breathing hard. "Dayne's house is about two hours that way." Colt points over the large hill.

"Great, let's try and make it there before dark," Cam adds.

Dayne agrees. "We can also get some food and rest before tomorrow's long trek."

Once they make it over the second hill, Dayne can see her house off in the distance, "There's my old girl." Dayne points to the other side of the valley, as they can barely make out the image of a little house.

As the three approach the little house, they notice the front door is left open. Dayne immediately grabs her sword out and holds it in front of her. "Stay here; I'll go in and make sure the house is cleared before you two come in."

As she enters the house, she notices that the kids are behind her, as they do not listen to a word she says. Slowly, they walk through the house, only to see stew and cake flung everywhere.

Cam snorts disgustedly, saying, "There must have been quite the struggle here. Look, there's even cake on the ceiling." He points to the ceiling as a big piece of cake falls to the floor with a splat.

Colt seconds Cam's deduction and adds, "Looks like more than just a couple of them to make this big of a mess."

After searching the entire house to make sure no one or thing is there, Dayne grabs three cleaning rags from the pantry and hands each kid one. She also gets a mop and a bucket of water, "Looks like we have some cleaning to do, kids, and it's not going to clean itself."

They clean for almost three hours before the house is spotless once again. While Cam and Colt finish up, Dayne makes a few frozen pizzas. Which, to the kids, hit the spot perfectly. With full stomachs and exhaustion setting in, they decide to turn in for the night. Dayne lets Cam sleep in Dak's bed. Colt takes the couch so she can watch the front door. Once the kids are settled in, Dayne finally stumbles into her bedroom.

She takes a much-needed shower, and when she hits her bed, she goes out for the night.

At the crack of dawn, Dayne is awakened by the smell of freshly brewed coffee and pancakes. She works herself out of bed and, with one eye still shut, shuffles to the kitchen. Cam is an early riser and has gotten up early to make breakfast. As a show of thanks for letting him and Colt spend the night, it had been quite some time since he slept in a real bed. Dayne sits there and enjoys every bite of breakfast. When she finishes eating, Cam brings out a steaming cup of coffee to finish an amazing meal.

"You didn't have to go through all this trouble, but I'm glad you did," Dayne jokes.

Colt sits at the table smiling with a stuffed belly. "Well, we can't go on an adventure without fueling our bodies up first." After a few minutes to rest her stomach, Colt is all giddy. "I went for an early morning jog and found the town the warriors are staying in. They are about a full day's walk, including nighttime."

Dayne laughs at Colt's eagerness and agrees. "Then we better not wait around. I'll go make some sandwiches and snacks for our adventure."

Once they are packed and ready to go, the three check their supplies at the front steps. Cam is weirdly looking towards the ground. Dayne asks, "What's wrong?"

"Look at the ground there; doesn't that look like an imprint of someone's body?" Cam points to the ground.

Dayne adds, "It looks like a smaller person is being attacked and piled on by bigger people."

Colt laughs as she points to the sky and says, "I like to play this game with clouds. Where I look at one and try to figure out what it resembles, look, that one looks like a bunny."

"Ahh, I think we're still a little groggy from getting up early," Cam remarks as he walks away from the house. Dayne agrees and follows Cam's lead.

About halfway up the first hill, Cam stops and looks back at the little house. He smiles and says, "That is almost a perfect night. It is almost as if I was in a normal family again."

Dayne has no idea what he is talking about so she keeps walking. Once they reach the top of the hill, they see the entire valley. They stand there, looking in awe.

Dayne asks, "Can you see the Horizon?"

Colt nods.

"That Horizon is painted there just for us," Dayne informs the kids.

Cam adds, "Well, whoever painted it deserves an applause."

The three stand there looking like they are caught in the Horizon's beauty and can't move. It has to be the longest Colt has ever stood in one place.

Just then, a bird bursts out of a tree nearby, startling them out of the trance that the Horizon holds on them. Cam looks down into the valley and notices a path that leads into the forest below, then turns to Colt. "Why don't you go down and check that path out and see where it leads to?"

"Sure thing, Captain." Colt salutes Cam and then is off down the hill.

Cam and Dayne reach the bottom of the hill much quicker than the climb to the top. Cam, curious about how Dayne arrived here, asks, "So, what's your story?"

"My story?"

"Yeah, your story. You know what the reason you and Dak were brought here to the Horizon?"

Dayne feels a little weird about telling a kid why she is in the Horizon. The more they walk, the more she thinks, why not? Besides, the kid has an old soul.

Dayne tells Cam her story. "Well, you see, it all started when I graduated high school and got married, all in the same summer, to my high school sweetheart. Everyone knew we would be together forever; it was no secret. Two months into our marriage, I got pregnant and didn't know how to tell Kannon or our families, who were already complaining we got married too soon."

Cam quickly asks, "Did you tell Kannon he would be a dad? I bet he was so happy; I know I would be."

"I left Kannon a voice mail on his phone since he must have been too busy at work to answer. I told him that as soon as he got out of work, he would meet me at our spot on the knoll overlooking Hidden Bridge. The knoll is the spot where we met and eventually got married, and that was where we were going to build our house and live happily ever after. It had this cute little tree where we would hang a tire swing for our babies. At night, you could see every streetlight Hidden Bridge had. It is like a bunch of lightning bugs just for us."

Cam sighs. "It sounds awesome."

Dayne nods in agreement. "Oh, it is. I was so excited and a little nervous to see Kannon's face when I told him our good news and that he was going to be a dad. I had gotten to the knoll about an hour before Kannon was to arrive. I didn't drive the car; I walked so I could get some exercise for myself and the baby. Once I made it to the knoll, I was a bit winded, so I sat at the base of the little perfect tree and rested for a bit. With this huge smile on my face, I sat there talking to my belly. Telling our baby how much he or she is going to be loved and how I couldn't wait to hold them in my arms. The breeze picked up as if it wanted to talk to the baby as well.

"Then something weird began to happen: a star fell from the sky. Which to me was crazy, because you don't see stars during the day. I thought to myself, this must be a good omen. Then sitting there all alone I began to talk to myself. 'I know you're excited but hold it together. There are no falling stars during the day.' But, sure enough, it was a falling star. More and more began to fall. I sat there amazed at what I was seeing. Suddenly, I felt this really sharp pain in my stomach. I thought no way the baby could be kicking this early in the pregnancy. I rubbed my belly, trying to calm the baby down. Maybe the stars were getting him excited as well. Then, I received a second sharp pain, which brought me to my feet. As I stood there, I noticed a crimson stain on the ground below me, where I had been sitting." Dayne stops telling her story as tears begin to fill her eyes. Cam now wishes he hadn't asked to hear it. He has no idea what to do or how to console her.

They walk quietly for a bit. Then Dayne begins to speak again. "I knew something was wrong with the baby, and I needed help. The pain was so great, I knew I'd never make it back to town. I pulled my phone out to call Kannon, but I got an even worst pain. Which made me drop my phone. With the pain so sharp, there is no way I could bend over to pick it up. I fell to my knees as the pain was unbearable. So much so that I couldn't see my phone to pick it up. I reached out for anything and eventually I felt this piece of metal and pulled myself up to it. It was the arm of an old park bench. With every ounce of strength I had left, I pulled myself high enough to sit on it. Once I did, all my pain went away. It was a miracle. I sat there dumbfounded, rubbing my belly and asking my baby if he or she was alright. Then a voice spoke beside me, and it was a little old man. He told me his name was Jim, and he congratulated me on my pregnancy. He looked at my belly and asked, 'May I?' As he began to rub my belly. Once he stopped, he congratulated me again and told me my baby would be an important man someday. I was so happy to find out that I was going to have a son that I didn't even question him.

"Then Jim explained to me about his world in the Horizon and how his world needed my son and me to save it. I thought this little man was crazy, so I told him I had to get back to Kannon. Jim, as nicely as possible, told me that I could never go back to my world. For if I did, my baby would not survive. But if I stayed in the Horizon, my baby would grow up to be a very important figure in his world. Then he explained the dire need that the kings were in, as well as the Horizon. I had no choice, and I stayed here to have a long life with my son. But I risked never seeing Kannon again. Or I could go back to my home and possibly live a long life with Kannon but lose seeing my son grow up. What could I do? He was my son."

"You made the only choice you could at that moment," Cam reassures Dayne.

Colt breaks up the discussion as she runs up to the emotional pair. "Found it. If you guys don't stop, you should make it there by sun rise." Colt dances around, holding colorful ribbons, which are purple and teal.

"Where did you get those ribbons?" Cam inquires.

"I found them in a field of flowers, and they asked me to take them and spread them as far as I can."

Dayne, not feeling so happy at the moment, suggests, "Maybe you can go back to the warriors and watch them so they don't go anywhere till we get to them."

Colt laughs. "If I do that, you won't know the way to find them."

They stand there thinking how they can find their way to the warriors without Colt's help. Finally, it comes to Colt. "I know! Why don't I tie a ribbon on a tree or bush every so often so you can follow my trail?"

Cam nods excitedly. "That's an awesome idea, Colt! But keep them close enough for us to find."

Colt giggles. "Sure thing, Cam. Tag, you're it." Colt takes off and is out of sight in seconds.

The two begin walking once more, and Dayne finishes her story.

"The next day, after talking to Jim, I woke up here in the Horizon, not pregnant, holding my baby boy. As soon as I looked into his beautiful eyes, I knew I had made the right decision, and the name Dak popped into my head. I spoke to him. 'Good morning, Dak! I'm your mother, and I promise nothing will ever harm you as long as you have me.' Dak looked at me as if he knew what I was saying. After a couple of weeks, Dak grew two feet taller and began to walk. Soon after that, he could talk. He was growing too rapidly. When I met up with Jim again, I asked him what was happening to Dak. Jim told me that here in the Horizon, children grow quickly, and special children grow even faster if the eat the blackberries."

Cam nods. "That explains his love for blackberries."

The two continue down the road, looking for ribbons.

CHAPTER 14

"When all you want to do is watch your child grow up, and you miss it in both worlds." - Dayne

Dayne and Cam continue their conversation about Dayne's story and why she needs to find her son. It isn't long before they approach the first of many ribbons.

Cam jokes as Dayne removes the purple and teal ribbon from the tree and uses it to put her hair up. "Boy, that Colt will never run out of steam. She's full steam ahead one hundred percent of the time. Our Little Engine That Could." Dayne nods, and Cam turns her attention to him. "So, what's yours and Colt's story? You heard mine already. So, spill it, old soul."

The two come to an old cow path running through an open hay field. To avoid Dayne's question, Cam replies, "Well, do we stay on the road or cross this field?"

Dayne puts her hand over her eyes to block the sunlight and looks into the distance for a ribbon. Far on the other side of the field, she points. "Does that look like one of our ribbons?"

"I think so…" Cam begins to head towards whatever it is.

Once they get closer, they can see it is definitely one of theirs, as Dayne removes it from the crooked little tree. As they continue into the high grass, Dayne once again asks Cam about his and Colt's story. Cam seems very reluctant to discuss his story. He rubs the back of his head while walking as if trying to plan how to tell Dayne. However, Dayne has been very persistent since she told Cam her story.

Cam finally breaks down and begins to explain. "We lived

just outside of Boston—Dad, Mom, and me. We never missed a Patriots game; it was like religion in our house. Dad always said we were the richest poor people he knew. We lived in this nice little town with a two-story garage house and two cars. They were in good shape and good on gas. You could say we were living life from one paycheck to the next.

"Dad had me throwing a football as soon as I could walk. I was going to be the next Tom Brady. Pop Warner came and went along with Flag. I was starting QB since day one. Man, did I have a great arm. Dad paid for football camps and training sessions with money he didn't even have. He'd always tell Mom not to worry; he'd figure it out. I was such a good quarterback that I was given the starting spot on varsity in eighth grade. I was a boy wonder, leading my team to the state championship in my first year. Newspapers wrote stories about me; they called me Brady Boy. Dad was already looking at colleges for me, knowing I'd get a full scholarship. Then, one day at practice, right before the championship. I didn't feel right. I told my dad and the coach something wasn't right. Dad said it was just nerves and I'd be fine by morning. Well, I wasn't. Morning came, and I was in even more pain. Mom took me to the doctor, but she was convinced it was just growing pains. What happened next was possibly my worst day ever. The next day, the doctor called us back to his office and gave us the news."

Cam stops walking and wipes his eyes on his shirt. Dayne wants to hear more but doesn't want to push him to finish. Cam begins walking again, and he continues. "He said I had stage three cancer, and I needed to start chemo immediately. My dad stormed out of the room as Mom just sat there hugging me and crying. I started treatment the following week. But they weren't working, and my doctor said I was getting worse. Dad was never around because the bills had become so much that he had to pick up a second and even third job. I was the one dying, but that disease was killing them as well. At night, I could hear Mom in her room crying, and when Dad was home, all they did was fight. Because of me, I destroyed our happy home. I would lay in bed and watch Dad out my window, stand in one spot, and play catch with the football by himself. He would throw it up, then catch it over and over again while I lay in bed, wishing I could just disappear.

"One night, as I lay in bed, looking at my trophies and thinking I would trade all of them to save my parents. So, I decided I would take matters into my own hands. Mom couldn't sleep, and I knew the doctor had given her sleeping pills. One night, I waited till she had fallen asleep, and Dad wasn't coming home because he had to work late. I snuck into her room, grabbed a handful, and then rushed out. I grabbed a pad and pen and sat on the back deck. I tried to write a letter to them, explaining how much I loved them and that I was doing this to save their lives. But the tears smudged it all, so I wrote *Save yourself. I love you. Brady Boy.*

"The first two pills I swallowed didn't seem to be too effective. So, I popped two more, which made me hallucinate, I think. I thought I saw the sky falling as stars landed all around me. Then, I saw a door appear at the end of my porch. I took three more pills as I sat there. I could swear I saw this fat guy come out the door." Cam shook his head. "And that's all I can remember. Next thing I know, I woke up here in the Horizon."

Dayne has nothing to say about that story, and she can't believe someone would take their own life, thinking it would save someone else.

The next few miles are pretty quiet as they come to a couple more ribbons. They stop for just a minute so Cam can run around a big old tree to relieve himself. The whole time, Cam keeps looking back around the tree to make sure Dayne isn't looking. Once he finishes his business, the two are back on the march.

"So, you saw a fat man on your porch?" Dayne asks, trying to start another discussion.

"With all those pills I took, it could've been an elephant for all I knew." Cam laughs as he nudges Dayne.

Dayne decides she needs to take a short break and maybe get into those sandwiches she packed for them. "How about a little rest and maybe a bite to eat?"

"I'm game." Cam has already picked his seat.

"I'm game, too," Colt says as she sits beside Cam.

"Where'd you come from?" Dayne asks.

"Oh, when I hear food, I'm there," Colt jokes, giggling.

"The lady only speaks the truth," Cam snickers.

The three settle down for a bite to eat and maybe a quick nap.

Dayne pulls out some sandwiches and holds them up. "I've got two PB&J's and a bologna with mustard."

"I call dibs on a PB&J," Colt blurts. Dayne laughs and hands Colt her sandwich. "Girl, you don't miss much, do you?"

"And you, sir?" Dayne looks at Cam.

"Whichever one you don't want will be fine. I'll eat either," Cam remarks.

"Well, I'm not a big fan of bologna, so here you go." Dayne tosses the sandwich to Cam.

They eat in silence, and when they finish, Colt stands, saying, "I really hate to eat and run, but…" Colt is off again and soon out of sight.

Cam suggests that they might as well grab a couple of hours of shut-eye since he is full and comfortable. Dayne agrees as she lays back and gets a little more comfortable herself. The two lay there looking at the starless sky as an occasional light orb floats above them, begging to be a star once more.

"These lights, when released, just float here in limbo?" Dayne questions.

"Yeah, I guess without the king's ability to send them to the sky to be a star, they just exist." Cam turns to look at Dayne. "Dayne, do you truly think we can win this? I mean, a lot is riding on a group of misfits that couldn't count on themselves."

Dayne doesn't answer him right away. "Well, we kind of gotta win. I guess that's why they came up with the saying, 'Go big or go home.'"

Cam looks at the sky. "Well, either way, someday we'll all be stars." Cam chuckles a little, not really agreeing with his own words. Neither one says much for a while.

It wasn't long before Cam breaks the silence again, asking, "Dayne, are you sleeping?"

"No, don't really think I can."

After a few more minutes, Cam adds, "I'm tired of being scared."

Dayne slides over and puts her arm over him as if he were her child. She can feel his body shake a little and can tell he is crying.

"The world is filled with monsters, and too often, we let them win. But, if we stand together against them, we might just scare a few of them away," Dayne says softly.

Cam tries to talk through his tears. "I didn't want to die. But it was the only way to save my parents."

Dayne reaches up and wipes her eyes with her sleeve, then places her arm back over Cam.

"I don't want to die here. But I would, to save you and Dak."

Dayne squeezes Cam a little harder without saying any words. They eventually doze off, but not for long, as a twig snaps behind them in the woods.

Dayne and Cam get to their feet immediately to see what it is. Nothing is there, so they figure it must've been the wind or a small animal. They brush themselves off and gather themselves before continuing.

Not wanting to continue their earlier discussion, Dayne says, "You know, you never told me Colt's story."

Cam shrugs. "I'm sure Colt won't mind if I tell it to you." As they walk, Cam begins.

"See, Colt was an awesome sprinter in high school. She pretty much owned every school record. She jokes that she lived on the track. The way I take it, she never lost a race. Colt had every college scout begging her to go to their school and offering scholarships. Her dad told everyone she was destined for the Olympics. Every night, she would practice after school till her dad got out of work and picked her up. They'd stop off and get smoothies on the ride home. Strawberry banana is her favorite. One night, after practicing, her dad called her and told her he was going to be an hour late. He told her to stay at school, do homework, or play on her phone until he got there. Colt told him her favorite show was going to be on in twenty minutes, and she didn't want to miss it. As a cool down, she figured she would jog home. Besides, it was only about five or so miles. Her dad wasn't having it, and he wanted her to wait for him. But Colt was persistent and finally got her way. Dad only agreed if she stayed on the main roads and called him every mile. Colt laughed and promised she'd call him." Cam stops then, staring off into the distance.

Dayne looks at Cam and says, "Are you going to finish the story?"

Cam shook his head. "She never made it home."

Dayne covers her mouth with her hand, not expecting that.

Cam sighs. "Her dad must be lost without his baby girl. He probably blames himself."

"What about her mom?"

Cam looks at the ground. "She never talks about her mother." He bends over to pick up a few stones to throw while they walk.

"Did Colt ever say what happened?"

Cam again shook his head. "All she says is that she'll never stop running again. Shit, first three weeks I knew her, she didn't sleep. I had all I could do just to get her to stop to eat." Cam throws his last couple of stones and adds, "So, I guess I'm kind of like her big bro. I'm more like her watcher than she is mine."

Dayne hugs Cam. "You're doing one hell of a good job, big bro."

Cam smiles out of the side of his mouth.

Suddenly, from out of nowhere, Colt joins the hug and shouts, "Group hug! I call dibs."

Dayne puts her arm around Colt as well and squeezes.

CHAPTER 15

"Nothing's cooler than meeting a real live teddy bear."
- Spin Doll

The weary warriors arrive back at the little cabin they call home and walk the front door one by one, with Bug holding the broken front door for Spin Doll. Once inside, they drop whatever they're carrying onto the floor and crash into their normal spots.

Hoss is glad to see them. "Well, glad to see you all made it back in one piece. Yeah, even you, Bug."

Before any of them can respond, Hoss grabs Bug in a bear hug. "Bug, you're back, you old son of a gun." He chuckles and rubs Bug's hair, messing it up.

Bug struggles to breathe and fixes his hair. "Yeah, I'm back. Someone has to help Dillo feed you."

Hoss picks Bug up and his feet dangle in the air. Then he tosses him in the air like a little kid and joyfully explains, "My friend, I promise ain't no one going to bully you while I'm around. Maybe we'll run into your classmates sometime so that I can explain that to them. What will you say, Bug, ole boy?"

Bug is a little embarrassed, disliking being tossed in the air, but he says, "That'd be great, Big man."

Spin Doll laughs as the huge man carries Bug around the room, refusing to set him down as if he were a baby. With Bug still in his arms, Hoss gives Kannon, Hunter, and Dillo all a hug as well. Hoss adds, "Gentlemen, it's so nice to see you made it back." Hoss puts his hand on the side of his mouth so as not to let Spin Doll hear him; softly, he whispers, "Who's the chick?"

Hoss drops the four men as he turns towards Spin Doll, saying, "Now, little lady, where's my manners? Would you like to have a seat and tell old Hoss about yourself?"

Bug jumps into the discussion. "Let me introduce you to the cutest lady in the Horizon. This little Warrior is Spin Doll."

Hoss places his hand up in Bug's face to tell him to quiet down. Then he gestures for Spin Doll to take a seat near him. "Now there's no way this pretty little thing is a Warrior. Please have a seat and rest those tiny feet."

Spin Doll sits next to Hoss, smiling and nodding in thanks. She can't believe the size of this mountain of a man.

"Please, tell me a little about yourself, little lady."

Bug leans over and whispers in Hoss's ear, "She can't speak. She hasn't got a voice."

"Oh, is that right? Most of the time, I don't want to talk to these guys either," Hoss jokes as he holds his hand out to shake Spin Doll's. Spin Doll places her small hand inside Hoss's hand and bows her head towards him. Hoss leans over and whispers, "It's ok if you can't speak. I'll do enough talking for the both of us." He nudges her with his elbow, almost pushing her out of the chair.

Dillo breaks in on the little meet and greet by asking, "Have you missed us? Has it been really lonely?"

Hoss smiles and answers, "Nah, it's not been that bad. Besides, I had company for a bit yesterday."

Kannon furrows his eyebrows. "Really, who?"

"Some young guy around seventeen or so. He knocked on the front door and politely asked if he could pick some blackberries we had on our bushes in the backyard. I told him to go for it, and if there were enough, I could use some as well. Really, I was starving. He thanked me and went out back to pick some." Hoss rubs his forehead, recalling the conversation. "It only took him about twenty minutes, and he was back at the front door. He had his shirt folded up and filled with berries. He walked in and dumped all the berries on the table, then thanked me and tried to wipe the berry stains off himself before heading out the door. As he walked out onto the road, he stopped and waved." I yelled to him, 'Pleasure to meet you, and thanks for the berries. Feel free to come back any time and pick more.' He waved once more and was gone."

Kannon asks, "Any chance you get his name?"

Hoss tries to think really hard. "Dan or Don or something like that. He says he can't hang out because his mom is waiting for him."

"Could it be Dak?"

Hoss touches his nose with his finger and shouts, "Bingo! That's what it is. Do you know him? Really good kid."

Kannon doesn't reply. All he can wonder is whether that could be the Dak he met or even the Dak that Dayne's in love with. Kannon goes over and looks out the window as he thinks, *That is the name of the little boy I met when I first got here. There's no way that he could be the same kid; and my Dak is really young. It does seem strange that his little kid, Hoss's teenager, and Dayne's man could all have the same name.*

Puzzled by this, Kannon stares out the window but isn't really looking out the window. He is lost in his own mind.

In the meantime, Hoss gets mad at not seeing any food brought home by the guys. "You're telling me you guys really didn't bring me home any food?"

Dillo pats Hoss on the shoulder. "Sorry, big guy, but we didn't bring you home anything."

Hoss's face instantly turns to disappointment. Bug jumps up and runs over to the hoodie he had hung on the back of a chair and pulls out a big piece of wrapped cake and hands it to Hoss.

Hoss's grins from ear to ear. "Bug, my best friend. Have a seat, old buddy." Hoss pats on the chair next to him for Bug to join him, then slaps Hunter's feet off the coffee table as he places his cake down. Hunter gives Hoss a dirty look but doesn't dare say anything to him.

The exhausted warriors sit around, quietly watching Hoss devour the piece of cake. Hunter is beginning to doze off as his head begins to get heavy.

Bug offers Spin Doll his blanket and Hunter's nice cozy chair. He then nudges Hunter to move. She graciously accepts as she settles down to sleep. Bug smiles at Spin Doll and then lies down on the floor next to a very unhappy Hunter. Kannon remains staring out the window as if the rest of the crew isn't even there. Hoss is already snoring, probably dreaming he had another piece of cake. Hunter and Spin Doll are also out as soon as their heads hit the pillow. Bug is just about out when he notices Dillo doesn't head to bed. Bug sits up to see Dillo at the table, shining his shell, so he gets up and joins his buddy.

"What's up, bub?" Bug says, trying to be funny.

"Not much. Just missing my gramps a little," Dillo responds.

Yeah, it's easy to miss someone you know you're never going to see again."

"Yeah, if it wasn't for you guys being here, it'd be even harder. I've never had any family except Gramps until I met all of you. This is what I've always wanted: a big family."

"Yeah, we're one big happy family."

Dillo smiles. "We'll be one big happy family forever now. Nothing can tear us apart. Life is really good here. I'm going to live here forever."

Bug punches Dillo in the arm and agrees as well. "Yeah, you're going to live here forever."

Bug takes the shell and sets it at the other end of the table. "But, for now, we need our rest, brother."

Dillo smiles and heads to bed. Once they're both laying down and it's totally quiet, Hoss lets out a massive fart, its stench filling the room. All the warriors cover their heads, trying to breathe.

Hunter reaches up and kicks Hoss.

"Excuse me, must have been something I ate," Hoss says with a laugh.

Bug yells, "That's nasty! You might have to go wipe."

Hoss giggles. "Hand me your hoodie."

Hunter begins to laugh from being overtired, and the rest join in laughing from being overtired as well. When they finally calm down, Bug jokes with Dillo. "Someday, you need to tell us his story."

Dillo stops laughing. "You want to know Hoss's story for real?"

Hoss snaps, "Go to bed. No one wants to hear my boring story."

Hunter puts in, "You know, I don't think you ever told me your story."

Hoss rolls over, ready to strike a deal. "If I tell you my story, will you let me sleep?"

They all sit up to hear Hoss's story.

"Ok, it all started when I joined the army. Man, was that a great day. My sarge told me I was the biggest soldier he'd ever had to train. My nickname was Hoss the Heavy Tank. I was so proud to put that uniform on once they found one big enough. Right out of boot camp, they sent us into battle. It was scary and difficult, especially being the biggest target out there.

Every night, you cherished those few minutes you got to sleep. One night, my camp was raided, and a lot didn't make it. Those of us who did survive wished we didn't, as we were taken to a not-nice place. The things I have seen and had done to me, I'd wish on no one. They would break men, day after day. But they couldn't break me, and trust me, they tried.

"One night, three other soldiers and I escaped. Once we had weapons in our possession, we took the whole camps' lives. It was a blood bath—so much so that my sarge said he couldn't tell if I won or lost. They gave us all medals and shipped us home. But home wasn't quite like I had remembered. Sure, everyone thanked you and was nice to your face. They truly didn't know or care what I had gone through. They weren't there when I woke up screaming with night sweats. Or when I barricaded myself in my house, thinking the enemy was just outside my door. I couldn't go anywhere without wondering if people were friends or enemies. I tried to get help but help ain't as easy to find as you would think. Just when I thought I was doing better, the least little thing would set me off. A car backfired, people arguing, shit. It even happened once at a shopping market when someone pushed their cart into the other carts at a cart return. I laid beside my car for over an hour. Now trust me when I say that nothing was the same for me when I came home. Many times, I sat with my rifle, thinking that would be my last day.

"I truly couldn't live in that world any longer. Then, one day as I was walking, trying to clear my head, I came upon a building with smoke pouring out of it. I noticed two little kids leaning out a third-story window yelling for help. They were crying, just like the kids overseas that were etched in my mind. My head was not right, but I had to save those kids. I opened the only door I could find that led inside the building. Flames blew out over my head. I knew the firemen would not make it in time, so I charged into the building. I could feel my clothes melting off me with every step. I made my way to the kids and tried to cover them as I headed back down to the exit. When I stepped out the door, the fresh air hit us and burned just as the fire did. My eyes hurt to open them. When I placed the kids on the ground, I could feel my skin tear. It was as if I were back in that prison camp. I could not go through that again. I asked the kids if anyone else was in the building. They said it was an abandoned building, and they were playing with matches and burning stuff. They said no one was left in that old building, but I could swear I heard more voices coming from inside. The crowd had gathered, cheering me on, just like when I came home. I'm sorry, but I just couldn't go through that again. Still hearing voices, I walked back into the building."

Hoss rolls back over to sleep, not saying another word.

They can't believe what they just heard. Silence fills the room as everyone lays down. In the darkness, Spin Doll is trying to be quiet but is sniffling. Bug wishes now he hadn't asked Hoss about his story. Everyone lies there waiting for sleep to come.

CHAPTER 16

"Sometimes you walk with a higher purpose than you know."
- Spin Doll

The three quickly make up some lost time, thanks to Colt finding a shortcut that shaves a good hour off the trek. As they walk, Colt fills them in on what she had seen at the Warrior's cabin.

"There's about six of them total. Four warriors and two watchers. Two of them sat at the table—a little guy with quite an attitude and a heavier guy cleaning this big shell. I think it was a turtle shell. I am pretty sure they are both watchers. The turtle shell dude is called Dillo, and the little attitude guy is named Bug. Which is funny because he looks like a little bug."

Cam blurts, "He's smaller than me?"

Colt nods. "Yeah, but not by much." Then she says, "I thought one of them had seen me because he had just sat staring out the window towards me. It was weird. Like he was looking right through me. I'm pretty sure his mind was elsewhere. A long, slender guy slept on the floor next to the couch. From the look on his face, he wasn't too happy. A beautiful girl in the chair was bundled up in what looked like a very cozy blanket. She looked tired, even though she was sleeping already. Finally, there was an enormous man on the couch. At least, I think it was a couch. I really couldn't see it under his mammoth frame. He was laughing in his sleep as he tossed and turned. I'm pretty sure he would've been a thrower on my track team.

"I waited till the last one fell asleep before heading back to you guys. Just as I was about to leave, a gentleman approached their front door. You could tell he was not part of their group, as he crept up to the door so as not to be heard. Even though I was very close to him, he didn't notice me standing there. He leaned over and looked in the corner of the window. I think to make sure a certain person was in there. Once he had seen enough, he went back to the door. I thought he was going to knock. But instead, he stuck a note to the door and quickly snuck off into the darkness. When the coast was clear, I went to the door to read it—not that I'm noisy. It was hard to read in the dark, but what I could make out was something about a one-on-one meeting."

"About a meeting? Did it have a name on it?" Dayne wonders.

Colt thinks for a minute. "Maybe it started with a K, like Ken or Kevin."

Dayne is beginning to get anxious. "Could it maybe have been Kannon?"

Excitedly, Colt nods. "Yup, that's what it is for sure. Kannon!"

Cam, looking confused, says, "Could that be *your* Kannon?"

Dayne shakes her head. "I doubt it. What's the odds he's here in the Horizon?" Even though she knows it is him. She doesn't want to tell the kids now, even though she has hinted it to Cam. She is not in the mood to explain everything again. Dayne asks Colt to please go back and follow Kannon and observe the meeting, so if they don't get to them in time, she can save him if it's a trap.

Colt doesn't wait for any more orders; she is gone before Dayne finishes speaking.

Cam looks at Dayne. "Look, from here on out, we won't be getting any rest stops for a while."

Dayne agrees and starts jogging. "We need to get to that meeting. I'm sure it's a trap, and we can't afford to lose a Warrior."

Cam jogs alongside Dayne for as long as he can hold up. Just as Cam is about to give up running, he and Dayne come to another one of Colt's ribbons. The only problem is that this one is lying on the ground. This definitely is a problem since they can't tell what tree it came from, and there are three different paths in front of them.

Cam nervously asks, "Which way? For all we know, this could've been blown around by the wind. If we make the wrong choice, there's no way we'll make the meeting on time."

They stand there, lost, not having any clue which one to take. Dayne thinks quickly. "Let's take this one to the left, even though it's against everything videogame. This path leads up the hill. Even if it's the wrong one, we can get a good look around for another ribbon in the distance. If we see one, we'll just come back and take the right path."

Cam agrees that's the best option at the moment. Dayne makes it to the top first, where she stops dead in her tracks. She says nothing as she waits for Cam to catch up. When Cam approaches Dayne, he stops as well. Sitting in front of them is a sight they'll never forget.

Where they stand on top of the hill, they can see the entire valley.

"Look at that! How can so much beauty be in one spot?" Dayne breathes.

Cam is speechless, taking in the valley. The whole valley is covered in purple and teal flowers, all about waist-high to Dayne. There is one single path that goes from one side of the valley to the other. It leads straight down the middle. As they approach the beginning of the trail, they see an old wooden sign.

It reads: Please stay on the path. Do not wander!

Dayne can't take her eyes off the valley of flowers. "Do you have any idea what this place is? It's even more beautiful than the Horizon."

Cam shrugs. "I once heard of a folk tale about a valley of flowers called 'The Valley of Never Lights.' I thought that was just a story like unicorns or Big Foot."

"Why is it called The Valley of Never Lights?"

"Trust me, you don't want to really know the answer to that question. It's kind of better if you don't know."

Dayne insists on knowing why such a beautiful sight could be named that. Cam puts his head down as he kicks a stone, trying to avoid Dayne's questioning. With Dayne just standing there looking at him, Cam gives in.

"The story I was told about this mystic valley is that in our world…" Cam pauses again. Dayne can tell he doesn't want to talk about it. But he continues. "In our world, when a child is unborn or taken as they are born, they do not receive a light. Instead, they are placed in this valley and forever become part of it. Each one becomes a beautiful flower as they should've been. They remain here safe and sound as the kings watch over them."

Dayne loses all feeling as she goes numb to Cam's words.

"Back in our world, if you chose Kannon over Dak, this is where Dak would've been placed."

"So, each one of these flowers—"

"Yes, each one of these flowers!"

Many minutes pass before Dayne can gather herself and begin to cross the valley. They follow the narrow path as tears trickle down both sides of Dayne's face. She walks through the valley with her hands down at her sides so she can touch every flower possible with each step. Each flower seems to giggle as she brushes them with her hands as if they are alive. Cam watches with amazement.

Dayne stops about halfway and kneels, finding a broken flower lying on the ground. As she picks it up, she can swear she hears it crying. Dayne holds it against her heart as if she is really trying to calm a baby down. She notices a stem that doesn't have a flower and places the flower in the stem. The flower and stem became one in her hands. It sounds as if the flower stops crying and begins to coo. This brings a smile to Dayne's face. As she kneels there, she can hear children playing and giggling on both sides of her. Tears continue down her face, but she is smiling.

Finally, Cam nudges her slightly to get her to continue on the path. Dayne stands and begins walking with her hands still down by her sides. Eventually, they reach the other side and begin to leave the valley floor. When they step out of the path, the flowers make a sound as if they are about to cry, begging them to stay. If it weren't for Cam, Dayne wouldn't have left. She touches the last few, and it sounds like they are asking her to please stay and not leave them. Cam continues to assist Dayne up the hill and into the woods.

They walk silently for a bit, and Dayne continuously looks behind them. She finally speaks, "It seems as if each flower has its own personality." Cam doesn't say anything. Dayne continues, "Each flower sounds just like a little." Cam once again cuts her off as he agrees, "Yes, I am thinking the same thing." Dayne puzzles, asking, "Why purple and teal? I think I see what looks like a firefly in each one. Is that maybe their own light growing someday to join the rest of their family in the stars?" Dayne stops walking. She then turns back towards the valley and begins walking back, as she insists, "I have to go back; they all need me!" Cam knows there is no stopping her, so he agrees to go back. But, only for a few minutes, then they have to leave. Cam tells Dayne, "We can't stay long; we must get to the warriors in time." Cam tries his best to talk some sense into her, but that has no effect.

They return to the valley where the flower babies are. There is nothing, no flowers. Just fields of grass and stone walls. Dumfounded, Dayne spouts, "They are right here. We saw them, thousands of them. We did see them, right?" Cam supports her by agreeing, "Yes, Dayne, we did see them." Dayne is now getting upset. She pleads, "They try to talk to me. The whole Never Light Valley tries to talk to me. I save one." Dayne turns to a loss for words. Then her disbelief changes to anger as she yells at Cam, "You made us leave! We could've saved them!"

Cam, wanting to calm Dayne down, says, "We can still save them by ridding the Horizon of the Jokers and helping the kings regain their power."

Dayne takes a deep breath and calms down, agreeing with Cam, and they head back towards the Warrior's cabin.

Once they reach the end of the woods, they spot another ribbon and know they are back on track. Cam watches as Dayne removes the ribbon and places them with the other ones they have collected.

Dayne says, "It's almost daylight. The warriors should be getting up soon. Any chance you have some energy left in those legs?"

Cam smiles and pulls his jacket off before bolting forward. "Last one, there is a rotten egg."

CHAPTER 17

"When a lost love is found, does it even know it's been lost?"
- Kannon

Dayne stops and removes what she hopes is the final ribbon and that town isn't much further. Cam stands beside her, panting for air. While Cam tries not to pass out, he notices Colt running towards them. Colt laughs when she sees how worn-out Cam is.

She points in front of them. "Come on you slow pokes; the town is just up there."

Dayne is relieved when she notices the town sign up ahead. "Did they have their meeting yet? Are we too late?"

Colt reassures them that the warriors haven't even woken up yet. The town sign reads, "Welcome to Hoyle." Dayne is surprised at how much it resembles her town of Hidden Bridge. They walk through the empty town as the sun begins to show its face.

Colt points towards the end of the street, saying, "It's the little cabin there at the end of the street, with the broken front door."

Dayne nods. "Let's hurry; we don't have time to spare."

The warriors begin to toss and turn as they wake up—everyone but Hoss, who refuses to move. He is out for the count. Bug sits up and tries to stretch as he rubs the back of his neck. "Damn, sleeping on the floor really hurts an old boy's back," he comments as he continues to stretch.

Hunter opens one eye and points to Hoss. "Shhh, Big man

is sleeping. Let's not wake the bear."

Bug stands up and tries to shake the sleep off. He rubs his eyes and gives a big yawn. Trying not to wake anyone else, Bug stumbles out onto the porch. He walks one end, then he uses the little boy's room off the porch. While scratching his butt, he is still half asleep.

"Now that's disgusting. No one should have to see that this early in the morning. You're one nasty little guy," Colt remarks.

Bug, startled by Colt, jumps and yells, "Kannon! Come here now. You're going to want to see this."

Kannon walks out on the porch, still trying to wake up, grumbling, "We told you before that no one cares how big a dump you took. There's no such thing as a Horizon record." Kannon, not too observant as well, walks to the end of the porch with Bug.

Bug points behind Kannon, and Kannon turns back to see Dayne and Colt standing at the front step.

Kannon's eyes almost pop out of his head with disbelief, and now he is wide awake. He yells excitedly, "Dayne, is it really you? I must still be dreaming. Bug, pinch me."

Not believing what he is seeing. Bug pinches Kannon hard. Kannon, in return, slaps Bug on the head.

"What the hell? You said to pinch you!" Bug cries as he rubs his head.

"It is a figure of speech, you idiot," Kannon replies while rubbing his arm.

Colt laughs. "Are you sure these are our guys?"

Dayne nods her head. "Yes, Kannon, it's really me. How are you doing?"

"Well, I was doing fine till some little idiot pinched me. Dayne, where have you been?"

"I've been here the whole time," she says with a shrug.

"I have so many questions—"

Dayne holds up her hands to stop him. "They'll have to wait. Right now, our main concern is finding the kings. Where are the others?"

Bug stands behind Kannon, making whipping gestures and trying his best to make a whip-cracking sound.

Kannon pushes him off the porch, then turns back to Dayne. "They are all inside. I'll go get them."

Since Kannon speaks so loudly, Hunter and Hoss can hear the whole conversation, along with Spin Doll.

Hunter mumbles, "Is that Kannon's wife?"

"Beats me; don't really give a crap," Hoss mumbles as he passes gas loudly in Hunter's direction and giggles. "Or do I?" Hoss chuckles.

Hunter's eyes bulge out as he covers his head with a blanket. Spin Doll covers her head as well while giggling at Hunter.

Kannon assembles the crew at the table while Dayne and Colt grab a seat next to Kannon. Kannon introduces his team one by one. "This is Spin Doll. She's unable to speak, so we consider her to be silent but deadly. Next, we have Dillo and his amazing armadillo shell. He's probably the most honest guy you'll ever meet. This here is Hunter, the sharpshooter. He can hit an ant in the ass from a mile away." Hunter tips his head towards the girls. Kannon continues. "This enormous man is named Hoss, the movable mountain. And last but not least, my best friend and watcher, Bug-I-pee-off-the-porch-because-I'm-nasty, or Kannon's bitch. He goes by either. And his bat that he calls Babe."

Dayne says, "It's a pleasure to meet you all. This is Colt; she is easily the fastest in the Horizon." Then Dayne points to the air beside her. "This is Cam. He's young but wise beyond his years."

The guys look at each other, thinking maybe Dayne is losing it, and Spin Doll just waves at the empty space. "Good morning to you, fine gentlemen and lady. Pleased to make your acquaintance." Then Cam appears in front of them.

Bug whispers, "I see ghosts."

Cam whispers back. "I assure you, I'm no ghost."

Hoss reaches out to shake Cam's hand, almost breaking him in half as he wisecracks. "Put her there, ghost dude."

Cam shakes Hoss's hand and then counts his fingers to make sure he has them all. Colt clears her throat and hands the note from the door to Dayne. Upon seeing the note, Dayne immediately hands it to Kannon and says, "This was on your door when we showed up this morning."

Kannon takes the paper and reads it out loud. "Kannon, hope this note finds you well. I've heard rumors that you've been in search of me. If you'd like to talk to me, meet me at the stone wall just past the next clearing when the sun is at its highest. Come alone since this is our problem and no one else's. I'll be waiting with bells on."

The note is not signed, but Kannon knows whoever it is, they're going to meet face-to-face.

Hunter isn't at all for it. He grumbles, "No way we are letting you go alone. Who knows who wrote this letter? It could be the Jokers for all we know."

Kannon puts his hand on Hunter's shoulder, reassuring him. "Thanks for caring about me, my friend. But I must do this alone."

Not one of them in the room agrees with Kannon's decision.

Bug looks at Dayne and begs her. "Say something to him."

Dayne forcefully states, "You can't do this alone!"

Kannon looks at Dayne with fire in his eyes as he snaps back at her, "Now you care about me!" He turns and storms out the back door then punches it, almost ripping the door from its hinges.

The room is instantly silenced as Dayne follows him out the door, slamming it shut behind her. Everyone in the room runs to the backdoor and presses their ears to try to hear what is about to go down.

Dayne says in a strong voice, "Are you done acting like a child?"

Kannon, fired up, yells, "I looked all over the world for you. I spent every dime we had. I lost the house and the car. I even emptied our savings to try and find you. I made sacrifices you couldn't even imagine, just for you. Then, when I do find you, you ignore me and run off after another guy. I loved you; we were supposed to be forever." With a shaky voice, Kannon holds up his wedding ring and adds, "This is forever."

Dayne struggles to find the right words. "I do still love you." She holds up her hand, showing her wedding ring.

Kannon shakes his head. "Are you just here to hurt me? Am I actually in hell right now?"

Dayne grabs Kannon's hand. "I'm sorry, but I cannot tell you everything right now. We need to find the kings."

"To hell with the kings. Find them yourself. You know, when I go meet this guy, maybe he'll release my light to help make your decision easier!" Kannon screams while pulling out his cannon.

Dayne stands back, scared because she's never seen this side of Kannon before. She tries to calm him down by reassuring him. "It'll all work out in the end. This I promise to you."

Kannon's eyes begin to tear up. "Why did you leave me alone in our messed-up world?"

Dayne now begins to tear up as well as she softly responds, "You think I *wanted* to leave you?"

"I don't know what to think anymore," Kannon mumbles.

Dayne reaches up and puts her hand on Kannon's cheek. "Of course I didn't want to leave you. You are my forever."

"But yet you did!" Kannon remarks, just as Dayne thought they were smoothing things over.

Dayne tries to explain. "I had no choice; you must believe me. Dak needed me more than you did."

"To hell with Dak!" Kannon blurts.

Dayne slaps Kannon in the face hard, turning his head to the right. Before either of them can say another word, they are interrupted by a voice behind Kannon.

"Now, are we going to kiss or fight? You know, we really hate to break up this hallmark moment. But nonetheless, we have a message for you." The voice belongs to one of the three Shadows.

Kannon fires on them, destroying the area behind the Shadows as his cannon shoots through them. "Trust me, this is not the right time for this," Kannon sternly states.

"Yeah, yeah, yeah, Whatever, slick. The Beast is hungry, so we're thinking maybe you'd like to be a meal for him. In two days, we'll meet in the south clearing for the Beast to properly introduce himself and maybe even get in a little warm-up. Oh, and bring your friends. The Beast really enjoyed playing with them last time." The Shadows laugh.

"How do you know we'll show?" Dayne snaps.

The shadow quickly replies, "Because if you don't, Dak will have a very bad day. If you know what we mean, and I'm sure you do."

Another shadow approaches and sarcastically states, "Maybe we'll get a little practice now."

The Shadows charge Kannon and Dayne, not knowing Dayne has The Releaser with her. Dayne easily disperses the shadow's lights with one swing, splitting three of them in half and releasing their lights.

The lone shadow runs off, yelling, "You have forty-eight hours, warriors! The Beast doesn't like to wait." Then its lights rise to the sky.

Dayne leaves Kannon standing alone, while she heads back inside to warn the others. Just before she enters, the group scatters from the door, pushing each other and knocking Bug to the ground. Kannon stands alone in the backyard, and he can hear Dayne tell the group what has just happened.

Cam's voice speaks from mid-air to Kannon's ears. "She does really love you. But you're not her only love. A heart can't be ripped in half."

Kannon knows now that her love for him is equally just as strong for Dak. Knowing this makes Kannon's heart hurt. He has to take some time to think as he walks into the woods and out of sight from the cabin. Cam figures it'd be best if he follows Kannon, just to keep an eye on him. A man in pain can easily let his emotions take over and do something crazy.

Kannon stumbles aimlessly through the woods, just thinking and walking. With his head down, he does not look where he is going and walks right onto a park bench, falls over it, and lands on the ground. He stands up and looks around to see if anyone had seen him.

Cam, off in the distance, chuckles low enough that Kannon doesn't hear him. Kannon, not seeing anyone around, sits down on the bench.

"Well, hello old friend," Jim's familiar voice chimes in.

"Jim, I think I'm losing my mind," Kannon explains.

"Nonsense. I can see it throbbing as you talk," Jim jokingly says with a giggle.

Kannon looks at Jim in a 'this is no time for jokes' manner. "Daynes is back!"

Jim smiles and replies, "Isn't that a good thing?"

"She's not back for me. She's back because she needs my help to save the kings and Dak," Kannon spits out disgustedly.

"We all need the kings back," Jim says reassuringly.

"Not all of us; let Dak save them," Kannon barks back.

Jim does not want Kannon to retreat to his former 'all about me' attitude, so he decides to tell Kannon a story. "One day, this lonely old man, who had nothing left, was about to take his own life. He was saved at the last minute by a text from his daughter, who had disowned him for many years. The text said 'I know we haven't spoken in quite some time, but I thought you should know you're going be a grandpa. Since I'm in no condition mentally to care for a kid, she's all yours.' Now, this man went from having nothing left to lose, to having everything to lose. This little baby girl saved his life, even though she didn't know it. His life changed for the better, and he finally had a purpose in life. Everything he did revolved around that precious little girl. On her first birthday, her grandpa bought her this beautiful little jewelry box. When she opened it, this little ballerina popped up and began spinning. Oh, how the little girl loved it. She would carry the box around with her everywhere she went. She would open it and begin twirling just like the ballerina. Even when the girl had grown up, the box was never too far away from her. She carried it with her always. Grandpa made sure she had a happy life. He took her to dance, soccer, and even karate. He wanted her to experience life to the fullest.

"Then came a day that would change both their lives. Grandpa's age finally caught up to him, and he couldn't do all this stuff with his beautiful granddaughter as he did before. Once he had stopped going to things, she did as well. This broke both their hearts, as the doctors gave Grampa only a couple of mere weeks to live. Now, a man who didn't want to live. Wanted nothing more than to live forever. One day, after his doctor's appointment, Grampa came home to a silent house. He yelled for his granddaughter but received no answer. He searched the house but found nothing. Then he found one of his ties in his closet, hanging alone but like something was supposed to be on it. Grandpa fell to his knees, thinking the worst. While kneeling, he noticed his granddaughter's jewelry box at the back of the closet on the floor. It was on its side and open. For the first time ever, the little doll that twirled was not there; she did not dance, and no music was playing. A small note lay beside it. Grandpa picked it up and read it. 'Thanks for always being my dance partner. The music will not sound the same without you. Love, your little ballerina.' Grandpa once again went from having everything to having nothing. He looked at the tie hanging, and he even tried it on. But then it hit him. Where was her body? It couldn't just vanish. Something seemed strange, so once again, he searched the closet. While in the closet, he found a small door that emitted just enough light for him to find. It was as if the door wanted him to find it. He tried to open it, but it would not open because something blocked it and kept it from fully opening. In the dark, he could not see what was stopping the door. He reached for the base of the little door. There, he found something wedged in the bottom of the door, keeping it from opening or closing. Not letting the door close, he stuck his fingers in it to hold it open. Then, with his other hand, he picked the object up. Once the object was close enough to see, he could tell it was the missing dancing girl from the box. How did such a small object hold that heavy door? Grandpa pulled the door open to reveal a grassy field, which was not at all what he had expected. As Grandpa stepped through it, the door slammed shut behind him. He knew that must be where his granddaughter was. He held the little dancing girl in his hand so tightly that it left an indentation in his fingers. To this day, her grandpa still walks the strange new place looking for his dance partner. He'll never give up looking."

"That's an awful story. How's that related to me?" Kannon asks.

Jim has to turn from Kannon for a minute to gather himself.

"Jim, how's that anything like my story?" Kannon is getting impatient.

Jim turns back towards Kannon as he pushes a handkerchief into his back pocket. Clearing his throat, he continues. "It's just like you but different. You had everything and then lost it. Now you get a shot at having everything once again and more. I'd had—I mean, *Grandpa*—had nothing, then he had everything. Now he has nothing once again."

"So, what do you want me to do? Forgive everything and act as if nothing has ever happened. Yeah, I'm pretty sure that won't happen," Kannon replies, shaking his head.

Jim is upset that Kannon truly didn't listen to his story at all. Now he's a little angry. "You need to find your dancing girl. That will once again reunite you and Dayne and bring you guys back to where you once were. It could be the littlest thing."

Kannon kind of knows what Jim is trying to tell him, but his stubbornness will most likely keep him from finding his dancing girl. Kannon stands up to leave, not saying another word as he tips his head towards Jim. Jim waves and Kannon notices a small indentation in Jim's hand. But, since he can't make out what it is, he leaves the bench and begins walking down the path that he has made on his way to Jim. Suddenly, he stops and looks back toward where Jim is, thinking, *That is just an old wrinkly hand.*

Cam sees Kannon appear from thin air, pretty much just like he does. He thinks, *Does Kannon have more powers than we know?*

Cam appears before Kannon. "There you are. They are all wondering where you had gone off to."

"I guess I was just out here dancing to no music," Kannon jokes as he pushes Cam, just playing around.

The two head back to the cabin to get on the same page with the rest and strategize a plan.

CHAPTER 18

"When you meet someone from the past, the past is all you know." - Kannon

Kannon and Cam walk through the back door and find the whole group sitting around the table.

Bug pipes in. "Glad to see you two could join us."

"Please, take our seats," Hunter suggests as he and Bug get up from the table.

Bug gives knuckles to Kannon as he grabs his bat to go get in a few swings. He informs them, "I'm heading outside to take a few swings and loosen up a bit. Looks like Daddy needs to send a few downtown tomorrow." He makes a half swing in the cabin, almost breaking an empty Starletta bottle. Everyone points for him to take it outside. Bug leaves out the front door as Spin Doll follows him.

"Make sure he doesn't hurt himself," Hunter jokes with Spin Doll.

Kannon grabs the salt and pepper shakers while using the table to show where they'll be and where the Shadows will be on the battlefield.

Hoss butts in. "All I need to know is where the Beast will be. Because his name is on the end of my boots."

Hunter smirks at Hoss. "Be careful what you wish for."

Hoss smirks back. "Oh, that's it, now you poked the bear. Maybe you better go polish your stick some more."

Hunter giggles. "Been polishing it all morning."

Kannon cuts in on their joking. "Guys, how about we take

this a little more seriously? Since the last time you guys met the Beast, he handed your asses to you."

Hoss leaves the table with no words, heading back to the couch.

Hunter goes over to Hoss, whispering, "This is bullshit. How about you go meet the Beast without us and then you can let us know how well that works out for you?" He slams the door behind him as he leaves.

Dayne shakes her head, not happy with Kannon's attitude. "What the hell was that? You better check your attitude at the door. You might not understand teamwork, but we need these guys."

"How did this become a *me* problem? We were all forced here to do a job that none of us asked to do. If you want the leadership job, here you go. Maybe your precious Dak can lead them. Oh wait, he's not here, is he?" Kannon stands and heads out the back door.

Cam looks at Dayne and Colt with wife eyes. "What the H-E-double-hockey-sticks just happened?"

Dayne huffs, "Too many cooks, not enough soup, I guess."

Colt shakes her head. "We traveled all the way here for this. I thought these guys were supposed to be heroes."

Hoss, listening in on everything, says, "Little lady, we didn't come here as heroes; and we probably aren't leaving here heroes. But trust me, you'll get everything I have out on the grassy field. Bet your ass on that." Then he turns back as if he is watching a TV that isn't there.

The three were taken aback by Hoss's words since it is the first time they know he isn't joking. Hoss punches the coffee table, shattering it into tiny pieces. He then stands up and walks out the back door, leaving just the outline of his body where the back door once stood. Once in the backyard, Hoss approaches

Kannon and growls, "You think you're big enough to run your mouth to them, little ladies, then go ahead, run that mouth, you disrespectful little shit. Guarantee you'll never do it again."

Dayne runs out the front door to get the guys to help calm Hoss down after hearing him speak to Kannon. Hunter, Bug, and Dillo run out back as fast as they can, trying to get in between the two men.

Hoss raises his voice. "I'll shove that cannon right up your ass, pretty boy. RUN THAT MOUTH ONE MORE TIME!"

The three are no match to stop Hoss from continuing to walk towards Kannon. Not knowing when to shut his mouth, Kannon says, "I'm the leader here, not you. If I tell you to jump, you jump. Nobody here is scared of your big ass. Lay around some more; try waiting on your own ass. All this talk, we haven't seen you do dick around here. Go lay on your couch; I'll be the hero here and save everyone. Wouldn't want you to tire yourself out."

Hoss stops in his tracks as he looks at everyone. "This is what you all think of me?" He puts his head down and walks off into the woods.

Hunter looks at Kannon wide-eyed. "What have you just done? He's the only chance we have to beat the Beast. Plus, he's our friend."

Kannon walks past everyone in the opposite direction as Hoss did. "He's your friend, not mine."

"What the hell is that? We just lost our lead-off hitter and our cleanup. We're going to have to tell the Shadows that the game has been canceled," Bug snaps. Then he and Spin Doll walk off in yet another direction.

Hunter looks at Dayne, scowling. "You brought all this shit here. We all got along fine till you showed up." Then he walks back into the cabin.

Dillo follows Hoss, leaving Dayne, Cam, and Colt standing there on their own to face the Shadows tomorrow.

Colt turns to Dayne and asks, "What are we going to do now? We can't fight them on our own."

"I'm going either way; they might have Dak. Which means I have no choice."

Cam looks Dayne in the eyes and reassures her, "When I told you I'd do anything for Dak and you, I meant it."

Bug walks back towards Dayne and tosses the fake crown he had at her feet. He confesses, "I found this at your house. You can have this back. I can stand fake people. Some Warrior you turned out to be." Bug turns around and walks off again.

Colt picks it up. "What's this? Have you been lying to us as well?" he asks Dayne, holding up the fake crown.

Cam shakes his head in disbelief. "What is this?"

Dayne has no idea what to say. She is caught being a fake and lying to her friends. She takes the crown from Colt's hand and shoves it into her pocket. "It's not that easy to explain," Dayne mumbles.

"Well, how about we give you a little time to think about your answer?" Cam suggests that he and Colt walk around the house and are gone as well.

Dayne stands there alone with no answers. How is she going to save her son now? Should she have told them all the truth from the start? But, in her defense, when she had met them, she didn't know if they were on her side or against her.

Kannon stops once he gets to the top of the hill. With nothing left to say, he continues to the meeting. He stops for just a minute when he sees Bug at the front of the house swinging his bat as Spin Doll gestures like she's routing for him to get a hit. That brings a half-smile to Kannon's face. He also can see the bushes moving off in the distance; it has to be

Hoss. Kannon thinks maybe he was in the wrong, but you don't talk to a superior like that.

Hunter is nowhere to be seen. Kannon can see Dayne standing alone in the backyard. She is looking in Kannon's direction, but he is pretty sure she can't see him that far away. He stands there, taking it all in, not knowing if he is walking into a trap or not. Kannon definitely does not want to leave possibly their last memory of him like that.

He turns and heads on to the meeting. About halfway there, Hunter steps out from behind a tree, startling Kannon.

"What are you doing here? The note said I had to come alone," Kannon explains.

"I'm not letting my best friend walk into a trap," Hunter responds.

"Well, if it is a trap, we definitely can't afford to lose both of us. I truly do appreciate the gesture, but I really must do this on my own," Kannon tells Hunter.

Hunter nods in understanding and gives knuckles to Kannon, then heads back to the cabin.

Kannon approaches the meeting place cautiously. The first thing he notices is a medium-built man leaning against an old Oak tree. Kannon doesn't notice anyone or anything else as he walks up to the man.

The man looks incredibly like Kannon. It's like they are brothers. The man steps away from the tree as Kannon gets closer.

"Well, nice to see you could make it, and you came alone. Finally, I get to meet the famous Kannon face-to-face. I heard so much about the man with a cannon for an arm. Must be honest, didn't think that is going to happen," the man greets.

"I'm not too keen on meeting people who leave random notes on my door," Kannon responds.

"Yeah, me neither. Sorry about that. But I have to say, I'm glad you can read." The man moves in closer to size Kannon up. "Well, your spelling could use some work."

Kannon ignores the dig and stares hard at the man while sizing him up as well. "You wanted me. I'm here. Now what?"

The man smirks. "I've heard rumors that you've been looking for me. Tell me now, ya like what you see?"

Kannon sighs. "That'd be good and all if I knew who you were. But I really can't say I'm too impressed so far."

The man holds his hand out to shake as he introduces himself. "Hell, I'm the famous Dak you've been hearing about. You know, the man you wish you were."

Kannon's eyes see red as his arm begins to change.

"Hey, wait up now. There are no weapons at this meeting," Dak quickly says, pulling out a staff with a spiked ball on the end and a shield from his backside.

Kannon smiles, gritting his teeth. "Yeah, then you heard right. I have definitely been the one looking for you."

The two circle each other, waiting for the other one to make the first move.

"I haven't the foggiest idea what Dayne sees in you. You're still a boy," Kannon growls with a sneer.

"I was thinking the same about you. Look how old you are, *Grandpa*." Dak smirks and Kannon loses it.

He quickly sends a rabbit punch shot at Dak, and as Dak deflects it off his shield, he sarcastically adds, "I hope that isn't all you got."

"Tip of the iceberg, my boy," Kannon remarks, toying with him.

"You seemed like a much nicer guy when we met to eat blackberries."

"So that was you. Should've ended you there instead of

coming here to waste my time," Kannon says with a snarl.

Dak swings his spike-balled staff, but Kannon blocks it with his cannon arm. "I guess your dad never taught you how to swing, did he?" Kannon says degradingly.

"Nah, my dad is a deadbeat. Left my mom and me when I was born. But he probably is a dick like you anyways."

Before they can actually start something, a rumbling sound comes from the woods on the other side of the field. The two men stop and look in the direction of the thunderous noise. Dak pulls his shield and maces up into a fighting stance toward the noise.

"What is it?" Kannon asks.

The noise gets closer and closer as Kannon joins Dak in a fighting stance.

Dak turns to Kannon. "The Beast is coming for me. Go, save yourself. This is my fight."

"How do you know it's the Beast? Why does he want you?"

Not taking his eyes off the trees, Dak says, "the Jokers have hunted me since as early as I can remember. I truly have no idea why. But they really want to release my light. The Beast is one of their pets; he's sent here to release me."

Kannon's arm begins to charge up, and he assures Dak, "Well, they won't be releasing it today."

Dak's only smirks.

The Beast busts out of the tree line like it is possessed, destroying everything in its path like a charging rhino. The only difference is that the Beast is taller than the trees. Its breathing becomes louder and louder the closer it gets. A small trail of drool flops in the wind as he charges.

Kannon fires a powerful shot, which does not affect the Beast, only bouncing off it and destroying a small group of trees. In seconds, the Beast is on top of them, and they both try to scramble out of its way. But Kannon is too slow, and the Beast sends him flying into the woods. Kannon bounces off a couple of trees, only to land face down, knocking him out cold.

He wakes to see he is being carried by Cam and Colt. Kannon struggles for them to put him down, yelling, "What are you doing? We need to help Dak defeat the Beast."

With his hands out to calm Kannon down, Cam says, "There was no Beast or Dak when we found you."

"What do you mean no Beast or Dak?" Kannon asks while holding his aching head.

"You were laying in the woods all alone," Colt answers.

"We need to get the group together now!" Kannon yells as he starts to walk towards the cabin.

Colt takes off like a shot, yelling, "On it, boss! They'll be ready when you get there."

When Kannon and Cam finally make it back to the cabin, Colt has assembled all of them but Hoss and Dillo. They go onto the porch, watching as Kannon paces back and forth.

"First things first," Kannon starts. "I met Dak today."

Dayne jumps in, alarmed, asking, "That's who wanted to meet you privately. Is he alright?"

"It's my turn to speak," Kannon snaps rudely.

Dayne backs up to let Kannon have the floor.

"I've been a complete jerk to every one of you. I put my agenda and feelings ahead of everyone. I'm sorry. I truly am. Dak and I did not hit it off. Actually, we were in a scrap when the Beast came out of the woods, charging us."

Bug excitedly cuts in. "You saw the Beast? Is he big? Does he have big fangs?"

"He's huge and unstoppable, pure evil. I hit him square in the chest with my hardest cannon shot, and it just bounced off him. Dak told me the Jokers and the Beast have been tracking him since he was a child," Kannon explains.

Bug jumps in again, still excited. "So, what happened? How the hell did you get away?"

Kannon shakes his head, confused. "I don't know. When the Beast hit me, he sent me flying into the woods. I must have hit a tree or something and got knocked out. I don't remember anything after that. Cam and Colt found me lying in the woods. I woke up as we were on our way here."

Dayne says, "Where's Dak? Is he alright?"

Kannon, Cam, and Colt just look at the ground, and Cam says, "Sorry, Dayne, we didn't see him anywhere."

Dayne collapses, and Hunter and Spin Doll catch her, carry her in, and lay her on the couch. Bug and Kannon remain outside.

"So, we don't stand a chance. Is that what you're saying?" Bug asks.

Kannon shrugs his shoulders.

Bug, now angry, begins pacing. "You mean to tell me that I just got all these new friends and family, and now the Beast will take it all away from me? Sorry, but I don't think so. Time to break some kneecaps."

Kannon knows there is nothing to say that will make Bug feel differently, so he stays silent.

Bug is so upset that he begins to spark. With sadness, he says, "Why us, really? Why us? Why hand us shit on a platter our whole lives, then tempt us with friends and family for a few days? What did any of us do to deserve this? To hell with this; I'm doing something about it." He takes off running, disappearing into the trees.

Dillo appears, and Kannon yells, "Dillo, you're back! I'm so sorry, my friend. Sometimes I can be a real ass."

Dillo isn't too eager to accept Kannon's apology and is all

business. "I'm not here for that. I'm here to tell you we found where the Shadows are. They're on their way." Dillo points over the cabin. "They are that way, about two miles away. You guys should leave this spot now! Nothing good will come from this battle. Both sides are going to lose key pieces. Maybe another time would be better."

Kannon places his hand on Dillo's shoulder. "Sorry, Dillo, but this is a fight we can't back down from. They have Dak."

Dillo shakes his head. "I'm sorry, my friend. If you must fight them, then I wish you all the best tonight."

"What do you mean tonight? The battle isn't till tomorrow."

"No, it's tonight. They're going to surprise attack you. I overheard a few talking. They're on the way here as we speak. Like I said, about two miles away."

Kannon rubs the top of his head with his hand, trying to think about his next move. "We can't defeat the Beast, can we?"

Dillo shakes his head. "You know, if what Bug and I heard is true, and the witch has a protection spell cast on the Beast, maybe we can get to the witch and release her light, and it will release her spell." He stops to think, then says, "I really wish I could help. But I just don't feel right on this one. Sorry, Kannon, but I do wish you guys the best of luck. If you find the witch, you might be able to end the Beast. It's your only hope." Dillo hugs Kannon and leaves the same way he had arrived.

Once Dillo is out of sight, Bug returns as if they are trying to avoid each other. Kannon asks Bug if he is all right. Bug replies, "Much better now. I went out in the woods and kicked a chipmunk."

Kannon, knowing he shouldn't, just has to ask. "You really kicked a chipmunk?"

Bug nods seriously. "Sure did. Whenever I used to get mad, one of my foster parents would tell me to go kick a chipmunk. I'll tell you what, you wouldn't believe the air you can get on them little suckers. Sure, they're not too happy with you. I mean, who likes to be kicked? But it's a dog-eat-dog world out here. Sometimes a man's got to do what a man's got to do." Bug pulls his pants up a little and walks into the cabin.

Kannon smiles and walks into the cabin with the news Dillo has just given him. He explains to the group how important it is to take the witch out. It truly *is* a life-or-death decision. None of the group has a good feeling about this, but they have no choice but to fight. Kannon leaves them to prepare. He sits on the steps, talking to himself about what might be his last day in the Horizon.

Colt approaches Kannon and confesses, "I shouldn't have run home that day."

Kannon, not knowing Colt is talking about her story, asks, "What day, Colt?"

Colt looks out into the yard, her eyes glazing over. "The day I came to the Horizon. My dad didn't want me to run home. But I really wanted to make it home before my favorite show started. It was the final episode. Ross was going to find out if Rachel loved him and if she was going to stay with him. Anyway, on my way home, a car came out of nowhere and struck my left leg, sending me to the ground. It felt as if I had a bad cramp in it; I couldn't put any pressure on it. So, I stopped and sat on the curb to try and stretch it out. While I was there, one of my college scouts pulled up to check on me, making sure I was alright. His car looked almost like the car that struck me. He was a really big fat man, and my dad didn't like him at all. This guy never missed one of my practices, and he really wanted me to attend his college. He offered to give me a ride home after insuring me it wasn't his car that struck me, and since I was running late for my show, I took him up on his offer. It was only a ten-minute drive.

"When we got to my house, he asked if he could quickly use our bathroom. He had a long ride home, so I figured it was the least I could do since he brought me home. But once he got inside my house, he wouldn't leave. I told him my dad would be home anytime, and he knew how much my dad didn't care for him. He laughed and agreed with me. Then, while we were standing at the door, I noticed stars falling from the sky. They were beautiful, like fireworks. The next thing I remembered was him carrying me through this weird door. Then I wake up, and I'm here in the Horizon."

Kannon is watching Colt speak, but he doesn't say anything. He lets Colt gather her thoughts before continuing.

"I should've never stopped running. That fat man was a bad man, wasn't he?" Colt wipes a few tears from her eyes and gives Kannon a hug, and then she is gone before Kannon can respond to her.

CHAPTER 19

"Never trust a man you meet in a hole." - Lakin

With four new shadow guards standing watch at the factory hole, Lakin awakens to nothing but what little light the top of the hole allows. Still groggy from the battle with the Beast and the drop in the hole, she tries to gather her wits together and figure out where she is. She feels around in the dark for anything that can help with the situation she finds herself in. Her hand grazes across something sharp, and she quickly pulls it back. Thinking it felt like teeth, she worries about what is in the hole with her. Slowly, she reaches back towards the sharp item. She feels a wet trickle down her arm when she picks it up. Lakin can feel the cut on her finger as it begins to sting. Holding the item up towards the hole light, she sees it is a crown just by the outline.

Why is the crown down in this hole? Lakin thinks.

Then she begins to feel around again, wondering if the king is also down here with her. It isn't long before she suddenly feels a hand . . . then a leg. Lakin quickly pulls her hand back, thinking, *Am I stuck down here with a dead king?*

Panic fills her mind as a voice from the dark says, "Are you alright, lady?"

Another voice says, "Yeah, lady, are you alright?"

Lakin tries to adjust her eyes to see in the dark as she asks, "Who said that?"

"Oh, I'm sorry, where are my manners?" the first voice says.

The second voice follows immediately. "Yes, where are my manners?"

Lakin grows even more terrified as the voices speak but tries to gather her courage. "Who are you, and why are you in this hole?"

The first voice answers, "My name is Mim. I'm keeping an eye on the kings. My Warrior tells me to."

The second voice follows suit. "Hi, my name is IC. I'm keeping an eye on the kings. My Warrior tells me to as well."

Lakin questions why the two are copying each other's words, and Mim quickly replies, "Sorry, didn't know we were. It's one of our bad habits."

IC follows with, "Yeah, sorry, didn't know we were. It's our bad habit."

Lakin shakes her head. "Are the kings down here with us?"

Mim quickly responds. "They most definitely are."

IC repeats, "They most definitely are, ma'am."

Lakin is confused. Are there two of them, or is there only one that just repeats herself?

One of the shadow guards yells down the hole. "Hey, keep it down. The kings are trying to sleep." The rest of the guards begin to laugh.

Mim yells back, "So sorry, Mr. Guard!"

IC yells, "Yes, we're so sorry, Mr. Guard." Both laugh at the same time. "Crazy old guard, always joking with us."

Without seeing the two, Lakin thinks they may have gone crazy being down in the hole for so long.

"It would be really nice if we had a light down here so I could properly introduce myself to you two."

Mim says, "Oh, there's a light switch on the wall beside me."

IC says, "Yes, I have a light switch on the wall beside me

as well.

Lakin stands silently in the dark, waiting for the two to turn the lights on. After a few minutes, Lakin blurts, "Can you turn them on, please?"

Mim and IC flick their switches on at the same time.

Lakin immediately holds her hand up to her face to block the bright light until her eyes adjust. When she can finally see, two little ladies are standing in front of her. Each one is about a foot tall. Mim and IC jump behind one of the kings, as Lakin is bigger than they thought and scares them.

Lakin, trying not to be rude, softly says, "Wow, I didn't realize you were that small."

Mim responds from behind the king, "I'm the bigger one. I'm two-tenths of an inch bigger than IC."

IC is also peeking around the king. "I'm the smaller one. I'm two-tenths of an inch smaller than Mim."

"Pleased to meet you, ladies. My name is Lakin, and I'm about four and a half feet taller than both of you."

Mim and IC laugh at the same time at Lakin's joke. Then they yell, "Pleased to meet you as well! You can call us Mimic."

Lakin laughs. "Alright, I'll call you Mimic! I like it because you two mimic each other."

Mim and IC look at each other, confused, and say, "We do? Oh, we do."

They all laugh and shake hands.

"Do people call you Mimic?"

Mim nods. "Yeah, our friends do. So, you must be our friend."

IC adds her two cents. "You must be our friend. Because our friends do."

Lakin is still not trying to offend Mimic, but she has to ask:

"So, are you sisters or possibly leprechauns?"

They respond in unison. "Leprechauns, definitely not. Disgusting, foul little people. No, we're fairies."

Lakin tries not to chuckle. "Don't fairies have wings or little pixie dust wands?"

IC looks disgusted as Mim answers, "Not all fairies have wings, and I really hope you are just joking about the fairy dust." Both fairies begin rolling up their sleeves like they will have a problem with Lakin.

Lakin holds her hands out in surrender. "I'm sorry, it's just I haven't ever met fairies before. You're both quite beautiful."

Mim and IC look at each other and smile before Mim says, "Why, IC, you are very pretty, and this girl knows beauty when she sees it."

IC grins. "Yes, you are very pretty as well, Mim. This girl does know beauty when she sees it."

The little ladies make Lakin smile because of their cuteness.

Lakin asks the ladies where they are from because in Lakin's world, there aren't people that small.

Mim and IC points to the sky, and IC says, "We're from up there. We live among the stars. We are known as star cleaners—or at least, we *were* star cleaners."

Mim nods. "When the Jokers made the stars fall, we fell as well."

Lakin is astonished. "You two live in the stars?"

Mim laughs. "No, silly, we live *with* the stars, not *in* them. As star cleaners, we clean them up and make them shine when they become dirty, making them sparkle again."

IC adds, "We make them shine. We fly from star to star, inspecting them."

Lakin is still a little confused. "How did you fly? You don't have wings."

"We have wings," they both answer.

"But didn't you say fairies don't have wings?"

IC jumps in, now angry. "We are not fairies! We are star cleaners!"

Mim, also angry, pipes in. "Star cleaners have wings. How else do you think we get from star to star?"

"Ok," IC says in a softer tone. "Look, we keep the stars clean because every star should be bright. When the Jokers pulled the stars down and turned them into Shadows, we fell as well. There used to be hundreds of star cleaners all over the sky. Once we arrived down here, we were hunted by the Shadows. If they caught us, they would pull our wings off so we couldn't fly. Also, they thought our wings were lucky, like a rabbit's foot. Trust me when I tell you, it is incredibly painful. Not being able to fly, we became sitting ducks for the master locksmith of doors. He is a very big man with metal teeth. He loved to catch us and eat us. He said we were a delicacy. The Shadows began catching us to barter with the locksmith. For every five of us, he'd let a shadow enter a door. Since the rumor was that we were the last two star cleaners alive, we were worth a great deal to the locksmith. We ran for our lives every hour of every day.

"Eventually, the day came when we got captured. On our way to be delivered to the locksmith, a Warrior crossed the shadow path. The Warrior quickly released the shadow's light, and we were saved for yet another day. Being so grateful, we offered to help the Warrior in any way we possibly could. Once she accepted our help, we became her watchers. She sent us down the hole to watch the kings and help heal them. Now, instead of star cleaners, we've become king cleaners."

Mim jumps in. "Kali is so beautiful, and she's a real

Warrior. Without wings, it kind of makes us like a no-horned unicorn from your land."

Lakin feels awful that they had lost all their friends and Warrior. "Well, until we find your Warrior, I'll be your protector, girls."

Mimic is ecstatic to hear that, and they dance around Lakin, who tries to quiet them down before the shadow guards yell again.

"Are the kings good enough to move? That is, if I can figure a way out of here for us."

Mim shakes her head. "The kings were put in a state of hypnosis so they can heal quicker without the worry of the Horizon."

"The kings can heal better while sleeping?"

IC nods. "Yes, it can definitely speed up the healing time."

Lakin has no idea how they are getting out of the hole. Even if they do, how could Mimic and she lift any of the kings out of the hole? The three sit there helplessly, having no idea where to go from here.

Trying to keep their minds off their situation, Lakin asks, "When we get out of here, and the Jokers are no more, will you two return to cleaning stars?"

Mimic answers, "How can we, without our wings? We'll forever be stuck here in the Horizon."

That doesn't help matters at all. It actually makes them all a little more depressed, and Mim and IC begin to bicker in a language Lakin has never heard before. She holds her finger to her mouth, motioning the two ladies to be quiet. Both stop talking and go silent before hearing a faint knock at what they think is the factory door.

Then, there is a very loud knock. They hear the faint creaking sound of the door being opened. "Hello, is anyone here?" a voice from the door yells.

"Stop! Don't come any closer. State your business or leave," one of the shadow guards yells back.

"Whoa, whoa, whoa, buddy. I'm one of the good guys. Just looking for a Warrior named Spin Doll. Maybe one of you has seen her? Small girl with some badass moves. What am I talking about? Of course you didn't see her. If you did, you wouldn't be standing here now, would you?"

The shadow warns once again, "I wouldn't get any closer, or you may just lose your light."

"Now, come on. We don't have to be like that. That's a mighty big hole. Say bub, what's in the hole?" the voice says, sounding closer.

"Stop!" the shadow yells, and Lakin and the girls hear a scuffle above them. It goes on for five or six minutes, then silence. The girls desperately hope the voice is the victor in the scuffle. Lakin and Mimic stare at the top of the hole, waiting for the results.

Finally, the voice says, "Now, see, guys, it didn't have to come to this. We could've worked out our differences like gentlemen. Safe journeys, my friends."

A head appears from above. "What are you all doing down there? Any chance one of you is named Spin Doll?"

Lakin yells, "No, sorry, no one named Spin Doll is down here! Can you please help us out? The Jokers threw us down here. I'm a watcher. I'm down here with three of the kings."

"You really have the kings down there? Well, why didn't you say so? I'll tell you what, I'll help you and the kings out of the hole. Then you can help me find Spin Doll."

"Deal!"

"The name is Fat Jack, little lady. Don't worry; I'll have you guys out quicker than a pig to mud."

Lakin guesses that Jack hasn't seen Mimic, so she quickly has the girls climb into a satchel one of the kings had on them. Once in the satchel, Lakin throws it over her back like a string backpack. She is worried that this Fat Jack isn't all he seems to be, and if that is the case, it'd be better if he doesn't see Mimic.

A few minutes pass before Jack approaches the hole again and yells, "You're in luck, little lady! I found a rope." He tosses one end of the rope down the hole to Lakin while tying the other around himself. "Tie the rope around you, then I'll pull you up."

Lakin yells, "As I said, I have the kings down here. I'll tie the rope around one of them first."

"Why don't we worry about getting you up here first? Then we can get help for the kings?"

Lakin wonders why Jack is so hesitant about saving the kings. "The deal is me and the kings; then we'll find Spin Doll for you. We really need to get the kings out now."

Trying to win his case, Jack yells, "I'll pull you up, then you can help me pull up the kings."

Lakin knows that is a stupid idea. "If we do that, who'd tie the rope around the kings? No, it must be them first."

Fat Jack, knowing he isn't going to change Lakin's mind, finally agrees to pull up the kings first. He has to work hard to pull that dead weight up that far. To an onlooker, it'd appear he was involved in a tug of war! He turns away from the hole and tugs as hard as he can.

As the first king reaches the top, he gets caught on the lip of the hole. Jack ties the rope to a conveniently places a hook to go over and help the king out.

"You got to give me a minute. I'm not in as good of shape as I used to be," he calls down.

Lakin doesn't answer but begins tying the rope around the

next king. She swears she hears Jack speaking to someone in a lower voice. He must be talking to himself, she thinks.

The next two kings go up smoother and quicker than the first, which Lakin finds odd.

While Jack places the third king down against the factory wall, Lakin climbs the rope to the top of the hole. She thinks she spots Jack kicking one of the kings.

"What are you doing to the king?"

The quick-thinking Jack replies, "He was falling over. I tried to stop his fall by placing my leg under him."

A not-too-trusting Lakin thanks Jack for getting them out of the hole and notices a few strange things that don't seem quite right. First, Jack, who is supposed to be out of shape, isn't breathing too hard. Second, there is a sweat stain against the factory wall, as if someone were standing there for a decent amount of time. Even though Jack isn't panting, he still has sweat stains running down his shirt from being so hot in the factory. The third and final weird thing is if Jack has freed the lights from the four shadow guards, where are they?

Mimic quietly asks Lakin without being heard by Jack, "Where are all the other Shadows? If this place is one of their major spots, why aren't they here? You would think in the hour Jack has been here, some of them would've passed through. It just seems too convenient."

Lakin agrees and whispers, "I'm with you. Something isn't right here."

Jack turns to Lakin, thinking he heard her say something. "What?"

Lakin quickly responds, "I said we gotta leave; this isn't a good spot for us to be right here out in the open." She suggests they get the kings away from the factory as soon as possible.

Lakin, being a very strong girl, picks the king up and tosses him over her shoulder before walking out of the factory. Jack places a king over each of his shoulders and stands. As he is walking out of the small factory door, he somehow bumps both king's heads into the wall before exiting. With not one shadow lurking, they make their way to the woods.

Soon, they find a nice, secluded spot to rest and set the kings down on the ground. Once they are all settled, Lakin properly introduces herself to Jack. "I'm Lakin. Thank you so much. You saved our lives and the hope for the Horizon." She reaches her hand out to shake. "How can we ever repay you, sir?"

Jack shakes Lakin's hand. "Pleased to meet you. I'm Jack. But my friends call me Fat Jack. I'm a watcher as well."

Lakin smiles, not truly believing he is a watcher. "Great. So, who are you a watcher for? My Warrior is Hunter."

Jack thinks for a minute, wondering if he knows who Hunter is. "My Warrior is a lady named Spin Doll who can't speak. Remember, we have a deal that you'll help me find her."

"A deal is a deal."

Mimic thinks it's weird to have two of the five warriors unable to speak. And, she thinks, Fat Jack's voice sounds familiar, but they just can't figure out why.

Lakin is so exhausted she figures she'll grab some quick shut-eye. She asks Jack if he'll take the first watch, and Jack, with no problems, says he'll be honored to. Lakin rolls in the opposite direction of Jack and closes her eyes. After a few minutes, without Jack hearing, Lakin asks Mimic to keep an eye out for Jack while she sleeps a bit. Since her back is to Jack, Mimic has a good view of Jack from the backpack.

Just as Lakin is drifting off, Jack startles her awake by asking, "Are we heading to where the fourth king is tomorrow?"

Lakin answers in a drowsy state, "I don't know who the fourth king is. For now, I'd be happy just getting the kings to a safe place."

Jack anxiously says, "We need to find the fourth king. The kings need to be powerful once more."

"We need our warriors first, then we find the king."

Jack, not really interested in listening to Lakin anymore, stops talking and turns in the other direction, acting as if he is watching out. Lakin falls fast sleep in seconds once Jack stops talking.

When Jack is sure Lakin is fast asleep, he sneaks from king to king, searching for something. He is agitated, appearing as if not knowing what he is searching for. Mimic watches as he stomps off into the woods. Mim sends IC to follow. IC follows Jack for a bit, and he stops when he's sure he's out of Lakin's view.

Mim wakes Lakin by shaking her head back and forth. Once Lakin is fully awake, Mim explains what her and IC's powers really are. "You see, we have a unique ability that we never told you about. No matter how far apart we are from each other, whatever one of us hears, the other can hear and duplicate the person's voice. We're kind of like high-powered walkie-talkies."

Lakin, trying to understand, notices Jack and IC aren't there with them. "Jack is supposed to be on the lookout."

"Jack took off the minute you fell asleep and walked far into the woods. So, IC followed him without Jack knowing. She just reported that Jack is meeting up with a strange figure as we speak."

"Can IC hear what they are saying?"

Mim nods. "Once they begin talking, we'll be able to hear word for word in their actual voice."

Mim begins to repeat everything in the exact voice she hears. Jack speaks first.

"Don't worry about the kings. They'll be back in their hole once they serve their purpose."

An unfamiliar voice responds. "They'd better be. As soon as you find out who the fourth king is and release his light, the better off we'll all be."

"Maybe I can free some of the warriors and watchers as well. Might as well have fun while I'm stuck in this shitty place."

"That was a close one when she climbed out of the hole. Your cover was almost blown right away."

Jack laughs, saying, "I'm not too worried about that. Plus, Lakin is not the brightest bulb in the box. She didn't even realize it was the shadow guards who actually were the ones pulling the kings out of the hole. You know I wasn't going to work that hard. Manual labor sucks."

"Either way, as soon as you're done with her, feel free to release her as well. Also, try to locate those two star cleaners and dispose of them before they cause us some unwanted issues."

Jack smiles. "Ahh, the star cleaners, so tasty and yet very filling."

IC remembers now where she heard Jack's voice when he was devouring her friends with his metal teeth.

Jack switches gears and asks, "How are my doors? Do you think these fools will ever figure out that I'm the one who pulled them through the doors? I mean, they are some pretty weak-minded people. But they were all I could find at the last minute. Shit, they already have given up once. So, I figured, what's one more time? Besides, they were so successful the first time."

The voice grumbles, "Don't worry about that wretched door collection. These bumbling idiots can't find your cave even if they want to. Look, it's only just around the bend from the witch's front door. They have to walk by it at some point. Even if they find it, they won't know whose door it is or have access to it. Your focus right now should be to find the fourth king, and once he's gone, you can pull as many helpless souls as you want from your doors. We personally don't give a shit."

Jack and the voice both begin to laugh as they walk away from one another.

IC takes off running so she can get back to Lakin and the kings before Jack does.

Lakin can't believe her ears. How can Jack enjoy their sadness? Jack brought them all to the Horizon to fail again. The kings have nothing to do with it. Lakin thinks, Hell, they might not even know we're here. All of us were brought here to help the Jokers find and release the fourth king so they could rule the Horizon forever. Even worse, Jack can continue terrorizing weak-minded people by making them step into his doors.

IC comes sprinting back as she dives into Lakin's backpack, begging Lakin not to let Jack eat them. Mim jumps in the backpack as well, remaining completely silent and hoping they can trust their new friend. Lakin can hear the twigs crack as she knows Jack is almost back. Quickly, Lakin pretends she is still asleep and has never awakened while he is away. Not seeing anything different, Jack lies down and pulls his hat over his eyes. Then he nudges Lakin as he jokes, "Tag, your turn to watch."

Jack begins snoring almost immediately before she can even pretend just to wake up. Lakin lays there terrified, wondering what her next move will be.

CHAPTER 20

"Good news always comes at the worst time." - Kannon

At the kitchen table, Kannon and Dayne begin making battle strategies using forks and spoons as the two sides. Hunter sits in his chair, cleaning his pool stick and playing one of his songs in his head. Cam, Colt, and Spin Doll sit on the edge of the porch, watching Bug hit stones with Babe. Bug crushes a stone over the treetops, then tosses his bat and begins to run bases like he hit a home run. His fans on the porch clap and cheer to play along with him. Just as he rounds fake third base, he gets hit in the face with a drop of water. Then another, followed by yet another. It is raining real rain. Amazed, the fans jump out of the stands to join Bug in his home run celebration. It has never rained in the Horizon the whole time they've been here. It's always been beautiful with sunny days and warm nights.

Bug yells, "Hey guys, it's raining! Come outside; it's really raining."

Dayne, Kannon, and Hunter rush out to join the celebration. Hunter's first thought is whether or not this is a good sign or a bad one. The good is softer ground, which will make it harder for the army to charge and stay cooler in case it's a long battle. The bad thing is it'll make them heavier and slower in the mud, making it harder to avoid or maneuver around. Either way, he is going to enjoy it while he can. Hunter looks towards the sky with a smile as he lets the rain bounce off his face.

Kannon smiles, watching Dayne dance around in the

raindrops. It's been so long since he's seen her that happy. When she comes to a stop, and the rain rolls down her face, her beauty takes Kannon's breath. He thinks if that's the last good sight he sees, he'll be content forever.

Dayne grabs Kannon's hand and pulls him over, which rushes back memories of their wedding day. They spin around and around till they can barely stand up. On impulse, Kannon leans in and kisses Dayne; to his surprise, she returns the kiss.

Bug gathers rain in his hands to throw at Spin Doll, as she does the same to get Bug wet. Cam sits on the porch edge, tired from following Kannon around. He smiles, even though you can see he is in a lot of pain. He isn't going to let the pain ruin this moment like it has all the rest. Colt notices Cam and immediately sits down next to him. "Are you all right, Cam? Do you need me to get you a drink or something?" Colt asks because she worries about him. Cam shakes his head to assure her he is, gesturing to Colt to have fun with the group. Colt smiles and jumps back into the celebration. Cam doesn't want to show her his pain; he wants it to be no one else's burden to deal with.

Once the celebration begins to die down, the crew gathers on the porch to listen to the rain. Little creeks begin to form where there is none as the rain refuses to let up. Raindrops from the roof's edge play a song in the newly formed puddles on the ground. Cam, feeling a little better, clears his throat. "I would like to tell you guys a poem that my bedmate and I made up in the hospital." Everyone moves a little closer to hear Cam over the rain.

Always enjoy the rain,
For it's quite unique and strange.
No one knows from where it comes,
But it's never twice the same.

It cares not to know your name,
Or put all on you the blame.
It will not remove your pain,
But it will wash away your remains.

The group sits in silence and takes Cam's words for their worth. Even though it is a peaceful rain, they can feel a storm coming. Shivers run down Spin Doll's arms, and Bug covers her with his hoodie. They all watch the rain in silence, fearing what is to come.

After an hour or so, Hunter says, "Since we don't know what tomorrow will bring, this might be the best time to get something off our chests—something that no one knows, but you'd like to tell if tomorrow doesn't come."

They look at Kannon since nobody except Dayne knows anything about him. He feels uneasy about going first, but he knows a leader leads. Kannon thinks for a minute, wondering how to tell the group his secrets. He finally decides to dive in.

"The one thing none of you know about me is this. When I couldn't find Dayne in my world, I went crazy. I was institutionalized for months. I had lost everything, including my mind. I drove to our favorite spot and yelled at the stars and moon like it was their fault. I blamed everything and everyone but myself. I sat against my car with a picture of Dayne in one hand and a pistol in the other. I thought that if I couldn't have Dayne in my world, I'd search for her in the next one. I pulled the trigger three times. I gave up, ended up here somehow, and now I can never return to our world." Kannon looks at the ground as Dayne stands and hugs him. The group can't tell if they are crying or if it is the rain wetting their faces.

After a few minutes, Cam volunteers to go next.

"All my life, I only wanted the simple things in life. But instead, I battled a disease that will never let you win. Through all the pain and treatments, I swore never to let it win. It hurt me, and my mom and dad were affected by it as well. They lost their money, the house, and even their love for each other. I felt like they wished I was never born. I brought them nothing but sorrow. I couldn't take the pain in their eyes anymore, so I stopped my treatments. I knew I wouldn't be long for my world with no treatments. But maybe if I gave my life up, then there'd be a chance for them to save theirs.

"Day after day, I would sit and dwell on all my missed opportunities as the disease took over more and more of my body. I'd never go on a first date or my prom. Never have a first kiss, first crush, or even be invited to a sleepover and stay up all night just to see if we could. I would never have a crowd cheer me on as I made the winning basket. I'd never drive a car or buy my first house. Never get a job interview or perform on stage. I'd never watch my kid take their first step or watch them fall so I could pick them up and tell them everything is going to be alright. Never fall in love and mean more to that person than anyone in the world. Most of all, what hurts more than the pain is knowing that no one would know I existed besides the doctors and nurses who took care of me. I would just become a name in the obituary that some guy would browse by while sipping his morning coffee.

"I gave up there and came here. This is my time, my new beginning. But the disease doesn't give up, as it followed me here. I don't want to die, and I have so much to give. The pain has already returned, so win or lose, this will be my last fight. My last dance."

Everyone is stunned, their hearts in their throats. Cam stands and walks into the rain-soaked woods to be alone with his thoughts. Once he is out of sight, the group can hear him crying, and then he yells, "Why me?! Why always me?"

The group is silent, tears rolling down their faces and staring at where Cam disappeared to; then they hear, "Fuck you, cancer. You just couldn't let me be happy for one day! Fuck you!"

Colt jumps up and runs into the woods to check on Cam. Kannon reaches up and pushes his hair off his face. Even Bug, who never shuts up, has no words. Hunter gets up to take a walk, punching the cabin wall on his way around the corner.

After a short while, everyone returns to the area and sits down. Even Cam comes back.

Hunter is willing to tell his secret next since this whole thing was his idea. "Most of you know that I lost my watcher to the Beast. You know how close we were. What you don't know is that was the second time I let my sister down. I couldn't save her from the Beast, just like I couldn't save her from the car accident I had got us into. She was in my car when I flipped it, trying to get me to slow down. We were thrown out of the car, and she lay there a mere few feet from me, but I couldn't move to help her. I watched as she died slowly, without me to comfort her. Even when we had gotten here, she still didn't blame me. She knew the grip the drugs had on me then. They were the only important things in my life. Every day, I worried about where I was going to get them. After I ran out of money, I stole from my family and friends. It didn't matter who I hurt or what I did to get them; I just had to have them. So, even though I'm in a new place, I'm always fighting the Beast."

Before anyone can respond to what he said, Hunter sits back down on the porch edge and points to Bug, signaling that the floor is his.

Bug nods. "Before I tell you my three flaws, does anyone have a question?"

"What's your real name?" Kannon asks.

Everyone laughs because no one knows what it is, and they know Bug isn't going to say. Bug fakes a laugh, then continues. "First, I have never played baseball. I know it comes as a shock to most of you, but it's true. All this talent is just natural. The second thing is that even with these incredible looks and suave and debonair words I use, I have never had a girlfriend."

Hunter jokingly says, "Say it isn't so, my friend," and everyone laughs.

Not realizing Hunter is messing with him, Bug says, "Oh, it's true, my long-legged friend. Don't get me wrong, it's not that I'm opposed to it." Bug winks at Spin Doll, making her blush and smile. "The third and final surprise is that I'm not much of a fighter." They all gasp, teasing Bug. But, once again, not catching on to the joke, he continues. "Yes, it's true. I couldn't fight when I got here. But after taking out a few Shadows, I've become somewhat of a badass." He strikes a pose and flexes his arm. Hunter reaches over, squeezes Bug's arm, and nods in agreement.

Knowing that Spin Doll is unable to talk, Dayne knows she is the final one left. She doesn't want to say anything, so she offers the floor to Colt, who quickly shakes her head. Even though Dayne doesn't want to, she realizes there is probably no better time than now.

She motions to Kannon, who walks over and stands behind her. After a deep breath, she says, "This secret has to do with Kannon, myself, and Dak." Kannon throws her a dirty look, pointedly staring at her. Dayne shakes her head at Kannon. "You know how much I love you? Well, I love Dak just as much."

Kannon is shaking and feeling anxious but angry at the same time. "Why do you have to bring Dak into this? How can you love him as much as you love me?"

Dayne reaches for Kannon's hand, but he pulls. With pleading in her eyes, Dayne says, "I can't see my life without either of you. When push came to shove, I picked Dak for a reason. If I had picked you, Dak would've died. If I picked Dak, you would still have a chance to find us. I had no choice."

Kannon shakes his head, disgusted. "You had a choice, and you picked him."

"I just told you I had no choice. Dak was going to die."

"So what?" Kannon yells, taking a step away from Dayne. "What is Dak to you? Why did it matter if he died or not? You didn't even know who he was. How could you fall in love with him so quickly? We had plans, and they didn't include Dak."

Kannon turns and stomps away, and Dayne yells, "Because Dak is our son!"

Kannon freezes mid-step. In a softer voice, Dayne says, "Dak is our son. He's *your* son. You're his father."

Without saying a word, Kannon falls face-first, landing on the wet, muddy ground. Hunter and Bug jump up quickly to help Kannon back to his feet. He's wobbly on his feet and has mud on his head but stands there speechless.

"Well, I didn't see that coming. Did you, Uncle Hunter?" Bug jokes, slapping Kannon on the back. "Congrats, Dad, it's a boy."

Finally, Kannon pulls Dayne into a hug so fiercely it seems he'll never let go. He has a thousand questions for Dayne, and she agrees to answer them once they are alone. The rest of the group joins in the hug, equally happy for the couple.

Before the group leaves Kannon and Dayne to talk, Bug, curious as always, says, "If Dak is your son, why is he as big as Kannon already?"

Everyone turns to Kannon and Dayne, raising their eyebrows in curiosity.

"There are no children in the Horizon," Dayne explains. "They grow at a rapid speed. Plus, blackberries increase weight and growth even faster; that's why only kings, warriors, and children can eat them. To the rest of us, they taste awful."

"I mean, don't get me wrong, if Dak misbehaves, I can't guarantee Uncle Bug won't put him over his knee and give him a once for," Bug jokes.

Everyone laughs, and Bug looks around to see what is so funny.

Kannon and Dayne walk away to find a place to talk. Dayne explains how she arrived there, how Jim had helped her, and why she and Dak have been on the run from the Jokers. How everyone believes Dak will be the new king. It was a lot for Kannon to absorb in one discussion, so he's still a little baffled as they rejoin the group.

Bug nudges Hunter, saying, "I knew it the whole time. I just figured it'd be better if she told him."

Hunter shakes his head and sighs while walking away from Bug.

CHAPTER 21

"How can evil erase beauty so quickly?" - Hunter

With the rain pouring down, the warriors decide to go inside to deliberate their final battle plans, each weighing in with their opinions.

"Why don't we leave the cabin for higher ground?" Bug suggests. "I mean, sitting here waiting kind of leaves us as sitting ducks."

For once, they agree with Bug and begin packing anything they can carry. They soon head out to a clearing a few fields over that overlook the entire valley and town, giving them a better chance to see an attack coming. The group decides to send Colt out to scour the area and make sure it's safe to set up there. Colt isn't gone long before she returns and agrees it is the best spot for their makeshift camp.

The hike is challenging, as the chosen spot is at the highest altitude in the valley. This location offers a clear view of the Horizon in all directions.

"It would be impossible for the Shadows to reach us without being seen," Kannon points out. "Hey, look, we can see the old cabin from up here."

Hunter laughs as he drops the sack he is carrying. "All this incredible scenery up here, and you guys want to look at the old cabin?" he jokes.

"Guys, you want to help me put up this tarp?" Cam calls out. "I really don't want to sit out in the rain all night since I'm feeling sick as it is."

Everyone lends a hand, and the tarp is up in no time. Plus, it helps keep their minds on something other than the Shadows and the battle soon to come.

With the tarp in place covering important items, they each watch in a different direction. Colt and Cam pick the east valley, Bug and Spin Doll watch the north, and Dayne and Kannon pick the south because it overlooks the town their little cabin is in. Hunter sits by himself, looking into the west. This way, he can watch the sunset briefly as the sun dances along the ground at the end of the Horizon. Everyone sits quietly, looking over some of the most beautiful terrain they'll ever have a chance to see.

Dayne begins shivering from being wet all day. Kannon puts his arm around her to help warm her up, and Dayne smiles.

"You know, I bet this little town is nice to live in when it is bustling," Dayne says. "This is the kind of small town we could've raised Dak in."

Kannon nods. "I could've been his Little League coach or taught him to ride a bike down that long, flat street." Kannon points to a street in the tiny town below them.

Dayne snuggles in a little closer. "That would've been great. I could've served snacks after the games and helped keep score."

Pressing his luck, Kannon says, "Maybe we could've given Dak a little sister as beautiful as his mom."

Dayne tilts her head back towards Kannon as he leans down and kisses her.

Hunter is bored, so he slides over by Kannon and Dayne and jokes, "Oh, please. Get a room, you two. Enough with that mushy stuff. We're trying to prepare for a battle here."

Kannon laughs, and he shoves Hunter a little. "Don't blame us because all you have to hold is your pool stick." This brings a chuckle out of Bug and Spin Doll.

Hunter, trying to embarrass Bug, yells, "What are you two giggling about over there? Look at you trying to figure out who will make the first move. Will you kiss the girl already?"

Kannon and Dayne snicker, then get up, asking Hunter to keep an eye out in their direction as well as his own.

"Sure. But where are you guys going?"

Kannon answers in a low voice, "We're going for a walk. We shouldn't be gone long."

Hunter whispers, "Oh, I get it. A little brown chicken, brown cow."

Kannon punches him in the arm hard, and they walk off into the forest. Hunter joins Bug and Spin Doll next, smiling at Bug and blowing him a kiss.

Bug sternly whispers, "Shut up; you're so stupid. We're taking it slow. We just met."

Hunter laughs, sarcastically stating, "Taking it slow! How can you take it any slower? It's like you're a ninety-year-old man trying to drive an uncharged electric shopping kart at the supermarket. Spin Doll is like that loaf of bread on the top shelf you can't reach. You need help getting that bread. Think of me as the nice gentleman who helps you get the bread."

Cam chuckles and gives Hunter knuckles on that one.

"Whatever," Bug grumbles.

Hunter walks to the other side of Colt and Cam. Sitting next to Colt, Hunter whispers, "Colt, how's he doing? Any better than earlier?"

Colt looks at Hunter and shakes his head. Hunter reaches around Colt and places his hand on Cam's shoulder. "Can I get you something, buddy? Maybe you could use my backpack for another pillow to prop you up? It might make you a little more comfortable."

Cam looks over at Hunter with his redden, sunken eyes and replies, "No, thank you. I'm just going to lay here and save what little strength I have left. I need to be able to assist you guys in the coming confrontation as much as possible. My friends count on me, and I will not disappoint them."

"Ok, buddy, but remember, if you need anything, ask me first. I got you."

Cam reaches over to knuckle Hunter as he smiles. "I truly appreciate you."

Hunter knuckles him back and wipes his eyes with the other hand before standing up and returning to his original spot.

After about twenty minutes, Kannon and Dayne return in a much better mood than when they had left.

Hunter jokes, "Wow, that was quick." Kannon gives him a "shut up" look.

After silently sitting for a bit, Kannon loudly says, "Hey, guys, check this out. That looks like Dillo heading back to the cabin."

Bug quickly stands up to get a better look and confirms Kannon's deduction. "Yeah, that definitely looks like Dillo."

They all begin to wave their arms in the cabin's direction. Since they are so far away, Dillo has no chance of seeing them. They all watch as Dillo enters the cabin. Cam tries his best to sit up and look as well, but the pain is just too much. However, he notices a cloud of blue slowly making its way toward the cabin, slithering through the woods.

Cam points at the blue cloud, yelling, "Guys! Guys, look!"

Hunter jumps up and places his hands around his eyes like he's looking through binoculars.

With a lump in his throat, Bug yells, "They're heading right for the cabin! Dillo's in there. He doesn't stand a chance. We've got to help him."

Colt takes off so fast down the hill that they can barely follow her with their eyes.

Dillo walks back onto the porch, looking for the group while drinking a pop, not knowing the Shadows approach the backyard. Colt swoops in and picks up an unaware Dillo, taking off as the Shadows reach the back of the cabin. She returns to the group just as Dillo finishes his pop.

Dillo tosses his pop bottle into the bush beside him, saying, "What's up, guys?"

Bug points to the cabin. They all stand there watching as the shadow army turns their beloved cabin into a shambles.

Kannon is puzzled. "Where is the Beast? He's not with them."

"He must be there; just look for the biggest one," Bug explains.

Hunter looks at Bug. "You really don't understand the magnitude of this Beast, do you?"

Bug smirks. "Seriously, how big can he be? I mean, Hoss is the same size. You guys told me that. Now, I'm thinking that on a good day, I could take Hoss. So why should I worry about the Beast taking on us all?"

Cam interrupts as he points down in the valley. "Ah, guys. I think I found the Beast."

They stand to get a good look at this so-called Beast.

Bug's jaw almost hits the floor when he spots the fifty-foot Beast walking through the woods, destroying everything in its path with each step. Without taking his eyes off of the Beast, he whispers, "How the hell are we going to fight that? You might want to send a letter to the kings saying I quit, good luck, and I hope you get your crowns back."

Hunter looks at Bug while he pulls out his pool stick. "You aren't. That one there is all mine."

"Good luck."

Kannon quickly pulls Bug, Colt, Dillo, and Cam into a huddle. "Come high or hell water, I need you guys to find that witch ASAP. We only stand a chance if you guys can locate and release the witch's light. We need to break that protection spell she has on the Beast. I mean it, guys. If you fail, we all fail."

Dillo's the first to answer. "You got it, boss. Now that Dillo's on the case, the witch will be erased."

"Time for a power shift, Captain," Cam says, trying to sound strong.

They turn and watch as the Beast reaches the cabin and destroys what is left in a matter of seconds.

Bug, still amazed at the size and ferociousness of the Beast, says, "Seriously, how do we stop that?"

"I told you," Hunter says with a smirk. "I called dibs on the big guy. Besides, you know what they say: The bigger they are, the harder they fall."

"Well, you better not let him fall on you," Bug retorts, turning to hug Hunter. "You've been a good friend. I'll miss you."

Just when Hunter thinks Bug is serious, Bug smirks, and Hunter punches Bug in the arm. "Jerk!"

Bug laughs. "Ready to get your ass beat, Hunter?"

"Have a little faith in your boy."

"No, I meant from me. I need a warm-up before I whip all those asses down there."

Hunter laughs as he pushes Bug down to the ground. Bug stands up, wipes the mud off his knees, slaps Hunter in the balls, then runs behind Kannon, yelling, "We're even, we're even! Kannon, tell him to stop."

Hunter, not feeling like running after receiving Bug's low

blow, agrees. "Truce."

Now, with both shadow armies combined, along with the Beast, the warriors' chances look bleak at best. It doesn't take long for one of the Shadows to spot the warriors on the hill. It points in the Warrior's direction, and the army charges them. The Beast lets out a hideous howl as he joins the Shadows in the charge.

Hunter looks at Bug as he puts on his shades. "Time to shine."

Suddenly, Dillo points to the right of the charging army. "Hey, what's that?"

The group looks over and sees a small army of the town folk, led by Dak, heading towards the shadow army. Hunter smirks as he whispers to himself, "You've got to love backup."

Kannon and Dayne are in awe, watching their son lead men and women to battle. Kannon has never been prouder. Then it hits them: Dak is heading straight for the Beast!

Kannon takes off down the hill with his sights on the Beast, but Hunter runs after him, yelling, "No you don't! I called the Beast. You go help your son. I got this."

Hearing this, Kannon changes direction and runs towards Dak. Spin Doll follows the two with fans out, like if she has enough speed, she will take off and fly. Dayne isn't far behind and already has The Releaser out, pointing towards the Shadows. Bug yells to Spin Doll, trying to get her to stop. But the noise from the charging army makes it impossible for her to hear him.

Before they can reach the shadow army, they hear the metal clash from Dak's makeshift army and the Shadows engaging in battle. Kannon tries his best to keep an eye on Dak as he fires shots and ducks a shadow's attack. Dayne begins releasing three or four lights with each swing she takes with

The Releaser. Spin Doll spins with her fans, looking like a circular saw cutting through the swarm of Shadows.

Kannon isn't as effective because almost all the Shadows are in mist form. He quickly devises a new plan of attack and begins shooting at the ground. He figures if he can't release them, he will at least slow them down.

The newly formed holes in the ground definitely make it much harder for the Shadows to attack. Dak and the townsfolk are already losing ground, as they are getting the same results as Kannon. Dak had planned ahead, knowing their weapons wouldn't have much effect on the mist forms. He had any townsfolk who could make a light flash move to the front line.

Kannon can't see what Dak and the townsfolk are doing, but it seems to be working, as they begin to push the Shadows back. Once he is close enough, Kannon sees that they are turning mist Shadows into solid Shadows, which makes Kannon relevant again in this battle. He fires into the shadow army, sending them flying in multiple directions.

Hunter dodges and shoots at the Beast with all his might, but he has the same results as their previous meeting. He only accomplishes making the Beast even more angry and clearly unfazed by Hunter's weapons. Hunter has no answers; he needs the witch released.

Bug stands at the top of the hill with Dillo and Cam, watching the battle unfold right before their eyes.

Colt has been sent off to see if she can locate the witch. It isn't long before Colt returns. "The witch is over there, on the backside of the battlefield." She points up the hill behind the Shadows' army. "She's over there behind enemy lines."

Cam takes a breath. "Well, it's now or never. Can someone please help me to my feet? It would be much appreciated."

Dillo quickly assists Cam in standing up. With Cam barely

able to stand, Colt offers to carry him. Feeling helpless in front of the guys, he has no option but to accept. Before letting her pick him up, Cam states, "We'll go around the outside of the battle and meet you two on the other side."

Bug never hears a word Cam says, as he is watching the battle unfold in front of him. His only thought is, as he speaks it out loud, "How are we getting through that? We'll be released in a matter of seconds."

Dillo grabs Bug's arm and reassures him. "Relax, It's mind over matter."

"If you don't mind, they don't matter. It's simple as two plus two."

Bug looks at Dillo, completely confused. "Sometimes I haven't a clue what you're talking about."

The four look one last time at the battle in front of them.

CHAPTER 22

"Sometimes you have to lose to win." - Bug

Dillo explains his plan for them to cross the battlefield safely. "I'll remove my shell, and you can climb inside it."

Bug stops him right there, disagreeing. "I'll never fit in that shell."

"The armadillo did. He is about the same size you are."

Bug is embarrassed that it is an actual option. After a few minutes, with no other ideas, Bug has Dillo take the shell off. Sure enough, Dillo was right: Bug fits perfectly. Watching this makes Cam smile through his pain.

"I'll have to have Colt help me get the shell on," Dillo says. "We'll just walk through the fight."

Bug nervously asks, "You sure this is the best idea we have? It doesn't sound too safe to me."

"What other choice do we have?" Colt says in agreement with Dillo. "We better get going. Time is a ticking."

"Grandpa always said, 'If I wear my shell, nothing could hurt me,'" Dillo reassures Bug. "Now, are you saying my grandpa lied to me? I haven't been hurt since I put this shell on."

Bug back peddles at that. "I would never say your grandpa lied to you. I'm saying your grandpa didn't know you'd be using your shell in this situation."

Colt assists Dillo in putting the Bug-filled shell on his back. Even though Bug is a little guy, it is more weight than Dillo is used to, and his first few steps are one step forward, then two steps back. Finally, he has the weight distribution to his liking, and they are off. Colt scoops up Cam, and the four take off after the witch.

Colt and Cam are at the bottom of the hill by the time Dillo gets his feet moving in the right direction. He begins to trudge down the hill and into the slippery mud. To Bug, it is forever before they reach the bottom of the hill where the battle is going on. As they approach the actual battle, Bug can hear and feel the vibrations of the Shadows' blades clanging against the shell. Dillo never slows his pace, moving one foot after the other.

Midway through the battlefield, Dillo stumbles once and falls to one knee. He is down for only a few seconds, then back to his feet and forges ahead.

Bug feels very moist in the shell and isn't sure if the rain is coming into the shell or Dillo sweating from the workout. He says, "Hey, Dillo, turn the water faucet off. I'm getting drenched back here. Also, have you ever heard of deodorant? It smells like shit back here." Bug doesn't know what is worse, the sweat or the smell. "Dude, we need to get you a bath after this."

Dillo doesn't answer, only continues to trudge through the mud and muck.

Once they reach the backside of the battle, Dillo slows his pace quite a bit. Bug isn't much help, as he acts like a child in the back seat of a car on a long road trip.

"It's like a sauna in here. Are we almost there? I think I have to go to the bathroom. Did you just fart? Because it smells like ass back here."

Finally, Dillo stops and drops to both knees from exhaustion. The shell falls off his back, exposing Bug. Bug climbs out of the shell, trying to get as much fresh air as humanly possible, and stretches.

"Wow! That took longer than I thought it would," Bug states happily. "Your grandpa is definitely not a liar. Look, I don't have a scratch on me."

Bug isn't paying attention to Dillo, who is still on his knees and not speaking. He turns back to see the battle from this point of view, and just then two Shadows come running toward them. Bug frantically reached back for his bat. Babe is not there; it must've fallen out on the battlefield. Bug covers his head with his arms and yells for Dillo's help. As the Shadows reach Bug, they disintegrate, leaving just their lights floating upwards.

Bug yells back at Dillo, "Good shooting, partner!"

Cam appears in front of Bug and announces, "I'd like to take credit for those two."

"I don't care who gets the credit as long as they're not here with us anymore."

Colt is suddenly coming towards them, pointing up the hill. "Up there is the witch. She can't see us while she's performing her spell."

Bug recognizes her immediately, as they were former acquaintances.

Colt hugs Bug and excitedly says, "I'm glad you guys made it across safely. How did neither of you get hurt with all the swords flying in every direction?"

"Oh, those weak ass Shadows were no match for us. Isn't that right, Dillo?" Bug jokes.

They turn to look at Dillo, who is still kneeling from where he had dropped Bug. Bug walks around and stands in front of him, saying, "Isn't that right, Dillo?"

Dillo remains silent, but his eyes are fixed on the witch. Bug grabs Dillo's shoulders and shakes him a bit. "Hey buddy, isn't that right?" Bug quickly notices a crimson color all over

Dillo's chest and arms. Bug becomes nervous. "Hey, buddy, Dillo, answer me. Please!" Bug shakes him a little harder. At that moment, Bug notices blood trickling out of both sides of Dillo's mouth. With no words, Dillo falls forward into Bug's arms.

"Kannon! Hunter! We need help over here. Something is wrong with Dillo!"

Neither Cam nor Colt knows what to do as they stand there and watch as Dillo passes away in Bug's arms, disintegrating.

"No, you can't have him!" Bug yells. "You can't have my best friend!" In a matter of seconds, Bug is holding nothing. Dillo's light hovers in front of him. Bug frantically tries to stop Dillo's light from rising by swinging his arms, attempting to coral it. With every ounce of effort Bug has, he can't stop the light from rising. Tears fill his eyes. "Wait! What about his shell? He needs his shell; his grandpa gave it to him. You at least have to let him take his shell. His grandpa gave it to him."

Colt and Cam try to console Bug, but he is jumping for Dillo's light. Knowing there is nothing anyone can do, they simply pull him into a hug. Bug, still trying to get to Dillo's light, pushes Colt and Cam aside, accidentally sending a weakened Cam to the ground. Colt tries to regain her balance and catch Cam, but she misses, and Cam hits the ground hard. Colt quickly tries to help Cam up, but this time, he has no strength to help her. She uses every bit of strength she has to finally get Cam back to his feet, but Cam knows he'll soon join Dillo. He feels the poison surge through his body, knowing he isn't long for this world.

Bug is no help. He sits on the ground, holding his hands out in shock. Colt knows Bug is out of commission and Cam is too weak to stand, let alone fight. She knows that releasing the witch's light is now all on her shoulders. Cam is sure Colt will need his help to rid this place of the witch; he has to make one last attempt.

Looking at Colt with his reddened eyes, Cam whispers, "I'll be your Doc Holiday, and you'll be my Wyatt Earp. This will be our last ride together."

Colt pretends she doesn't know what he is talking about. "Do you have enough energy left in that old body to release the witch? I'll try and keep her focused on me." Cam nods, so Colt says, "I'll distract her while you go invisible and sneak up behind her with this dagger, then free her light. When the bitch is gone, we'll get you the help you need. I promise. Besides, the kings will owe us."

Cam smiles, knowing he can't beat his illness, but does not want to sadden Colt, and says, "That would be really nice. Thank you, my friend."

Colt hands Cam the dagger, worried about whether he can hold it. Cam places it in his belt loop and then vanishes. Colt worries that this will be the last time she sees her friend. She takes off and reaches the witch about halfway before she spots Colt. The witch immediately stops the protection spell and begins casting lightning bolts at Colt. Colt dodges the barrage of lightning being thrown at her; she doesn't know how long she can keep this up. With the witch occupied, Cam finally gets behind her, stumbling the whole way. The witch, not focusing on her backside, makes Cam almost sure to be the hero of this story. Cam slowly stumbles towards the witch, losing the strength to hold the dagger and dropping it just mere feet from the witch. His dreams of being someone's hero fall along with the dagger. The witch spins around as Cam appears. Being too weak to stay out of sight, he smiles and waves.

"I'm your huckleberry," Cam whispers as he falls into the hands of the witch.

The witch fills his body with electricity. Colt watches Cam's body shake from the bolts of electricity sent through him as he clings to the witch.

Colt dashes the witch. On the way, she picks up what seems to be an old metal fence post. The witch has no idea of the speed at which Colt can reach her as Colt plunges the metal post deep into the witch's chest.

They hear Cam's voice as clear as a bell state, "You can't kill me, witch; I'm already dead."

Colt never let's go of the metal post as the witch vanishes and her light rises to the sky. That's when Colt realizes that the post went not only through the witch but through Cam as well.

As Cam vanishes for his final time, Colt can see him mouth the words, "Thank you."

Cam's light follows behind the witch's up into the air.

Colt stands there, knowing they have broken the protection spell. But at what cost? Her best friend's light. Not able to control her emotions, Colt drops the metal post and runs off into the woods.

Bug finally regains his sanity and, with tear-filled eyes, wanders up the hill to where the witch once stood. Not knowing what just occurred with Cam's demise and Colt's quick exit from the group, Bug searches the area where the witch once stood. Standing in the field alone and not knowing what his next move will be, he wipes his eyes on his hoodie sleeve and watches the battle turn for the better as the warriors begin to push the shadow army back down the hill. Bug thinks that this is why you always take the high ground.

Suddenly, something near his feet catches Bug's eye. He bends down and notices a second piece of the heart. He picks it up and holds it into what sunlight is left, and it sparkles on his face. Then he puts it in his mouth and swallows it like the previous one before. He laughs out loud, speaking to no one but himself. "You know, a good friend once told me if you want to keep something from someone, just swallow it."

Bug reaches into his front pocket and begins fumbling for something. He pulls the item out of his pocket and tosses it in the same spot he picked up the piece of heart. Smiling, he says, "Trade you."

Bug laughs and walks down the hill towards the battle, never looking back. The closer he gets to the battle, the more he lights up. With a cocky attitude, he yells, "Oh, Shadows, I think you're about to have a bug problem!"

CHAPTER 23

"How can someone who's considered dumb outsmart his enemy?" - Hoss

The battle rages on, with the Shadows holding a slim advantage with their numbers. Dak and the townsfolk are dwindling in numbers. Dayne and Spin Doll have all they can do to swing their weapons, slowing from exhaustion with every swing, even though the shadow numbers grow.

Kannon, still trying to help Hunter against the Beast, is sent flying through the air by a huge backhand he had received, compliments of the Beast. Hunter only seems to annoy the Beast. It is as if he is one of those little gnats that fly around in your face that you, for some reason, can't catch. Kannon lands far down the hill, almost beside a charging Bug, who is flashing like the paparazzi on a hot shoot. Bug's flashing makes Kannon relevant in this battle. He turns the Shadows solid, and Kannon sends them up. They are the perfect team.

Hunter, for the most part, avoids the big swings from the Beast until he loses his footing and falls on his back, throwing his pool stick off into the distance. With the Beast standing over him and his pool sticking out of reach, Hunter's thoughts flash back to the first meeting when he lost Lakin. Fear fills his body, and he feels like he can't move. The Beast raises his fist over his head, with plans of crushing his adversary. Just as the Beast is about to shut Hunter's coffin door, Hunter tries to crawl away but still can't move in the slippery war-torn ground. Kannon's eyes grow in disbelief that he is about to watch his friend parish, and he can do nothing to stop it. Suddenly, the battlefield goes deathly quiet, and everyone stops fighting the warriors, the Shadows, and the townsfolk. They all look as the Beast stands above Hunter. Bug turns away, not being able to watch another friend leave him. The Beast savors the moment as he lets out a blood-curdling growl, and the Shadows begin to cheer him on. But, for a quick second, they can see a band of light travel down the Beast, removing the invincibility spell the witch had placed on him.

Spell or not, Hunter's time in the Horizon is coming to an end. After a flurry of more growls, the Beast brings his big fist down, and Hunter's eyes close as he braces for impact. Everyone draws a huge breath. Hunter raises his hands to try to stop the releasing blow. Right before the Beast's fist reaches Hunter, a large shadow looms over him, sending the Beast reeling backward. The stunned Beast quickly looks up to see what hit him. There stands an equally sized and very intimidating-looking Hoss, who sarcastically says, "Tag, you're it."

The Beast, not one bit intimidated, gives out a loud growl and charges Hoss, who, in return, charges the Beast. When the two mammoths collide, the onlookers can feel the ground tremble beneath their feet. They all race to get out of the way of these two building-sized monsters. Hunter has never felt so delighted to see his old friend Hoss. He quickly crawls out of harm's way, leaving his pool stick behind.

The two stand toe to toe, trading haymakers with each other. The sun begins to rise over the hill, revealing just silhouettes of the ultimate battle. The Beast swings and misses as Hoss ducks, then catches the Beast with an uppercut. The Beast's head spins sideways as teeth fly from his mouth. This makes the Beast stagger backward, feeling a pain he's never felt before. The battle is turning towards the warriors' side as the Shadows watch their monster feel pain for the first time.

The Beast raises his fist to swing, but before he can land the punch, Hoss spears him as the two tumble toward the bottom of the hill, taking many of the shadow's lights with them. Neither one of them stop swinging through the entire tumble as they both rose to their feet and continue the fight. With a plethora of powerful swings, the Beast finally connects a hit on Hoss's face, sending him back a bit, while making him even angrier.

Hunter rejoins the fight, firing shot after shot into the Beast's backside, reigniting the whole battle. Hunter's shots make the Beast shriek in pain as they dance across his back. Caught between the two and not knowing which one to fight, the Beast begins to charge Hunter, seeing him as the smallest and most likely the easiest target to release first. Hunter unloads everything he has on the charging Beast. Hoss, chasing after the Beast, catches a glimpse of a familiar object in the middle of the upper field. He freezes, hoping it isn't what he thinks it is. The battle is no longer his concern as he runs towards the object. As Hoss approaches the object, it becomes more and more familiar to him. Hoss drops to his knees as he picks the object up. Giant tears begin to roll down his face and crash into the ground. No one notices the giant's pain as the battle continues to unfold.

Closer and closer, the Beast approaches Hunter. Hunter begins running towards the Beast, firing with everything he has. Blue goo flies from the Beast's body but doesn't seem to slow him down whatsoever. The closer Hunter gets to the Beast, the more shots riddle the Beast's body. Before reaching Hunter, the Beast begins to stumble, and his pace starts to slow down.

Hunter relentlessly continues unloading on the monster. As they reach each other, the Beast stumbles one last time and slides face-first right up to the end of Hunter's pool sticks, where he stops dead in his tracks. The look in the Beast's eyes shows he knows he's lost the fight. With his final breath, the Beast blows Hunter's coat and hat back. Hunter's pool sticks are placed firmly against the space between the Beast's eyes. Hunter leans over and whispers to the Beast, "I'm gonna make you a star." Then, he pulls the trigger and releases the Beast's light. A moan can be heard from miles away. Slowly, the battlefield watches as the Beast's light floats into the morning sky. The Shadows can't believe what they just witnessed since they were told the Beast was unbeatable. After witnessing this devastating loss, the Shadows all retreat into the woods. A few stragglers who don't realize they are retreating are released and join the Beast in the air.

A pool of blue goo lay where the Beast's light is released. Hunter, being the closest, gets the brunt of it, covered from head to toe in goo. Kannon and Dayne run to Dak, and they both embrace him. Dak, with a puzzled look on his face, embraces them back. Bug runs to Spin Doll, who is exhausted and sitting on the ground. He pulls her into his arms, not knowing whether to smile because she is safe or cry because Dillo is gone. Spin Doll squeezes him tight, not knowing what he has just been through. She is delighted that nothing happened to him.

Once they ensure everyone is alright, they notice Hoss in the middle of the upper field, looking towards the sky. They all run to him and see the big man is in pain.

"What is it, Hoss? Are you injured?" Kannon asks.

Hoss sniffles as he turns around and holds his hands out in front of him. When he opens his hand, he reveals Dillo's shell.

They all gasp and immediately hug Hoss, knowing how much Dillo meant to him.

Hoss looks at Bug accusingly and yells, "You were supposed to protect him! He counted on you!"

Bug, feeling just as awful as Hoss, explains how Dillo carried him in the shell across the battlefield safely. Then, when Bug finally got out of the shell, he saw that Dillo was covered with stab wounds and blood from head to toe.

He says, "I never realized how tough of a guy he was. He never made a sound while carrying me. He just continued walking till we were on the other side. You were right about Dillo being a loyal and trusting friend. He sacrificed his life for all of us and for you and Hunter to defeat the Beast and bring Hunter some much-needed revenge."

Hunter, still wiping blue off himself and not hearing most of the conversation, adds, "Shit, so none of us lost our light but Dillo."

Hoss looks at Hunter like he is next to lose his light. "But Dillo? Did you really say that? Friend, we are about to not be friends."

Kannon jumps in quickly to de-escalate the situation, standing between the two. "Do you two really think Dillo would want this to end this way?"

Hoss looks at the tired group. "Someday, when they tell stories of this day, make sure they know of the selflessness of Dillo giving his light up to save the Horizon and bringing an end to the Beast." Hoss pauses momentarily as he stares at Hunter, then adds, "This simple man only knew of two things. The love he had for his grandpa and the meaning of friendship."

No one has a dry eye; their hearts break for Hoss's loss of a brother.

Hoss stands while holding Dillo's shell in his open hand

and looks at the sky. "Tell Grandpa how strong you were and how, with or without the shell, you became the man he wanted you to be. Fly high, my friend, until we meet again." Then he turns towards the woods, where the Shadows retreated, and yells, "No more will we run! No more will we hide! No more will we fear the darkness! From now on, the darkness will fear us."

Hoss crushes Dillo's shell to pieces in his hand, and bits fall to the ground. He lowers his voice but remains just as loud as he repeats, "From now on, the darkness will fear us." He slams the remaining shell pieces to the ground as he turns and walks to the top of the hill to the makeshift camp.

With the threat of the Shadows diminishing and another victory—if you can call it that—under their belts. The warriors join Hoss at the camp to rest and prepare for what's to come.

While sitting around, Bug's curiosity gets the better of him. "Has anyone seen Cam or Colt?"

Everyone shrugs. Hunter tries to lighten the mood by saying, "I hope Hoss didn't sit on them."

Everyone is so tired that they just laugh from exhaustion as they sit under the tarp. Everyone but Hoss. The rain begins to let up and one of the most beautiful rainbows appears from one side of the valley to the other side. With so much sorrow being dealt to the group, it is nice to be rewarded with something so beautiful.

Hunter begins to sing, "What a wonderful world." Kannon lays on the ground holding Dayne, and Bug and Spin Doll sway back and forth together and watch the rainbow. Hoss lays on his back with his eyes closed, with almost a smile on his face.

Dak thinks, *This must be what they call the calm before the storm.*

Hunter finishes his rendition, then covers his face with his hat.

Kannon looks at Dayne. "How can so much beauty coexist with so much darkness?"

Dayne kisses him. "Darkness will only exist if we let it. When we rid the darkness in our hearts, we are only left with love."

They close their eyes and grab some much-needed rest as the rainbow watches over them.

CHAPTER 24

"When you make a deal with the devil, make sure the devil knows your dealing." - Lakin

Morning arrives, finding Lakin very tired due to Fat Jack not being honest with her last night. She now knows he can't be trusted. Slowly, she sits up and stretches, making it look like she has slept well through the night. Immediately, she reaches for her sack to check on Mimic. She is relieved to find them still sleeping, safe and sound. *At least someone got a good night's rest,* she thinks. While rustling through the bag, Lakin startles Mim at first, making her jump, and in return, wakes IC up as well. They are at ease once they realize it is only Lakin.

Fat Jack is sitting by a small fire he made, cooking something on a spicket. "Well, good morning, sunshine. Glad you could join us on this gloomy rainy morning."

Lakin smiles and sits on Jack's opposite side.

"Ya hungry, little lady?" Jack rips off a piece of whatever is on the spicket with his knife and hands it to Lakin.

She quickly responds, "No, thank you. I don't eat meat. But I appreciate the offer."

"Suit yourself. Means the more for me." Jack pops the piece of meat in his mouth. At the same time, while chewing with his mouth open, he asks, "What's up with that old sack you carry around? I notice you rummage through that quite often. If I had to say so, I'd think you had a pet or something in there."

"Oh no, nothing like that. I just have a couple of personal

items inside, that's all. I get nervous that I might lose them, so I check on them every so often."

From the look on Jack's face, he isn't buying that at all, but he nods and resumes eating.

Lakin wonders if the kings had eaten. "Have they eaten anything? I'm sure they're starving," she inquires.

Jack looks at the kings and rudely replies, "You mean the three stooges? Nah, I'm not their nursemaid. If you want them to eat, be my guest. I'm not feeding anyone but myself."

Lakin thinks that is awfully rude of Jack, so she grabs three pieces of meat from the carcass and walks over to feed the kings. Jack gives her a dirty look, but as soon as her back is to him, he tries to look in her sack. Noticing Jack, Lakin quickly slaps Jack's hand, then takes her sack with her as she tends to the kings. Jack's face turns red with anger.

The kings aren't too eager to eat. But eventually, she gets each one to take a couple of bites.

Jack scoffs. "What a waste of time and food. They'll never be the great kings they once were. Shit, they won't even be a shell of their former selves. It's a shame to let them suffer. Maybe we should just take them out back of the woodshed and give them a once for." Jack finishes what food is left, then pulls down his suspenders and tells Lakin he'll be back in twenty before heading into the woods and out of sight.

IC jumps out of the sack and scampers after him, unknown to Jack. Mim slowly climbs out with a big yawn as she tiredly states, "I don't like IC following that fat man. What if she slips up, and he catches her? He might eat her, for all we know."

"I wouldn't worry. IC is way too smart to ever get caught by the likes of him."

Mim nods.

Fat Jack meets up with the same character as before. But

this time, there are two of them. IC wants to get closer to see the faces of those to whom Jack is speaking.

Mim yells to Lakin, "IC says they're about to speak, and you might want to hear this!"

Lakin finishes with the kings, so she quickly sits down to listen.

Jack speaks first. "This is a bunch of bullshit, making me lug these dead ass kings around the countryside. Why don't you just let me dispose of them *my* way? I've never eaten king before; bet they're gamey and full of grizzle."

IC can see the figures from behind, but she needs them to turn around to see the faces of the tall, slender couple.

One of the men says, "We personally don't care what you put in that dump you call a body. Our only concern is whether or not you've heard anything about the fourth king. Or are you just making buddies with the good guys?"

"You should've seen breakfast this morning. Is it me, or are the townsfolk getting slower? Then, to beat all, I let her feed it to the kings." Jack laughs as he picks some breakfast from his teeth. Lakin's eyes widen, now knowing why the kings didn't want to eat the meat.

The other character jumps in. "We need to know who's the fourth king, not some townsfolk nobody gives a shit about."

Jack rolls his eyes. "Yeah, yeah, yeah. This Lakin chick ain't saying shit. Her only concern is for the three kings we have in our possession. But she's definitely hiding something in that sack she's been carrying. I don't know what it is, but it smells delicious."

One of them looks in IC's direction as if he heard something. After a few minutes of seeing nothing, they continue their discussion.

Jack regains his thoughts and says, "It's funny. I kind of

thought I smelled star cleaners coming from her sack. But that's impossible; I ate them all."

Mimic's eyes widen as well, now realizing where they have heard the voice before. She whispers, "That's the monster with the metal teeth. He's the reason there are none of us left. We need to leave now; it's not safe here for us."

Lakin puts her hand on Mim's back, trying to console her, and they listen as Jack continues.

"Maybe her sack does have a star cleaner in it. I must find out."

The second voice breaks up Jack's thoughts by replying, "We offered you your fill-on star cleaners and, of course, your chain of keys. All we wanted was the fourth king. Now, a deal is a deal, so get your fat ass in gear and get us the fourth king. Or we might just lose a key here and there. I mean, it *is* an old chain of keys."

The first voice pipes in. "So, find the king, or else, fat boy."

Jack begins to smile with a jaw full of shiny teeth. "Or else what? You know, I've never tried Joker before, either. So, I'd watch your tone of voice with me, clowns."

IC knows now who Jack is speaking to. The Jokers.

Omin gets up in Jack's face, saying, "Call us clowns one more time."

Jack whispers, "Clowns!"

Sin says, "Well, now, look at that. I think we just lost a couple of keys. What good is having all those doors but no keys?"

Jack quickly retracts. "No, not my keys. I need them. I apologize for my mean and unfair remarks."

Omin laughs at the stupid oaf. "I didn't quite hear you right. Maybe you owe us an apology. Now!"

Jack begins to grovel even more. "I'm so sorry, Jokers. I

don't know where my mind is. Please forgive me. I get like that when I miss brunch. As for the fourth king, I'll get the info right now. Please, don't lose my keys."

Sin pats Jack on the head. "Good dog. Now go fetch before I slap you on the nose. Bitch!"

Jack quickly walks off, and the Jokers hear him say, "Probably tastes funny anyway."

IC knows she can't beat Jack back to Lakin, so she decides to stick with the Jokers, which pays off immediately.

Sin says, "I really don't like working with that pile of shit."

Omin nods. "True statement, brother. But we need him and his brother for just a little longer. Then we'll let them play with the Beasts."

Sin laughs. "As long as the idiot doesn't bring them to the Castle of Four Castles, the kings will never wake."

Lakin looks at Mim, but neither of them has ever heard of the Castle of Four Castles.

"No one has ever mentioned a castle. We need to get the kings there," Lakin says.

"Won't the Jokers be there?"

Lakin nods. "It's almost certain. That's why we never come across them. They've been in the castle."

The Jokers head off in the opposite direction as Jack does, and IC follows, hoping they will lead her to the Castle of Four Castles or their hideout.

Suddenly, Jack turns around and yells to get the Jokers' attention while heading back, looking puzzled. Sin and Omin turn back to see what the slob wants now.

"What could you possibly want?" Omin asks.

Jack is a little out of breath, and he doesn't notice IC as she ducks out of sight once again.

"Before we part, any chance I could get one or two of my

keys? You know, like a good faith kind of thing."

Sin scowls at a begging Jack and says, "Are you serious? You think we carry the keys with us?"

"Well, I was kind of hoping?"

Omin, not happy with Jack's wanting, shouts, "Shut your mouth and do as you're told, you fat disgusting troll! You'll get your keys when we feel that you've earned them. Now be gone, dog."

Jack begins to growl as drool drips from the sides of his mouth. Sin, not worried in the least, rolls his eyes, saying, "Oh, please. That might work on the star cleaners or the weak-minded humans you take advantage of. But believe me when I say this: that little growl act has no effect on us. Besides, who has ever heard a pig growl?"

Omin adds, "Don't make us put the collar back on you, dog! I'm sorry, piggy."

IC thinks Jack looks like a dog on a leash whose food is just out of his reach. In a really low voice, Jack warns them, "When I finally get my keys back, you two clowns might want to avoid me at all costs. We'll see who squeals like a pig in the end."

Omin laughs. "Are you trying to threaten us?"

Jack smiles as he replies, "I don't make threats. I eat them."

Sin has to get his two cents in with that not making much sense. "When we gain total control of this Horizon, you might want to avoid us. Who knows, you might look good in a cage. You can be our very own piggy bank." Both Jokers laugh.

Jack grins. "You may want to stick to the evil you know and not the evil you don't."

The Jokers get goose bumps up their arms and say together, "Silly pig, we are the only evil we know."

Then Sin teases, "Sorry we can't stay and poke the pig

some more, but we really must be going. We have to see how many warriors were freed today by our Beast. Too-ta-loo."

Jack stomps off in the other direction. IC follows the Jokers once she knows the coast is clear.

Mim is so frightened that she says, "Hurry, we must leave. He's going to eat us."

"Relax. He doesn't know that we know who he is," Lakin calmly tells her. "We can tell him we know where the fourth king is, and then we'll lead him to the warriors. Once we reach the warriors, we'll let them rid this world of him."

Mim snugly tries to slide into Lakin's pocket, knowing eventually Jack will check Lakin's sack. Since that didn't work, they hid her in the king's clothing that Lakin is carrying.

Jack returns, acting as if he is having stomach problems and using that to explain how long he was gone. He picks up his two kings and says, "Let's get going; we need to make up some ground. We aren't getting anywhere by sitting here all day."

"No worries. We'll get to where we are going soon enough." Lakin wants to lead Jack to the warriors, but she contemplates finding the castle and helping the kings regain their whereabouts. After deliberating over the two, she chooses the castle.

But Jack has his own plans: He will lead them back to his cave of doors and then free them all, thinking he will deal with the Jokers later.

Lakin says, "When I was stuck in the hole, I heard the shadow guards talking. One said they heard the fourth king heading for the castle. Do you have any idea where that would be?"

Jack looks puzzled. "Oh, really. Why am I just hearing about this now? What's this about a castle? Why haven't you mentioned this earlier?"

"I had to wait till I knew I could trust you. These last couple of days, you've seemed like a stand-up guy. I believe now that I can trust you."

Jack smiles at that. "Can you trust me enough to show me what's in the sack?"

"Sure, why not?"

Lakin hands Jack her sack, and Jack opens it, hoping to find a star cleaner. But he only finds a couple of little knick-knacks and a comb. Disgusted, he hands her back the sack. Since he brought her to the Horizon, he knew those things didn't come with her. She is lying. Now, they both realize they can't trust one another. He needs to find the fourth king to retrieve his chain of keys. She needs to get the kings back to the castle successfully. They are at a stalemate.

After walking a bit more, the rain begins to fall faster.

"Aw, great. More rain. Just what we need. Nothing like making this dead weight even heavier. Like these kings aren't already heavy enough," Jack complains.

Lakin worries Jack will not be able to keep his composer much longer, and a confrontation is soon about to start. After another fifty steps, Jack drops the kings to the ground and turns back to Lakin.

"Do you have star cleaners in your sack? I know what I smell."

She tries to play dumb, responding, "What are star cleaners?"

Jack immediately knows what she is doing, but he figures he'll play her little game. "Star cleaners are these foul little creatures that are a menace to this Horizon. But let me tell you, they taste great. Especially with a little bit of honey and ketchup."

Knowing that he doesn't truly believe her, Lakin still tries to play clueless. "Little creatures? Why would I keep foul little creatures in my sack? That doesn't make any sense. If I did, don't you think they'd have to eat or use the bathroom?"

Jack knows she is lying to him because his nose has never lied to him before. His eyes redden as he asks her again, "Do you or do you not have a star cleaner on you? Trust me, it would be wise to tell me the truth."

Lakin, refusing to give up Mim, answers, "No, I most certainly do not have a little animal in my sack, let alone one of these disgusting little creatures you call star cleaners." She backs up away from Jack as she displays her whips. "I know what you are," she confesses.

Jack smiles, now showing his shiny teeth. "Then you know what's about to happen."

"I know what you're capable of doing but trust me when I say you don't know what I'm capable of doing."

"Oh, but I do. Who do you think brought you and your worthless brother here? The tooth fairy?"

Lakin, confused, states, "What? *You* brought us here. Why would you bring us here? You could've just ended us there. I mean, really, why bring us here?"

"I pull in weak people who have already given up. Since I couldn't find the fourth king on my own, I figured, why not ten more sets of eyes? Plus, if I got hungry, dinner would be served. You know, it's really funny. The ones who give up in your world just seem to taste better than the ones who put up a fight."

"Why would you think we'd help you? Especially now that we know what you are."

Jack growls and takes a step closer to her. "Because if you don't, I won't get my keys back from the Jokers. That means I can't open my doors and devour souls back into your world. I'd have to feed here, and the food here is not so good."

"Well, your only chance of getting your keys back lies with me. But I have an idea. You help me get the kings safely to the castle—"

"How do you know about the castle? The Jokers had the witch put an invisibility spell on the castle and surrounding kingdom. Even though I know about the castle, I'm not allowed through the gates."

"You know why you're not allowed in the castle? Because that's where they hid your keys. How about we make a little deal, just you and me? No one will ever have to know about it. You help me get the kings to the castle, and in return, the warriors and I will get your keys back."

"Why would you give me my keys?" Jack barks. "You'll just betray me. Then I would have to release all of you, including those Jokers."

"Because if we return your keys, you can return us home."

Jack thinks for a minute, and it's like a light bulb pops above his head. "I'll tell you what. Maybe you can be useful after all. There's this little old guy that goes by the name Jim. He's stuck here in the Horizon. When I was collecting his granddaughter for this mission, he stole my favorite key from me. The one key. It is a special key, and it's the only key that can open any door. It makes the other keys obsolete. The Jokers don't know of this. It can be our little secret."

"How did this little old guy get your one key?"

Jack mumbles, "He followed me into the Horizon and blocked my door with a little plastic doll. I didn't notice it till I realized my key had been stolen. He offered to trade me for his granddaughter. I kind of refused, thinking I got a two-for-one deal. He found a way to keep it hidden from me."

"If the key is that important, why not make the trade?"

"Because he wanted to trade back in his world, where he

could trap me and save countless souls. I'm not giving up all those free souls. So, do we have a deal?"

"You help me get the kings to the castle, and I get your one key back from the old guy named Jim. Sound about right?"

Jack smiles and holds out his hand to shake and make the deal legit. She has no interest in shaking his hand, and she refuses to. "Deal!" Lakin knows that even though an agreement is set in place, Jack can't be trusted and that he will no doubt double-cross her.

Jack picks up the two kings. "Follow me; I know of a shortcut. The castle is only a day's walk away."

Lakin picks up her king and Mim and follows very hesitantly from a distance, keeping Jack in her sights and in front of her.

CHAPTER 25

"When you leave this world, you truly never know who's going to miss you." - Dak

Being exhausted, sore, and bruised, the warriors sleep the entire day and early into the next. Morning comes quicker than they had hoped for. The good thing is that all the rain from the previous day has dried up and is gone for now. The sunshine awakens them to a good morning and empty stomachs. Dak and Kannon are the first two up and moving. They decide to fetch breakfast for everyone. Dak explains to Kannon that he has seen a small farm near them. He wonders if they head out now and can return before the rest are up and moving. Kannon is more than delighted to walk with his son, who doesn't know Kannon is his dad. He thinks this is the perfect time to talk with Dak and explain any questions either of them has.

Without waking anyone else up, they head out to gather some breakfast for the group. Kannon is chopping at the bit to tell Dak he is his father. They walk at least a couple of miles without making a sound. The whole time, Kannon runs scenarios through his head about how to tell Dak. Neither knows much about each other, as they struggle with starting the conversation, which makes for a somewhat dull walk to the farm.

Eventually, Kannon gives in and tries to break the ice. Knowing it is a now-or-never situation, he says, "So, that's a pretty nice sword you've got there. Who taught you how to use it so well?"

As he answers, Dak pulls it and swings it back and forth in front of him. "This old thing? Just an old, worn-out sword. My mom taught me everything I know. Since my dad wasn't around." He swings it a few more times, then continues. "I think she traded it from some old peddler that came by the house. She knew how much I wanted it when the man pulled it out to show us. To think, she got it for two pies and a pot of stew. I think we got a good deal on it. But I'm not quite sure; Mom's pies are very good."

Kannon is surprised to hear Dayne taught him to swing that sword so well. "Your mom taught you that? What about your dad? Where is he this whole time?" Kannon wants to hear what Dak truly knows about him.

Dak shrugs. "Didn't know much about my dad. I've never met the guy, but if I do, I'm sure to have a few words for him. But Mom said he is quite handy with a firearm. Mom also told me some stories about him, but nothing that seemed out of the ordinary."

"Like what stories did she tell you?"

Dak continues, even though it's not something he is too keen on talking about. "Mom said I'm a spitting image of him. But you don't want to hear some old stories about a guy neither of us knows."

"I would love to hear some stories about your dad. Besides, it'll make the walk go by quicker."

Dak realizes Kannon isn't going to leave him alone, so he continues. "Well, you see, they were high school sweethearts. They got married right after graduation, even though everyone told them they were too young. Dad was a reporter for their local news channel, and I think maybe a volunteer fireman. I guess he was an all-around likable guy. That night, she was going to tell him about me, but a weird occurrence happened.

She said that all the stars began to fall from the sky, which made for the story of the century. Dad was called to cover it. Since he was new and just getting his feet wet, he couldn't pass on the opportunity. He and Mom planned to meet at their favorite spot, out in some cow field. Can you believe their favorite spot was in an old cow pasture? Mom waited a long time for him. But Dad couldn't get away from work. She said the stars were falling all around her and that she needed to find some shelter because she was scared the stars would land on her.

"Suddenly, she noticed a random door in the middle of nowhere. To me, that sounds too hard to believe, but why would she lie about it? She made her way to the door and opened it. The view from the inside looked calm and a lot less dangerous. So, she walked through, and it brought us here, in the Horizon."

Kannon wonders why she didn't try to come back through the door for him. "Why didn't she just go back through the door to me—I mean, your father? If she loved him so much, why didn't she go back to him?"

Dak again shrugs. "I don't know. I think the door disappeared, so we could never go back. She decided to make the best life we could right here. It was awesome growing up in the Horizon. At least it was until the Jokers showed up and destroyed it all." Dak took a few more steps and added, "Mom told me not to worry, that my dad would find us once he was done chasing his storms. But now that he's missed so much, I don't think we really need him."

Kannon wants to hug Dak but instead just adds, "That's a cool story."

Dak sighs. "I know most of it isn't probably true, and my dad is probably some deadbeat who only cares for himself. But it's all I know. My dad, the storm chaser."

"Did she tell you his name?"

"No, sir, but she did tell me I'd know him when I saw him. I guess he looks a lot like me, or I look like him. I've never found him yet, but I'm sure I will someday."

When Kannon builds up the nerve to tell him, they arrive at the farm. They wave to a weathered old man working out in the field.

Kannon yells, "Hello!"

The old man yells back, "Hello yourself. What brings you guys by today?"

Dak answers. "We were wondering if we could have a word with the owner."

The old man stops what he is doing and approaches. "I'm the owner, but whatever you're selling, I'm not buying."

Trying to be as pleasant as he can, Dak says, "Oh no, sir, we're not selling anything. It's more that we want to buy something."

"You got any money?" Dak and Kannon shake their heads, so the man says, "Well then, how are you looking to buy something with no money?"

"You see, sir, we just finished a large battle with the Shadows. Luckily, we held them off to fight another day. We're just looking for a few eggs and maybe some milk to help rejuvenate our fighters. Any chance we could get a dozen or two?" Kannon asks.

The farmer rubs his chin, shaking his head. "Aw, I don't know. Been giving my eggs and milk to this simple young man who comes by every morning and helps me feed the animals and gather eggs. If I give them to you, I won't have any for him." The farmer leans in and whispers to Dak, "I don't think he likes my geese much. But it's funny to watch him try to avoid them with that big turtle shell on his back." The old farmer chuckles just thinking about it.

Kannon knows right away he is talking about Dillo. "I'm sorry to inform you, but the young man you're talking about is part of our team. He was released early this morning. His name was Dillo."

The old man is silent for a minute, then, with sorrow in his voice, says, "Well, that's just awful news. Seems like no matter what world you're in, the good guy always gets the short end of the stick. Such a nice boy; he wouldn't hurt a fly. I'm going to have to break the news to Maw. She's taking quite a shine to the simple soul. I guess you can have the eggs and milk then. Maw just baked some cookies for him. You might as well take them also."

Dak says, "Thank you so much, sir. If you don't mind, we'd like to help you finish the morning chores as a repayment."

The farmer appreciates the help and gives them all the eggs, milk, and cookies they can carry. As they are about to leave, the farmer shakes their hands and says, "Please tell the young man's family that we are very sorry for their loss. What kind of evil could hurt such a simple man? Be safe, warriors, and may your fight end with happiness."

Dak sets his armful down and hugs the old man. As they walk away from the somber moment, they look back only to see the old man going back to his field. They stand and watch the old farmer stop to wipe his face with an even older handkerchief. He stuffs it back into his back pocket and then returns to work.

Once out of sight, Dak remembers he had left his sword near the gateway of the barnyard. He places everything he carries on the ground and says, "Please keep an eye on this. I'll be right back. I forgot my sword. I took it off to help with chores and forgot to strap it back on."

Dak runs down the path that leads to the old farmstead. When he reaches the gateway, his sword lies right where he left it. While strapping his sword back on, he can see the farmer and his wife standing in the field, hugging. Even though they don't know he is there, Dak can see their tear-filled faces and hear Maw's pain. He quickly leaves before they can see him, and a lump builds in his throat.

When he returns, Kannon points out, "Wow, that was quick. Did you see the farmer?"

Dak shakes his head. "Nah, he must've gone inside or something. We better get back to the group; they should be getting up by now."

On their way back, Kannon knows he must tell Dak he is his father. Their discussion with the old farmer proved that you never know when you will be released, so you should tell the ones you love that you love them every day. Kannon knows he almost lost that chance with Dayne once before. He will not lose it again.

"You know, I'm from Hidden Bridge as well. I grew up there."

Dak looks at Kannon in surprise. "So, you knew my mom from before? That means you knew my dad. What's he like? Were you guys friends? Man, why didn't you tell me this before?" Dak begins to get excited, and before Kannon can answer any of the questions, Dak blurts out, "So why are you and Mom so friendly with each other? Is there something I need to know? Aren't you worried someday my dad will show up and find out about you two and kick your ass?"

Kannon shrugs, not knowing which question to answer first. He tries to tell him outright. "Well, to be honest with you, Dak. I'm—"

Dak suddenly trips and splits some of the eggs he carries, interrupting Kannon. Once Dak regroups and has everything situated, they head off again.

Dak says, "So, did you really know my mom, or did you just know *of* her?"

"Yeah, I knew your mom. Hidden Bridge isn't all that big. Everyone knows everyone. Shit, sometimes people hear things about you before you do them."

"So, when's your birthday?"

Kanon sighs but plays along, wondering when Dak will put two and two together or if he should try to blurt it out again. Instead, he says, "My birthday is July fourth."

Dak stops dead in his tracks. "Wait a minute. You and my dad both knew my mom, both grew up in Hidden Bridge, and both have a birthday on July fourth. What a small world, huh?"

"Not only that, but we are the same height. We kind of look alike, and we have the same middle name."

Dak looks at him as if he is joking. "What's a middle name?"

This catches Kannon off guard. "A middle name is just that: a middle name. You have your first name, which is Dak. Then you have a middle name; mine is Lee. Then you have your last name."

Dak looks confused, knowing nothing of having three names. "Here in the Horizon, we only have one name. Mine is Dak, and yours is Kannon. That's it; nothing more."

Kannon can tell that the discussion is taking a turn for the worse. He thinks now is not the best time to talk about it anymore. A few minutes later, the camp is back in sight; they can see smoke coming from the fire. Dayne is the only one up, so she must've made the fire. She walks down a little bit to greet them and help lighten their loads. Kannon hands Dayne his eggs, and Dak gives her the milk and freshly baked cookies he is carrying.

"Perfect timing. I just got the fire going well. Fresh cookies, as well. You guys must've hit the motherlode. I'll get cracking on those eggs immediately," Dayne says.

The smell of the still warm cookies is enough to awaken Hunter and Hoss. They get up and join Dayne by the fire.

Hoss yawns, saying, "It's going to be a big day today."

Hunter smiles and replies, "Because today's opening day on Shadows."

"Nothing like the first day of hunting season with a handful of tags to fill," Hoss jokes.

They both laugh and fist-bump each other.

Bug yells, "Guys, trying to sleep here. You all mind shutting your yaps? Trust me, you guys don't want me to get up on the wrong side of the bed. That would mean ass whooping's for everyone. Dayne, don't encourage them, or you can get the same. Just saying."

Hunter smiles again, then lowers his voice. "Hey, guys, I think we have a bug problem. What do we do when something is bugging us?" Kannon and Hoss smile, and they all scream, "Bug pile!" All three run and pounce on Bug, squishing him awake. Spin Doll rolls out of the way, giggling to safety and leaving poor Bug to take a beating.

Bug screams, "Get off me, you friggin idiots! You're going to hurt someone, jumping on them while they're sleeping."

Just for saying that, Hoss makes Bug kiss the ground till he says he is sorry for yelling at them.

While the boys play, Dayne and Dak have a discussion over the fire. She asks, "Did you tell him you know he's your father?"

Dak laughs and says, "It never really came up."

She gives him her best mother's glare. "Tell Kannon you know about him being your father."

"Just a little longer. It's been fun messing with him. I think he's about to crack."

Dayne shakes her head and then turns to flip the eggs. Standing there, they hear the boys plotting to Bug pile Dak next. Dak immediately takes off in the opposite direction as the three men chase after him. They leave Bug picking grass out of his mouth and bitching. Spin Doll doesn't help Bug's mood any when she drops a handful of grass on his head as she walks by to join Dayne by the fire.

Dak runs past the girls and grabs Bug to use as a sacrifice. The three warriors also run by, huffing and puffing. They are more than happy to accept the Bug sacrifice as they pile on Bug once more. This time, Dak joins the Bug pile as well.

Dayne yells, "Guys, get off Bug. Look at him! He's turning blue. Let him breathe. Besides, breakfast is done."

They all jump off Bug and run to get breakfast. Bug lies on the ground, looking like he has just lost a battle. By the time he regains his bearings, most of the food is gone. Bug stomps around the fire, extremely mad, because not one time but two times he gets Bug piled for no good reason.

While trying to piece together a breakfast from the scraps that are left, Bug yells, "I know you guys have to gang up on me! Only because none of you can take me one on one because you know I'd be whipping all your asses." Before Bug can notice the guys setting their plates down, the guys Bug pile him once again, making him drop his food into the fire.

Bug is spitting fire, he is so mad. "Thanks, guys. Now I have nothing to eat, and you know it's opening day. This is just bullshit. How about we grow up a little, huh? I'll tell you what.

Tomorrow, when you all wake up, I'm gonna have something waiting for y'all. You want the smoke; you're gonna get the smoke. Don't sleep on this Brahman bull. Ain't a one of you who handle me for eight seconds; I'll guarantee that."

Kannon helps wipe the grass from Bug's backside, trying to calm Bug down. "Relax, Great White Hunter. Spin Doll has a plate of food already set aside for you."

Bug isn't in as bad of a mood when he sees his plate of food. They leave Bug alone to finish his breakfast.

Once Bug finishes and everyone is full, they pick up the camp. The plan is to head for the barn, where Bug and Dillo had rescued Spin Doll. Spin Doll doesn't seem so happy to return to that place, but Hoss promises to leave nothing left of the barn when they finish it. Each of them takes in the beautiful sight on the top of the hill one last time before heading out.

As they begin to walk away, Hoss stops for just a moment and tips his head toward where Dillo's shell pieces lay. Then, they are on their way to bring the fight to the Shadows. Soon, they are out of sight, with only the smoke from the fire's cinders visible. As they walk off, Bug suggests they first stop at the witch's cabin.

CHAPTER 26

"Never order out when you can have a home-cooked meal."
- Fat Jack

IC does everything she can to keep up with the Jokers without being spotted. She tries her best to listen to their conversation as they walk.

Sin complains, "I can't stand having to deal with that fowl mouth lump of shit. We should just cut our losses and relieve him of his light. He's just stupid and arrogant enough to ruin our whole plan."

Omin laughs. "Very true, brother. He typically thinks with his stomach. But even *he* can't be that stupid to cross us. You know the funny part about this? I can't, for my life, remember where I set those keys for him. Besides, my worrisome brother, with all the problems the warriors are having with the Beast, how on the Horizon will they handle the rest of the Hereafter Horde?"

Now, looking slightly more at ease, Sim responds, "You're so right, brother. I mean, I'm scared of Horde myself. If we don't gain full power of the Horizon soon, we may have to deal with them ourselves. Also, if our supply of townsfolk doesn't run out soon at the castle, the Horde will not be willing to venture off. But you know that buffoon Jack will somehow lead the warriors to the castle."

"Well, if he does, lead the warriors to the castle. We'll sit back and watch the battle of the century as Octoro destroys them one at a time and makes them watch. Besides, it'll have to feed the babies something. Then we'll disperse the rest of the Shadows and be done with them all. We really do need a vacation to somewhere warm."

"My brother, we've just arrived from somewhere warm. Besides, the warriors haven't a chance without the fourth king. And to think they have believed all along that it's this Dak kid."

They both begin to laugh hysterically. Between snickers, Omin adds, "Now, brother, let's resume our stay at the Castle of Four Castles resort, shall we?"

Then, the two laugh again in the evilest tones as they pick up their pace.

IC is now running relatively quickly to keep up with the quick-walking duo. She receives a lucky break when a shadow approaches the Jokers. The shadow, out of breath from running, tries to speak.

"My liege, forgive me for the interruption. But the Beast is no more. The warriors have freed it."

Sin looks at Omin, anger in his eyes. "Did he just call us Lees? What the Horizon is a Lees?"

Omin chuckles. "No, brother, he called us his liege. It means king or leader."

Sin, feeling a little dumb, responds, "Why didn't he just say king or leaders then?"

Omin scowls at the shadow. "And our army?"

The shadow lowers his head. "Over half have been freed as well, sirs."

Sin questions, "And what of their losses?"

The shadow slowly nudges back as he answers. "We think we freed two of them, or at least we believe we had."

Sin steps closer. "You think you released two? You think!? Which two do you think?"

The shadow begins to stutter nervously, knowing how bad

his report sounds. "Sirs, we think the one with the turtle shell and the invisible one."

"Oh, you think the invisible one," Omin says sarcastically.

"Yes, sir, the invisible one. You see, we kind of can't tell."

"How can't you tell? You either freed him or you didn't!" Sim yells.

The shadow knew he'd regret answering the Joker's foolish question. "Yeah, we can't tell, sir. Since he's invisible and all."

Omin begins to smirk, knowing how stupid Sin felt when the shadow made him look dumb.

Sin, trying not to react to looking stupid, changes the subject by asking, "Who did they have at the battle?"

The shadow, feeling pretty good that he just bested a Joker, replies, "Dayne, this enormous guy that is as big as the Beast, the pool stick guy, the man with a cannon on his arm, the turtle shell guy, this really fast girl, Mr. invisible—or at least that's what we call him—and this little guy who flickers. Kind of like when a little kid finds a flashlight and they continue to turn it off and on, and even though you tell them to put it down, they ignore you and keep flicking it on and off."

Omin and Sim look at each other before a frustrated Omin says, "Was that all of them?"

"There is this guy who showed up. He led a small army of townsfolk. I think they called him Dot or Dan, or maybe it is Dick. He certainly acted like a dick."

Sin, trying not to smile at the shadow's answers and tired of dealing with the dimwit, simply asks, "Was it by chance Dak?"

The shadow stops throwing names out and says, "You know, now that you say the name, I think you're right. Dak sounds right. Thanks! That would've driven me nuts all day."

"No problem; that's what we're here for," Omin responds

sarcastically.

Sin jumps in. "Is that all you have for us, or is there more incredibly shitty news you'd like to share?"

"One of the Shadows overheard a couple of them talking. We think they're heading for the barn next. One of them said it was time to bring the fight to the Shadows. Also, they weren't talking really nicely about you either. Oh yeah, and some old farmer gave them a bunch of food. Which is crazy because you guys told all the townsfolk that if they help the warriors, they will regret it."

Omin is confused. "The barn… There's nothing at the barn. Just our pet's old cage and the witch's tongue, which I still can't believe you touched."

Sin snickers. "I didn't touch that old thing. I'm pretty sure it was you. Now, as far as the old barn. Send some Shadows to welcome them properly. Maybe even put a few at the witch's house to warn the barn when they're coming."

"You sure you don't want to send one of the Hereafter Horde?" Omin asks. "I'm sure they'd be willing to get out and play today."

Sin thinks for a minute. "Nah, I don't want to send one of them. But I would send two. You know, so they don't get lonely. That way, they can play together. You know, like a play date."

Omin laughs. "Brother, you are pure evil. I love it."

"Come, brother, let's retreat to the castle. I need to rest; we've had a busy day, you know?" Sim boasts as he and Omin walk past the shadow, leaving him behind.

Omin yells back to the shadow, "Go get the Shadows and take them to the barn. Next time, if I were you, I'd come back with a much better report."

IC waits for the lingering shadow to be on his way before

she tries to catch up to the Jokers. Once she does, she is totally spent. IC can't for the life of her figure out what the Jokers are doing. They are standing on a dirt path entrance to a huge open field. She looks as far out in the field as possible but sees nothing but fields. Then she can't believe her eyes. The Jokers begin to dance randomly. IC thinks they have just lost the last bit of marbles they have left. Out of nowhere, an enormous, beautiful, and extravagant kingdom appears. The Jokers enter the front gates when they finish dancing. From what IC can see, through the open gates, are shops and vendors galore. The streets look like they are cobblestones, and banners fly high above the walls. Light poles look to be made from gold. IC has never seen such a place. Far off through the streets of Shadows and townsfolk, IC can spot an amazing castle made from four separate castles.

"This is where the kings must rule from," IC says softly. She desperately wants to enter, but it will be impossible to hide from all of them.

As the gates slowly close, she can hear thousands and thousands of Shadows cheering for the Jokers. It is now the Dark Kingdom. She knows it is time to head back and report her findings to Lakin. As she turns to leave, there are three smiling Shadows in front of her. Before she can say a word, they quickly throw a blanket over her and carry her through the gate just before it closes. Then, they disappear with her into the sea of Shadows.

Meanwhile, Lakin and Jack's partnership is not going as planned. She has a strange feeling he isn't leading them to the castle. Cautiously, she follows him as they come across a strange little house.

"Who in their right mind would live here? It looks atrocious!" she exclaims.

Jack grumbles and continues to walk on. "Some old nasty witch lives here. Trust me when I tell you we don't see eye to eye on anything. But don't worry; I'm not stopping here. My cave—the castle, I mean—is just around this bend."

Lakin remembers the first conversation she heard between Jack and the Jokers. Jack's cave is near the old witch's house! Now she knows what the fat man is up to. She thinks there is no way she will let the kings near the evil lair.

"I need to stop and rest for a moment. My legs are cramping from all this walking today. Plus, the kings need a rest."

Jack angrily shouts, "A rest from what? These kings haven't done shit to be tired! As far as your cramps go, keep walking, or they'll tighten up on you. Besides, we're almost there, and then you can rest."

"But I really need to rest. I need to use the lady's room," she insists.

"The entrance is just up here around the bend. Suck it up, buttercup." Jack continues walking with the kings.

Lakin knows if they go into Jack's cave, none of them will come back out. She has to do something quick. Lakin drops the king to the ground, pretending she tripped and hurt her ankle. Jack knows it is all an act to get him to stop.

"Are you serious? C'mon, it's just around the corner. If you can't make it, I'll take these two to the entrance and then return for you two." Jack continues to walk out of sight around the bend.

Lakin yells, "Give me a minute! I think it's just a scrape." She is trying desperately to buy some time to figure a way out.

"Well, you sit right here if you want. I'm taking these two with me. Besides, it's almost lunchtime, and I'm not missing a meal." Jack smiles as he eyes one of the kings.

Against her wishes, he rounds the bend. Going against her

better judgment, Lakin picks her king up and follows Jack around the bend. When he sees that she's following him, Jack's smile widens.

He stops in front of a door built into the hillside and sets his kings on the ground, rubbing his hands together as he talks to himself. "Home sweet home."

Lakin places her king beside Jack's two and takes a step back while reaching for her whips.

"Whoa, whoa, whoa, little lady. Hold your horses. This isn't the castle; it's my home. My little piece of the Horizon. I'm just stopping to check on my doors and grab a bite to eat. Shoot, if you're interested in seeing how your final outcome finished, I could let you peek in your door. You're more than welcome to come in and see the behind-the-scenes of before and after." Jack smiles as he fumbles with the doorknob.

"No thanks. I think we're good out here. Besides, the fresh air is good for the king's lungs."

Jack opens his door and enters the cave. "Ok, suit yourself. But don't say I didn't ask." He quickly slams the door behind him.

Lakin finds a place to sit next to the kings, needing a quick rest while watching Jack's door. After a little while passes, her eyes become heavy, and her head begins to drop, pinning her chin to her chest. Mim exits the king's pocket and attempts to shake her awake. It is no use. Lakin has fallen asleep.

Suddenly, a hideous scream comes from the cave and startles Lakin awake. It sounded like a fight broke out in there. Screams pour from the cave. The girls don't understand anything that is yelled since the screams aren't in the language they know. This goes on for a good fifteen minutes, and Lakin and Mim can't believe their ears, even though they can't understand the words. It sounds like the voices are yelling for someone to stop. Soon, all is quiet until a large burp comes from the cave.

Lakin gets to her feet while pulling out her whips. She stands as quietly as a church mouse, motioning to Mim to get out of sight. They hear a very light whisper coming from somewhere. It is quite faint, as they can barely hear it. They look around but can't pinpoint where it comes from. At first, they think they might be losing their minds because of hanging out with Jack.

After a few more words and not finding the source, Lakin thinks her eyes might also be going or playing tricks on her. She could've sworn she saw one of the king's fingers moving. She and Mim quickly rush to the king's side. Sure enough, the finger is moving. That's where the whispers came from. Lakin leans down and places her ear to the king's mouth. Even though his voice is extremely low, Lakin can hear what he is trying to say.

"Three to the left. Then, three to the right. Then you must dance with all your might." The king immediately passes out, leaving the girls wondering what he means. Either way, they can't let Jack know a king has woken.

Lakin quickly hides Mim back in the king's pocket, then checks on the other two kings and tries to get them to drink something. After fighting to get them to take a few sips of water, she packs everything up and turns to check on the cave entrance. Standing in front of them is a young lady who looks like someone Lakin has met on her travels. Startled, she quickly pulls her whips out.

"Who are you? How'd you get here without us hearing you?"

"Relax! I'm one of the good guys. Or at least I was one of the good guys. I'm not too sure now. My name is Colt. Pleased to meet you,"

"Name's Lakin. I'm also one of the good guys. You look very familiar."

Colt tries to figure out where she has seen Lakin before. Then, it hits her like a pile of bricks. "You're the watcher the Jokers tossed in the hole."

"How'd you know that?"

Colt smiles because she figured it out. "You were pretty out of it when we met. They were laughing at you because you lost a fight against the Beast."

"Well, you don't have to worry about that ever happening again," Lakin replies. She feels weird that this girl knows all about her, yet she knows nothing of this girl. "What do you mean I don't have to worry about the Beast anymore?"

Colt begins to get fidgety standing in one place too long. "The Beast is no more. It had its light released by warriors yesterday. Hoss and Hunter beat it really bad; it stood no chance without the protection spell."

Lakin can't believe she heard her brother's name come out of this girl's mouth. "You said Hunter and Hoss, did you not?"

"Sure did. Hunter and Hoss are two warriors who act like brothers but aren't. It's a blast to hang with them, and they're so nice, polite, and funny."

Lakin thinks to herself, Hunter is nice and polite. No way can they be talking about the same Hunter. Then she remembers something she can ask Colt to confirm whether or not it is the Hunter she's thinking of.

"What's Hunter's favorite thing to do?" Lakin blurts out.

Colt thinks for a minute, then says, "He really likes to release Shadows, but that's not his favorite thing. I'd have to say it's sing into his pool stick."

Lakin becomes warm, and a smile breaks out from her

toughness. Then it clicks in Colt's mind. She puts two and two together and realizes this is Hunter's sister, whom he thought had been released. She immediately pulls Lakin into a bear hug.

"You're Hunter's sister! He will be so glad to see you. He thought you were released in the battle against the Beast. I'm so happy you weren't."

Neither can stop smiling. Lakin has many questions for Colt, but they hear the handle turning from the cave door before she can say anything. Colt rapidly explains to Lakin that even though she won't see Colt, she'll never leave her, and she is gone in the blink of an eye.

Jack opens the door and steps out, wiping his mouth with a napkin that he tosses to the ground. "Now that hit the spot. Nothing like a little Chinese for lunch." He laughs at his joke and picks up his kings. With the king firmly on his shoulders, he asks, "Who was here? Who'd you talk to?"

Lakin, still not good at trying to play dumb, says, "What do you mean? Nobody's been here but the kings and I."

Jack looks at her, knowing she's lying to him. "Really? Then whose footprints are those on the ground in front of you?"

"Oh those, those were from a young lady who ran by us. She didn't really say much. I think she is running from something or looking for someone. Either way, she was here, then gone. Didn't have any time to catch her name."

The Wiley Jack knows exactly who it is. "A girl running, huh? You didn't catch her name? Let me help you with that. Her name is Colt. You can say I knew her daddy well. You sure you didn't talk to her much?"

Lakin shakes her head as she picks up her king.

Jack mumbles, "Right!" He begins to walk, and Lakin follows along.

CHAPTER 27

"Words lose their strength if not used at the appropriate time."
- Cam

With little to no resistance, the group reaches the clearing, where they spot what appears to be a tiny house.

Bug points off into the distance towards the view of a house. "That's the witch's house."

Everyone squints their eyes as they try to see it. Once they have gotten close enough to scout out the tiny house and see no movement around it, Kannon begins to devise a plan. He grabs Hunter, Bug, and Dak and sends each one to the side of the little house they surround. This way, whatever direction a shadow would run out from, they could release them.

Hunter whispers loud enough for the three to hear him but not loud enough to alarm whatever is inside, "So, this is the mighty witch's house. What a pile of shit. Hey, Bug, are you sure you don't want it before we destroy it? It would make a nice honeymoon suite for you two lovebirds."

Knowing Hunter is just busting balls, Bug replies, "No thanks! Been there, done that."

Kannon signals for the guys to prepare their weapons as his cannon begins to charge. Hunter pulls out his pool stick and puts on his shades as Dak draws his sword and Bug winds up for a homerun.

Kannon informs the guys that they charge on three, and Hunter states, "Time to shine."

Kannon begins the countdown as Bug grips Babe tighter.

"Three, two..." Before Kannon can get "one" out of his mouth, Hoss's big boot stomps the tiny house into nonexistence, startling the men.

Bug yells, "Where in the Horizon did that come from? How'd we not hear your big ass coming?"

Hoss grins. "I'm pretty light on my feet for a big guy." Then he twists his foot, making sure there's nothing left of the tiny house. The men stand there watching as three lights trickle out from the sides of Hoss's boot and rise to the sky.

Dak says, "Well, lookie there. There were some Shadows in there, after all."

Bug adds, "Poor Shadows. What a way to go out. I don't think Hoss has washed those feet in at least a year. Along with his big stinky ass."

"Watch it, or I'll clean them by using you."

Bug quickly walks away but has to get the last word in edgewise. "I wish you would try. I'd hand that big ass a once over."

Hoss chuckles. "What's that? I can't hear you. Were you saying something? It sounded as if you wanted another Bug pile."

Bug begins to sprint, and they all laugh because none of them are even chasing him. From where Dayne and Spin Doll stand, they can barely tell that a house once stood there. Kannon waves to them to join them as they head towards the barn.

Once Dayne and Spin Doll catch up to everyone, they head to the barn by following an old cow trail, which doesn't look like it's been used for quite some time. Weeds and grass fill most of the trail, leaving a few spots of dirt to guide their way. They approach the barn from the witch's side, which means they'll have to sneak to the front of the barn without being seen.

One at a time, they crouch and slowly work across the barnyard. Bug crawls on his stomach, pretending to be a soldier.

Once everyone is accounted for and hidden from being spotted in front of the barn, Kannon says, "Everyone arms up, and if it moves, make sure it never will again."

Seeing the barn again brings a tidal wave of emotions back to Spin Doll. Every painful memory rears its ugly head, and she begins to shake nervously, goose bumps racing up her arms. A tear starts to trickle down her cheek, and Bug catches it with the side of his finger before hugging her.

"Don't worry. I promise, ain't nobody ever going in a cage again," he says softly.

Hunter places a hand on her shoulder. "For once, I agree with Tiny here. Nobody will ever be put in a cage again."

Hoss bends down to talk to her. "When we come out of that barn, nothing in it will cease to exist. That, little lady, is a promise from me to you."

Even though Spin Doll knows they're right, a sliver of doubt remains in her mind.

Standing just outside the barn door, they can hear the Shadows hootin' and hollerin' like they're celebrating something.

Bug whispers, "Well, here we are. Who's going to knock?"

Kannon smiles. "I'll knock." He sends a shot into the front of the barn, leaving a car-sized hole for them to enter. Shadows scatter in every direction, pulling their weapons as if they knew the warriors were coming. Dayne and Hunter are the first to enter, slashing and shooting anything in their way. Lights rise and escape the barn through a broken window up high. A couple of Shadows try escaping out the side doors, but one stomp from Hoss, and they are a memory.

Dak and Spin Doll are told to stay back and only join if needed, but there is no way they will sit back and let someone else fight their battles, so they rush into the barn. Bug swings his bat for a dinger every time. Losing him in the crowd is hard since he is lit up like a Christmas tree. Bug's flashing light changes the mist to solids, which makes the Shadows sitting ducks for Kannon's cannon. There are over a hundred of them, if not more. But their numbers are dwindling with every swing and shot the warriors take. With the strategic positioning of the warriors, the Shadows can't reach them to inflict pain. The entire battle only takes about twenty minutes as the warriors paint the inside of the barn blue with goo.

The battle is over before it even begins. Hunter stands in the middle of the barn, wiping goo from his face, and complains to Kannon. "Asshole! You didn't give me a chance to put my shades on or use my catchphrase. Pretty inconsiderate of you, jackass. Just blowing shit up without even a warning. Next time, you wait for the catchphrase, or I just won't enter."

Kannon simply stands there, trying not to laugh, but Hunter isn't finished.

"I'm not kidding. I'll sit my ass out and watch. I don't need this kind of bullshit. See, it's really simple: catchphrase, then enter. Look at me! You got me all blue up here looking like a badass Smurf."

Kannon smirks. "I got it; no catchphrase, no enter. What if one of us uses a catchphrase?"

Hunter glares at him. "It's truly not the time to mess with me. I'm fucking blue." With that, he stalks out of the barn to clean off.

Hoss laughs and calls out, "Why so blue?"

Meanwhile, Bug is frantically searching for Spin Doll. "Has anyone seen Spin Doll? I can't find her anywhere."

None of the warriors know her whereabouts, but they join in the search for her. Bug is about to have a breakdown. "I promised her. She's got to be here. We need to find her. Look everywhere; leave nothing unturned."

They search the barn with a fine-tooth comb, and someone yells, "We ain't found shit!" Everyone chuckles, even though it is a serious moment.

With a chuckle, Hoss whispers, "Nice! A "Space Balls" reference," referring to his favorite movie.

Suddenly, there is a massive crash in the middle of the barn. Everyone runs to find a shattered cage lying in bits on the barn floor. They immediately look up to where the cage once hung and see Spin Doll standing on a beam and looking down at the broken cage that once held her prisoner. An evil smile pastes her face, and everyone stares silently.

She softly says, "No more bullshit cages ever again."

The group doesn't move, their jaws open, still not believing she spoke.

Hunter returns to the barn, still wiping blue off him, and when he looks up to see what everyone is looking at, he asks, "What's that little hook next to Spin Doll even used for?"

Bug is still looking at Spin Doll as he says, "Spin Doll just spoke."

Hunter slaps Bug on the shoulder. "Well, then, that sucks for you. Because now she'll never shut up." He laughs and walks over to Kannon. "Any idea what is on that little hook up there?"

"Well, obviously something small had to be hanging there, but now it's not."

"Then I guess we'll never know."

Hunter walks back out of the barn, and Hoss says, "Well if it isn't Grouchy Smurf."

Spin Doll begins to spin until she moves so fast that she floats to the ground. When she lands, Bug immediately rushes to her and pulls her into a tight hug.

"Are you alright? You had me so worried."

Spin Doll nods and returns the hug. They stand in the middle of the floor, holding each other until the last Warrior leaves the barn. Bug looks into Spin Doll's eyes, never wanting to let go. She kisses him on his forehead and smiles.

Bug can't contain himself any longer and says, "Spin Doll, I love you!"

Spin Doll is surprised but grins and gives him another kiss on the forehead. Then, they walk out of the barn together, holding hands.

The warriors stand in a staggered line, staring at what is left of the barn. They're all exhausted but glad to see everyone made it out safely.

Without looking at Hoss, Bug says, "big man, will you do us the honor?"

Hoss nods, then runs toward the barn, yelling, "Cannonball!"

Everyone watches happily while Hoss performs a belly flop onto the barn, sending it crashing to the ground. In almost the same fashion they did with the witch's house, they leave the barn just as flat.

Kannon feels good about winning. "Well, that's two down. Soon, there'll be no place for the Jokers to hide."

With the factory next on the list, they head back up the hill.

Dayne knows she has to tell the crew about her time at the factory, so she stops walking and says, "Can I have a second to address everyone, please?"

Tired, they gather around Dayne to hear what she has to say and take a much-needed break. Dayne begins by telling them how she had been caught spying in the factory and how the Jokers weren't going to release her. "If it weren't for Colt and Cam saving me, I probably wouldn't be standing in front of you right now." She also explains how the shadow guards watched a giant hole that held their pets.

Then Dayne walks up to Hunter and places her hands on his shoulders. "Hunter, there was a young lady who had whips on her hips. She was in very bad shape—bruises from head to toe, cuts, ripped clothes, and bleeding from her mouth. She couldn't stand on her own. We were all tied up, and I was in no position to help her. We could only watch them drag her to the hole and toss her in. She never put up a fight. I think she didn't even know she was there."

"Why are you telling me this? What's it have to do with me?" Hunter asks, confused.

Dayne puts her head down, knowing she can't look Hunter in the eyes as she answers. "Her name is Lakin, and she looked a lot like you. I—"

"My sister! You're telling me you've seen my sister!" Hunter shouts. "You're just telling me this now. Why didn't you tell me when we first met? Why didn't you tell me? My sister could be lying in a hole on the brink of her life, and you didn't tell me. Why?" Hunter is so angry that hatred is running through his veins.

Dayne tries desperately to explain herself. "I know, I should've told you. But you would've gone off halfcocked and gotten yourself relieved of your light. I was thinking of *you.*"

Steaming now, Hunter spits out, "Who the hell are *you* to tell *me* what I can and can't do with my own light? Fuck you!" Everyone gasps, but he isn't finished. "The only one you care about is yourself and your kid, you selfish bitch. You even shit on your own husband by leaving him out of everything for years. If it was your family in that hole, I'd *die* trying to save them. But it's *my* family, so fuck me. I guess it's true when they say you can only count on family. Well, bitch, from now on, don't call me family." Hunter furiously starts to walk away.

Bug tries to intervene and help calm the situation down as he pleads with Hunter. "Hunter, we're not just a team here; we *are* family. You really don't think for one minute that if Dayne thought she could've helped Lakin, she would've."

Hunter's anger blinds him to what Bug is trying to say. "Fuck you, Bug. Trust me, now's not the time you want to voice your opinion. Sit the fuck down. Nobody asked you. She could've helped Lakin, but her precious little boy comes first." Hunter turns to Dak. "To think you might be a king. My ass, you're a king. My sister is lying in a hole, maybe no longer with us because we all must prance around this fucking prison trying to save *your* ass, so you can help some low life's who didn't even want their own lives. You're no king, boy!"

Kannon steps between Hunter and Dak. "We're not doing this!"

Hunter glares at Kannon. "What the fuck do you think you're going to do? I will release you in a matter of seconds. But I get it. You can protect your family but fuck mine. I see how it is." Hunter walks off as he pushes Kannon's shoulder aside.

Kannon looks at Dayne. "You should've told him. He's not yours to protect. Family supports family, or did you forget that?" Then he walks off, following Hunter's path.

Dak shakes his head, not wanting to speak to his mother, and then he follows Kannon and Hunter. Everyone falls in line and follows, leaving Dayne speechless, watching them walk out of sight. Feeling awful, she puts her head towards the ground and follows them from a distance.

CHAPTER 28

"A real friend will be there in times of need; without them,
I'm sure we all would bleed." - Lakin

Jack and Lakin carry the kings up one hill and down another for over half a day. Lakin's legs are getting wobblily; she isn't sure how much further she could go. Eventually, Jack leads them to an opening attached to the largest field she's ever seen. It goes as far as she can see. Lakin wonders if it will ever end.

To her surprise, Jack set the kings down gently on the grass. She follows suit by placing her king beside the other two, then cautiously waits for Jack to sit before she does, keeping him out of arm's reach. They sit there looking out into the field, with dinnertime passing and the sun not too far away from calling it a day.

Lakin's patience runs out, and she finally says, "What are we doing here? We're just sitting here looking at a field."

Jack looks surprised, then answers, "Wait a minute, princess. Our deal was that I would bring the kings to the castle, and then you would find me my one key or the fourth king to trade for my chain of keys. I lived up to my end of the deal, now pay up, sister. It's your turn, lady. Shut up and put up."

"You brought me to a big empty field. This doesn't look like any castle or kingdom I have ever seen."

Jack stands and points to the field. "There's your kingdom, princess!"

She sarcastically laughs. "So, this is just another one of

your stupid tricks. Did you think you could lure me to some secluded place and free us?"

Jack's face becomes red as anger begins to join his smile. "Listen, lady, you asked me to bring the kings to their castle, and I did just that. Here it is, the whole field is their kingdom. Feel free to venture out there. I dare you!"

Lakin trots to the edge of the field and then looks back at Jack. He gestures for her to keep going. To prove him wrong, she stomps forward and smashes her face against an invisible wall.

Even though it hurts pretty badly, and she thinks she may have broken her nose, Lakin isn't going to give Jack the satisfaction of being right. She places her hands up against the wall, flat on the cool surface that feels like stone. Without looking back at him, she asks, "What is this? I can't seem to go any farther."

Jack laughs, knowing it has to hurt. "I told you…it's the kingdom. The kingdom has twenty-foot walls all the way around it and a sixteen-foot moat around the inside of the wall. There is only one gate to get in and out of there, and it lies near that old goat path somewhere over there." Jack points in the direction of the gate. "But good luck. I've tried everything to get in, but trust me, we need one of these kings to show us. So, we sit here with our thumbs up our butts, or you get one of them to help. I'll be sitting over here, so let me know what you come up with."

Lakin walks along the wall with her hand skimming it, trying to feel for a gate. She continues late into the night, walking and feeling, coming up with nothing that feels like a gate.

Jack grows tired of watching her and soon falls fast to sleep propped up next to the kings. When Lakin is sure he is asleep, she helps Mim out of the king's pocket to get some fresh air. While doing this, Lakin never took her eyes off Jack.

She places Mim on her shoulder and again approaches the kingdom wall to search. They are unaware that Jack isn't really asleep. Whenever she turns her back on him, he opens one of his eyes. When she turns back towards him, he pretends to be fast asleep.

Mim finally whispers to Lakin, "Are you sure he's asleep? I feel like I'm being watched."

"Oh, but you are being watched," Jack says from behind them.

They quickly spin around to see Jack staring at them with a larger-than-life smile, drool dripping off his metal teeth. "Well, Well, Well! Look at what we have here. A star cleaner and a liar. I believe when I asked you if you had a star cleaner in your possession, you told me 'no' multiple times. I do believe this to be true."

Lakin shakes her head. "No, what you asked me was whether or not I had a star cleaner in my sack. And at that time, I most certainly did not. She is in the king's pocket, not mine. So, you see, I didn't lie to you."

Jack's face continues to redden. "Now, how are we going to have an agreement if we can't even tell each other the truth, hmm? You know, liars almost taste as good as star cleaners."

"I did not lie to you. She was not in my possession!"

Jack walks around them, tapping his chin with his index finger. "Now let me see, how can we rectify this situation and let you regain my trust? We had a deal, and I supplied my side of the deal. But now I'm eagerly waiting for you to deliver your side. Since you failed on your part and lied to me, I have a proposition. You don't have my one key or my chain of keys, and you damn sure don't have the fourth king! How about I take that little star cleaner off your hands, and we'll call it even? After that, I'll leave, and you won't have to deal with my beautiful face again. But you must watch me devour your little friend. Trust me, the screams make the whole meal."

Lakin pushes Mim a little farther back on her shoulder as she slowly grabs her whips. "I don't think I like the new deal, so I will have to pass. But I appreciate the offer."

Jack laughs as he continues to circle the two ladies. "See, that's the funny thing about the new deal. I don't think you understand it. I didn't ask if you wanted to take the new deal. I was telling you what the new deal was. I truly do understand the confusion; I really do. But I'm going to be needing that star cleaner. Now!" Jack swings his hand at Mim, but Lakin deflects it with her whip.

Jack shakes the pain from his hand and grumbles, "Well, if that's how It's going to be, and you don't want to pay up on the deal, I'm going to have to insist on eating both of you and I mean both of you. But don't worry, I'll still let you watch your friend be the appetizer."

Jack lunges at the pair, but Lakin is too quick for him. He falls flat on his face, which hurts his pride. Slowly, he gets back to his feet and chuckles. "Now look at what you've done. You made me get my dinner clothes dirty. I'll tell you what, just to sweeten the deal. How about I give you a little insight into your life before I eat you both?"

Lakin doesn't move, not wanting to take the bait. But Jack carries on anyway. "Lakin, my dear, you'll be my main course; the star cleaner can be the desert. Let what I'm going to say now be the appetizer. When your brother and you got in that little car accident, it wasn't his fault at all."

Lakin is confused. Her brother had been driving. "How wasn't it his fault?"

"I mean that it wasn't his fault. Just what I said. You see, my little morsel, I'm the one who cut his brake lines. I also put sticky glue on the floor under his gas pedal. You know, that shit sticks to everything. I was peeling dried glue from my hands for a week. When he pushed the gas pedal down, it stuck to the floor. He couldn't stop, and you should've seen your faces. *Ahhhh!* Now *that* shit is funny."

Lakin stares at Jack, her heart beating in her chest. She can't believe what she's hearing, but his story seems so…sincere.

Jack gives an exaggerated throat-clearing before he continues. "Even though your brother had been clean for over three months, I put a few empty liquor bottles in his back seat to give the newspaper something to write about. You wouldn't be here today if it weren't for your brother. See, he was supposed to be my special of the day, and you were merely an appetizer. Kind of like a two-for-one deal. I really didn't need you, but you know the price of food these days.

"Well, I turned my back for a minute, and your brother sneaks out of my kitchen with you. The worst part is that he stole my pool stick on the way out, making it hard to entertain. Nobody wants to play pool while having to swap sticks all the time. Either way, the funny thing about this whole deal is that neither of you would die in your world. You would probably be watching reruns and eating popcorn in your boring apartments."

"You mean to tell me we weren't part of the king's orders?"

Jack laughs at that. "Shit, the kings don't even know you exist. Every one of you is here because of *me*. So, how I see it, you kind of owe me."

Jack smiles and lunges once again. This time, he catches Lakin off guard and grabs a piece of her shirt. She is too close to use her whip. He pulls her closer to him as she tosses Mim out of harm's way. Jack's teeth begin to shine, his mouth open, his head leaning back like a bear trap. He pulls Lakin slowly towards his mouth. She fights, but he is just too overpowering. Jack's teeth begin opening and closing, making a clanking noise.

Just as he begins to raise her to stuff her in his mouth, kicking and screaming, Colt flies in, knocking Lakin to the ground and out of Jack's hands. Jack's mouth instantly goes back to normal, and he shouts, "You little bitch! Always sticking your nose in someone else's business."

Colt quickly grabs Lakin's hand and pulls her out of distance from Jack, who furiously screams.

"You never interrupt a guy when he's eating! That's extremely rude!"

Colt, trying to make a joke, says, "Sorry to not let you eat while I run."

Jack laughs, giving her credit for that one. "Not bad, little one. I've taught you well. But how about I share a little bit about *your* story, hmm?"

"How about we say we did but don't."

Jack begins anyway. "Your story wasn't your fault either, you know. Your pops did help me in some way with you. You and Pops would stop and get smoothies every day after your training session. Strawberry banana, I believe. Well, when Pops would go get the smoothies, he added a few ground-up sleeping pills for you. By the time you got home, you were ready for bed and fast asleep. Those pills were so strong you wouldn't even flinch when he gave you your steroid shot. You were like a walking—I mean *running*—medicine cabinet. Every day, you'd get stronger and faster, and every night, he'd pump you full of poison. A few of the scouts suspected you of steroid use and wanted you tested, but your dad refused the tests. Then came that day your father couldn't pick you up, so you decided to run home on your own. The only thing was you didn't make it home, did you? A mile into the run, your heart stopped. You collapsed beside the roadside. Luckily, I was there to pull you through my door. Somebody could've easily seen you and done CPR trying to be a good Samaritan. Pretty sure you would've survived, but we'll never know now, will we? So, you see, Colt, you owe me as well. Getting you away from that mean old Pops. Maybe I should change my name to Lifesaver."

Colt can't believe her dad would do that to her. But it does explain why she runs faster every day. Lakin yells at her to take Mim and go find her brother, Hunter, so Colt instantly scoops up Mim and is off, leaving Lakin to fend off Jack herself. Jack definitely likes his odds now. Every time he lunges, Lakin cuts him with her whips. It isn't long before Jack's hands and arms are dripping with blood from all the whipping. Finally, on one of the attacks, Lakin slips and falls, making her easy prey. Jack pounces on her and she fights with everything she has to get away, but he firmly has his grip locked in, both hands holding hers.

"That's it, fight and tire yourself out. It makes it easier to chew once they give up."

He pulls her closer while leaning his head again, opening it like a trap. The clanking of his teeth is the only sound she hears. Jack lifts her off her feet and begins to stick Lakin's head in his mouth, the only part of her visible being her shoulders to her feet. Her body begins to go limp.

Suddenly, a voice speaks from behind her disappearing body. "Put her down, or you won't see the light of day."

Jack's eyes make it hard for him to see who spoke since he

has an eye on each side of his head from his jaws being opened so wide. Either way, he isn't going to stop since he hasn't eaten supper yet.

Just as he starts to chew, Lakin is ripped from his hands and thrown to the ground. She lies there gasping for any air she could get in her weakened body. Jack's head takes normal form, and he adjusts his eyes to see who is stupid enough to disturb his dinner. Standing behind Lakin are the three kings. They look much larger standing than slumped on the ground. Jack immediately runs into the woods and out of sight.

The king with the spade on his vest yells in a deep, loud voice, "Run, little pig; your days here are numbered."

The three surround Lakin, quickly inspecting her to make sure she is whole. Once she gathers her wits and realizes who saved her, Lakin immediately drops to her knees in front of the revived kings, and softly says, "My kings, thank you for saving my life."

The king with the diamond on his vest says, "No, my child, it is you who saved us. You will forever have our gratitude. Please rise, child."

Lakin stands and asks, "May I give the kings a hug?"

The king with the club on his vest smiles. "It would be an insult if you didn't."

Lakin hugs each one as if it were the last hug she'd ever give, and the kings wonder if she will ever let them go.

CHAPTER 29

"When you walk alone, leave footprints so others can follow."
- Hunter

Hunter walks a few miles before Kannon catches up with him, and then they walk side by side for about ten minutes without saying a word.

Looking straight ahead, Hunter says, "Go back to your family; they need you."

Not looking at Hunter, Kannon replies, "I'm walking with my family."

They continue walking as they refuse to look at one another. While they walk, Hunter's emotions catch up, and tears slowly creep down his face, making the road blur. Kannon stumbles to find words to console his friend. Hunter knows he said things that he should've kept to himself. But, as always, his mouth beats his head to the punch.

"I'm sorry, bro," Hunter says, still looking forward.

Kannon finds a small stone in the road and kicks it. "I know you are, buddy." He watches the stone he kicked quickly roll away. The stone brings to his attention what looks like one of Jim's Park benches, just off the path in the woods.

Kannon. "You see that park bench over there?"

Hunter doesn't see anything and wonders if his buddy is feeling alright.

"C'mon, I'll show you what I'm talking about," Kannon insists while pulling Hunter off the roadway towards the bench.

Hunter is more concerned for his friend, as he still sees

nothing the further they walk into the woods.

Kannon stops at the bench, pointing and explaining, "This bench right here."

Hunter only sees Kannon standing in the woods, pointing at the ground.

"Really, there's a park bench right in front of us. But I guess only I can see it. Probably because it's my safe place. When I sit on it, this little old man named Jim comes out and gives me advice."

Hunter is concerned that the Horizon has finally gotten to his friend. He is sure that Kannon has truly gone mad from this place.

Kannon turns around like he is going to sit on his imaginary bench. "C'mon, try it. What do you have to lose?"

Hunter figures, screw it; if Kannon is going off the deep end, why not join him?

Kannon smiles. "On the count of three, we're both going to sit on the bench. One! Two! Oh wait, do you want to say your punch line first?"

Hunter shakes his head, worried that when he sits on this imaginary bench, he'll tumble into the little ravine behind them, making his punchline look stupid.

"Ok, great. Here we go. Maybe you'd better hold my hand, just in case."

Kannon grabs Hunter's hand and begins to squat a little. Hunter's only thought is if that someone walks by right now, they'll see two men holding hands in a little wooded area, squatting to take a shit together.

"One! Two! Three!" Kannon shouts.

Lo and behold, they actually sit on a park bench. Hunter's first thought is, *I am actually just as crazy as Kannon.* But Kannon explains that when he first arrived in the Horizon, Jim was the first one he met and that showed him what happened to the king and what role he was to play in it. Kannon wonders why Jim isn't here. Maybe Jim only appears with one guy on his bench, not two.

They sit and watch as Dak walks by, followed by the others. Hunter can't believe that they can't see them sitting there. Not much later, a lost and troubled Dayne walks by with a face full of tears. Hunter wants to run over to hug her and apologize, but he said what he said, and he can't take it back.

"Truth hurts. Sometimes, it can even break a person," Jim states.

Hunter jumps, almost landing on Kannon's lap. Kannon laughs. "Yeah, he got me just like that as well."

Hunter can't believe his eyes. There, sitting on the arm of the bench facing him, is a little old man. Jim holds his hand to greet Hunter. "Pleased to make your acquaintance, Hunter."

Hunter shakes Jim's hand. "You know who I am?"

Jim laughs. "Sure I do. Who wouldn't know the great Hunter?"

Hunter sighs. "I'm not too great at this moment."

"Ahh, I know words can hurt, but they don't release your light." Jim pulls an old rag from his pocket and wipes a spot off on his bench. "Now these words you said… Did you mean them?"

"Not all of them." Jim wipes another spot on his bench. "So, some were from the heart and the others were from the ass. It's hard to tell them apart sometimes. It's good to let feeling out. If you hold them in and they get built up, they may explode. Kind of like a bottle of pop. If you keep shaking it, BOOM!"

Listening to Jim is what Kannon needs to get his mind right. He was taught long ago to listen to experience. Kannon feels something different this time. It feels like Jim needs him and is trying to say something without saying it.

Kannon says, "You don't seem like yourself today; where's the giggling, Jim, I know? Something bothering you? Anything we can help you with, we're all ears."

Jim halfheartedly smiles. "I feel as if I'm not long for this world. I'm very tired of looking over my back."

Hunter patiently asks, "What do you mean by that?"

Jim climbs over Hunter's lap and sits between the guys. Nervously, he begins to speak. "You know what? I know everything there is to know about you guys, yet you know nothing really at all about me." Jim clears his throat and then continues. "I'm not here to be your safe place or voice of reasoning, even though I'm very good at it. No, I'm just a lonely old man wanting some company. I'm not supposed to even be here at this particular time."

Kannon is puzzled. "I'm sorry. I really don't know what you mean by that. Why aren't you supposed to be here?"

Jim sits back, places one leg over the other, and continues to talk. "Let me start from the beginning. You see, I have this beautiful, young, full-of-life granddaughter. She is my whole world. Every day, I would take her to the park to play. We only went for a few hours, but it would always last the whole day. She would ride the old metal merry-go-round for hours. I would spin her around and around with no care in the world. Whenever it was time to leave, she graciously asked me to dance with her. We'd dance around and around for quite some time. She would begin to sing with the voice of an angel. People would gather around us to hear her sing."

Jim smiles as if he is really dancing with her. "Well, eventually, word got around that people should come to the park to listen to her sing. But if more than ten or twelve people were there, she wouldn't sing. I think they call that stage fright. Eventually, word got back to her dad; all he could see was dollar bills. He immediately sent her to get voice training. We could no longer go to the park and play because her dad wasn't letting her give free concerts. If people wanted to hear her, they'd have to pay. He made her practice day and night. He would be rich with all the auditions and performances he had lined up. I was told we could no longer hang out; he said she was too busy and didn't want me around. I knew that was a lie, but what could I do? He was her father. Since my son-in-law wouldn't let me see her, I bought her a little wooden music box. Every time she opened it, a little doll would pop up and spin in circles. It would play the most beautiful melody. I believe it played "You Are My Sunshine." She loved it and was never without it. She kept it hidden from her father, deep in her pockets, knowing he'd take it from her if he knew about it.

"Time came for her first big show. I was worried because she would never sing in front of a lot of people. Until that night, the park was the biggest crowd she had ever seen. Of course, I bought a front-row seat. I was such a proud Grampy. When the curtain rose, and she saw the crowd of hundreds and hundreds of people, she froze and stood there. They began to boo as she ran off stage. I ran backstage to check on her. She was sitting in the darkest corner of the building, playing with her music box as she watched the little doll spin. Before I could get to her, her dad ran by, pushing me to the side and grabbing the music box from her hands. He was furious about the money he had just lost because she was not singing. She had made him look stupid in front of all his friends. He told her that he would ruin something of hers since she ruined something of his. He smashed the little music box on the ground, shattering it into pieces. As he dragged her away, she tried desperately to pick up the pieces of the little box."

Hunter asks, "Where was her mother through all of this?"

Jim's eyes are full of tears that won't run down his face. Smiling through the emotional pain, Jim answers, "Ahh, my beautiful daughter. She was my whole world. There wasn't anything I wouldn't do for my little girl. She lost her light, giving birth to baby Cali. I guess she figured that if she had to go, she would leave me Cali in her place. Grampy took care of Cali from birth since her dad was either working or drinking. He took my daughter's death pretty badly. He blamed Cali for not having his wife."

Kannon interrupts. "What happened after he smashed the music box?"

Jim wipes his eyes with his cleaning rag, pauses for a moment, then answers, "He locked her in her room as punishment. I was told to stay away from her for good. I was not to have anything to do with her. But she would write small notes to me and stick them in her window facing out so I could read them. Every day, I would walk by, reading them from the street. Almost every one of them read: would you like to dance? She would wave and laugh as I danced around in a circle. She would then join me from her room, spinning around and around. Oh, how I missed my Cali.

"When her dad figured out what we were doing, he taped up her windows and called the police. She was a prisoner in her own home. The police told me her dad put a restraining order against me, and I was never to see her again. A couple of nights later, her dad said he had found her in the closet. Immediately hearing the gossip, I ran to the house. Her dad was on the front porch playing the victim, saying he couldn't believe his little girl would do this. I pushed him aside and went up to her room. There were notes she wrote to me all over her room. One said,

Sorry, Grampy, I don't feel like dancing today. I fell to my knees right in front of the closet. I couldn't believe I had lost both my beautiful girls. If this was true, where was her body? Nobody mentioned anything about her body.

"With the windows still taped and a dimly lit bulb flickering, it was very dark in her room. Through the tears, I noticed a little sliver of light coming from the back of the closet. As I moved a few boxes and a small pile of show clothes, I saw an outline of a door. It was being held open by something smaller that was blocking it. I slowly pushed the door open just enough to pick the small object up, placing my foot in the door to keep it from closing. Immediately, I realized that the small object was the little spinning doll from her music box. Why would she leave that for me to find?

"Slowly, I stepped through the door and into a strange-looking cave with many more doors. When I was fully out of the doorway, it quickly shut behind me, leaving me with no way to open it. I began to inspect the cave, which led me to a fat man sleeping in a reclining chair. I thought that had to be one well-built chair. He had cages stacked on top of other cages, and they were filled with people. Actually, it was all of you. Quietly, I crept closer, the whole time rolling the little doll in my fingers. I noticed a single key laying on his stomach. So, I snuck up and snatched it without waking him up. The way he seemed to be holding it, I figured this key must have been a special key. It wasn't long before I realized the key opened every single cage just by touching it to the cage's locks. You guys were in a weird state of mind, kind of like zombies.

"Once I found the door to the outside, I began carrying you guys two at a time out of the cave to safety, trying my best not to wake the fat man. Then I placed you all in random places so the fat man couldn't find you. After freeing you and still not finding Cali, I returned to the cave to search for her and found her on a shelf in his kitchen labeled *Breakfast*. She was labeled *breakfast* as if he was going to eat her for breakfast. I thought to myself, *What kind of place am I in?* Like a surgeon, I held my hands steady and carefully unlocked Cali's cage. The cage made a loud click sound, which woke the fat man up. With Cali in my arms, I rushed out of the cave and quickly hid behind a couple of trees. The fat man came out of the cave door like a bull who had seen red. Screaming at the top of his lungs, he swore he would find me and eat me slowly. I don't know which one made him angrier, me freeing you all or me having his key." Jim holds up the key as proof.

"Later, I found out that since I didn't lose my light back in our world, I was not supposed to be here in this world. I'm guessing that's the reason I can't be seen." Jim polishes the key with his rag.

"Then why can we see you?" Kannon questions.

"Maybe you didn't totally lose your light back in our world either."

Kannon and Hunter don't know what to do with that answer, so they just look at each other.

Jim hands the key to Hunter. "Here, take this, please. Guard it with your light. This key will open any lock or door it touches. Maybe if you can make it by the fat guy, some of you can go back home to our world. I'm sure the fat man will find me soon enough, and if so, I will accept my fate."

Hunter slowly takes Jim's key and places it in his pocket. "Why me? You don't really even know me. I mean, I'll guarantee he doesn't take it from me, but…"

Jim doesn't answer but fiddles with something in his pocket before pulling out a small wooden box, which he hands to Kannon. "If you ever come across Cali in your quest, please give this to her and tell her Grampy will always love her. Also, never stop dancing, no matter what."

Kannon takes the box and places it in his pocket. "Is this a goodbye? If so, thank you for being there for me. Cali is one lucky girl to have you as her Grampy."

Kannon and Hunter hug Jim, assuring him they will do as he has asked. Jim smiles. "I hope this is not our last goodbye, but you never know. Be good boys and bring those kings to the kingdom. And if by any chance you find Cali, please tell her Grampy is dancing."

Then Jim is gone, this time maybe for good. Hunter and Kannon sit on the bench silently, trying to process everything.

They look at each other and loudly proclaim, "The kingdom!"

CHAPTER 30

"Just when you think you have everything put together, you find an extra piece in the box." - Kannon

IC wakes from being bounced around inside that dirty, smelly old sack she is captured in. Trying to figure out what is happening to her, she suddenly remembers seeing the three Shadows. Thinking the worst, she desperately tries to find some light in the sack. But there is none as she continues to be bounced around. She feels around, only finding small useless items in the sack. Nothing that could help her escape. She can hear many voices as if she is among a crowd. On one of the bumps, the bag catches on something, tearing a small slit in it. The slit is big enough for her to somewhat see out of. IC soon realizes she must be inside the kingdom's walls because she has never seen such a market. It is filled with Shadows and townsfolk, all buying and selling their wares. She must've been carried past hundreds of Shadows. Finally, her captors came to a stop. She is then set on a scale to be weighed.

"I'll give you seven trinkets for it; take it or leave it," a voice barks.

"Only seven? Yeah, I can't take seven. Give me eight and we have a deal," another voice bargains.

"Sorry, seven or nothing. Unless you'd like to bet on it."

"What's the bet? And what are we playing?"

The buyer explains. "If you win, I'll give you twenty trinkets. But if I win, the Joker gets the sack and it'll be fed to the Horde."

IC thinks twenty trinkets must be a lot because the seller accepts the deal.

The buyer explains the rules. "I'll deal you one card. Then I'll deal myself one, plus each of the Jokers one. If any of our cards are higher than yours, you lose. But if your card is higher, you get to keep the sack and get twenty trinkets."

The seller agrees, even though he doesn't have a choice. The buyer begins, flipping over the seller's card first.

"This first card is yours. It's a queen! Sorry, but this kingdom doesn't have any queens. It only has four kings. Well, actually, three kings. So, let's draw another one, shall we? Your new card is a ten!"

The seller seems fine with that.

"Now for my card, I get an eight!" The buyer doesn't seem to be pleased with that draw. "Now for the Jokers. Sin gets a seven!" The buyer is even less pleased with that draw, and the crowd cheers. "Now for Omin's turn. He draws a six!"

The buyer angrily throws the rest of the deck on the makeshift table. The crowd erupts as the seller rejoices with a little celebration dance. The buyer throws the twenty trinkets on the table, covering the bet. While the seller picks up and counts his money, the buyer signals a shadow to come to him. IC overhears the buyer telling the shadow he called over, "When he gets out of sight, collect my money and the sack. Then, toss him to Skulk. He needs a new play toy since the last one just lays there now."

The man nods his head and leaves the celebration.

When the winner picks up his sack full of winnings, the Shadows pat his back and congratulate him on his way out of the market. He rounds the corner to find four Shadows waiting for him. He tries to run, but two more Shadows stand behind him. Before he can say anything, he is bound and gagged. They pull the twenty trinkets, plus two more, from his pocket and toss the sack containing IC onto a cart. Two robbing Shadows walk off, pulling the cart behind them, which holds IC. They return to the crowded market.

As the men pull the cart through the crowds, IC watches through the hole in the sack. The kingdom is not in the best shape; garbage is thrown in the streets, and Shadows lie everywhere. IC thinks, *there is no way the kings would've allowed this.* Then she notices they must be coming up on the inner kingdom and closer to the castles since the roads all turn to cobblestone. The cart begins bouncing her around like she is in a popcorn machine. This makes it almost impossible to see out of the hole, let alone keep her food down from the night before. Every time the cart stops, they pile more items, pushing IC further under the pile and blocking her view. It isn't long before the cart stops for good as they begin unloading it into two piles. One pile goes into the castle, and one pile doesn't. IC is placed on the castle pile. She wonders how her friends will find her.

Outside the castle, Colt sprints through the woods so quickly that all Mim can see is a blur going by. Finally, Colt stops right in front of what used to be the witch's house.

Mim gathers her wits and says, "I don't think anyone lives here."

Colt laughs. "I'm thinking the same."

They can tell it is the work of Hoss. Mim is shocked to hear that Hoss is one man.

Colt says, "Hang on. We're heading over to check out the barn."

Mim clutches tightly, and they're off. In a matter of minutes, they're at the barn. It looks like it had received the same treatment from Hoss as the witch's house. Mim asks Colt if Hoss hates buildings. Colt smiles and shakes her head. Colt figures the next stop should be the factory. Most likely, because that's the last place they would look.

Mim again grabs Colt and yells, "Off to the factory!"

Colt takes off like a starting pistol was set off. She knows she has to find Hunter, as every second she wastes could be Lakin's last. They race down the path towards the factory, Colt's mind running as fast as her legs are moving. She tries to think of the reason her dad has to put that poison in her body. The Fat man has to be lying to her. There's no way her dad would do that. It just doesn't make sense. She is his little girl.

As they round the bend, Hunter and Kannon stand in the middle of the road. Colt races by them, then turns back around, stopping directly in front of the two. The cloud of dust that follows finally catches up to her, and the guys fan the dust from their faces.

"Slow down, rocket. Where's the fire?" Hunter asks.

Colt replies so fast that the guys don't understand her words. Hunter raises his hands and gestures for Colt to slow down. She tries, but her nerves won't let her.

Mim slowly climbs from Colt's back to regain her spot on Colt's shoulder. This surprises the two men at first. They think Mim is a large bug, and both draw back their hands to swat her.

"Now, which one of you is Hunter?" Mim asks.

Hunter lowers his hand. "I am. And who do I have the pleasure of speaking with?"

Mim blushes. "I'm Mim, and your sister sent us here to find you. She's in grave danger."

"My sister! Where is she?"

"Your sister saved mine and my sister's life. She carried the kings to the kingdom's walls. She also made a deal with a very bad man to get all the kings brought to the castle at once.

Now that they have the kings to safety, she doesn't have her part of the deal. The fat man wants her light in replacement of what she had offered him. When we left, she was winning, but for how long, who knows? The fat man is relentless. He's much more powerful than she is. Hurry, she needs your help."

Hunter looks at Kannon, who is quick to assure Hunter, "We can handle the factory. Your sister needs you more than we do now."

Hunter nods and grabs Mim to take with him so she can show him the way. It doesn't take long for them to be out of sight. Colt agrees to stay and help the group with the factory, since now they are down a Warrior.

Kannon begins to jog so Colt doesn't have to walk. Worried about her, Kannon asks, "Are you alright? Cam is a good guy who got a raw deal in life."

Colt nods, not wanting to really talk about it. Kannon can tell it is a sore subject, so he changes the discussion. "I'm glad to hear Lakin is still with us. That'll be a good plus for Hunter's sanity. There's nothing worse than losing—" Kannon catches himself from saying the wrong thing. Colt only smiles, then runs up to see the rest of the group. Kannon smacks himself in the head. "Idiot!"

The first person Colt comes across is Dayne, depressed and alone. Colt doesn't like seeing Dayne in that state of mind, so she gives Dayne one of her world-famous hugs. Dayne needed that more than Colt knew. Dayne explains what happened at the barn and how everyone hates her now.

Colt assures Dayn that she did what she had to do. Hunter most likely wouldn't be with them if she didn't keep it a secret.

"Don't worry, you make a decision for the betterment of the Horizon. You can't always be liked, but you can be right, whether they want to see it now or not," Colt reassures Dayne, who smiles. Then Colt adds, "Sometimes we have to make choices that may hurt the ones we love, but it's the only way to ease their pain."

Dayne knows she is talking about Cam more than Hunter and her. She smiles and says, "How can a young girl be so smart?"

Colt smiles as well. "I'm smarter than my age. Maybe I have an old soul, too."

They both laugh with tears in their eyes, and Dayne responds, "From the mouth of Cam."

Kannon catches up with the girls, and, trying to catch his breath, he gauges their moods. Are they happy or upset? Are they laughing or crying? He shakes his head, trying to speak between breaths. "Women!"

The girls punch him playfully, sending Kannon reeling a couple of steps back. He holds up his hands in surrender. "Sorry, I give up." They all laugh and run to catch up with the others.

It isn't too long before they catch up with the others since they are all sitting on a stone wall along the roadway, eating blackberries from a large bush Dak found. Their faces show how good the blackberries are and how hungry they are. Kannon, Dayne, and Colt quickly grab a handful and join them at the wall.

Colt tells them what is going on with Lakin and why Hunter had to go. Dayne wonders if they should go help Hunter before they charge the factory.

But Bug, being Bug, asks, "So where is Cam? Is he here? Cam, if you're here, come on out and show us that pretty mug of yours."

Kannon shakes his head and whispers, "Bug, enough. Cam is not here."

Spin Doll pulls Bug back to his seat. Bug is confused. "What? What'd I say?"

Dak hugs Colt, giving her his condolences. "He was a good man who cared about you and all of us, probably more than he should've. May his star shine bright forever."

Then Bug realizes and goes quiet. Hoss, knowing it, doesn't really want to know it. He punches a large rock beside him, splitting it as both sides fall off the stone wall.

Kannon walks over to Hoss. "You know, for a place so beautiful and scenic, it brings its share of sorrow with it." Hoss nods in agreement since they're all together, sitting around with stuffed bellies. Kannon thinks it'd be a good time to go over their plan of attack on the factory.

"Now, this factory is much larger than the barn. We're not going to be able to go in guns a-blazing, especially without Hunter in our lineup. I'm sure the Jokers have gotten word about the witch's house and the barn by now. The forces at the factory will definitely be beefed up."

Colt pipes in. "If I had to guess, and I'm just guessing, I wouldn't be surprised if the Jokers send some or all of the Hereafter Horde."

Bug jumps in, then. "What's the Hereafter Horde? That doesn't sound too good."

Kannon is also confused, not knowing anything about this Horde. Colt tells them what she and Cam overheard when they eavesdropped on a few Shadows.

"There were originally four of them in this Horde. The Beast is actually one of them. So, I'm betting the rest really want to meet us. We were told they called the king's castle the Castle of Four Castles. But that's not the case. It's called the Castle of Four Towers. Each tower is guarded by one of the Horde. The Jokers wanted to ensure the kings couldn't waltz back in and take over what they had stolen. They went to the four corners of our world and brought them back here to the Horizon. The Heart Tower is guarded by Skulk, a large, rat-shaped creature with the strength of a thousand rats. He is easily the heaviest of the Horde. He is also extremely elusive for his size. He has a large, spiked ball on the end of his tail that he crushes his enemies with.

"Next in the Diamond Tower is Dice. Dice is a red and black snake and about as long as fifteen buses. His fangs are made from diamonds and can shear through anything. The thing that makes him unique is his eyes are actual dice. They continue to spin, stopping occasionally to reveal numbers. Trust me, you do not want them to land on snake eyes. The Beast is the guard for the Club Tower. We all know where he is now."

Bug feels a lump form in his throat, and everyone is silent, staring at Colt.

"Finally, The Spade Tower guard is the most feared of all. Octoro has a spider body with a bull's head. His horns are the sharpest weapon ever created. On the end of each arm is a stinger that shoots a sticky substance, and once it attaches itself to you, it renders you helpless for some time. Also, Octoro is rumored to not feel pain and can throw a web from behind himself. Avoid this monster at all costs."

Kannon says, "So you really think one or more of them could be there?"

Colt nods. "Yes, definitely. If not the Jokers themselves."

Bug nervously chimes in. "Ok, seriously, guys. Are we really going to try this? I mean, a couple of Shadows is one thing. Fighting the Joker's zoo is another. How can we fight one of these, let alone the army of Shadows? Something doesn't sound fair here. They have razor and diamond body parts. I have a wooden baseball bat. Unless the monsters throw curveballs, I ain't doing shit to them. No wonder the kings were overthrown; they didn't have monsters on their side."

Colt holds her hand up. "Actually, the kings do have a Beast. It's a dragon called Savior of Souls, but they call her Char."

Dak smiles. "Have you seen her with your own eyes?"

Colt nods. "She's got beautiful scales, purple and teal. Her wings and eyes are made from gold. She flies like an eagle, and her talons have the force to tear anything to pieces. She's as close to majestic as you'll ever see."

Bug feels a little better knowing they have a dragon on their side. He walks over to Hoss and pats him on the leg, saying, "Well, then, that means we have two monsters of our own. The dragon and our big buddy right here. Isn't that right, Hoss?"

Hoss hasn't been paying attention to the conversation. He turns towards the group with blackberries covering his face. It is impossible not to laugh, and they all burst out laughing.

"Yeah, we have the Berry Beast. We call him B. B. for short," Kannon jokes.

Hoss, having no idea why they're all laughing, chuckles with them.

Everyone cleans themselves off and heads for the biggest fight of their lives. Colt runs ahead to do a little recon. Dak hugs his mom to let her know she's still his mom.

Bug walks up to Kannon and says, "We might have a problem if Dice is there. You see, I'm incredibly scared of snakes. If Dice comes out, I may, in fact, shit my pants."

"Listen to me. If you actually shit your pants, the bright side is Dice probably wouldn't eat you," Kannon says with a chuckle.

CHAPTER 31

"When you're asked to dance, dance like no one's watching."
- Lakin

Hunter and Mim arrive at the very spot that Mim had left Lakin. There is no one there, just some scuff marks on the ground to prove there is a fight. Hunter immediately begins to yell out Lakin's name, stopping for a second to listen but getting silence in return. This continues for some time, as he searches the surrounding area. He then spots a path in the woods that looks freshly made. Finding nothing, Hunter and Mim decide to go check it out, and, following the freshly made path, they run off into the woods.

The kings bring Lakin to an old, unused fire pit. Rocks circle the pit, with very little ash inside them. Lakin thinks it is a little weird that none of them touch each other and seem to have been placed perfectly.

The diamond king asks, "Do you remember what we told you, child?"

Lakin remembers a little about three to the left and three to the right but can't remember the rest. The club king points to her to stand in the middle of the fire pit and face the invisible kingdom wall.

The spade king explains. "Now, child, do as I say. Place your left foot on the stone directly in front of you. Then, one at a time. Proceed to your left three stones and be sure to touch each stone in order."

Lake places her left foot on the center stone and then counts each stone as she touches them one at a time to the left. Each stone lights up as she touches it.

"Next, my child, place your right foot on the stone directly in front of you. Then do as you did on the left side, but this time only go to the right."

She does as she is told. This leaves seven stones lit up.

The three kings all at once instruct, "Now dance with all your might."

Lakin begins to dance like she's never danced before. With a rumbling from the ground, a stairway opens, revealing a path that leads down under the kingdom's wall. The kings go first, as she lets them lead the way. She follows closely behind, not wanting to get lost in the dark tunnels.

After running for about ten minutes, Hunter and Mim come to a clearing, where it appears another struggle took place. Hunter looks around, searching for a clue.

Suddenly, they hear a scream nearby, and it sounds distressed. Hunter and Mim hurry in the direction of the scream, and they come across a fat man with a deformed-looking head. His head from his upper teeth to the top of his head is on a hinge, making his mouth look like an open manhole. They arrive in time to witness a pair of legs sliding down into the man's mouth. His metal teeth make an eerie clanking noise. They can't tell who the legs belong to through the splattered blood on his face.

Hunter instantly pulls his pool stick out as the fat man's face again takes a normal shape.

"What are you doing, you sick bastard?" Hunter yells.

"Name's Fat Jack. C'mon Hunter, you know me; we go way back. Haven't you ever seen a man eat before?"

Hunter ignores what the slob says and asks, "Where's my

sister? Was that her?"

Jack laughs. "I wish. That little bitch has her day coming. Nobody makes a deal with Fat Jack and then does not pay after Jack delivers on his part. Maybe you'd like to pay her debt."

"Maybe you'd like to try to collect it. If that wasn't my sister, then who was it?"

Jack burps. "I'm sure she is someone's sister, but not yours, unfortunately. I've eaten a lot of sisters, brothers, dads and moms. Really, don't ask them their names anymore. Makes your food taste different if you have a bond with them."

"Since you know who my sister is, where is she then, asshole? The last time she was seen was with you."

Jack frowns. "Aw, yes, the girl who doesn't pay her debts. You know, something like that makes the whole family look bad. I can tell you what should've happened to her." He rubs his stomach with both hands, taking another step towards Hunter.

Hunter fires a shot in the air, readying the stick.

"Whoa, now Yosemite. Your sister left with those ungrateful kings. I'll tell you what, if there weren't three of them, I would've had a buffet. How about you pay off her debt by handing me that delicious-smelling star cleaner you have in your possession? Man, it's like you each have one. Is it like a family thing? If so, how do I get invited to the reunion?"

"If you ever touch a single hair on my sister's head, I'll free you where you stand," Hunter growls.

Jack takes another small step towards Hunter, leaving him almost within reach. "If it wasn't for the kings, you wouldn't have to worry about your sister's hair again."

Jack reaches out just as Hunter fires a shot into Jack's arm. The fat man stumbles backward and screams, "You shot me! Who the hell shoots somebody nowadays? What's wrong with these young kids today? Doesn't anyone fight with their fists anymore? You know that friggin hurt. Look, now I'm bleeding. I'll never get this shirt cleaned. You stupid bastard; you really shot me."

Hunter smiles. "Oh, relax, I didn't feel a thing." He pulls a rope from his sack and tosses it to the ground before Jack, pointing his stick at Jack's face.

Glancing at the rope, Jack says, "And what the hell do you think I'm doing with that?"

Hunter, still smiling, informs Jack, "Thought maybe you'd tie your feet with it. That is if you know how to tie. Oh wait, maybe you can't reach your feet. Those things at the end of your legs that you probably haven't seen in quite some time."

Jack growls, "No, I can't reach them. Why don't you come tie them for me?"

Hunter shoots him once again in the same arm, and more blood trickles out. Jack, now in even more pain, reaches over and grabs the rope, trying to tie his feet the best he can with one arm. Hunter walks around the fat man sitting on the ground with his feet tied. Standing behind Jack, Hunter hands his stick to Mim.

"If he moves one muscle, free him."

Hunter grabs Jack's hands and ties them the best he can behind his back. Jack seems more concerned about trying to lick the blood from his shoulder. Hunter, grossed out, unties Jack's feet as he helps him stand up, then takes his stick from Mim and places her back on his shoulder. He points his stick at Jack's back.

"Now, we're going to take a little walk to the factory. A few friends would like to meet you and say hi."

"I can't believe you shot me," Jack whines as they walk.

"Relax, it's only a flesh wound."

"Ahh, flesh. Have you ever tried it? It's really good with mustard."

Hunter disgustedly pushes Jack down the path.

They aren't even halfway back to the factory before Jack begs for a break. Hunter refuses, knowing he must make it back to the factory in time to help his friends.

"We need to stop and take a rest. I'm not feeling too good; it might be from all the blood I've lost. You know, because some asshole shot me,"

"Keep walking, or I'll shoot your other arm. It'd be a shame if you couldn't use your arms to eat with."

Mim notices they have already returned to where she and Colt met the guys. "We're making good time. Maybe we *should* stop for a minute."

"Are you on his side or mine?" Hunter jokes.

Mim doesn't get it; she simply says, "I'm on your side, of course."

Chuckling, Hunter finally agrees since he has to relieve himself anyway. They find a big tree and tie Jack to it.

"I'm going to just be over there. If you try anything funny, I'll put a shot in your leg so you won't run again."

"Yeah, yeah. Just piss already, will ya? I have to go when you're done," Jack grumbles. "And don't be gone all day. I have a weak bladder."

Hunter went one way, and Mim went the other. When Hunter returns, Jack is not there. He chewed through the rope with ease!

Mim notices Jack's absence when she emerges from the woods and yells, "Where is he? We must find him! He's going to find me and eat me." She is shaking with fear.

Hunter calmly places her on his shoulder and says, "Relax. I'm sure we won't see him anytime soon."

He then notices a trail of blood leading toward the witch's house. Hunter says, "We can track him for a minute, but we don't find anything soon. We need to head out and help the others at the factory."

Hunter jogs back down the road, stopping where he had last seen Jim's bench. The bench isn't there, but he does notice the blood stopped just before it. With no bench in sight, Hunter figures Jack ran into the woods, trying not to be spotted by anyone. Either way, he had to have gone back to the factory. Hunter knows he can't waste any more time. Mim agrees, and they run back towards the factory, leaving Jack to run and hide.

Back at the bench, Jim appears, thinking his friends returned with more questions. He is wiping the armrest when he hears a voice.

"Hello, old friend."

Jim looks up and is surprised to see Fat Jack standing next to the bench. "What do you want? How'd you get in my space?"

"What, no hello for a long-lost friend? I think we have a little business to discuss," Jack states as he smiles, showing his metal teeth.

Jim tries to back away, but Jack quickly grabs him. "Now, now, friend. I believe you have something of mine, and I'd like it back. Now!"

Jim knows he doesn't stand a chance against Jack, so he pretends he doesn't know what Jack is talking about. "What could an old man possibly have that you could want?"

Jack laughs. "Nice play, stupid. I wonder how grizzly you'd be since there's not much meat on those old bones anymore. Ok, this is what's going to happen. You're going to hand me my one key. Then I'm going to eat you, but not because I'm hungry; just because I can. It's nothing personal." He chuckles before continuing. "Then I'm going to sit here and wait for any of your buddies to come along and probably eat them as well. You know what they say: eat your troubles away. Then, and only then,. Will I find your granddaughter, and—"

"I don't have your dam key!" Jim screams. "How many times do I have to tell you that?"

Jack is angry now, so he shows his teeth and growls. "What do you mean, you don't have my key?" Jack slides closer to Jim as Jim slides up on the armrest.

"I gave the key away. I don't have it anymore."

"Where is it!" Jack yells as his head begins to deform.

Jim dives to make a getaway as Jack's teeth make a loud clanking sound, followed by more clanking sounds.

In the meantime, Hunter reaches the team's break area and notices half a bush of blackberries is gone. He laughs, unsurprised, and says to Mim, "They've definitely been here. This has Hoss and Dak written all over it." Hunter quickly picks a handful of berries for Mim and begins running down the road.

Not too far ahead of them, the group finally reaches the outer area of the factory. Kannon sneaks over to where Colt is kneeling behind some thick bushes. Colt rapidly informs Kannon of what she's seen so far. To his delighted surprise, she hasn't seen any of the Horde yet.

Colt informs Kannon, "I've counted close to five hundred Shadows, but I couldn't get a good look toward the back. I don't know what, but something doesn't feel right. I feel like we're being watched."

They look around the area and, not seeing anything unusual, slowly sneak back to the group to inform them of Colt's findings. Kannon tells everyone that Colt hasn't seen any of the Horde, only Shadows. Bug sighs, relieved to hear the news.

Kannon goes over the plan of attack. "Hoss, being that we'd need a huge hole to get you in the factory, you'll stay out here. We can't have you in there knocking stuff down that may hit us."

Hoss salutes. "Ok, captain; the outer factory will be secured."

Bug laughs. "Yeah, keep that big ass out of my way. I'm feeling froggy."

Kannon grabs Bug's face and sternly whispers, "Bug, this is not the time for jokes. You need to be ready steadily. Flash like you've never flashed before."

Bug laughs and jokes again. "Who'd thought I'd grow up to be a flasher?"

Everyone raises their hands, even Spin Doll.

Kannon rolls his eyes but continues. "Colt, we need you to use your speed and clean up every shadow Hoss can't catch." Colt nods in agreement. "Dayne and I will knock on the front door." Kannon points around to the back of the factory, explaining. "Spin Doll, you go in the back door, spinning and forcing them our way." Spin Doll nods her head in compliance.

"Yeah, what'll you have me do?"

The team turns around to see Hunter coming out of the woods, two light orbs in the sky behind him. Hunter looks at Kannon and grins. "Found a couple of spectators in the stands that weren't rooting for the away team."

Everyone is so happy to see Hunter! Bug excitedly asks, "What's that on your shoulder?"

Hunter clears his throat. "Ladies and gentlemen, I'm proud to present—"

"Cali! I found you!" Mim shouts, jumping down and

running to Spin Doll. Spin Doll scoops her up and kisses her on the cheek.

"I take it they know each other," Bug comments.

Mim, not letting go of Spin Doll, yells to Hunter, "Thank you for finding my Cali!"

Kannon wonders where he's heard that name before. Then he wonders: can Spin Doll be Jim's lost granddaughter, Cali? He will have to wait and have that discussion with her after the factory fight.

Bug is confused. "Spin Doll, why is she calling you Cali?"

Spin Doll places Mim in this pouch that hangs around her neck. "I'm Cali's watcher. Well, my sister and I are Cali's watchers. Sitting in this pouch by Cali's neck allows me to say what she wants by feeling the vibrations in her throat, like an interpreter. When Cali was captured by the Jokers and placed in a cage way up high, they took her voice and hid it away. Then they tore our wings off and tossed us into the hole to be eaten by the kings. But the kings would never do such a thing. We were stuck in that hole for seventy-one days until Lakin found us and rescued us and the kings. Now I've found my Cali. I can't thank you guys enough."

Hunter nudges Bug, saying, "You know what this means, don't you?"

Bug smiles. "Yeah, it means I'm not the shortest watcher anymore."

Once the excitement wears down, it is time to set the plan in motion.

Kannon and Dayne walk up to the factory door, and Kannon turns to Dayne. "You want to knock, or shall I?"

Dayne smiles. "I would, but you do it too."

Kannon begins to charge his cannon, then turns to Hunter and asks, "Would you like to send us off?"

Hunter pulls out his shades, smiles, and announces, "Time to make them shine."

CHAPTER 32

"I received the royal treatment, alright." - IC

After over two hours of loading and unloading the cart, IC's sack is moved from the big cart to a smaller cart. It isn't long before she is on the move again. With all the packages now out of her way, she can see out of the hole once again. While moving down the street and into the center of the kingdom, IC can see four very tall towers standing in the center of it all. They are exquisite, each one showered in colors and trimmed in gold with its own symbol etched into it: a club, diamond, spade, and heart.

She gazes at their beauty the whole trip as they grow closer with each step, looking as if she is being taken to the Heart Tower. IC can't help but wonder if the inside is as beautiful as the outside. Once stopped, she is picked up with a couple of other sacks and carried into the tower and up many flights of stairs. Due to the other sacks being pressed up against hers, she can't see anything out of the hole, leaving her to simply wonder how beautiful the inside looks. After many steps, she hears a door open.

"Right this way. Here, dump it into this. Make sure the foul thing doesn't get out. Are you positive it can't get out on its own? Ok, that'll be all for now. We must leave before they arrive."

IC can hear the door close; then, she is dumped into an old birdcage. The voice she hears is a small, chubby shadow that IC watches as it goes around the room, straightening up.

There's another birdcage the same size as hers, but that one is covered by a cloth. It's not too far from her, but far enough so she can't reach it, and she can't tell if anything is in it because the cage is covered by a cloth. She continues to look around and sees a large window behind her that overlooks most of the kingdom. Since IC is at the very top of the tower, she can see for miles.

The shadow maid finishes and leaves, closing the door behind them. Trapped with nothing to do, IC watches the bustling of the kingdom below her. She can smell all the wonderful aromas coming from the vendors, making her hungry—and her stomach lets her know. As if someone had heard her stomach, the maid comes back into the room and sticks fruit into IC's cage and the second cage. Then it closes the door behind it and is gone. The shadow is too quick to feed for IC to get a good look in the other cage.

She sits in silence, eating her berries and staring at the other cage. Eventually, IC can't take it anymore and asks, "So, what are you in for?" Thinking it was funny, she chuckles to herself.

When she doesn't get an answer, she tries again. "Name's IC. I was a star cleaner. Now that they tore off my wings, I can no longer fly. I guess I'm nothing."

Again, she doesn't receive an answer. Still not knowing if anything is in the other cage, IC turns back towards the window and watches the kingdom. This doesn't stop her from talking. "You know what? I have a sister who looks just like me. She's so awesome. I really couldn't ask for a better sister. Well, now that I'm here in the penthouse, and she's out running around outside of the kingdom walls, I probably won't ever get to see her again. I really miss her silly smile and the way she bosses me around. How about you? Any siblings you want to talk about?"

Still, no answer from the other cage. But IC continues. "Not too talkative, are you? Well, that's ok. I'll talk enough for both of us. Guess what? You're talking to a real-life watcher. My Warrior's name is Cali. She and the other warriors are going to save the kings. They're finding the fourth king as we speak. This kingdom will be saved in no time. I bet they're on their way right now to save me. Oh, don't worry, they'll rescue you too. My Warrior Cali doesn't speak much, either. My sister and I do all of her talking. I think it's because she's muted. It'd be cool if I got your name. Then, at least, I'd know who's ignoring me." With no answer, IC goes quiet for some time.

"My name is S.O.S." the voice from the other cage answers.

IC's face lights up, and she happily responds, "Pleased to meet you, S.O.S."

"My name is not S.O.S.; it's S.O.S. But my friends call me Char."

IC laughs. "Sorry about that, S.O.S.—I mean Char."
Silence.

IC begins to talk to herself. "Well, look at that, IC. You made a new friend, good job. You and Char are now cage buddies." Then she stares out the window in silence with a big smile.

Just as IC is about to take a little nap, the door swings open, revealing the Jokers. She can't believe her eyes. Standing in front of her are the two who destroyed the Horizon and all her star friends. How did she end up in the Jokers' room? IC waits for them to give up any information that can help the warriors.

The Jokers seem very angry as they knock over chairs and clear everything off the table and counters.

Sin yells, "These warriors were supposed to be the bottom of the barrel. We had Fat Jack pick them because they gave up in their world. What the hell makes them so eager to fight in this one?"

Omin is angry as well. "How'd they defeat the Beast? There's a reason he's called *the Beast*."

Sin kicks over the waste basket. "We need to end the big one's light. If we release him, then the rest will fall."

Omin picks up the waste basket to kick it over again and asks, "If they are heading for the factory, why don't we send Skulk and Dice to introduce themselves to the big man? Maybe, if we're lucky, they can release all of them, and we'll live happily ever after."

Sin walks back around and picks up the waste basket again as he answers his brother, "That actually sounds like a great idea; how'd you come up with it? Did you ask our buddy S.O.S.?" Sin taps on Char's cage, making it swing back and forth.

Omin walks by, kicking the wastebasket over again, as he disgracefully yells, "How can we lose the kings? They can't walk, talk, or move. They are actual lumps of shit. Yet we can't find them. I blame this whole thing on your mother." Omin slaps Char's cage again to make it continue to swing.

Sin picks up the waste basket and notices IC. "What the hell is that ugly-looking thing?"

Omin glances at IC. "Oh, that's one of those star cleaning things that Jack likes to eat. Ugly little suckers, but he swears they taste good. This one doesn't have wings, though."

Sin replies, tapping on IC's cage and making it swing as well. "At least it can keep S.O.S. company."

Omin laughs. "Maybe S.O.S. will eat it. That'd be so cool."

Sin taps each cage once more, making them continue to swing, as he tells IC and Char, "You guys keep an eye on this place while we're gone. And no parties, you hear?"

Omin follows Sin out. "We got to go see a couple of old friends."

Omin closes the door behind him, leaving Char and IC alone.

A few seconds later, Omin walks back in and taps the cages. "We'll be out late, so don't wait up for us." He walks by the waste basket and kicks it over as he leaves, slamming the door and mumbling, "We really need to find better cleaners."

IC worries that their plan to take the warriors out may work. She yells toward Char's cage, "We need to get out of here fast! We must warn the warriors about the ambush."

Char's cage continues swinging back and forth with no sound coming from it. IC yells again, thinking maybe Char didn't hear her. "Maybe you don't care about the men and women fighting for us. What about the kings who need our help saving the Horizon? You might not care, but I damn sure do. I'm not letting some fancy birdcage stop me from helping my friends."

She runs back and forth, getting the cage to swing even more, causing it to lift off the hook a little each time. Eventually, the cage slips off the hook and crashes to the ground. When she regains her wits, IC notices the cage door is ajar. The door opens just enough for her to slip out of the cage. She is a free star cleaner.

IC quickly looks around for something to open Char's cage. "Don't worry. I'll find a way to get you out of that cage."

Char says, "Go save your friends."

"I *am* helping a friend."

"My cage is unbreakable. A witch put a spell on it, making it my prison for the rest of my days."

IC laughs. "You mean the witch that the warriors freed the other day. Yeah, I don't think she's doing many spells nowadays."

Char perks up and asks, "The witch is no more? Are you sure of this?"

"Sure, as I'm holding the keys to your cage. Now, are you ready to save some warriors and kings? Or do you want to wait for the Jokers to return?"

IC uses the tipped-over waste basket to reach up to Char's cage. IC reaches up enough to pull the cloth off the top of the cage, revealing Char. She can't believe her eyes, and she begins to stutter. "You… You're a dragon!"

Char isn't only a dragon, but she is possibly the most beautiful creature IC has ever seen, with bright purple and teal scales and shiny gold wings. She is absolutely perfect, and she is IC's friend.

IC unlocks the cage, and Char steps out of it for the first time in over a year. With a giant-sized smile revealing Char's golden teeth, she spreads her wings as gold dust sails through the air. Char jumps over to the open window as the breeze from the kingdom rejuvenates her once-confined wings.

Looking back at IC, she asks, "Well, friend, you ready to save some warriors?"

IC instantly smiles as she jumps on Char's back. The pair step from the window's ledge and find themselves in a freefall. Faster and faster, the cobblestone street is approaching.

IC yells, "You can fly, right?"

"I used to be able to. Here goes nothing."

Char spreads her wings as far as she can, and both close their eyes, IC holding on as tightly as she can. Fearing they are about to hit the street, Char extends her wings a bit more, making them catch the wind. This quick-thinking maneuver keeps them just inches from the road's surface. They open their eyes and see they're soaring through the crowded kingdom streets. Char begins dodging in and out of the walking Shadows before she finally gains control and shoots straight up above the massive crowd. Once they are high enough, Char straightens out, and they soar over the kingdom, looking at all of its beauty.

"I really didn't think we were going to make it," IC confesses.

"That makes two of us."

They both take a deep breath, and the kingdom below gets smaller as they fly off into the Horizon.

Meanwhile, under the kingdom, Lakin follows the kings through a maze of tunnels. Every tunnel and turn looks like the one before it. Lakin thinks if kings didn't know the way, she'd be lost down there forever.

Finally, the tunnels come to an end, and they step into a huge room filled with luxuries galore. Food and drinks fill the tables; there are lavish beds and heated pools. Each bed holds a fresh set of clothes. The kings immediately sit at the tables and feast till they can't move. Lakin picks at her food as she thinks, *Besides the kings, I'm the only one who knows of this place. Why would they let a common person enter this?*

Lakin can't believe that there is a hidden oasis under the kingdom. She is shocked and awed to see how handsome the kings are once they cleaned up.

The king of spades speaks as he sits in the pool of heated water. "My child, go fetch your warriors and bring them to us. Let them eat, sleep, and soak till their hearts are full. We must prepare for war and need them at their best."

The king of clubs says, "I'll lead you out of here till the door. Then you will be on your own till the meeting of the warriors." Lakin follows the king to the door, and he says, "Remember, three to the left, then three to the right. Then stand and dance with all your might. Each one must perform this task to enter. If done wrong, the path will take your light. We will part ways here. But soon, we'll meet again. May your travels be safe and steady."

The secret door closes, leaving her standing alone in an unfamiliar place. Lakin quickly looks around to see if anyone has spotted her, then pulls her hood up and walks into the woods.

CHAPTER 33

"Every great plan should have a what-if." - Kannon

With the cannon charged and ready to go, Kannon looks to everyone for a thumbs up. Dayne nods as she draws The Releaser out. Hunter smiles as his weapons are out way ahead of time. Spin Doll gives a thumbs up, and Bug begins to flicker. Dak runs around back to assist Spin Doll while waving his thumb in the air. Hoss stands patiently, waiting for cleanup duty, and Colt patrols the perimeter. Everyone checks in and is ready to go.

Kannon smirks. "Well, I guess I'll knock." He fires a shot into the front of the factory, leaving a gaping hole where the door once stood.

Hunter and Dayne rush in first, slashing and shooting as Dak and Spin Doll swing wildly through the back. Kannon and Bug follow right behind Hunter and Dayne. They all rush to the center of the factory, bringing them right up to the hole with not one shadow there to release. A painted sign stands there. Everyone surrounds the sign.

"Where the hell are they?" Kannon yells.

Dayne reads the sign. "Our turn."

Bug looks at Kannon. "What does that mean? 'Our turn.'"

Instantly, on his last word, Shadows charge the factory from every possible entrance. Hundreds of them pour in and begin attacking the warriors. Shadows are even crawling out of the hole. The warriors fight valiantly with everything they have as a sea of never-ending Shadows continues to file in. After an hour of swinging and shooting, the warriors are getting exhausted, trying to keep the Shadows from reaching them. Surrounded and bloody, the shadow numbers begin to push them back towards the hole.

With their backs to the hole and Shadows still entering the factory, things look very bleak for the warriors. They free so many Shadows that the floor becomes slippery from all the blue goo, making it harder for the warriors to keep their footing on the edge of the slippery hole. The goo pours into the hole and runs past the warriors, turning it into a pool of goo.

Spin Doll stops spinning to catch her breath and has to reposition her feet to keep from falling into the pool of goo. That little hesitation allows one of the Shadows to slip a rope around her head. More Shadows grab the rope, pulling her into the sea of Shadows and out of sight. None of the other warriors see what is happening as they are dealing with their own battles.

Bug is the first to lose his footing and plunges into the goo. Kannon reaches to try and catch him but soon follows after being struck from behind. Kannon makes a much larger splash than Bug did. When he comes up for air, he can't see a thing because it is even darker in the hole. Not being able to swim, Bug frantically tries not to sink. Kannon pulls him to the wall, and Bug grips the wall like a fly stuck in a spider's web.

Kannon tries to see the battle above, but the darkness and goo make it impossible to see. Soon, the overwhelming number of Shadows force the remaining warriors into the pool of goo. One after the other, they splash into it, clinging to the wall to avoid the projectiles being thrown at them from above.

Kannon begins to shoot into the wall, trying to make a hole in order to protect them from the shadow's weapons. Bug loses his grip and plunges back into the middle, where it is the most dangerous. Dak quickly pulls him to safety under the newly formed ledge Kannon made. Now, with them all under the edges and out of harm's way, it has become a waiting game. The Shadows stand around the top of the hole, pacing back and forth, stalking their prey. Unable to see the warriors from any side, patience grows thin in the Shadows. Dayne, Kannon, and Dak huddle together, knowing what fate will come to them. Hunter tries to talk to Bug, but Bug does not pay any mind to him, only hugging the wall with every muscle in his little body.

One of the Shadows yells down the hole, "Hey, warriors, you know this is the end of the line. We win, and you lose. Someone must be first to go. It would make it easier for the first one who is freed. They won't have to watch their friends be freed in front of them. C'mon, Dayne, show the men that you're the only one down there with balls."

They hear the Shadows laughing above them. After a few minutes, the shadow yells, "I'll tell you what: since we're such nice guys, how about you give us King Dak, and we'll let the rest of you go? What do you say? That sounds like a pretty fair deal to me. I'll give you a few minutes to think it over." After a minute or so, the shadow once again yells down the hole, "Well, you ready to take my offer?"

Kannon instantly yells back, "We're good. But why don't you jump in and join us? The water is nice and warm."

"I'm going to have to pass on that, being I didn't bring my bathing suit and all. I'll probably just wait here for y'all. Go ahead, enjoy your last swim."

While they sit there in a stalemate, the goo seeps into the ground. It isn't too long before the warriors can stand on the hole's floor. Hunter pulls Bug from the wall to show him he can now stand. Even though Bug's feet are now on the ground, he still grasps the wall. One of the Shadows leans over the hole, trying to see them, as Kannon shoots randomly, not looking up the hole, just missing the shadow and sending a message that they aren't about to give up.

"Well, we've waited long enough. I've been thinking, and a few of us will take you up on that offer to join you."

The Shadows begin to drop into the hole, but the warriors free them before they hit the bottom. This, in return, begins causing the hole to fill up with goo again.

Hunter yells, "They'll never stop till they drown us all!"

Kannon shoots toward the hole to make it wider and deeper and buy them some more time. Dayne makes him stop, fearing one of them will get hurt by the debris.

Kannon stops and looks desperately at Dayne. "I'm not losing my family again."

Dayne hugs him, trying to calm him down so he doesn't do anything stupid.

Suddenly, the ground begins to shake. All the warriors turn to Kannon with a *"What did you do?"* look. The Shadows take off, running in every direction to escape the factory, leaving the hole unguarded. Warriors come out from under their ledges and stare up the hole, trying to figure out what is happening above them.

Suddenly, two massive dark figures quickly pass over the hole, eclipsing any light they have. The noise is so loud that it sounds like a thunderstorm is coming from the factory. Something or some *things* are destroying the factory. They hear walls coming down, and pieces from above fall into the hole.

Then, from nowhere, a rope drops into the hole. Colt's head pops over the edge, and she yells, "Hurry while they're at the other end of the factory! We don't have much time!"

The warriors climb out of the hole, one after the other, starting with Dak. Once they are out, they realize they have front-row seats for the greatest heavyweight match ever. They watch Hoss and Skulk throw haymakers at each other, trying to extinguish each other's light. Hoss tackles Skulk into walls, taking out support beams. Both monsters are ripped open, and blood and goo cover their bodies. The warriors want to help Hoss, but they can't take a chance on striking him by accident. They all run out of the tumbling factory before it comes down, leaving the giants to fend for themselves.

Everyone leaves the dangers of the collapsing factory and steps into the waiting arms of the shadow armies. The battle continues like it never stopped; only now, the warriors aren't surrounded, and they can actually see what they are shooting and swinging at. Being so outnumbered by the Shadows, the warriors can't help Hoss with his fight, but eventually, they start to balance the battle out.

They are about to gain the upper hand when another member of the Horde suddenly comes out of the woods. Dice emerges from the woods so quickly that Colt can't react quickly enough to avoid her. The impact is so fast and hard that it shears Colt's left leg off from the kneecap down. Dice continues into the factory as if she never knew it had happened.

Colt falls to the ground, screaming in pain, and reaches for her leg that isn't there anymore. Bug is the first one to reach her. He tries to stop the bleeding while still swinging at the Shadows. Dak fights his way to her as well, trying to fend off the Shadows while Bug ties her leg off to try and stop the bleeding. Using his hoodie, Bug tightens it with every bit of strength he can muster. With the blood slowed but not completely stopped, Bug tries to locate Colt's leg, slowly working his way back to the factory entrance that Dice had made when it entered the building. Bug peeks into the factory to find Dice staring back at him. Bug freezes in place, and Dice's eyes begin to spin. When Dice's eyes finish spinning, they stop on a three and a six. She quickly turns back, leaving Bug. Dice returns to the monster's battle and joins in helping Skulk defeat Hoss.

Kannon and Hunter fear the worst for Hoss as they try to work their way back to Bug and the entrance to the factory. When they finally approach the entrance, they can see Skulk on top of Hoss as Dice continues putting gash after gash into Hoss's body with her fangs. Hunter fights off the Shadows while Kannon unloads shot after shot into the direction of the monsters. More of the factory begins to crumble as some of Kannon's shots hit their mark. Now, the factory is barely held up, as most of the support beams are weakened by the monsters. The far end of the factory has already crashed to the ground, leaving the front to soon follow it.

A loud screech is heard by everyone from the sky above. It is like nothing the warriors have ever heard before. Dice instantly slithers out of a hole in the back of the factory as Shadows disperse quickly. It is every shadow for themselves. All the warriors, but Colt and Bug, search the sky for the sound but see nothing but clouds. They wonder what could put that kind of fear into their evil enemies.

Hunter asks Kannon, "What more can these Jokers throw at us?"

"I don't think that's one of theirs."

Finally, the factory tumbles down, and Hunter sees Skulk and Hoss thrown into the hole. The factory drops on top of them, leaving a cloud of dust behind. Hunter watches the hole intensely as he sees Hoss's big hand reach out and grab the ridge of the hole. Slowly, his hand creeps back into the hole. Hunter tries to make his way to his fallen friend, but too much debris is in his way. Knowing how much his friend needs him and not being able to reach him destroys Hunter, watching two light orbs rise from the wreckage and smoke and float up in the air. They all join in watching the orbs through Colt's screams and know this is a battle they lost in more ways than one.

Dayne runs to Colt's side. Colt is now in shock, still feeling for her leg. They retie her leg to stop the bleeding for now. Dayne holds Colt's head on her lap and strokes her hair while Dak begins to search for the leg. Bug still stands frozen in fear from his meeting with Dice. Kannon limps to Bug as he tries to shake some sense back into him, getting him to come back to reality.

Hunter sniffs the air and asks, "What's that awful smell?" Kannon points towards Bug, and Hunter covers his nose. "Dude, did you shit your pants again? Go over in those trees and clean yourself off; you're a grown-ass man."

Bug puts his head down and walks over behind the trees. Mim climbs out of the tree, holding her nose as well. "Has anyone seen Cali? I don't see her anywhere."

None of the warriors knew her whereabouts, as they had lost sight of her during the fight. They wait for Bug to return to check with him, but he hasn't seen her. Fearing they have lost Spin Doll, the warriors feel beaten even more than they ever have.

CHAPTER 34

"Watch out for the wolf wearing the sheep's clothing." - Lakin

After stumbling through the unfamiliar dark forest, Lakin finally recognizes an area she knows. Now that she is on the right track, her priority is to find her brother and then the rest of the group. She can't wait to tell them about the kings and the secret entrance. The last thing she remembers is that Colt and Mim were heading for the barn. So that's where Lakin plans to look first. She figures if they aren't at the barn when she gets there, she will head for the factory next. She is nervous since Fat Jack's cave is near, and she will have to cross paths with it.

While walking down the old, broken, paved road, Lakin can hear several voices approaching her. She quickly leaves the roadside and hides behind a small group of trees. Praying it is her brother and the warriors, she quickly learns it is not. Quietly, she watches as twenty or so Shadows march by carrying something in a sack on their shoulders. They stop directly in front of her and place what they carry in the middle of the road. It sounds heavy, and it makes a thud when they drop it. The Shadows gather around it, making it hard for Lakin to see what the 'something' is. Quietly as she can, she moves to higher ground for a better view. Her new spot makes it much easier to see what they have dropped. She watches as the Shadows untie and stand a figure up.

To her surprise, it is Spin Doll. She watches as Spin Doll brushes herself off and throws the ropes at the Shadows, yelling, "You fools! Why did you bring me here? The plan was working perfectly, and you idiots screwed it all up!"

The Shadows begin helping her brush off as they plead, "My lady, your brothers feared for your safety. Especially with all that fighting going on at the barn and the factory. If we had let anything happen to you, it would have been our lights for sure."

Spin Doll angrily says, "They all believed I was the real Spin Doll. What fools! Even that stupid little creature that rides on her shoulder thought I was the real thing." Spin Doll begins to stomp around, still complaining. "Oh yeah, whichever one of you put that rope around my neck, be prepared to speak to my brothers. You fools could've marked my beautiful face."

The Shadows are nervous and point to each other in blame.

Lakin can't believe she is listening to Spin Doll talk. She thinks *That is not the kind of voice I pictured Spin Doll to have.* Then, to her surprise, Spin Doll begins to change, morphing into another lady. This lady is hideous and downright ugly, so unlike Spin Doll.

One of the Shadows says, "Cozzex, you look even better in your true form."

Cozzex scowls and grumbles, "Those fool warriors never saw me switch spots with the real Spin Doll in the barn. I almost blew my cover when I spoke after cutting that stupid cage down. My only concern at that time was avoiding the witch's tongue while I was up there. But my brothers must have been lying since I've seen nothing of the sort—just an empty hook."

One of the Shadows meekly adds, "Don't worry about the real Spin Doll; the Jokers returned their pet back to her cage. The only difference is this time she's at the top of one of the towers and not in the stupid old barn. I'd like to see them try and rescue her now."

Cozzex, still wiping her face off, replies, "Good. She's

back, just hanging around again. I truly hope my brothers punish her for escaping. She *so* deserves it. Now, run ahead, fix my room, and tell my brothers I'm well and will see them soon. Also, tell them that I loathe them with all my heart."

The Shadows nod, turn, and march ahead, leaving Cozzex standing alone on the road.

Lakin watches as Cozzex stands there as if she is pondering something or waiting for someone, perhaps. Eventually, she says into the air, "I know you were watching. Did you like the performance? It wasn't my best. But under the circumstances, it was still a solid performance, nonetheless."

Lakin worries that Cozzex knows she is there and is speaking to her. Just as Lakin is about to speak, a voice answers Cozzex.

"Bravo, bravo. You could have won an award for that performance. My, how you shine, my little star." Then Fat Jack steps out from a wide tree, clapping his hands.

Lakin stands frozen in place with fear.

"What's wrong with your arm, boo bear?" Cozzex asks as she touches Fat Jack's injured arm.

"One of those warriors shot me twice; can you believe that?" Fat Jack complains.

"I told you before you shouldn't play with your food," Cozzex scolds him as a mother would to her child.

Fat Jack rubs his injured arm, still complaining, though Cozzex moves on to the next topic. "What about the kings? Are they history yet? How'd they taste? The Horizon is in desperate need of a queen's touch. Once we release all the warriors, the kings, and my piece-of-shit brothers, there will be no one left to stop me. I mean us."

Fat Jack begins to laugh. "I can't believe how gullible your brothers are. They are practically handing you the Horizon, and the whole time thinking you were helping them. While, in reality, you were their biggest threat."

Cozzex rubs her finger down Fat Jack's cheek, whispering, "Remember our plan. You promised to save my brothers for last so I can watch you eat them personally. I'd love to hear their final screams as they beg me to make you release them." Cozzex holds out her arm. "Look, I'm getting goosebumps just thinking about it!"

Fat Jack leans in toward Cozzex, hoping for a kiss. She backs away and messes his hair playfully, then she turns and walks in the direction of the Shadows. Fat Jack, still smitten with love, doesn't realize Cozzex is playing with him. While Cozzex walks out of sight, she blows him a kiss and says, "Till we meet again, boo bear."

Fat Jack waves back with hearts in his eyes. A strange smell enters the air, and he begins sniffing, smelling something familiar. He looks around, hoping to identify the smell but finds nothing. Confused, he turns and heads back to his cave. Lakin waits for the coast to be clear, then takes off running to find her friends and explain Cozzex to them.

With the factory destroyed and the Shadows running, the warriors begin to investigate their injuries and build an extremely hot fire to staunch the serious wounds they received from the battle. Once the metal in the fire is hot enough, they begin to cauterize the wounds. Dak volunteers to be the first test dummy. They quickly work to get his back mended as he bites down on a stick he found on the ground. A few seconds seem like forever as the pain makes him bite the stick in half. Once Dak's back is remedied, Kannon places the metal back into the fire in preparation for the next Warrior.

Hunter and Dayne manage to sew up their own wounds to avoid the hot iron, thus leaving Colt the only one left to face the hot iron. The men know all four will have to hold Colt down while Dayne applies the hot metal. At first, Colt doesn't put up much of a fight. But, as soon as the hot metal touches her open wound, the sound and smell of flesh mending can be heard. It is all the men can do to hold her down. Who would've thought a tiny girl like her could be so strong?

Colt's screams ring through the forest, reaching the walls of the kingdom and alerting Lakin to their whereabouts. Dayne has only one issue with the procedure: when the hot metal briefly touches Colt's skin, ripping the wound open, only to be fixed again.

Once the horrific procedure is complete, Colt doesn't speak. She simply lies there, avoiding eye contact with everyone. Now that everyone has mended and eaten until they are full, it is time to get some rest and get their minds right.

Dak and Bug are the first to fall asleep, with Dayne soon to follow. Hunter and Kannon are too overtired to sleep. Worrying about Colt, they sit, poking the fire with sticks.

Hunter speaks low enough for only Kannon to hear. "I am worried about Colt. She hasn't said a word since the battle. She wouldn't eat or even acknowledge we were here. It's like she's in her own little world."

Kannon pokes the ash and sends a few sparks into the air. "Yeah, she doesn't look right. Running is all she loved, and now they've taken that away from her. I guess if they can't release us, they'll still try to break us."

Both men stoke the fire and join Colt, staring at the empty sky. Kannon finally gives in and falls asleep next to Dayne.

Still unable to sleep, Hunter sits and stares into the dancing flames, wondering how they can help Colt. His first thought is that the kings can somehow help the situation once they reach the kingdom. Maybe they can somehow give her a new leg. He pokes the fire again, making the sparks dance.

Suddenly, he hears a voice behind him. Hunter jumps and quickly pulls out his pool stick.

"Hope there's a spot open by that fire for me." Then Lakin steps out from the darkness.

Hunter is so delighted to see his sister that he throws his pool stick down and tackles her, knocking them both to the ground. When he finally stops hugging her and they make it back to their feet, Hunter asks, "Are you ok? Do you need something to eat? Sit here and I'll get you some food; we just put it away so it should still be warm."

Laken happily replies, "I definitely could use some food unless you cooked it. If so, I'll pass." She laughs as she quickly takes the food from his hands and wolfs it down.

They talk for a few hours until it is time for the sun to wake up. In a short time, Hunter informs her of everything, including the factory battle. He explains how they lost Cam to an awful disease that followed him to the Horizon, how Dillo lost his light due to his fortitude and love for his friends, how Hoss gave up his own light to release the light of our enemies, Skulk, and the Beast. Then, he explains how Spin Doll's fate is unknown to them.

Saddened by what she had just heard, Lakin tells of her path back to them and how the kings await their return.

Colt doesn't sleep the entire night; she just lies there looking at the empty sky and listening to the two, acting like they are at a sleepover.

At the first sight of daylight, when the warriors wake, Hunter introduces his sister to each Warrior. After all the hugging and welcoming is over, they waste no time picking up camp and heading out to the kingdom, going in the direction Lakin had told them the kings were waiting. To help keep up with the rest of the group, Dak finds an old wheelbarrow ideal for transporting Colt. Once Colt is settled in the makeshift stretcher, they head toward the witch's destroyed house to locate the path north to the kingdom. They walk for quite some time, with little to no conversation.

Kannon can't stand the silence, so he finally says, "You know, back in my world, I thought I was winning in life the whole time but ended up losing everything. Now I'm here in the Horizon with nothing but have been given another chance to win back everything I thought I had."

Bug looks at him in disgust. "We all gave up everything in our past worlds. I'm tired of losing. From now on, if I'm going out, I'm going out on top! We have to be winners. Because we owe it to Dillo, Cam, and Hoss—the ones who gave up their lights for us to have a shot of going out winners."

Hunter smiles. "We deserve to have our name in lights. The kings or not, I'm beating the Jokers and replacing the stars."

Bug says he feels Spin Doll is still alive because he can feel it in his bones. Hearing Spin Doll's name come out of Bug's mouth reminds Lakin of what she witnessed.

Lakin walks up beside Bug and says, "You know the Spin Doll that was just taken from the factory battle? That wasn't the real Spin Doll."

Bug stops walking and stares at Lakin. "How can that not be the real Spin Doll?"

Everyone gathers around Lakin as she explains what she witnessed. Bug is beside himself. How could he have let them take her again after he had made a promise to her that she'd never be put in a cage? He starts running toward the kingdom, leaving the others far behind. They chase after him, knowing the kind of trouble he can get into if left by himself. This does not amuse Dak since he can't keep up while pushing Colt in the wheelbarrow.

CHAPTER 35

"Everything is not always what it first appears to be." - Bug

Bug isn't slowing down as he runs through the woods, passing tree after tree. It takes Kannon all he can do to catch up to Bug, and once he does, he tackles him as a means to stop this mad fit Bug is in.

"Kannon, get out of my way! I'm not playing with you. I'm serious. Let me go! I've had all I can take."

Kannon holds tight, trying to reason with him. "Bug, stop! Wait for the others; we need to stay together."

Bug fights to try and get out of Kannon's hold. "I need to help Spin Doll! I promised her no more cages. What kind of man am I if I can't keep my word? It's the only thing I have left. You have Dayne and Dak, Hunter has Lakin, and Colts is a zombie. Where does that leave me? Shit, even Mim has IC."

Kannon still hasn't released Bug even after his plea. "Bug, I'm not letting you go off and get hurt or, even worse, lose your light because you're not thinking clearly. How will you help Spin Doll by losing your light?"

Bug knows Kannon is right, but he still can't help continuing to plead as tears fill his eyes. "Kannon, I need to go. They put her in a cage again. How could I not tell that it wasn't her? You have to let me go! It's my job to protect her like it's yours to protect Dayne. She's my everything!"

Kannon releases Bug, knowing that he wouldn't stop if it were Dayne in the cage. For once, Kannon thinks Bug is right. Once released, Bug begins to walk away.

Kannon tries to reason with him once more. "I know you will save her, but I'm asking you as a friend. Please wait for the rest of the group. Then we will all go together and save her. I promise you."

Bug stops for a second until Kannon finishes speaking, then he walks away.

Kannon quickly pulls the little wooden box out of his pocket and opens it. Faintly hearing a melody from the box, Bug stops and turns to Kannon.

Bug asks, "What is that, and why do you have it?"

Kannon walks up to Bug and hands him the little wooden box. "The old guy, Jim. The one that I often talked with. He gave this to me and said that when I saw Spin Doll, I should give this to her. He also said that she would know immediately what it was. Then he explained that he was her grandpa and followed her there. Supposedly, whenever she hears this little box play, she dances in circles."

Bug holds the box in his hands, listening as it plays.

Kannon stands silently, letting Bug inspect the box.

Bug, without taking his eyes off the box, asks, "If you had this the whole time, why are you just now telling me about it?"

Before Kannon can come up with a good excuse, he notices over Bug's shoulder, further back in the woods, a bench sits covered in vines and old leaves like it is camouflaged. Kannon tells Bug to hold onto the box; it is now his responsibility to get it to Spin Doll. He then makes Bug promise to stay and wait for the group while he checks out the almost-hidden bench.

Not completely happy with the request, Bug agrees as Kannon heads toward the bench. Kannon notices that it looks similar to Jim's bench, the only difference being it looks dirty and unkempt—totally opposite of Jim's well-maintained bench. Kannon clears the bench of leaves, then wipes off the spot and sits. Patiently, he awaits Jim's appearance.

After over ten minutes of waiting, Kannon mumbles, "This must not be one of Jim's benches. Not with it being dirty and all. I don't think he'd survive seeing this dirty of a bench."

Kannon decides to leave since the only thing happening is wasting time. He stands up and hears a voice behind him.

"Leaving so soon? I haven't even had a chance to introduce myself. The name's Jack, but my friends call me Fat Jack."

Kannon turns to see a man extending his hand to shake. Kannon, startled, yells, "You're not Jim! Where's Jim?"

Jack tries to push Jim's little boot off the bench without Kannon seeing it. Kannon witnesses the boot falling to the ground and slides away from Jack.

"Name is Jack, not Jim." Jack lets out a large burp, then pounds his chest with his fist. "Jim's a little disposed at the moment. Is there anything I might be able to help you with?"

Kannon, worried about his friend, yells, "If you touched one little hair on Jim's little head, I'll—"

"You'll what? You, sir, won't do shit but sit there and shut your mouth while I talk. Do I make myself clear?" Jack smiles, revealing his metal teeth.

Kannon feels a little intimidated now. "So talk, Big man. I'm all ears."

Jack pauses for a moment, then slides closely to Kannon and he cunningly says, "I only want what's truly mine. Nothing more. Nothing less." He pauses to make sure Kannon is hearing him. "See, that little morsel of a meatball, Jim, suggested you might know the location of my stolen key. Now, you give me the key, and I'll let bygones be bygones, and we'll both be on our merry little way. What do you say, friend?"

While Jack is speaking, Kannon tries desperately to change his arm into his cannon, but since this is a safe zone, weapons aren't allowed. Instead, he nervously says, "I don't have your key, but I may know who does."

Jack growls, "If you're trying to pull one over on old Jack here, don't, or I'll be having meatball for dinner. Oh, how I love Italian food." Jack nudges playfully. "But it doesn't love me. If you know what I mean."

Kannon doesn't laugh at Jack's joke. "I'll go see if my friend has the key. I'm pretty sure he does, as we were talking about it earlier."

Jack slides closer to Kannon so now their legs are touching. He leans over and whispers, "Let's say thirty minutes, my place. Oh, and bring your friends. It will be like a party. I do hope there'll be food there, because it isn't a party without food."

For the sake of Jim, Kannon has no other choice but to agree to the meeting. Now that Jack has gotten his way and is going to get his key back, he quickly vanishes, leaving Kannon sitting alone on the bench with Jim's little boot, which he shoves in his pocket. Then he stands and heads back toward Bug to explain the meeting they have with Fat Jack in a half hour.

Kannon returns from the unexpected meeting to see Bug standing with the rest of the group.

"Took you long enough. What, did you fall in?" Bug jokes.

Nobody laughs, and Kannon calls the group together to explain his encounter with Fat Jack and how they must meet with him soon to save his friend, Jim. He pulls Jim's boot from his pocket to back up his story.

"Why do we care about this old guy?" Bug quips. "You know, we kind of have our own problems. Maybe we should deal with our own dust-covered demons and focus on getting Spin Doll back first."

Kannon doesn't disagree with Bug but reminds him that that Jim is Spin Doll's grandpa and he is only in the Horizon to find his granddaughter. Bug changes his tune after hearing how important Jim is to Spin Doll.

After a quick vote, the group agrees to head for the cave to rescue Jim. Hunter is the only one concerned.

"Are we really going to risk going to Jack's cave for a guy who isn't even supposed to be here? You know it's going to be a trap. We can't afford to lose anyone else."

Kannon quickly responds, "It's definitely going to be a trap. So, if none of you want to risk it, I can go alone. If you guys can get Colt and yourselves to the kings, I'll stay and deal with Jack myself. After I get Jim, we'll meet up at the kingdom."

The group is not 100% convinced that Kannon should go alone, so they agree that Dak, Dayne, Lakin, and Mimic will take Colt to the kingdom. Hunter and Bug will go with Kannon if it *is* a trap. The two groups split in different directions, Dak leading his north to the kingdom and Kannon and the other two west toward Jack's cave.

It isn't long before the three men reach the entrance to Jack's cave. They play even or odds to figure out who will knock on Jack's door. Per usual, Bug loses. Kannon and Hunter stand behind Bug, their weapons drawn, fearing the worst.

Bug knocks hard, then runs behind Kannon and Hunter. Standing quietly, they hear footsteps approaching. The door swings open, revealing Fat Jack wearing an apron that reads 'Kiss the Cook.' Upon greeting the men, Jack wipes his hands on a towel, smiles, and displays his metal teeth.

"I'm disappointed. Only you three? It's a shame the rest couldn't make it. I guess that means more food for us. The cookies will be done in no time. But, while we wait, where's my key?"

With a fully charged arm, Kannon answers, "I told you before when you asked, I don't have any key."

Jack's face quickly loses its smile. "We had a deal."

Kannon barks, "Where's Jim? Wasn't that your part of the deal?"

"What's wrong with our youth today? None of them can commit. It's like their words mean nothing to them. Sorry, there is not a participation trophy for life. If you make a deal, stick to it. It's just that simple." Jack turns and looks at Hunter, then speaks directly to him. "Just like your bitch of a sister. You two are full of lies. Maybe it's just a family thing. Do you all just sit around at family reunions, lying to each other?"

Hunter smiles at Jack while adjusting his pool stick. "Maybe we just don't make deals with trash. Answer the man's question. Where is Jim?"

Jack rubs his stomach and answers, "Oh, he's here with us."

Hunter's eyes widen as he mumbles, "I think it's time to finish what I started."

Jack lowers his tone, saying, "I'm sure you'll find things a bit different this time." He looks to the left, and Hunter's eyes follow. With Hunter distracted, Jack takes his chance and lunges at him, pushing him into the tree behind him and making him drop his pool stick.

Kannon fires an unaimed shot at Jack, missing him and clearing a new path through the woods. Bug swings his bat and connects with Jack from behind, sending the fat man reeling a few steps. Jack quickly shrugs it off and throws Bug into Kannon, sending them both to the ground. Jack then spins back around, grabs a still-stunned Hunter by the neck, and lifts him into the air above his mouth. Jack's head flips back into eating mode as he slowly draws Hunter to devour him. Hunter struggles to get free, but Jack's grip is too strong.

Kannon and Bug tried to gather themselves. Bug quickly takes another swing, which bounces off Jack. Kannon charges his arm while Hunter kicks with everything he's got. Before Kannon can get a shot off, a loud thud is heard behind the scuffle.

Everyone stops and turns to see what made such a loud thud. Standing in front of them is a larger-than-life dragon. Jack's face forms back to normal as he drops Hunter and immediately begins to back up. Jack's trembling voice shouts, "Char! You're supposed to be locked in a cage at the top of the tower. Gentlemen, we'll have to adjourn our meeting to a later date." Jack turns as quickly as he can and runs into the woods.

The dragon draws her head back and releases a stream of fire into the woods, disintegrating everything in its path. Bug, Hunter, and Kannon sprint into the woods in the opposite direction. They run through the woods, ducking and dodging trees and bushes, all the while hearing loud footsteps gaining on them from behind. Closer and closer, the steps thud, and the sprinting men realize they are losing ground.

The tired men round a blind corner, trying to lose her, but immediately stop when they realize they're at the end of a path. Standing on the edge, they look down over the cliff. What looks to be too much of a drop for them to possibly survive, the men contemplate jumping as the footsteps and sound of breaking trees grow closer and closer. They huddle together, still debating whether to jump, when the footsteps suddenly stop, and it is quiet again.

Bug whispers, "What happened? I don't hear anything. Did it leave?"

No one answers, but both begin to charge their weapons. Bug is still trying to ask questions but Kannon places a finger up to Bug's mouth to shut him up. He whispers, "Someone needs to take a look around the corner and see if it's still there."

Both men shake their heads, but at the same time, Kannon and Hunter push Bug out in front of them. Bug looks back at them disgustedly, shaking his head and giving them both middle fingers. The guys point their weapons toward Bug and gesture for him to peek around the corner.

Bug whispers, "How about you both suck a dick. I'm too young to be eaten. I have like almost a girlfriend."

Bug's pleas are ignored as the others continue to gesture for Bug to look. Knowing they will make him do it, Bug turns to face his demise.

Slowly, Bug looks around the corner, his hands trembling and his teeth chattering louder than if he were talking. He sees nothing and happily turns back to give the guys a thumbs up, then jokingly flexes as if he had scared the dragon away. Slowly, unknown to Bug, the dragon's head peeks around the corner and hovers above Bug. Kannon and Hunter begin to point behind Bug, trying to warn their friend, but Bug thinks they're pointing at his awesome celebration and continues to pose.

Suddenly, the dragon blows a puff of smoke that engulfs Bug. Bug walks out of the smoke, coughing and waving his arms and attempting to clear the smoke. His eyes grow big as he realizes where the smoke came from. Refusing to turn around and see for himself, Bug takes off running for the cliff. Kannon and Hunter catch him before he can jump, saving him from what could be a worse fate. They cowardly huddle together as they await their fate in the dragon's hands. The dragon draws her head back while taking a deep breath, and Bug drops to his knees and begins to beg for his life. Hunter closes his eyes and braces for the worst while Kannon fires a shot that bounces off the dragon's scales, having no effect.

Bug mumbles to Kannon, "You know, for a big guy with a big gun, you're worthless."

The dragon leans forward and releases a smoke ring that circles the trembling men. Their eyes are closed when the smoke ring hits them, but Bug screams a high-pitched scream like a girl. "Oh, it burns, it burns so bad!"

Kannon and Hunter both stare at Bug, not believing that sound could come from a real person. They look up at the smiling dragon and are surprised as they see Mim pop up from behind the dragon's head.

Hunter, trying not to startle the dragon, asks as quietly as possible, "Mim, what are you doing on this D-R-A-G-O-N?"

IC laughs and answers, "I'm not Mim. Mim is my sister. My name is IC; pleased to meet you."

Kannon gives a little wave. "Ok, IC, what are you doing on the back of this D-R-A-G-O-N?"

IC is still giggling as she says, "Riding her, silly. Her name is Char, and she can spell."

Char whispers, "My name is Char, and I'm a D-R-A-G-O-N. Pleased to eat you–I mean *meet* you."

Both girls begin to laugh, and Bug is still unsure what the hell is going on since he still has his eyes closed and is begging on his knees.

Kannon and Hunter drift over toward IC and Char without Bug noticing. They point at Bug, trying to direct Char into screeching at the groveling man. Char loads up and screeches toward Bug with all she has. They all watch and laugh as Bug pisses himself.

Hunter yells, "You're so nasty!"

Everyone laughs again as Bug finally opens his eyes. Now knowing he is the butt of their joke, Bug stomps off angrily to clean his pants. While Bug is away, the four take the time to get acquainted.

Once Bug returns, smelling much better than when he left, Char introduces herself to him and asks if they'd like a lift to the kingdom.

Looking like he won the lottery, Kannon states, "You want us to ride on your back?"

Hunter squeals like a teenager. "O-M-G, this is friggin' awesome; best day ever!"

Char chuckles and directs everyone to climb on and sit behind IC. Hunter climbs up first and lowers his hand to Bug while Kannon boosts Bug up from below. Kannon is the last to be seated making sure Bug sits between him and Hunter. With a quick flap of her wings, Char lifts off into the air, adjusting to the added weight and trying to get higher. The men's ridiculous conversation amuses her.

Kannon says, "Why do you still smell like piss?"

Bug sarcastically answers, "Ah, I don't. Hunter does. Also, we did just have a 5-ton dragon chasing us."

"At least you didn't shit your pants again," Hunter adds.

Bug yells, "Oh, like you've never shit your pants before!."

Kannon looks at Hunter for his answer. Hunter looks back at them and shouts, "What? No, I have never shit my pants."

Kannon tells Bug, "Don't touch me with those pissy hands. Matter of fact, don't touch anything."

Hunter leans toward Char, trying to get further away from Bug, and apologizes for Bug having to ride on her. He turns to Bug, warning, "If you touch me with those nasty hands, I'll throw you off the dragon."

"Relax. I wiped them off on a big leaf." Bug puts his hand on Hunter's shoulder, wipes it down his back, and jokes, "Now they're clean."

Char cannot believe the stupid conversation she is listening to as she finally gains the height she needs to fly.

Bug yells to Char, "Hey, dragon, does this flight come with a meal?"

Char quickly drops and then rises, making the men lose their stomachs.

"No thanks. I'm not hungry anymore."

Hunter adds, "I wouldn't do that again. You never know when he's going to shit."

Bug wipes his other hand down Hunter's back as Char flies off into the Horizon.

CHAPTER 36

"Even the most unexpected wishes sometimes get granted."
- Dak

The men are amazed at the view of the Horizon and all the places they've seen. They never know how far the Horizon reaches. They fly over the barn and the factory. When crossing the factory, Kannon thinks just for a second that he sees part of the factory roof move. But then his attention focuses more on the beautiful landscape. Bug points as they fly over Dayne's house and their old cabin. Kannon yells, "There's our campsite and the farm Dak and I got the eggs from." They all go quiet as they notice a part of Dillo's shell lying in the field, making them think of their friend. With the men not expecting it, Char makes a hard right, making Bug lose his grip and fall. Hunter and Kannon are quick enough to catch him and secure Bug back in his seat. IC looks at the smiling faces, knowing this is one of the few rewards the warriors will receive. With the wind blowing through their hair, just for one moment, they are carefree. Char makes one more pass around before heading for the kingdom.

Kannon points and yells, "That's our group down there!"

Bug joins in. "There are Dak and Dayne.!"

Hunter quickly asks Char to land by them if she can. She abruptly lands in a small clearing, and the men quickly jump down and run to the rest of their group.

Kannon reaches Dayne and spins her around in his arms. "Look, Babe, we have a dragon!"

Once Kannon's excitement settles, he quickly introduces everyone to Char.

Hunter adds, "Hey, Mim! We have something for you as well."

"What could you have that I could possibly want?"

Then Hunter points at Char's head. They all look as IC pops her head up. Mim can't make it to her sister quickly enough. They embrace as if they haven't seen each other in years. Each one speaks a hundred words a minute.

After the greetings and reunion, the group has a quick discussion of what is next. They agree it's best if Char takes Colt, Mimic, and Lakin to the kings. When all are safely loaded, Char takes to the air and is gone. Kannon and Dayne lead the remaining warriors to the north into the woods.

Lakin points to a ring of rocks, insisting Char lands next to it. Immediately after Char lands, Lakin slowly helps Colt down, who shows no emotion while riding on Char's back. Mimic jumps off excitedly into Lakin's arms. Lakin knows she has to watch over the girls until the rest of their group arrives. She figures there is no safer place than the king's lair. Char flies to the top of the highest treetop and watches as they try to enter the secret pathway. They immediately have an issue with the entrance ritual. Colt can't complete the rock pattern with one foot, and Mimic is too small to accomplish the task. Lakin has to get to the kings and explain their dilemmas. Since she is the only one capable of completing the ritual, it lies solely on her shoulders. Lakin goes three to the left, then three to the right. Finally, she dances with all her might. Char joins Mimic in laughing at Lakin's dancing abilities. The secret door slowly opens as Lakin enters to retrieve a king for Colt.

Char agrees to watch the three while Lakin goes to retrieve the kings. Lakin only gets lost once in the maze but returns with the king of diamonds in good time. Lakin explains why Colt and Mimic are unable to complete the task. The king agrees to allow Lakin to do the ritual for each one. But first, he has to meet with each one privately to see where their loyalties lie.

After having a private discussion with Colt, the king returns to the secret entrance to discuss Colt's wishes with the other kings. It isn't long before all the kings return and sit on the circle of rocks with Colt. This time, Lakin and Mimic will be allowed to join. Lakin and Mimic sit while listening to Colt speak to the kings.

Colt says, "My kings, I truly appreciate your giving me this opportunity to ask an unusual favor of you. I've tried since arriving in the Horizon to fight the good fight. From my world to this one, I run. That is what I do and what I'm known for. It's what I'm good at. Now, without my leg, I'm no longer a runner. I'm no longer able to help anyone. I'm no longer Colt." She stops for a second to gather her thoughts, then takes a big breath and continues. "I lived my life always on the run. Now, I just want to stop. I'm tired and need a rest. I'm asking you— no, I'm *begging* you—if it is possible to swap spots with someone else's life light."

The kings huddle to discuss what the young girl is asking of them.

After much deliberation, the king of clubs says, "We've never seen or heard of such a thing. You are willing to give your life light to another who has had their light released?"

Colt nods, and the kings turn back to their discussion. Lakin can't believe what Colt is asking, and she whispers to Mimic, "Is Colt really willing to trade her light for another's to be returned?"

The kings finish their discussion and turn back to Colt.

One says, "My child, your light is yours to do with however

you see fit. But I need you to understand that once the swap has taken place, it can never be reversed. If the one you honor with this gift returns and, by chance, loses their light once again, you will both lose your lights, never to return."

Colt doesn't hesitate and answers, "My friend, Cam, has had his light stripped from him in both worlds by an evil disease. He thought he had escaped it when he left his world, but it still found him here. By giving him my light, he may have a chance at a pain-free life that he has never experienced before. Then he'll have a chance to do all the things he missed. He might find true love or have a sleepover, go to a prom, be called Daddy, or dance in the rain with some buddies. With this last chance, he will take nothing for granted and live each day to the fullest. What little everyday things we take for granted, he will surely cherish. Yes, my kings, I do know what I'm giving up. But I will smile knowing what he'll be getting. I wish to continue with my request."

The king of diamonds places his hand on Colt's hand. "My child, in doing so, you will inherit all of the released light's pain. Every awful thing he has endured will now be passed on to you. You will burden his disease. Is this your final wish, my child?"

Colt nods in agreement. Lakin can't believe her eyes or ears. Is what she heard true? Colt is giving up her light and switching spots with Cam?

The king of spades says, "My child, never in all our lifetimes have we seen such a display of unselfishness. Nor have we been asked such a profound request. This must be quite some friendship you possess. I truly hope this light you are offering finds the man worthy enough to embrace it. After quite a lengthy discussion, we've decided your wish may be granted."

Lakin rushes to Colt's side. "Colt, what are you doing? You're not really going to go through with this, are you?"

Colt smiles. "I'm no good anymore with only one leg. I'm a broken Colt. What do they do with a racehorse that can't run? If I can give my Warrior a do-over, then my job here in the Horizon is complete. I'm a watcher; it's what I was brought here for. I need my Warrior and all the warriors to succeed and win in the end."

Lakin cries, tears making it hard to speak. Finally, with a shaking voice, she says, "I love you, Colt. You may not have finished your race but won all our hearts. I promise to remind Cam every day of how good a friend he had. Goodbye, my friend, until we meet again."

Colt gives Lakin the last hug she has left as they both are unsuccessful in holding back their tears.

Lakin backs up when the kings surround Colt. The kings begin to chant in a language that is unfamiliar to Lakin. Colt begins to scream in pain while absorbing all of Cam's pain—Cam's two lifetimes of the disease being forced into Colt's little body. Mimic covers their ears to try and drown out the shrieking screams.

Then Colt is no more.

They watch Colt's light rises into the sky. Lakin whispers, "I can't believe she's gone. How can so much strength come out of such a little body? May you always be the brightest star, baby girl." The three girls bow their heads as Char lets out a screech across the Horizon. They stand and watch till they can no longer see Colt's light.

The kings return to the secret entrance one at a time, with the last king adding, "The wish has been granted. It has been done." Then they are gone.

Lakin tries to wipe the tears from her eyes while she looks

for Cam. Not finding anything to prove that Cam returned, Lakin looks up. "Did the kings pick the right orb of light? What if they had the wrong orb, and Colt gave her light for nothing? Why isn't Cam here? That was the deal."

Mim and IC are beside themselves, dumbfounded at what they have just witnessed. Mim softly says to IC, "She just gave up everything. How can some just give up like that?"

IC answers, "Her everything is running. When she lost the ability to run, she lost her everything."

"We lost our wings; that was *our* everything. We haven't given up yet, so why did she?"

IC doesn't have an answer to Mim's question. She simply says, "In my eyes, she'll forever be a hero's tale. I personally will make it my job to inform everyone what we witnessed here today."

Mim shakes her head. "How can any life not be worth living? We are only given one; through hardship or happiness, it's the greatest gift we are given." The two hug each other as part of their hearts has left with Colt's light.

As the girls stand silent, watching the many lights above them, patiently waiting for Cam's light to emerge, Mim whispers, "What if it didn't work? With all those lights up there, how can the kings be sure of their choice?"

Suddenly, they are startled when they hear the rustle brush nearby. Lakin quickly pulls her whips out as Mimic hides behind her. They are very relieved to see Kannon and the rest of the gang step out from the brush.

Bug waves and says, "Where's Char? You know, she could have come back for us. Now I'm so tired from walking through the woods I can hardly stand. Really, girls, you shouldn't hog the dragon."

Lakin points to the top of a very tall tree next to Bug. They look up to see a much smaller Char swaying back and forth on the treetop. Bug waves and says, "Appreciate you coming back for us. Now my legs hurt." He then turns his attention to Lakin. "Huh, where's Colt? Did she already meet the kings? Are they going to fix her? If anyone deserves to be fixed, it's her. I bet she's even faster now."

Lakin quickly cries out, "Colt is gone!"

Everyone looks at Lakin, feeling confused. Hunter says, "What do you mean she's gone? Like gone with the kings?"

"She's gone for good. She's gone! When we met the kings, instead of asking to be fixed, Colt asked if she could switch her light for Cam's."

Bug nervously chuckles and says, "How can she switch? Cam already lost his light. You can't trade something for nothing."

"She asked if she could give her light to Cam. She is a watcher, and her job is to protect him at all costs. The kings were even stunned. This was the first time this had ever been asked of them. After a lengthy discussion, they agreed to grant Colt her wish. But it came with a stipulation. By switching lights, Colt would have to endure all of Cam's pain in one large dose. She still agreed, and they proceeded with her wish. All we could do was stand here and watch as all of Cam's pain poured into Colt's screaming body. After what seemed like forever, we watched Colt's light rise in the air and join the rest of the lights."

The stunned group is at a loss for words, but the silence is soon interrupted by Hunter. "How could she leave us without saying goodbye? To just give up her light like that... Why would the kings even agree to it? They are supposed to be the heroes in this world."

"I guess when you lose the one thing in your life that made

you feel alive, you have no life to live. So, being the big-hearted person she is, she gave her life to someone who wanted only to live. Now her generosity gave Cam a chance to be real."

Dayne says, "She knew in her condition that she would only hinder us in the fact we'd have to fight and protect her at the same time. Giving us a healthy Cam also gave our lights a better chance. I truly think she saved us all."

Dak adds, "She couldn't think of seeing any of us perish, so she increased our chances in battle. Fly high, my beautiful friend. May you only stop running long enough to give a hug."

Bug lets his sadness turn to anger and yells, "No Hoss! No Dillo! No Colt, and possibly no Spin Doll. Where the hell is Cam? No Cam! We're told all this shit about those kings and how if we save them, they'll save us. Well, someone damn sure isn't keeping up their part of the deal. Kings! Kings! Oh, kings, get your asses out here and do your part. From here on out, I ain't doing shit till they give us answers! The only thing you're helping us do is lose our lights. Save this place without me. I'm fucking done." Bug sits on the ground and looks to the woods, away from everyone's eyes.

His rant put a little fire in Kannon's mind. "Where's this kingdom we've heard all about?"

Hunter grumbles, "Probably more bullshit that is fed to us. Besides Shadows and an ugly fat man, we haven't seen shit. Why Cam, and not Hoss or Dillo, who lost their lives for us? If you can bring back one, then why can't you bring them all back?"

Dak answers, "Cam gave his light for us as well, or have you forgotten?"

Hunter barks back, "Cam's light was gone before that battle. He was just skin and bones walking. He truly didn't have a choice."

Bug mutters, "Where's this super golden kingdom?"

Lakin points to the field, saying, "This giant field is the kingdom. As far as the eye can see."

Before she can finish, Bug runs into the field. Lakin yells, "Bug, wait! The kingdom is—"

SPLAT!

"—invisible."

Bug stops abruptly at the kingdom wall, knocking himself out.

Kannon and Dak run over to help revive Bug and help him to his feet.

"If it's invisible, how do we find a way in?" Hunter asks.

Lakin tells them that it's only invisible until they are inside. She also shows them the secret entrance to the king's hidden lair. Lakin touches the stones in the correct order and then dances until the door opens. Seeing the door open, Bug takes off, running for it. But before he can get to it, Lakin tackles him. Helping Bug up, she explains that they each must enter separately after completing the code. If they enter without doing it, they will lose their light.

They line up, letting the girls go first. Bug is the first guy to try it. Kannon whispers to Hunter as Bug begins to dance, "Look at that little guy go. He's got some real moves."

Hunter chuckles. "Must be all that practice with the broom."

Bug overhears their jokes, and as he enters the secret pathway, he flips Hunter off and jokes, "We know you can sing, but can you dance?"

Kannon is the last to enter because he doesn't want the others to watch him dance.

Once inside, Lakin does her best to lead them through the maze. She only makes two wrong turns and corrects it quickly, but not before Bug points out that she screwed up twice. It isn't long before they reach the door to the king's keep.

Kannon gathers the group before they enter. "Now, remember, we are guests. Let's make sure we're on our best behavior. Politeness and manners go a long way. Bug, no stupid remarks."

They all look at Bug, who pretends to zip his lips. Laken slowly opens the door.

CHAPTER 37

"Sometimes it's hard to tell: who are the real bad guys here?"
- Sin

Inside the kingdom, there's a much angrier vibe. Sin and Omin enter their room by kicking in the door, only to find Char and IC not in their cages. Sin knocks the cages to the ground while he screams in the air. Omin ignores Sin as he walks to the open window and looks over the kingdom grounds.

"Brother, soon they'll be at our door."

Sin calms down and joins his brother at the window. "Why won't they just give up? It's in their blood to give up. That's what they do; it's who they are."

Omin looks toward another tower. "The reports still haven't arrived from the factory. I'm hoping we'll get some good news for a change."

"So far, ain't nothing good about this damn place. But when control is fully ours, we'll make this place a home."

Omin agrees. "We need to remove all this color. This place needs more gray."

The two sit there sulking when a knock at their open door reveals a shadow holding a piece of paper. Omin unkindly gestures for the shadow to enter.

Without greeting the shadow, Sin says, "Well, what's the good news?" Omin walks behind the shadow, adding, "There better be good news."

The shadow swallows hard before speaking. "We lost a good number of troops and Skulk as well. But, until the dragon came, we were winning. All is not lost; their giant is no more, and Dice left the fast girl with only a leg to stand on. Let's just say she won't be winning any races anytime soon." The shadow stands, proud of his joke about the fast girl.

Omin punches the wall and yells, "Shit, we lost Skulk! He is always my favorite. It's true; the best ones are the first to go."

Sin taps his fingers on the windowsill, and the reflection reveals a very angry face. He barks orders at the shadow. "Call every last shadow and tell them by order of Jokers to return to the kingdom and prepare for battle at once. Then go and wake our little friends Dice and Octoro. Oh, and do not feed them. I think it's time to end this silly game and release all their precious lights."

Omin, with a sinister smile, adds, "Now is the time, brother, to finish what we started."

Sin joins his brother with his own evil smile. "I'm going to make our soon-to-be fourth king, Dak, place his crown on my head in the center of the kingdom."

The shadow stands still, waiting for his final orders when a very unhappy Cozzex pushes him down from behind.

"Well, well, if it isn't my lazy, do-nothing brothers. Here I am out in the middle of this shitty little war, risking my life, while it looks as if you two double-teamed a wastebasket. Are you tired, Omin? Did that basket hurt your feelings?"

Omin glares at Cozzex and mumbles, "Now is most definitely not the time to start shit with me, sis."

Sin jumps in. "Where's your fat boyfriend? I'm sure he's out bullying something much smaller than he is."

"Maybe he's crying on someone's shoulder about his stupid keys." The two Jokers have a quick laugh on Fat Jack's behalf.

Cozzex, trying to one-up her brothers, states, "Oh, would

that be my fat boyfriend who ate the kings?"

Both Jokers stop laughing and say, "Tell us this is true, and he'll have his keys today."

"From his mouth to my ears, the kings are no more."

Before they can celebrate, another knock is heard on the Joker's door. Sin looks at Omin and asks, "Were you expecting company?"

"Never this late, brother."

Cozzex walks to the door and looks in the peephole, but she can't see anyone. She turns back toward her brother just as another knock is heard. Cozzex, thinking someone is messing with her, quickly opens the door. There, in the Joker's doorway stands sweet little old Jim.

Jim strolls in and asks, "Mind if I join you gents? I could really use a drink to wet my whistle."

Sin happily shouts, "Jim, did you hear the news? We've already won. The kings have been released!"

Jim chugs down his first drink and answers, "I don't know where you received that news from, but some girl named Lakin and Cozzex's fat boyfriend, my brother, brought them kings right up to the kingdom's walls." Jim walks over to the window, already sipping his second drink.

Once he sees Spin Doll hanging in a cage just outside the Joker's window, Jim squeals with excitement. "Where did you get my pet? Oh, how I've missed her."

Sin proudly says, "Back at the barn. She came back to see her cage one last time, but we had a plan of our own. We made Cozzex shape-shift into your pet's look-a-like and then switched places with her during the barn battle. The plan worked perfectly."

Jim smiles at Spin Doll, giving her a creepy wave. Spin Doll sits there quietly, just taking everybody's info in.

Jim continues. "I heard the fourth king just reached the remaining three kings and must be sworn in and take an oath."

Cozzex, not wanting to believe her boyfriend lied to her, says, "Listen, old man, you're the one who lies. You've been lying to our friends since they got home. Only one person isn't telling the truth. Isn't that right, Jim? You talk out of both sides of your mouth. Sounds like a spy to me. Go ahead, Jim; tell them the truth. The floor is all yours."

Jim, giving a half-smile, then responds, "So, all of a sudden, we're telling the truth? Ok, here's the truth. Jokers, your sweet little sister and my brother Fat Jack—or, as I call him by his real name, Terrorizer—were plotting to eliminate you two after you won. She told Jack to eat you both at the end so she could hear your screams."

Both Jokers look at Cozzex displeased. Sin asks without hesitation, "Sis, is this true? You think for one minute that you are going to outsmart us?"

"Brothers, who you gonna believe—blood or some old guy? Maybe Jim's the one who should be eaten."

Jim pours another drink. "Listen, bitch! Your brothers are in a partnership with me and my brother, Jack. In order to take over the Horizon, we need four to replace the four, which makes you a fifth wheel. Now, Jokers, I do not feel the partnership is taking off as it should. Seems we need to cut some dead weight."

Cozzex is shocked that her brothers could trust this old man over her. She tries one last-ditch effort, yelling, "Jim, what do you actually do around here? I mean beside sitting on park benches."

Jim smiles as he finishes yet another drink and responds to Cozzex, "You think you performed well as a pet? I'm the only show stealer here. I have both sides eating from my hands. No one knows I'm the real door master. My brother just does as he's told. You may know me by my real name, Torment. I pulled the stars from the sky; I planned the first king's death. Without me, none of this happens. Now, you're starting to bore me. Boys, please get rid of her to prove your loyalty to our partnership. Try not to make a mess; that blue goo gets all over. It is a pleasure to meet you, Cozzex. Too bad this is where your story ends. Boys, if you please."

The two Jokers approach Cozzex and ask her to leave. She begins to fight back as each Joker grabs an arm and walks her out the door and down the hall. Jim smiles as he can hear Cozzex pleading with her brothers, followed by stabbing sounds and screams.

While the Jokers are gone, Jim looks at his pet. "My little pet, what's wrong? Cat got your tongue? You know, to get your pretty voice back, all you must do is find that little dancing girl in a box and smash it. What's really funny is the warriors have it, keeping it safe for you. Ah, what fools. They're protecting it for me. And to think, they believe I'm your grandpa. Little do they know you had the perfect life—loving parents, friends, good grades, a nice job, and money in the bank. You had everything, that's why you're my pet. You're the feather in my cap. I tormented you for a whole year before I got you to break, and then you still didn't want to give up." He pauses to make sure she's really listening. "I had my brother tie you up in that closet. You put up such a fight, not wanting to give up. But don't worry. Your little secret will be safe with me. Your family still doesn't know about the little girl you had. I'd give you your voice back if only you'd tell me where you hid her. I'm sure she's missing Mommy. Being only two years old and all alone, she must be scared, hungry, and cold. I truly hope she doesn't get sick. I'd hate to meet her in this awful place. I'll tell you what. You write down where she is, and I'll have my brother check on her."

Tears roll down a helpless Spin Doll's face, but before Jim can finish, the Jokers walk in and grab a towel to wipe off the goo.

Sin stares at Jim as he threatens, "You and your brother better come through or trust me, you'll see real evil."

Jim smiles. "Watch your tone, boy."

Omin snaps, "Bitch, stick to the demons you know, not the ones you don't. Trust me, piss us off past the limit, and we'll be the only two surviving this, Horizon." Omin shoves Jim back a step, and all three men's faces quickly get serious.

"That will be the one and only time you will touch me. Now, I'm going to leave before I do something to end this partnership." Jim stands up and walks to the door. He stops briefly but then continues without another word.

The Jokers turn off the lights and adjourn to their rooms. Spin Doll sits quietly in the darkness, not knowing how to get her voice back or where her Baby Bee is.

CHAPTER 38

"The man who would not be king." - Bug

Lakin almost has the door to the keep open when Bug busts in like a kid in a toy store. The first thing he notices is the pool and runs straight for it, diving in fully dressed. The three kings, sitting on makeshift thrones, laugh at the sight of Bug floundering around in the pool. The rest of the group approaches the kings and kneels in front of them.

The king of clubs speaks first. "Rise, my warriors. My name is Truncheon, and I welcome you with open arms."

Next to speak is the king of spades. "I am known throughout the land as Furrow. May my house be your house."

"Many in this realm know me as Paragon, the king of diamonds," the final king states.

Dayne feels a weird sensation rolling over her body as if she's been here and has given this same greeting in the past. Before she can make sense of it, Kannon stands.

"Your majesties, my name is Kannon. I would be the chosen leader of this fine ensemble of men and women. This is my beautiful wife, Dayne, and our son, Dak, who I believe you are most interested in. Next, we have our sharpshooter, Hunter, with his sister, who you've already been associated with, Lakin. The two little ones are known as Mimic. This is Mim, and here is IC. Before losing their wings, they were star cleaners."

Before Kannon can finish, a voice from out of mid-air says, "I, my kings, am known as Cam. I'm full of wisdom since I have an old soul." Cam appears in front of the kings, kneeling.

Furrow speaks. "Rise, Cam, and welcome. These people seem to be full of love for you. You must be special."

Cam is puzzled. "My kings, why am I here? My light is released some time ago."

Furrow places his hand on Cam's shoulder. "Someone above us loves you more than you'll ever know."

Truncheon explains, "A young girl named Colt offered her light for yours. With this trade, she also agreed to accept all of the pain you have endured."

Cam is shocked by what King Truncheon told him. He yells, "You can't let her do that! This is *my* disease to bear, not hers. In no world would a leader ok this. My kings, you were wrong to do such a thing."

Paragon quickly says, "It has already been granted. Never again speak to us in that manner, or she will have given her light for nothing."

Cam looks around at all the warriors who are staring at him.

Leaning on the edge of the pool, Bug clears his throat quite loudly. Hearing this, Kannon quickly says, "Last but not least, let me introduce you to Bug."

The kings chuckle at the sight of a wet Bug. Paragon says, "So you're the famous Bug we've heard so much about. It's so nice to put a face to the name."

Bug, surprised that the kings had heard of him, replies, "Thanks, kings. You've really heard of me? Of course you did. When there's a big man on campus, everyone knows him."

Furrow says, "No. That is just a jest. But really, don't pee in the pool. Your reputation arrived before you did."

Bug, now dissed by the kings, dives back under the water.

Paragon explains the sections of the keep, showing them to the eatery, which is lined with buffets of every food you can imagine. Next is the sleep hall area, which has enough big, soft, warm beds for all. The pools are the last to be shown, as Bug is already in one of them. This hidden keep is better than anywhere they have lived in the past.

Paragon says, "Now that you know the layout of the keep, feel free to inspect. But before you all run off, do any of you have a request of the kings?"

Kannon, puzzled, speaks up. "Sirs, a request?"

Truncheon nods. "Requests, my boy. When most people first meet us, they ask for a request."

Furrow says, "A request, in your words, means would you like to know your final outcome; for example, how your reason for being here is handled back in the real world; how it affects the people, places, and even inanimate objects."

All the warriors nod, wondering if the world they left behind really misses them or not.

Furrow starts with Hunter. "Hunter, or as we know you as William L. Jackson, you sure are a musical star. After your disappearance, people fell in love with your voice, and it earned you a gold record. Your award hangs on your manager's wall, and your earnings go into his pockets. You've made him a very wealthy man."

Paragon turns to Lakin. "Lakin, sister of Hunter. Like the rest, you have not passed in your world. A long, child-filled future can still be written in your story. Your book is far from finished."

Truncheon approaches Mimic. "You two are very important to us. If you survive the final battle, we will call on you two once again and replace what was stolen from you. When you rise in first light, your wings once again will be yours." Mimic jumps for joy from the news that they will be getting their wings back.

Paragon moves on to Bug. "You, young man, were not as

alone in your world as you thought, for you have a family that you know not of."

"I was a foster kid; I didn't have a real family."

Paragon shakes his head. "No, you are wrong. You have a mother and father who love you with all their heart. You also have two brothers and a sister. You also have a nephew who shares the same name as you."

Bug shakes his head. "You have the wrong guy. I don't have any family. My parents passed away when I was born."

"You were removed from your parents when just born by a couple who took you without permission. The two who took you from your family perished soon after the theft and paid dearly here in the Horizon. You were found abandoned without a name. The lady who found you thought you were cute as a bug. So that's how your new name came to be."

Bug, deep in thought, talks to himself. "I was kidnapped and forced to live through the system because of people I didn't even know."

Paragon continues. "Your true parents, still to this day, look for you and pray they will find you. They have never stopped looking."

Bug is flabbergasted. He actually has a family and a nephew who share his name. Bug asks Paragon if he knows his real name. Paragon nods, leans down, and whispers it to Bug.

"Really? That's my real name? I have a real name! I would never have guessed such a name."

Hunter says, "What's his real name? Is it something like Wilber or Orville?"

Paragon shakes his head. "When he's ready to reveal and take his original name, only then will you know what it truly is."

The kings turn to look at Kannon, Dayne, and Dak because

it is their turn to request. Before Kannon can ask his request, Truncheon says, "You, sir, are a man who had everything but is not allowed to keep any of it. Now, you come to the Horizon with nothing but have taken everything. Your leadership was shaky in the beginning but, as did you, grew into a strong alliance with your group. A leader must be followed, and you, sir, are."

Kannon bows his head as a thank you.

Next, they look at Dak, as Paragon says in a deep, serious voice, "Dak! You, son, are brave, strong, loved by the townsfolk and carry leadership abilities only very few are blessed with. The strides you've made in the Horizon since you've arrived have been nothing but amazing."

Furrow jumps in. "You are a boy above men. Stories will be spoken of you long after your life's end. The boy who leads men."

Truncheon finishes. "You, son, are the one to help us regain our thrones. That is why we're asking you to lead our soldiers. Please accept our offering to command our guards."

Dak kneels in front of the kings, feeling confused. Was he to be king or not? Dak wonders that but doesn't say it out loud. Instead, he bows and says, "It will be an honor my kings."

Dayne is their next target. Paragon steps forward. "Dayne, mother to the son. Without your strength and will to help Dak succeed, this place would have been much different. You sacrificed so much for so little in return. This group is luckier than they know. Soon, they will come to realize."

The kings finish with Cam, Truncheon saying, "You, sir, are playing a game with someone else's turn. This gift is not to be played with. You owe it to the young lady to succeed in battle and experience what life really can offer. Do not take for granted this light you hold."

Cam, feeling like he's been scolded, says, "Sirs, I will honor this light with all that I am. All the gratitude and thanks could never be enough. This light will be cherished in the manor it is given."

Furrow nods. "Let's be sure it is, shall we."

The kings address the group one final time before adjourning to their quarters. Truncheon speaks loudly to the group. "We thank you all for what you've done and are about to do. Let it be known that the Horizon will be saved because of you and the sacrifices of warriors who aren't with us today. May the night sky hold the stars once again." Then the kings turn in for the night.

When the doors closes, Bug says, "Is Dak the king? If not, we went through all this without the fourth king. I'm so confused. How can we defeat all these Shadows, Jokers, and whatever else they throw at us? Pick any of us to be king, and let's go get some. I need some air. This is too much to lay on us all at once. How the hell do I get out of here?"

Lakin offers to show him the way out, as the two leave.

Dak, not understanding exactly what just happened, asks his mom, "What just happened? Am I not the fourth king?" Dayne doesn't have an answer, so she hugs him.

Kannon welcome Cam back, and the two head for the buffet. Hunter found a real bed and falls fast asleep. Mimic is all a buzz with the chance to regain their wings.

When Lakin and Bug reach the keep's entrance, Bug says, "Can you give me a while to just be alone and think?"

"I'll be back in an hour, but you should really get some rest."

"I can rest when I lose my light."

Lakin hugs him then heads back to the keep. Bug turns and walks with his hand skimming along the invisible kingdom wall. After a while, he comes to a small creek and sits on the bank of the creek, tossing small stones into the water that he finds on the ground beside him. Quietly he sits, thinking about where Spin Doll is and what his mom and dad look like. Soon, he begins to talk to his reflection.

"Look at you, feeling sad about your life when it wasn't even supposed to be your life. Jumping off that bridge would've been pretty selfish. You could've taken away someone's son, brother, and uncle that they never would've gotten to meet. Kevin John Case, you are a piece of shit." Bug stares into his own reflection, wondering if the man in the water looks like a Kevin. He throws a stone into the reflection, making it go away.

A voice from the bank on the other side of the creek says, "Can't sleep either, I see."

Bug replies, "No, sir, been through a lot of shit lately. If you have a minute, can I ask you a question?"

"Shoot; I've got nothing but time."

"Do you think if someone who can't handle life and what it throws at them just one day decides to quit and end it, are being selfish?"

For a moment, there is no answer. Then the voice says, "I don't really know. I mean, it doesn't sound like they thought how it would affect their friends and family. I mean, your life is the only true gift you're actually given. I've seen people who were homeless and families penniless with no food on their table and the unloved fight every day for a chance to have any one of those things and they didn't give up. I personally lost my father because he gave up. I've hurt every day since, wondering if I was part of his reason for leaving me. I've put hours of thought into why he would do such a thing. Yet I still worry if he made it up there or is still wandering with the same problems tormenting him. I really wish I had seen it coming. Maybe I could have done something to stop him and made him happy once again. But I guess, like him, I'll carry this 'why' with me forever."

Bug feels awful. Is that what he did to his family? Will they always wonder why they can't find him? He takes a deep breath and says, "It wasn't your fault. The demons your father carried belonged to him alone. He probably thought he was helping the situation if he wasn't in the way. Maybe your dad didn't want you to have to deal with the demons as well. What your dad went through is not because of you. Not every chalk line silhouette is because of someone else."

"Thanks. I truly do appreciate that. If I may ask, how do you know so much about this?"

Bug answers, "Because I was like your dad. I almost gave up."

The voice softly responds, "Sorry. I didn't know. But may I ask why?"

A tear trickles down Bug's. "I had no family, no money, no friends, no love, and no diploma."

"But you did have family, you said."

"I had family I didn't know about."

"If you didn't give up and found your family, you would have had family, friends, and love. I was once told that your life is what you make it. If I had met you back in your world, I would have loved to have been your friend. Even though I can't see you, you sound very nice."

Bug smiles. "Thanks. You sound very nice as well. I guess I should be getting back to my friends. They're probably wondering where I've been. It is nice to meet you. By the way, my name is Kevin."

"It is nice to meet you, Kevin. My name is Luke, but here

in the Horizon, I go by another name. I better be getting back to my twin brother; he worries about me. If, by chance, we meet on the battlefield tomorrow, what we must do does not mean we choose to do it. Stay safe, my friend, till tomorrow."

Bug freezes when he realizes who he is speaking to. "I'm glad we're friends tonight because tomorrow is another day. The names we go by now, tomorrow will all be changed."

When the Joker turns to walk away, Bug catches a glimpse of something shiny in the dark. He has to find out what it is, so he asks Luke, "Hey before you leave, what is that shiny thing I just saw you holding? Was it a skipping stone? Because I collect skipping stones."

Luke answers, "No, it's not a stone. It's just an old piece of glass. It had two more pieces that went with it, but they got lost, and without all the pieces, it's worthless. I don't know; it may be good for skipping. I'll tell you what, I'll try and skip it to you, and if it makes it to you, you can keep it."

Luke skips the piece of glass toward Bug, but it comes up short and sinks into a shallow spot in front of him.

"It didn't make it, but thanks for trying."

"Yeah, didn't think it would, but nice talking to you."

Bug listens as Luke gets farther and farther away. Once he knows for sure that Luke is gone, he jumps into the creek in search of the piece of heart. After pulling up about fifteen rocks, Bug finally retrieves the piece. Like the two pieces before, Bug swallows the third one. This time, Bug doesn't feel good. His stomach is doing flip-flops, and he thinks he may throw up.

Bug feels his way along the kingdom wall back to the entrance. There, waiting for him, is Lakin.

"Where have you been? You had me worried sick. Why are you so wet?"

"I was tossing stones in this creek and accidentally fell in."

Lakin shakes her head. "What am I going to do with you?"

Bug smiles while grabbing his stomach. Lakin is quick to ask, "What's wrong? Why are you holding your stomach like that?"

"Maybe I ate too much too fast. I'm sure it'll be fine by morning with some good sleep."

When they return to the keep, Bug finds new clothes waiting for him and a big old bed to sleep in. He quickly changes and jumps into bed. It only takes a few seconds, and he is out for the night.

CHAPTER 39

"Nothing like having the upper hand that, in return, slaps you in the face." - Fat Jack

Fat Jack approaches the main gate to the kingdom, still talking to himself and glancing back with every other step. He paces when he reaches the gates and mutters, "Dragons! Now they have dragons. Guns, whips, cannons, and now dragons. These Jokers better have their shit together because I'm not going down like this. Whatever happened to the ones who supposedly gave up easily? No, this new young crowd wants to shoot shit and use dragons."

A shadow speaks up, who has been listening from a distance. "Ah, dragons have been around forever."

Jack gives the shadow a why-are-you-talking-to-me look. The shadow, realizing he may have overstepped, quickly leaves.

Jack walks in a circle, chanting and then dancing like a fool until the kingdom gate opens. He looks to the right and then the left before entering, only to make sure he is not being followed and no one sees him dancing. He slips into the kingdom, the gate slamming shut behind him. Jack quickly works his way through the crowded streets on his way to the towers.

The streets seem to be even more crowded than usual—Jack waves and greets Shadows like he is a famous movie star. After finally reaching the Tower of Hearts, Jack immediately heads for the top floor. Exhausted and worried, Jack stops halfway up to catch his breath and mumbles, "Whoever designed this tower should be punched in the face for not adding an elevator. Twenty floors and no elevator! Bet your ass it wasn't a fat man."

He moves onward and upward, grumbling the whole time until he reaches the Jokers' room. Angrily, he begins to pound on the door. To Jack's surprise, Jim, wearing a robe and slippers, opens the door and looks half-awake as he mumbles, "Stop pounding; you want to wake up the Jokers."

Jack lunges in and immediately heads for the ice box. He opens it to find no drinks, then slams the door shut. Jim takes a sip of his hot coffee, sits in a chair, and looks out the window.

"I'll take a coffee also. Mind pouring me one, brother?" Jack barks as he slops on the couch, looking at Jim.

Jim points to the streets below and replies, "There's a nice shop down there that has the best coffee in the kingdom. Do be a gentleman and grab a few crème-filled ones while you're down there. Oh, and the Jokers like their coffee with two creams and two sugars."

"Are you serious? I just got up here. Yeah, I'm not thirsty anymore. I'll pass."

Jim scowls at Jack. "I wasn't *asking* you; I was *telling* you. Now, before the Joker's wake. Don't make me *tell* you again."

Jack rolls his eyes and mumbles as he walks out the door.

Sin stumbles from his room. "Was someone just here? I thought I heard you talking to someone."

"Jack was here, but I sent him for coffee and some crème-filled."

Omin is sleepily coming from his room, saying, "Did someone say crème-filled?"

Jim answers, "Jack went to get some along with coffee."

Omin jokes, "He better get a few. He'll probably have to stop halfway up for a breather and a snack."

All the men chuckle, knowing it is probably true. Sin rubs the sleep from his eyes, and Omin notices his brother's heart necklace has the piece of heart missing.

"Hey, you're missing your heart," Omin jokes.

Sin reaches up, feeling for it, then remembers he gave it to some kid last night at the creek. "Yeah, now I'm heartless."

"No matter; it was worthless thanks to the witch losing the other two pieces."

Jim looks over and says, "Good riddance. That thing was creepy anyway." The Jokers don't disagree.

They all peer below at the shops as Jack argues with the shopkeeper about how he will carry everything at once.

Sin turns to Omin, saying, "Bet you he tries to carry everything at once instead of making two trips."

Omin laughs and replies, "I'm gonna lose, but I'll take that bet." They fist-bump to seal the deal.

Soon after, the front door swings open, revealing Jack to be even more exhausted. He leans against the door, trying to catch his breath, and gestures to come in as two Shadows carry in a basket of crème-filled and box of coffee cups. The Shadows quickly place the items on the counter and leave.

Jack shuts the door behind them and then collapses to the floor. Each Joker grabs a coffee and a crème-filled, then sits at the window. Jim gets up, grabs a crème-filled as well, and then returns to his seat.

Sin sips his coffee and asks, "Did you get two sugars and two creams? Because this doesn't taste like it has enough sugar. Jack, can you be a gent and go fetch a sugar pack?"

"Can you lick my balls?"

Sin scoffs, then continues to look out the window. Omin and Jim try hard not to laugh at Jack's reply.

After finishing breakfast and Jack recuperates, they discuss the coming war.

"In the days to come, this place will never be the same. So, enjoy it while you can," Jim tells them.

Jack speaks up. "Now they have a dragon. A fire-breathing dragon."

Sin kicks the cage on the floor. "I know. Someone let her out of her cage."

Jack is puzzled and points to the cage. "You had that little cage holding the dragon? Boy, you're some kind of stupid, aren't you?"

The Jokers slowly look at Jack as Omin says, "Watch how you speak to us, boy. It could be the last thing you ever say."

Jack laughs. "Oh, please. I eat guys like you two for breakfast."

The three men stand, sizing each other up until Jim jumps in. "Hey, enough with the tough-guy shit. This war will be at our door today, and we sit here bitching like tough guys who have never been in a real fight. Sit down and get your shit together. Now!"

The Jokers slowly sit back down, but Jack decides to leave and find Cozzex. "I'm off to see Cozzex. You guys figure out what we're doing and just tell me my job later." He slams the door behind him.

Sin looks at Jim. "You didn't tell him about Cozzex? He's going to fly off the handle when he returns. Let's hurry this up and leave. I'm not dealing with that shit today."

Jim talks out the window to a lifeless Spin Doll, who is listening to everything said. "How am I going to win the Horizon with these buffoons? Now you understand why I had to get rid of Cozzex, don't you? With the control Cozzex has gained over Jack, I would have been outnumbered and possibly not needed. These fools will hand me over the Horizon; then

I'll no longer be in need of their services. Then you and I can rule the Horizon together. With Baby Bee as well."

Spin Doll turns her face away as he draws back into the window.

Omin is fidgety, thinking about Jack coming back all fired up, and he says, "Ok, we need to tell everyone in the kingdom to prepare for tonight. Clear the streets and make sure to have the turrets lit. We need every shadow in the Horizon here and ready at sundown."

Jim agrees. "Make sure Dice and that creepy crawly Beast is ready. Have our guards surround the four towers; they cannot reach their thrones."

Sin jumps in. "If the four kings each reach their thrones, they will reign over the Horizon evermore. Tell every shadow to destroy any king they see. We only need to take out one king, and the rest will fall."

Once all the plans are in place, the Jokers head out to begin setting up for the kings' and warriors' endings.

Jim stays behind, still admiring Spin Doll, while sipping his final coffee drop. He can hear the stomping coming toward the door, which suddenly flies open.

A hostile Jack enters, growling, "Where are they? Those sons-a-bitches released their own sister. I'm going to enjoy eating them. Get out here, you cowards! Daddy's hungry."

Jim places his coffee cup on the table before addressing Jack. "Someone had to go. We'll only be able to crown the four of us. Cozzex made five, and we couldn't have that, so one of us had to go. The Jokers wanted you to be released, but I insisted we needed you. So, I'm very sorry. I know how much you loved her."

Jack left by slamming the door behind him and ripping it off the hinges. Jim is a little nervous since he's never seen his brother so angry. Jim picks up his little hat and waves to Spin Doll as he walks through the broken door.

Once the room is empty, Spin Doll tries to break the lock. She needs to get free and help the undermanned warriors. She has to tell them about Octoro and the dysfunction in the ranks of the evil side. Most of all, she has to save her Baby Bee. Even though the fall might end her light, she begins swinging the cage to try and free herself.

CHAPTER 40

"Trying to fit 50 pounds of shit into a 10-pound bag just doesn't work." - Kannon

Morning comes quicker than any of the warriors have anticipated. Dayne is the first to wake up and sees clothing left on her bedside. It is so regal and beautiful, colored in shiny silver with hints of purple and teal throughout. She hurries to try everything on and is happy the clothing fits perfectly, making her look like something from a comic book. Now fully dressed, she heads for the food buffet and waits patiently for the rest.

Dak and Kannon are next to wake up and soon come out dressed in their super suits as well. Kannon fidgets a little as his suit does not seem to fit.

Dak asks, "Dad, are you alright?"

"Not really, son. These super pants are crushing my balls," Kannon answers. He looks ridiculous—his pants are not reaching his ankles, and his shirt is three sizes too small. His stomach hangs out, and he can't get the pants to button. "This can't be right; everything is way too tight," he complains while trying to stretch the suit out.

Bug emerges from the restroom dressed in an outfit three sizes too big for him and yells, "How am I going to fight in this? My legs don't even reach the end of the pants, and this shirt will fall right off me. These are, like, size *not me,* when normally I wear a medium."

Bug trips over the long pants as he attempts to walk, and

Dak and Dayne laugh at the two, who are obviously wearing the wrong outfit. Eventually, they figured out the issue.

Hunter walks in and says, "I have to admit, that shit's funny, guys, but why are you wearing each other's suits?"

Bug screams at Kannon, "Dude, get out of my suit! You're stretching it out!"

Kannon laughs at his mistake while he pries himself out of Bug's outfit. By the time they change, Lakin, Mimic, and Cam join them at the buffet. Kannon, now more comfortable in his actual suit, is ready to eat. Bug, on the other hand, enters the eatery in a sour mood.

"Your big ass stretched my shit out," he complains. "Now everything is loose. If my pants fall off me during the battle, I'm joining the other side and fucking you up."

Hunter laughs as he grabs the duct tape, heading towards Bug.

After filling their plates, they sit at the large table together. Everyone bows their heads before they begin to eat and listens to Hunter.

"May the kings regain their strength, and may our fallen friends soon find their places in the sky. May evil not replace us as we go from calm to chaos."

Everyone raises their heads and digs into their plates of food. Knowing this could be their last meal, they eat in total silence, the only sounds in the room being forks scraping on the plates.

When the meal is almost finished, Bug says, "This may have been the best meal I've ever eaten, not because of the food, but because of who is sitting at this table with me. If I've never said it, thank you all for being my friend. Also, while in battle, if Lakin's whip can find Hunter's ass just once, I'll be a happy man."

They raise their glasses to toast Bug's words, and Kannon stands.

"In my old world, I couldn't wait to leave, but in this world, I don't ever want to leave. You are all my family now. May we defeat this evil and once again fill the night sky with those who truly belong there." Once again, they raise their glasses to toast.

Before anyone else can speak, the kings enter the room. Dak quickly grabs three chairs and pulls them over to their table. They stand until the kings are seated.

Paragon says, "By night's arrival, we shall be at war."

Furrow continues. "May the angels not give up on you today."

Bug interrupts by saying, "Angels? What do you mean, angels?"

Truncheon says, "Why, all the townsfolk are angels. The angels roam the Horizon until they become a star. Some must earn their shine whether here or back in your world."

"If they're angels, where are their wings?"

Paragon answers. "Once they earn their wings, they fly up to their spot in the night sky and receive their starlight."

Kannon, also confused, asks, "They turn to their star form?"

Furrow laughs then replies, "They don't change form. They remain in their image and receive their starlight."

Truncheon finishes. "Their starlight surrounds them like a bubble, so they can look down at their world and loved ones."

Mim adds, "That's where we come in. Our job is to always keep their starlight bubble clean so the stars will never lose sight of their loved ones."

The group is finally on the same page and understands what stars truly are.

Bug changes the subject by asking, "So, did you pick your

fourth king?" The three kings nod but don't answer, so Bug jumps to his own conclusion by stating, "Congrats, Dak. Or shall I say, King Dak!"

Dak smiles, hoping the kings will confirm it, but Paragon swallows his food and says, "Dak cannot be king. He is the marked angel."

Hunter jumps in then. "A marked angel? What's a marked angel?"

Truncheon answers, "A marked angel is a being whose whole existence has taken place in the Horizon, making him a pure angel."

Kannon asks, "How many marked angels are there and what's his purpose?"

Furrow shrugs. "Dak is the only marked angel the Horizon has ever had. He is to lead the remaining angels into battle against evil."

Dak feels honored and betrayed at the same time. He knows it is an honor to be the only marked angel, but he was raised with the idea he was to be king. Unsure of his situation, he asks, "If I truly am the leader of angels, why do I not glow or have wings?"

Paragon replies, "Oh, your light will shine once you step in the kingdom and the angels see you and accept you."

Furrow adds, "Your wings you already have. They've been with you since birth."

The three kings point between Dak's shoulder blades, and Dak removes his shirt, revealing to the rest of the group a small set of wings on his back that look as if they are tattooed on.

Furrow continues. "They will sprout from your back when needed."

Kannon leans over and whispers to Dayne, "You have never seen a set of wings tattooed on our son?"

Dayne just shakes her head.

While the group inspects Dak's back, Cam turns to the kings, saying, "Well, if Dak is not a king, then which one of us is?"

Truncheon says, "The fourth king will be revealed soon." The three kings stand and leave.

Bug asks Dak, "Do you think you'll be able to fly?"

"No idea. I didn't even know they were there."

Cam inspects the tattooed wings. "Do they hurt at all?"

Dak pulls his suit back over the tattoo. "No, not at all. But, if I'm not the king, which one of you are?"

The group looks around, wondering who the new king will be.

Hunter finally says, "Kannon. It's got to be you. You've been in charge since the day you arrived in the Horizon. We know it's not Dak or any of the ladies since they said king and not queen. They'll never make me king. I'm the bad guy in our group and I mean, look at Bug and Cam. Shit, they look as if they could be on a Saturday morning program, eating cereal. That only leaves you, big guy. I guess we should kneel in front of you now and kiss your ass."

Bug grumbles, "What's that shit I can't be a king? You know you'd love to kneel in front of me again, Hunter."

Hunter quickly adds, "No offense, guys, I really didn't mean anything by that statement. Cam, you definitely have the brains to be king, but you're the size of Bug. Also, Bug, if I knelt in front of you, I'd still be taller."

Cam says, "No sweat. You didn't hurt my feelings."

Bug just huffs and heads back to his room.

After Hunter's speech, Kannon begins to think Hunter must be right. It's got to be him. Kannon needs a little time to think about it, so he says, "This is a lot to think about. I'm going for a walk to clear my head."

Cam adds, "Mind if I join you? Once we get outside, I'll go my own way and leave you to your thoughts. Besides, I'm chomping at the bit to take a run through the woods and maybe find a creek to wade into."

Knowing how little Cam actually had gotten to do while he was sick, Kannon agrees to let him wander out of the keep with him. The two are off to spend what might be their last day in the Horizon.

CHAPTER 41

"A friend of my friend is my enemy." - Kannon

Once outside, Cam bolts for the nearest path and is soon out of sight.

Kannon walks for a bit along the invisible kingdom walls. His short walk leads him to a recognizable park bench, and he immediately thinks of his lost friend, Jim. Kannon sits on the old bench and starts talking like his friend is there.

"Boy, Jim, I wish you were here. Man, do I have a lot to talk to you about. You won't believe it, but after all this time, Dak isn't really the next king. Yeah, I can't believe it either. This place turns out to be just like my old world—nothing is what it seems. Spin Doll isn't even Spin Doll. She was kidnapped once again by the Jokers. I guess the Jokers' sister shape-changed to look like Spin Doll. Imagine the enemy walking right beside us that whole time. Oh yeah, and now we have a dragon on our side, but we lost Hoss in the process."

Kannon sits in silence, peacefully watching his surroundings. After a moment, he whispers, "Sorry, Jim, I should've protected you. I didn't mean to let you down. But I have a plan for tonight. If you were here, I would've consulted with you and seen if you thought it would work." Kannon pauses then says, "Ahh, who am I kidding? My plan is probably garbage. It will most likely blow up in my face and get more of my friends hurt. Boy, I really could use some of your advice right now."

Jim's voice suddenly comes from the other end of the

bench. "Kannon, my boy, nice to see you again. It seems like forever since I last saw you."

Kannon jumps up. "Jim, you're back. Is it really you?"

Jim spits on the ground in front of them and replies, "Kannon, I need to explain something to you. I'm not really who you think I am. With the final battle approaching tonight, I'm gonna lay all my cards on the table. This is only because I like you and feel I must ask you to please not be there tonight."

Kannon sits again, confused now. "What do you mean don't be there? I'm the leader and possibly the fourth king. This is why you brought me here."

Jim starts to get annoyed. "You're not the fourth king, and I need you to please not to be there."

"I'm definitely going to be there. Why would you ask me differently? You brought all of us here to defeat the Jokers. Now you don't want us to. I don't get it. What's the deal?"

Jim snaps at Kannon. "I brought you here to find the fourth king, not destroy the Jokers. Your job is to locate that king, and that's all."

Kannon has a blank expression while he states, "You really don't want us to destroy the Jokers? This is not you, Jim. Maybe running from Fat Jack has your mind all boggled."

Jim slams his fist on the arm of the bench in frustration, yelling, "Will you just listen to me?! Do not come to the battle tonight!"

Kannon wonders if the man in front of him is really *his* Jim. He notices this Jim is so angry that he can almost see smoke coming from the man's ears.

Jim growls, "I was not running from Fat Jack. Jack is my brother, and his real name is Torture. My real name isn't Jim. It's Torment, and together, we are known as TNT. I'm not a good guy, matter of fact. I may be the evilest person you've met here in the Horizon. For some unknown reason, I like you and don't want to see you get released."

Kannon, really confused now, tries to change his arm in case he needs to defend himself, but in the safe space, weapons can't be used.

Jim notices Kannon is nervous and says, "Think of me as that little guy who sits on your shoulder. One is evil, and one is good. I'm the evil one who slays the good one. I was there the night you pulled the trigger. To be honest, I really didn't think you had it in you. You really surprised me. I was also the one who talked Dayne into bringing your son to the Horizon. You know, a little secret about that is that Dayne wouldn't lose your son. The blood she saw was just an illusion that I made up. Same with your buddy, Bug. Those classmates who took his diploma? They didn't rip it up. They had it framed, and they waited at his house with a collection of money and a huge graduation cake. They didn't knock him off his bike. I did. Just like I persuaded him to go to that bridge, where I ripped up a fake diploma and pushed him toward the edge. Shit, I even threw a bat at the imbecile. I missed him, and the idiot picked it up and took it to the bridge with him."

Kannon can't believe what Jim is saying. *No way this is really Jim. It must be one of the Joker's tricks*, Kannon thinks. He wants to ask about the rest of the crew, but Jim continues before he can say anything.

"Hunter songs never had a different name on the radio. Making him think that and having some bad guys chase him… that was classic. Now, Cam is easy since he had one foot in the grave already. Hoss's mind was so scrambled when he returned from overseas; it was like taking candy from a baby. Dillo was my mercy project. Poor guy didn't know any better. Now, there is a pure soul. I don't know what Colt told you, but having Fat

Jack, as you call him, hit her with a car while she was running alongside the road worked better than planned. You should've heard all the crying. It sent shivers down my back. Once she lost her leg, pushing her over the edge wasn't much of a problem. Now for my crown jewel, Spin Doll. She had everything—awesome, loving parents, good grades, on the cheer team, and stuck with a child that wasn't hers."

Kannon jumps in. "She had a child?"

"You didn't know Cali has been hiding a baby? Yeah, well, neither did her family. For all we know, the baby might be here in the Horizon. By any chance, have you heard any babies crying lately? I believe the coach of the cheer team left her with that burden. It was kind of a forced thing if you know what I mean. Yup, she named him Baby Bee. We, in the Horizon, call him The Storyteller."

Kannon shouts, "Why would she do what she did to get here if it meant leaving a baby all alone?"

Jim smiles. "That's the best part. I had Jack attempt to kidnap the baby. He failed, but Cali couldn't even go to anyone since no one knew about little Bee. To make things worse for her, I took her voice and stuffed it into that little music box. Then I gave it to you. When you open the box, it'll eventually start singing, "You are my sunshine." That is actually Spin Doll's real voice. Without being able to protect little Bee and literally unable to tell anyone, I talked her into coming to the Horizon and helping me find the fourth king. I told her if we find the king, I will open the door that leads back to her room, and we'll never bother her and little Bee again.

"Before entering the Horizon, she hid little Bee away so no one could find him. When she realized I'd had tricked her and planned on never letting her leave, she tried to work out a deal with the Jokers to release me. Foolish girl—she never realized the Jokers work for me all along."

"The Jokers, Jack, and you are all a team? Why would you do this?"

Jim stands on the bench and clenches his fist as he answers, "For power; it's always been about power. Why only harass the souls in your world when I can do it forever here in the Horizon?"

Kannon couldn't believe Jim was the mastermind behind all of this. The whole time Jim was speaking, Kannon knew he had to get back to the group and tell the kings.

"What if I release you here and now? That would end this war before it begins."

Jim laughs. "Foolish boy, why do you think I made this a safe place? You know, I really did like you."

Before Jim exits, he says, "If you're going to be released tonight, be the first one. This way, you won't have to watch your friends and family perish in front of you. Unless you're more like me, I know and like to watch. May we meet on the battlefield, son. As you might realize, this will be your last safe place. From here on out, no place is safe. Tell King Dak we're coming for him."

Jim is gone in the air, leaving Kannon sitting all by himself.

Kannon quickly runs back to the kings to inform them of Jim and his deceit. Reaching the entrance, Kannon begins to yell for Cam to join him. There is little time to waste, and Kannon can't wait any longer to tell the kings. He begins to dance, and Cam appears, and the two enter the keep.

CHAPTER 42

"There's a part in everyone's story that has a chapter read silently." - Spin Doll

Kannon and Cam quickly make their way into the keep, and Kannon yells, "Everyone to the table! Mimic, go get the kings!"

Mimic rushes off to fetch the kings while the group assembles at the center table. Kannon turns to Bug and orders, "Bug, I need that music box!"

Bug, wondering why, pulls it out and reluctantly hands it to Kannon, who tosses it to the floor and stomps it into bits. Bug screams as he tackles Kannon, "What are you doing? That's Spin Doll's! Her grandpa gave it to her."

The two wrestle for a few minutes until Kannon gains the top position and pins Bug to the ground.

"It's not a gift from her grandpa. We were tricked into believing that. It's her voice that they trapped in the box. Jim is not her grandpa. He's her captor; he put her in the cage and locked her voice in this box."

Bug stops resisting and stares at Kannon's lips as if reading the words coming out. Kannon stands up, helps Bug to his feet, and straightens himself.

The kings come into the room, and Paragon says, "What is the meaning of this disturbance?"

Kannon respectfully answers, "Sorry, kings, but I have information I feel might serve our purpose."

Furrow nods. "Then proceed, Kannon. The floor is all yours."

Kannon bows his head to say thank you, then continues. "The old gentleman I've frequently spoken to, Jim, is not what I believe him to be. He's the reason we all are here in the Horizon. He has deceived and lied to each and every one of us. Hunter, the DJ actually did say your name. Jim made you hear it differently. The men chasing you were Fat Jack and him. They pushed you off that road. And Bug, that wasn't your diploma at the bottom of High Bridge. Your real diploma is waiting at your foster home, along with all your graduating classmates, and a huge cake. It was to be a surprise. They really did care about you."

Bug jumps in. "Why'd they knock me off my bike?"

"They didn't. Once again, it was Jim and Jack making you see the untruths. Dayne, my love, that night you crossed over, you weren't losing Dak. The pain and blood were all an illusion. They made us all see and feel in ways we never would have. Bug, I'm sorry. I should've explained Spin Doll's situation to you before smashing the box. She is a good girl, has a great family, and is a cheerleader. She was forced to protect the baby from evil. They tricked her as well. When she arrived here and refused to help Jim with his plans, they locked her voice in that wooden box and placed her in a cage so she couldn't tell anyone about their misdoings. They think of her as a trophy."

Bug is more upset that they destroyed Spin Doll's life than his own. Kannon knows he must mention the baby; he can wait till he and Bug are alone.

Kannon turns to the kings. "My kings, the plan is to release Dak at all costs. They believe him to be the fourth king. He is their primary target. Jack and Jim and the two Jokers have planned to fill your shoes and become the four kings."

Truncheon narrows his eyes and says, "Then they may

want to change their plans. Dak, the marked angel, is not the fourth king."

Paragon states, "When the time is right, we'll reveal the king and not anytime sooner."

Furrow adds, "Now, if interruptions cease, we will return to our duties."

The kings leave the warriors standing there, wondering what they are to do next.

Back at the kingdom tower, Spin Doll feels a hot wave of air blowing through her. Her hair is pushed back, and she has to catch her breath. Even though it is just wind, she feels different.

"Wow, what is that?" she speaks out loud. Stunned that she actually spoke out loud, she continues. "Someone must have crushed the box and released my voice. I know somehow Bug had something to do with this. Now to use my newfound voice to my advantage."

Fat Jack bursts through the door just as she finishes talking. Spin Doll hopes he has not heard her.

Jack yells, "Jokers, Jim, anyone here? The kingdom is filling with Shadows from every corner of the Horizon. There must be five thousand or more. There's no way the kings and that worthless crew can win against those odds. By tomorrow morning, I'll be a king. Get ready, Horizon, here comes King Jack." Fat Jack dances around the room as if he has already won the war.

Spin Doll says, "Jack, is that you, honey?"

Jack stops dancing and looks out the window at Spin Doll. Smiling, he says, "Are you talking to me, pet?"

Spin Doll quickly replies, "Honey. It's me, Cozzex."

Jack is confused. "You're not Cozzex! You're Jim's pet."

"Darling, Jim's pet can't speak. My brothers made me look like this pet again in case the warriors make it this far to rescue their friend. Not knowing it's actually me, I can simply release them one at a time."

Jack grins, thinking it makes sense. "Babe, I thought I lost you forever."

"Honey, let me out of this smelly cage so I can stretch and get something to eat. I really must use the little girls' room as well."

Without hesitation, Jack pulls the cage back inside the window and pops the lock. He grabs Spin Doll's hand and helps her out of the cage.

Hearing Jack dance and sing, she heads into the bathroom, searching for anything that can be used as a weapon. The only thing she can find is an old, used hairbrush. Quickly, she smashes it on the wall, shattering it, then picks up a larger piece that has a jagged, sharp edge. Getting Jack's attention, she lures him to the bathroom.

CHAPTER 43

"There are two kinds of fighters: those who throw a punch and those who catch it." - Hunter

The tension is so thick in the king's keep you can cut it with a knife. No one is talking, each doing their own prep.

Bug sits in pain on his bed, buckled over and holding his stomach. Seeing this, Kannon asks, "Bug, what's wrong? You haven't eaten at all today. I see you take food, but your plate looks untouched."

"Yeah, my stomach feels weird. It's like when you finish eating Thanksgiving dinner and want to sleep and not move."

Kannon laughs. "It's just butterflies; we all have them."

"No, I really think something's wrong. I'm in real pain." Bug figures it must have something to do with him eating that third piece of the heart, but he isn't telling anyone about that. He rolls over and faces the opposite way from Kannon. "I'll be fine; just going to rest for a bit."

Kannon pats Bug on the back of his leg and heads for the door. Before closing Bug's door, Kannon reminds Bug, "We came to the Horizon together, and we'll dam sure leave together."

Bug doesn't respond as Kannon closes his door.

Kannon heads to the center of the room and raises his hand to get everyone's attention. "Can everyone come here, please?"

Dax and Hunter gather chairs for everyone, and everyone joins Kannon.

Cam raises his hand like he's in school, and when a

confused-looking Kannon nods to him, Can says, "Where's Bug? Shouldn't he join us?"

"Bug is dealing with an upset stomach. He'll be fine in a couple of hours. It's probably just butterflies. Now, I need to get something off my chest. Between Jack, Jim, and the Jokers, the Horizon is filled to the brim with evil. Tonight is all or nothing. Once we enter the kingdom, there's no turning back. When those gates close, we will be outnumbered by the thousands. They have a giant snake that took everything away from Colt. So, now it's only fitting that we take everything away from them. They will come for Dak, thinking he is next to be king. Unless we can figure out how to change all the Shadows to solids, I'm nothing more than a distraction. I'll take the snake; you guys find and destroy the Jokers."

Dayne interjects. "We cannot protect each other inside the walls. There'll be too many Shadows. So, when the kingdom gates close behind us, it'll be a free-for-all."

Hunter looks at Dak. "Yo, Special Forces, any chance you know how many angels you command?"

Dak shrugs. "Knowing the amount of townsfolk, I'd say 300 to 400. But that's just a guess."

Cam says, "The four towers should be our main goal. By my calculations, if Dak and his army can withstand the onslaught of Shadows long enough, it might give us time to make our way to each castle and secure them for each king. Dayne, Kannon, and Bug can make a straight line for the Heart Tower. Hunter and Lakin can secure the club tower. Mimic, you two take Char and control the diamond tower."

Kannon cuts in. "What about the spade tower?"

"I'll take the spade tower," Cam answers. "They can't release what they can't see."

Everyone agrees and continues to make final preparations.

Hunter smiles and adds, "A released light can't fight."

The kings enter the hall and sit quietly until everyone enters the room. The only one they have to wait for is Bug, who finally comes out of his room, still holding his stomach. Kannon helps Bug sit.

"Bug, are you sure you're alright? Do you need some water?" Kannon asks.

Bug shakes his head and doubles over.

Hunter turns to the kings. "Sirs, I don't think Bug will be able to help. He should probably sit out this one."

Paragon looks at Bug, then says, "Small one, you have consumed something that is not made for consuming. With the swallowing of the glass heart shards, you now have two hearts fighting inside you over your body."

Hunter and Kannon look at Bug, and Hunter says, "Bug, you didn't swallow the third piece, did you?"

Kannon adds, "Where did you even find it?"

Bug looks up at his friends and confesses, "The other night, I took a walk down by a small creek. I sat on the bank and skipped stones across it." Bug stops for a moment, his pain worsening. "But," he continues, "there was this guy on the other side, sitting there and watching the water. We had a conversation about families and some other shit. I watched as he threw what I thought was a shiny stone. It stopped almost to my side of the bank, so, being who I am, I had to see what it was. I asked him if I could have it if I found it in the water. He said he was fine with that, so I retrieved it. Sure enough, it was the third piece of the heart. Like the pieces before it, I swallowed it quickly, before he'd want it back. Long story short, the guy on the other side was a Joker, but he didn't know who I was."

Dak says, "You met a Joker, and he was nice and gave you

something? That doesn't sound like a Joker to me."

"Yeah, like I said, he didn't know who I was."

Truncheon begins to speak. "Small one, the Jokers knew that the three pieces could never touch one another."

"What do you mean? You think the Joker knew it was me? That the guy gave me the piece of heart so I would join the three pieces?"

Furrow chimes in. "Yes, small one, that is precisely what he is saying. You're like a fish. The Joker dangled the shiny bait, and you swallowed it like a little fish."

Kannon is very concerned for his friend. He looks at the king and says, "Is there any way to retrieve it from his stomach?"

Paragon shakes his head. "I'm sorry, but no. By now, the heart has become a parasite, and Bug is its host. Soon, it will take over every aspect of Bug's body and brain."

Dak interrupts, not wanting to know Bug's outcome. "Excuse me, kings, but have you chosen your fourth king by any chance?"

Paragon says, "No, son, we haven't, and there's a good chance we won't for some time still."

Hunter is agitated at the answer. "What do you mean 'some time?' We will be at war within the next three hours. What the fuck are you waiting for? The last man standing?"

Furrow responds calmly. "At this time, this war is yours, not ours. Until we have chosen, there'll be no war for us."

"What the hell are you saying?" Bug yells. "This war is not for you. This war is only *about* you. You're the reason for this whole shit show. And now you're not going to fight? What is wrong with this place?"

Before anyone can interject, Bug continues his rant. "Are every one of you crazy as a loon? Kings, let me explain this to you as simply as I can. If you ain't fighting, then I damn sure ain't fighting! You ever hear of the phrase, 'kiss my ass'?"

Just as upset, Kannon says, "Wait, you really aren't going to help us? Are you shitting me? We've lost friends for you."

Truncheon answers, "Not till we're ready. Do you not understand?"

Hunter butts in and adds his two cents. "You mean to tell me that we were forced into coming to the Horizon to help you, and you're going to sit and watch? We did just as we were asked to do. Now you're going to send us out to be released with no backup. What kind of rinky dink shit is this? Maybe we help the Jokers and release your asses right here, right now."

Furrow frowns and snaps, "Stand down, or you too can feel our wrath."

Dayne, now fired up as well, says sternly, "Whoa, big guys, you're willing to use force on us, but not the bad guys. I think it's a good time for us to leave." Dayne gathers what she has brought and quickly heads for the exit. Everyone follows but Dak, puzzled as to what just happened.

"My lords," Dak says to the kings. "I'm honored to be given such a prestigious promotion. But if my friends and the angels under my control do not stand a chance, why would you send us into the mouth of evil without your help? Though I disagree with your words, I will go fight for your names. But real kings fight for their people's names as well." Dak exits, leaving the kings behind.

Once they all are out of the keep, Lakin angrily says, "All this shit I went through to save their asses, and they're just going to hand my ass over to the Shadows!"

Cam tries to calm the fired-up group down by saying, "People, mad or not, we have a war knocking on our backdoor. I, for one, will not go out without a fight. Colt did not give her light so ours could be thrown in the fire. If tonight is the night I'm released, I'm taking as many of them as I can."

Cam walks toward the kingdom entrance, and Char flies down from the top of the tall tree and lands beside Kannon, saying, "Now that I'm free, they'll never cage me again. I will await your orders, Kannon." Char then follows Cam with Mimic on her back.

Kannon, Dayne, Hunter, Dak, and Lakin stand in a circle looking at one another. Bug sits on the ground, holding his stomach and grimacing.

Kannon says, "You know we all won't make it out alive."

"I may not make it to the war alive. Something feels like it's growing inside of me," Bug grumbles.

Kannon ignores Bug, saying, "Dak, I'll do everything in my power to protect you. Hunter and Lakin, if we don't meet again for unseen reasons, know this: I will never forget our friendship. Dayne, my love, from the last world to this one, our love conquered all. I promise you this night will not separate us either. A love like ours can't be defeated. The Horizon will be our forever home."

Kannon turns to Bug, extends his hand to help him to his feet, and then pulls Bug into a hug. "I may not have known you in our previous world, but I'm truly blessed to know you in this one. Be safe, my friend, for we will have a laugh after this night."

Bug returns the hug and adds, "Kannon, my first true friend, I love you, and I'll miss you."

With emotions running high, the group walks off to join Cam, Char, and Mimic at the kingdom gates.

Inside the gates, the two Jokers are preparing in the basement of the four towers. Sin walks to Octoro's dwelling and says to the shadow guards, "You've made sure it hasn't been fed? We need it hungry and angry."

The shadow guard responds, "Sir, it hasn't moved in days. Is it alright?"

Omin says, "Open the door and check. Isn't that your job?"

"Yes, sir."

Sin calls out, "It's time to wake up, old friend. The good guys are coming, and they taste even better alive."

The shadow slowly opens the enormous gate, which clanks against the wall as it fully opens. The shadow enters the dark room, unable to see anything. Then, the Jokers hear a scream and watch as a light orb rolls out of the gateway and rises in the air.

Sin claps his hands and shouts, "Oh, goodie, it's awake!"

Omen yells into the gateway, "Octoro, time to come out and play!"

Both Jokers stand flat against the wall as the giant spider creature emerges from the gateway. They watch it leave the basement and begin to climb the Heart Tower. The Jokers, filled with glee, run up the stairway and away from the prison cell, not noticing a large sack hanging from the cell ceiling. They bust through their door and run to the window to watch the spider make its way to the top, then they grab a seat and stare out the window at the monstrous Beast beginning to weave a web. The room is still dark since they forgot to turn on the light when they entered.

Jim's voice comes from the corner of the room. "Glad to see you both made it back."

Sin startles and turns. "What the hell are you doing sitting in the dark all alone?"

"Seems we've got something to talk about, boys." Jim tosses Jack's teeth on the floor at the Jokers' feet.

Omin backs away. "What the hell is that?"

Jim steps out into the light of the window. "Oh, that. Those were my brother's teeth."

Sin is disgusted and snaps, "That's sick. Why do you have Jack's teeth?"

With a crazed look, Jim replies, "Really, you want to know why I have Jack's teeth? Maybe the same reason I'm going to take Sin's eyes and Omin's head."

The Jokers jump to their feet as they pull out their blades. Sin nervously shouts, "Are we seriously going to do this, old man?"

Omin adds, "I knew we couldn't trust this old shit and his fat brother."

Jim laughs. "Old shit and his fat brother. Guys, I'm sorry, but I think this is where our partnership ends. Like I said, I'll be taking your eyes and your head." Jim points at Sin, then Omin.

Sin, trying to reason with Jim, says, "Why would we release Jack when we were so close to war?"

Omin adds, "Where's your pet? Maybe she has something to do with it."

Jim stops for a minute to consider it. Then he puts his knife away and walks out of the door, not saying another word.

Sin looks at Omin and asks, "What the hell just happened? He just left. Was he still with us or not?"

Omin shrugs. "No idea, brother, but let's just be glad we don't have to deal with both crazies anymore."

They both put their swords back in their places and sit back down at the table. Little beads of sweat run down each face of the Jokers as they return, watching Octoro spin its web.

Kannon and the rest of the crew catch up with Cam and Char at the front gate of the kingdom. They all stand, trying to figure a way in. Each one offers an option to try and open the invisible gate, but none seem to work.

Bug, still feeling awful, states, "How are we supposed to win a war when we can't even find the entrance?" No one has an answer for him.

Char decides to fly up above the wall to take a look and find the door. While in the air, Mimic takes in everything to report to the warriors. Char lands and explains, "The kingdom is filled from wall to wall with Shadows. There must be ten thousand of them with townsfolk randomly scattered amongst them."

Kannon asks, "Is there any chance you can drop us in one at a time?"

Char doesn't think that is a good idea because with that many Shadows, she'd be dropping them to their release.

While they stand there with no answer as to how to breach the gate, it appears suddenly in front of them. For some reason, the invisible wall is now visible.

Dayne says, "Well, so much for the element of surprise. Shall we knock?"

Before anyone else can speak, the entrance gate begins to open. Everyone draws their weapons, and Char takes a deep breath. The gates open about two feet apart, then stop. The warriors stand ready to fight as Spin Doll steps out from the gate. Relieved to see her, the whole gang hugs her. Everyone but Bug, that is.

Bug yells, "How do we know it's really her? Why did the Shadows just let her waltz out?" Bug makes a lot of sense, and they all back up and draw their weapons out again.

Spin Doll walks up to Bug, reaching for his hand, but he refuses to give it to her.

"So, tell me, real Spin Doll, if you truly are the real Spin Doll, what do the warriors call it when they all attack me?"

Spin Doll smiles and then answers, "A Bug pile."

Bug stands there for a moment, amazed to hear her voice. He then replies, "That was an easy one. How about one more? What did I keep in my pocket that grosses you out?"

Spin Doll makes a sick face and replies, "Someone's old tongue."

Bug's face lights up; she has gotten it right. It is his Spin Doll, and her voice is as beautiful as she is. Bug runs and hugs her as he says, "My beautiful Spin Doll, I'm so sorry I let them put you in that cage again. I love you so much."

Spin Doll returns the hug but adds a kiss. After the long kiss, Spin Doll replies, "I love you, Bug."

Bug stands in amazement. Not only does he get his first real kiss, but she tells him she loves him!

Everyone feels so happy for Bug. It is his best day ever.

Kannon doesn't want to break it up, but they are about to go to war. He turns to Spin Doll and says, "Spin Doll, how does it look in there?"

Spin Doll shrugs. "I honestly don't know how we can defeat all of them." Then she tells them how the Jokers, Jim, and Jack are working together and how the Jokers released their own sister, and Spin Doll had released Jack and escaped.

Bug asks, "How did you defeat Jack all by yourself?"

"He thought I was Cozzex, and he hugged me. While we stood there embraced, I took my makeshift shank and stuck him in the back of his neck. As he rolled around trying to retrieve it, I ran to the kitchen and grabbed a larger knife. I stabbed him repeatedly until his light lifted out the window. The only thing left was his metal teeth. I hid them in the cage they had locked me in."

Bug grins and hugs Spin Doll again. "That's my girl."

Kannon regroups the crew as they again stand in front of the gates. He says, "Bug, why did you have an old tongue in your pocket?"

"It was the witch's tongue. Besides, I traded it back to her."

Hunter grins. "You are so nasty."

"Shut up, Hunter, before I teabag you."

Everyone smiles and then gets serious about preparing for what is on the other side of the gate.

Kannon grabs one side of the gate as Hunter grabs the other side. They slowly pull them apart to reveal a kingdom of Shadows standing, waiting to fight, as if they are trapped from leaving the kingdom. The warriors stand in a line facing the waiting enemy.

Kannon asks, "Any last words?"

Bug takes Spin Doll's hand and looks into her eyes. "May I have this last dance?"

Spin Doll smiles. "Yes, you can have *all* my last dances."

Dayne looks at Kannon and states, "Forever."

Kannon nods his head and repeats to her, "Forever!"

Lakin steals Hunter's catchphrase by saying, "Time to shine."

Cam softly says, "Colt, I need your legs now."

Dak begins to slightly shake as his body begins to sprout wings and his whole body turns to crystal.

Hunter looks at his friend and adds, "Now that is awesome. Your shit just turned to diamond."

Dak raises his hands and spreads his wings, then yells, "Forgive me, Father, for I'm about to sin!"

Hunter adds, "And if he likes it, he'll probably do it again."

Dak smiles and leads the way as he charges into the open gate. The rest follow the two into the heart of the battle, as blue goo flies over the now-closed gates.

CHAPTER 44

"Calm has left as chaos takes its place." - Dak

A shadow runs through the crowd and up to the Jokers, yelling, "They are here! They are here! They've entered the gate!"

Sin smiles and whispers, "Finally, something fun."

Omin looks at his brother and asks, "Shall we welcome our guests?"

Sin, still smiling, replies, "In a minute, let's not rush it. Besides, we have all night."

Off in the distance, they see light orbs rise one after another.

Dak, slashing his way through the crowd, stops, raises his hands, and yells, as sounds clank off his diamond body, "Angels, now is the time! Wings rise, my friends."

All the townsfolk begin to take their crystal angel forms, and the war is now real. Dayne swings The Releaser, taking lights with every passing. Hunter and Lakin stand back-to-back, ensuring nothing can sneak up behind them. Char shoots fireball after fireball as Shadows climb onto her. Mimic tries to help but isn't helpful at all. Spin Doll keeps the Shadows from reaching Bug as he flashes as quickly as possible. Still holding his stomach, he stops every minute or two to catch his breath. Kannon releases every solid figure he can see, all while searching for the snake. Cam walks through the massive crowd, eliminating a light with each step while totally invisible. Everyone is holding up their end and extinguishing Shadows at record speed.

Dayne looks at the towers in the distance. There is a spider's web that extends from tower to tower. Right in the middle of the web is Octoro, waiting to strike at any moment.

Lakin yells, "Look at the size of that spider! How are we going to beat that?"

Hunter, releasing lights, says, "When I see a spider... I squish it."

The Shadows are relentless, their attack never slowing. Hours pass as the moon lights the battlefield. What little ground the warriors seize quickly vanishes when they become exhausted.

Kannon yells to Dayne, not knowing if she can even hear him, "We need to get closer to the Jokers! Where is Cam? Where are those kings?"

Dayne doesn't answer, nor does anyone else. Char throws shadow after shadow off her back and uses her wing strength to clear space. She makes room only for it to be filled again in seconds. Mim and IC swing their little makeshift swords, trying with everything they have to keep the onslaught of Shadows off Char's back. With an unsuspecting move, Char turns quickly, destroying a few vendor shops, and Mim loses her balance and falls into the sea of Shadows. IC reaches to grab her, but she is lost in the darkness. With so many Shadows and light orbs, Mim surely perished.

Lakin cracks her whip through the crowds, taking five or six Shadows with each swing. With her and Hunter now pushed apart, her backside is exposed, making it harder for her to swing in both directions. Tired, she begins to lose the fight. The Shadows are too much for her. She can feel their blades tear into her skin. With a few more blows, she will lose the use of her right arm. Backing up, trying to reach her brother, Lakin stumbles and falls back onto the ground. Like a pack of wild dogs, the Shadows tear her in every direction. Soon she is engulfed in Shadows and is no more.

Hunter makes his way back to Kannon and Dayne, asking, "Have you seen my sister?"

They shake their heads but never take their eyes off the charging army.

Kannon kneels beside Bug and asks, "Are you alright?"

Dayne and Hunter keep the Shadows at bay while Kannon attends Bug.

"The pain; it's gotten way worse. It hurts bad." Bug can barely be heard in the chaos.

Kannon tries to pick Bug up so he's not so trampled.

A very weakened Bug says, "Kannon, thanks for being my friend. Please tell Spin Doll she'll always be my last dance."

Kannon yells, "Bug, you're not giving up, are you? You're my watcher; you have a job to protect me!"

Bug begins shaking so badly that Kannon cannot hold him, and he falls to the ground. Kannon, feeling helpless, just watches as his friend gives up. Bug's body begins to swell, and his skin becomes redder as if he is heating up.

Hunter yells, "Bug, get up! This shit isn't over yet, my friend."

Bug, still swelling and almost completely red, speaks one final time. "Hunter, I'm sorry, but this time, I'm gonna be the hero of the story. Now, please run."

As Bug continues to expand, Kannon, Dayne, and Hunter take off running away from Bug. The Shadows engulf Bug, and he expands even more. With a loud exploding BOOM, Bug bursts as giant flash of light expands in every direction, covering the entire kingdom and changing every shadow to solid while sending all the warriors flying to the ground.

When Kannon and the remaining warriors gather to their feet to see Bug has solidified every shadow, a smile comes to Kannon's face as he states, "Bug, my old friend, you saved me once again. Way to have my back one final time." He cocks his cannon and begins to fire massive rounds into the sea of Shadows.

Hunter smiles and remarks, "Nice to see you join the fight, princess."

They charge onto the towers while Char finally gets the Shadows off her and takes to the air.

Dak and his angels hold strong and push toward the towers as well. Off in the distance, you can hear, ever so often, the sound of breaking glass as an angel loses their light to the war. Even hours into the battle, Dak pushes forward, never taking his eyes off the Jokers. The tide has seemed to change, thanks to Bug's final unselfish conclusion.

CHAPTER 45

"Even the biggest win can count as a loss." - Cam

Cam makes his way to the Jokers unseen, slowly moving into position and standing behind them. Listening to every word they say, he draws his two knives and slowly moves closer to release them.

Sin yells to one of his shadow guards, "I think it's about time to wake up, Dice! Why don't you go tell him it's feeding time?"

Omin laughs as he adds, "These warriors definitely have some fight in them, don't they? I'm really enjoying myself. Think we should join in the festivities?"

Sin doesn't answer because he is excited about releasing Dice.

Cam stops closing in on the Jokers and puts his knives away. *Is that the Dice that destroyed Colt's life? I must go and see this Dice for myself,* Cam thinks. *Colt must have her revenge; it's the least I can do.*

Cam begins to follow the shadow who is sent to awaken Dice, but before leaving, he says, "Gentlemen, till next time."

Sin and Omin look around to see where the voice has come from, and Sim says, "I thought I heard that shitty little kid's voice again."

Omin replies, "We must be too stressed from all this hostility. That kid was released weeks ago. I think your crazy is affecting *my* crazy." Both Jokers laugh, then continue to watch the war.

Cam follows the shadow down into the dungeon and to the very last cell. The shadow looks incredibly nervous as his shaking hand tries to unlock the cell door. The shadow drops the key, and when he bends to pick it up, Cam speaks.

"Here, let me help you with that."

The shadow looks around, trying to figure out where the voice is coming from. Cam appears in front of him and quickly releases him. Then he looks in the cell window to see part of a giant snake in his view. He once again vanishes as he turns the key and unlocks the cell door. As Cam steps into the cell, he closes the door behind him and listens for the lock to click.

Dice can sense a figure and says, "You must have a death wish, boy, entering my confinement."

Cam slowly moves around the snake, trying to find its head. "So, you're the deadly Dice. Well, once I'm done with you, they'll have the dead part right."

Dice lifts his head from his coiled body and answers, "Boy, you gave up when you stepped in here. You know you won't leave. Why don't you show yourself, and I promise to make it quick."

Cam continues to move, so Dice can't pinpoint his scent. "Do you remember a girl that you had taken a leg from?"

"Oh yeah, she wasn't a battle at all. She wasn't even my target. Consider that one a freebie?"

Not taking his eyes off the slowly searching snake, Cam says, "Well, that girl was my best friend."

"Don't worry. Soon, I'll reunite you."

Cam slices Dice's body. As he quickly dives to the side, Dice snaps its fangs in Cam's direction. Cam dusts himself off, unfazed.

"See, you bleed just like everyone else. I don't see what makes you so special. Before I'm done, I'll prove you can be released as well."

Dice, now getting annoyed by the boy, replies, "I was going to take the whole girl, but you should be glad I left some for you. You know, so you can say your goodbyes."

Cam continues to move, not standing still to be an easy target. His only mistake is stepping in some of Dice's blood, which leaves footprints. Dice lunges in the direction of the bloody footprints, but Cam is too quick and dives, slicing off the tip of Dice's tail.

"You little bug!" Dice screams in anger. "Now I will eat you slowly, starting with your feet so you can watch."

"Oh, there'll be death in this cell tonight, but not mine."

Dice lunges toward Cam's voice, but Cam eludes the strike, leaving a new wound on Dice's neck.

"It seems like you're losing a lot of blood," Cam says with a sneer. "I can make this easier for you. All you must do is apologize for releasing Colt, and I'll send you quicker, so you don't have to go through the pain. Though I do hope you wait a little longer."

Cam, while changing directions, accidentally drops the cell key, alerting Dice to his whereabouts. Dice lunges, scraping Cam's shoulder as the snake smashes its head into the stone cell wall, stunning itself for a second. Cam takes this advantage and sticks Dice at the bottom of its mouth, leaving a large gaping cut.

Dice screams in pain and anger as blood begins to pour out. "I'll release you and your friends now, you little coward. Now you will die my way."

With so much blood covering the cell and Cam, he is an easy target. He quickly tries to wipe the blood from his body, but Dice lunges, sticking both fangs into Cam's back and filling him with poison. Cam, in the process, gets two good stabs between Dice's eyes, leaving his knife stuck in the snake's head. The snake shrieks as it shakes its head back and forth, trying to remove the knife. Cam falls to the ground. The more Dice struggles, the deeper the knife pierces. Cam's body is filled with poison, a feeling he has dealt with his whole life. He manages to stand, even though the poison has consumed much of his body.

Dice yells, "I ingested enough poison in you to release everyone above us! How are you still standing, boy?"

Cam smirks. "I lived with worse poison in my body my whole life. But can you live with that knife embedded in yours?"

With a last-ditch attempt, Dice lunges, crushing Cam into the cell wall, but also accomplishes pushing the knife into its brain deeper and releasing himself. The snake vanishes, but instead of the light rising, it sinks into the ground.

Cam, barely clinging to his light, is lying there, unable to move. He calls out to Colt. "Colt, my best friend, you traded your light for mine to give me a life I never had. I hope you're proud of me, but maybe I was not supposed to have a happy life. I defeated your enemy and retrieved your honor. But, no matter what happens, I cannot escape the poison. In my world or this, it finds me and releases me. May our next journey allow us more time together." Cam's body ends the fight as his head drops and releases his light once more.

CHAPTER 46

"When the odds aren't even, always bet on the underdog."
- Spin Doll

A shadow soldier runs up to the Jokers. Out of breath, he informs them, "Jokers, I'm sorry to report that we have lost Dice and most of the area near the entrance gate."

Sin fires back, "What happened to Dice? He was fine earlier; you must be mistaken."

The shadow nervously replies, "I'm sorry, sir, but he has perished in his cell. We could not locate him, but there were two separate blood stains throughout the cell. I still believe we will have enough forces to extinguish them, as they have also taken losses."

"Octoro! Your turn."

Omin adds, "Now is the time we should join the fight as well, my brother." He pulls out his sword and runs into battle.

Sin yells, "Brother, let's not be too hasty!" He sits back in his seat and takes a sip from his cup.

A loud screech from above makes Sin and the entire battle look above them. They all witness Char torching the giant cobweb attached to the four towers. Octoro falls to the ground below with a huge thud that shakes the ground beneath them. Char continues incinerating the web while getting close enough to a window high in the Heart Tower.

IC quickly jumps off Char and into the tower window. Octoro fires multiple webs at Char as Char fires back, burning the webs. Rapidly, Octoro shoots more webs than Char can burn, which consumes Char, sending her crashing to the ground and making her unable to move her wings. The Shadows cover Char, stabbing her from all angles. Her powerful scales protect her as she swings her wings, sending Shadows flying in all directions. Char ascends into the air and widens her fire range.

IC yells to her, "Char, fly away before you get released! You're the Horizon's last remaining dragon. Please leave. I can't watch you fade away."

Knowing IC is right, Char turns and flies off into the moonlight.

With only Kannon, Spin Doll, Dayne, Hunter, Dak, and whatever angels remain, the battle will be over soon. The warriors begin to lose more ground as they are pushed back ever so close to where they began. With the odds stacked against them, they need a miracle.

Dak yells to the angels, "If this is our last stand, then make it one they'll talk about for the years to come!"

Suddenly, the entrance doors swing open, and the three kings stand dressed for battle. Seeing the kings, the Shadows begin to back away.

Omin runs out of the pack, breathing hard, "The kings are here. Now we can finish you all at once. What a lovely day this is. You know, this is the one time it's not good to be the king."

Octoro stands overtop of Omin, waiting for the word to be given.

Sin yells, "Brother, give them a minute to say goodbye! I do so like a sad ending."

The kings ignore the Jokers and their army as they walk up to the tired warriors. All three kings kneel before Dayne, and Paragon says, "Dayne, would you give us the honor of being the Horizon's first lady king?"

Stunned, Dayne doesn't know what to say as Kannon and

Hunter also kneel. All the angels and Dak kneel as Spin Doll follows suit. Dayne, still stunned, looks at the kings in front of her, kneeling and holding the crown towards her. Dayne takes the crown with shaking hands and places it on her head. The crown immediately forms around her head, and she feels a jolt of energy shoot through her body.

Dak smiles and whispers, "My mom is a king."

Dayne says, "Rise, my fellow kings. We have a war to win."

The kings join her as Sin yells from the back, "What the hell's this? There's no such thing as a lady king. Attack!"

Dayne smiles. "Hey, Jokers, the bitch is back, and this time, I'm bringing friends."

The shadow army, along with Omin and Octoro, charge. To Kannon's surprise, the kings are even better than he had thought with their blades as they were making quick work of the Shadows.

Octoro charges after Hunter, knowing he is the one who released the Beast. Hunter's back is against the kingdom walls. Octoro races towards him, sizing him up for a web.

"I'm going to enjoy eating you little by little, fly," Octoro says in a deep voice.

With his back against the wall, Hunter feels the wall begin to move, pushing him toward Octoro. Then, the wall pulls him away from the spider. Octoro goes in for the kill, and Hunter dives to his right, just avoiding the attack. Now facing the spider and the wall, Hunter can see the wall moving back and forth. Hunter runs into the crowd of Shadows, followed by Octoro and the wall. The crumbling wall leaves Octoro in a cloud of dust. He is barely visible to Hunter and the rest of the battle.

The dust clears, revealing Hoss and Skulk standing where

the wall once did. Octoro charges them as the two, in return, charge him. The warriors can't believe their eyes. Hoss is back, and he has brought a friend. With Octoro being larger than either giant, it takes both of them all they have to push him back. Blood flies from all three giants as the moonlight captures every grueling swing. The war is back in full swing. The Jokers are ending every angel they see.

Sin yells to Omin, "Let's get the boy!" Sin points to Dak. "You get on one side, and I'll take the other side. Keep him between us; he can only stop one of us, and the other will release him."

Omin nods, and they both circle around an unsuspecting Dak.

Off in the distance, Kannon can see the Joker's plan developing. He tries to yell at Dak, but the battle is too loud for Dak to hear. The Jokers begin to run toward Dak, and Kannon sprints toward his son as well. The closer the Jokers get, the more their eyes widen. Just as they reach their target, Dak is pushed from the side onto the ground face-first. Dak quickly rolls over to see his father's body hanging from the swords of the Jokers, with the big moon behind his dad's silhouette revealing that each Joker has pierced Kannon—Sin from the front and Omin from the back.

Dak is in shock and can't hear any of the battle. It is like everything stopped. Unable to move, Kannon looks at Dak and mouths, "I love you, son. Take care of your mom."

The Jokers hold Kannon in the moonlight as if he is a trophy for everyone to look at. Kannon's dangling feet show his light trying to hang on. Knowing this is the end of his best friend, Hunter places a well-aimed shot into his friend's heart to end his torture. Kannon's body slowly vanishes as he tries to gulp for air. Then, they all watch as his light trickles into the night sky.

Dak's is stunned. It is like he is staring through the Jokers. Then Sin and Omin begin to run back toward the towers and direct every shadow to end Dak's light.

Dak walks through the Shadows as if they aren't putting up a fight at all. The Jokers run into the Heart Tower and lock every door behind them. When Dak finally reaches the towers, Jim stands in his way with a bigger figure and a burlap sack over his head.

Dak stops. "Jim, move aside, or I'll go through you as well. I will release the Jokers tonight."

Jim smiles and replies, "Oh, I don't think so. You see, this creature standing beside me has other ideas on how this will end. Dak, let me introduce you to—"

Jim stops when Dak folds his wings over his shoulders to cover his chest. Still smiling, Jim pulls the sack off the creature's head, saying, "This here is the Hangman, or as you might know him by his nickname, the Boogeyman."

Dak takes a step while fear rushes through his mind. He's seen this Hangman before…in his nightmares as a child. With the Hangman and Jim standing between him and the Jokers, Dak lunges forward, swinging his sword at the creature. The Hangman steps aside, easily avoiding the attack, and places a noose over Dak's head. Then he turns to be back-to-back with Dak. The Hangman bends over, pulling the noose and lifting Dak's feet off the ground. Dak fights to get loose but is losing air with every move.

Hunter sees his friend losing his life, so he pulls up and aims at the Hangman's head. He pulls his trigger just as a shadow pushes into him, sending his shot off target. The bullet travels through the crowd and just misses the Hangman's head but shears the rope enough for it to snap, sending Dak tumbling to the ground.

The Hangman turns toward Dak to finish the job but is stopped by Jim yelling, "Leave him be! The Shadows will finish him off. Besides, we have our own objective." Jim points in Spin Doll's direction, and the Hangman follows his orders and heads her.

Spin Doll notices the Hangman heading her way, with Jim not far behind. This time, she is not going without a fight. Spin Doll charges the Hangman with her swinging fans. She sends two deep cuts across the Hangman's chest that heal themselves right in front of her. She sends two more slices into his body, but they don't seem to faze him either. The Hangman pushes her to the ground and immediately places a noose around her neck.

Jim says, "So, my Hangman is not as easy to release as my brother was. You know what this means, don't you? Let's go see if we can find this baby of yours. You know what they say—an eye for an eye."

Spin Doll, feeling the noose around her neck and hearing Jim's words, makes her body give up again. The Hangman drags her along the ground as he follows Jim out of the kingdom gates.

CHAPTER 47

"Sometimes the littlest thing can make the biggest
difference." - IC

IC jumps through the window and lands in a room she is
familiar with—the room she and Char were caged in. Now,
there is only one cage. She thinks this is where they had kept
Spin Doll. She searches for something to use as a weapon in
case she has to deal with a shadow. She pushes a chair over to
the kitchen counter and climbs up, thinking there must be a
knife or something in one of the drawers. She finds a knife
block on the counter, but it is missing the largest knife. IC grabs
the smallest one and hides it in her pocket. She even names it
Shark Tooth.

While searching, noises come from outside the room, like
someone is approaching quickly. IC quickly hides in one of the
drawers, leaving it slightly open so she can see and hear who
enters. The door busts open, and the two Jokers stumble in, out
of breath.

Sin says, "Crystal angels, dragons, and giants—this just
isn't fair. All we have is a huge spider and a million Shadows."

Omin adds, "And they made a lady a king. Who does that?
How were we to know the new king was a lady? There's no
such thing. I call bullshit! We were hornswoggled."

Both Jokers rush to the window to see the battle below, and
IC pushes the drawer open just a touch more to hear better.

Sin says, "Brother, we will win this war if we can keep the

warriors and kings from turning on each heart-shaped spotlight in each tower."

Omin turns and looks at this brother, asking, "What do you mean? Are you saying each tower has its own heart?"

"Why, yes, brother. Those enormous beacon lights at the top of each tower are the tower's heart. Each light covers a quarter of the Horizon. Then the guardian, or in our case, the king of that tower, fully regains their strength."

Omin nods, understanding. "So, no light, no king. Why don't we just smash the light?"

"The lights can't be damaged. If they could, don't you think we would have tried that first before we released a king?"

Omin smiles and gloats, "That was truly awesome when we released that cannon guy, holding him up there for all his friends to witness like he was on display."

Sin begins to picture it as well and adds, "I wonder how long he could have endured the pain. That stupid marksman had to ruin our fun. I think we should release him next."

IC can't believe what she is hearing. Is Kannon really gone? Listening to the Jokers' discussion, she now knows what to do. She must light the four towers' hearts. Slowly, she slides out of the drawer and creeps across the counter and down the chair. With all the yelling from the Jokers and their attention solely on the battle, IC easily slips out of the room and into the hallway.

Not knowing which way to go, she chooses left, which she knows is against all the logic of a gamer. But her thought is you can't always go right; some good stuff must be on the left. She works herself down the hall, trying not to make a sound.

At the end of the hall, IC finds a lone door with no doorknob. She tries to push it but has no luck, and pulling it doesn't work either. IC stands there stumped, thinking how she will open the door. She leans back on the wall opposite and studies the door. She says to herself, "It can't be that hard to open this door. What can I be missing?"

Unable to figure it out, IC places her hands over her eyes and tips her head back to face the ceiling. Ready to give up, she uncovers her eyes, and a red button is on the wall about two feet higher than her. Instantly, she knows that must be the switch for the door. But it is too high for her, and she definitely can't reach it. There is nothing around for her to use to get a boost.

She tries getting a running start, but that doesn't work, as she bumps her knee on the wall and limps around like she is wounded and feeling upset. Standing there with no options, she hears the Jokers leave their apartment and head her way. There is nowhere for her to go. She is a sitting duck.

IC stands in the corner and closes her eyes, waiting for the worst.

Sin says, "Well, this door is still sealed. The alarms we put on them are still armed."

Omin responds with, "That is a good idea, brother. Putting one-way switches with alarms on them. If someone enters them, they can't leave unless someone lets them out. They'll never get all four turned on without dealing with us."

"No, brother, the best part is that the kings can't enter the towers till the light is on. So, someone other than the kings must activate them. I'm sure they're not smart enough to figure that out. Once they're trapped inside, we enter and free them. It's just that simple."

They both laugh, thinking once again that they outsmarted the kings. The Jokers leave and head back into their place, still not noticing a cowering IC.

IC slowly opens her eyes and wonders how the Jokers

didn't see her. Then she notices that she's floating; her new wings are working! She can finally fly again.

IC begins flying in circles and spins, realizing how much she misses her wings. Once she is done testing them, IC heads straight for the button. Immediately upon pushing it, the door opens and the alarm sounds. She quickly flies into the room and sees a thick rope hanging down from a hole that leads to the room above. She can hear the Jokers running down the hall toward her. With not much space left in the hole due to the thick rope filling it, IC tries to squeeze through but only gets halfway. With her legs visible, she's bound to get caught.

IC continues to struggle as the Jokers shut the alarm off and knock on the door. Sin talks from the other side. "I don't know who's in there, but you won't be when we get in there."

Omin adds, "We'll huff, and we'll puff. Guess who? You guessed it; we're the big bad wolf. The better to eat you with."

Sin slaps Omin in the back of the head as he states, "That's one of Fat Jack's lines."

Omin rubs his head and apologizes.

They blast into the room just as IC slips through the hole. Sin yells, "There's no one here! What's going on?"

Omin adds, "We've been tricked."

As the two Jokers hear a click and the door locks behind them, Sin says, "Grab the door before it locks."

Omin replies, "Too late; we're locked in." B

The Jokers begin to pound on the door, hoping someone hears them and lets them out. A small pushing battle begins as they blame each other for being trapped.

IC searches the light for a switch before realizing the rope needs to be pulled to turn the light on. There is no way she is strong enough to pull the rope, so she quickly comes up with a plan. Since no one is coming for the Jokers because they are all down in the war, she will offer them a trade.

IC yells down the hole, "Hey, Jokers, I'll make a deal with you."

The Jokers look toward the hole, having no idea who is speaking to them.

IC yells again. "I can't see anything up here. If you can turn the light on so I can find my way out of here, I'll get out and open the door for you."

Sin yells up, "Are you crazy? We ain't helping you do anything. We'll wait for one of our Shadows."

They wait about twenty more minutes until they realize no one is coming.

Omin yells, "Ok, we'll turn on the light, but you better come open the door as soon as we do."

IC agrees, and the Jokers begin to pull the rope. With a loud click, the light turns on, filling Dayne, on the battlefield, with newfound strength, lighting up a quarter of the Horizon, and releasing every shadow standing in the light.

IC stumbles around, trying to regain sight as the bright light blinds her for a few minutes. She then yells, "I'll be out in a minute, then I'll get you guys out!"

Frantically, she searches for something to cut the rope. She lucks out and finds a piece of broken glass, which must have broken from part of the light. The glass is very sharp and slices through the old dry rope like a hot knife through butter.

Sin, getting impatient, yells, "Come on; we need to get out! If we're not out before I count to ten, we're shutting off the light. Ten, nine, eight, seven…"

IC tries cutting faster, but the rope is so thick it takes longer than she thought.

Sin continues counting. "Six, five, four, three, two, one."

As the Jokers yank on the rope, it falls to the floor. IC cuts it enough that when the Jokers yank, the rope breaks.

Omin screams, "Let us out! We had a deal!"

IC doesn't answer; she climbs out onto the roof through a hole between the light and the wall. She can still hear the Jokers yelling while she looks for a way to get to the next tower. She knows her new wings won't be strong enough yet to fly that far since the towers are quite a distance apart.

Down on the ground, the war is raging on. Hoss and Shulk aren't fairing too well against Octoro. Hoss runs in and crushes Octoro with a large part of the wall, knocking Octoro back a little. Octoro has Skulk in his grasp with three of his legs. Shulk fights with everything he has, but Octoro is too strong for him. Hoss tries to dropkick Octoro to get him to release his buddy, but the spider knocks Hoss's attack away. Octoro slowly crushes Shulk to death, and Hoss can do very little to stop it. After having no success in stopping the giant spider, Hoss watches as Shulk is released, and his light floats up in the air.

Octoro turns his attention to Hoss, then throws him against part of the kingdom wall that is still standing. Hoss is bloody and bruised, fighting a battle he can't win. With being a giant, you wouldn't think that would happen as often as it does.

Pinned against the kingdom wall, Hoss is just about to be injected with Octoro's poison, so he pushes with all his might, but for some reason, Octoro is easily drawn away from him.

The giant spider is losing ground and power, and it is all thanks to Dayne. She runs under the giant spider and slices open its abdomen with The Releaser. Her newfound power made her ten times stronger. With Octoro now on his back, Hoss and Dayne pound and slice until the spider finally gives up and sinks into the ground. Octoro has been released without having a light. With a quick celebration, Dayne and Hoss turn their attention to the towers.

CHAPTER 48

"When everything is destroyed in the battle, there are no spoils to go to the victor." - Dak

Dayne takes a quick breather, trying to wipe all the blue goo from her vision. The battered and beaten Hoss trudges on toward the towers. Dak and the remaining angels push on by making a wall of angels. They move in unison, one step at a time. Stopping for a moment behind the angel wall, Hunter gets a much-needed rest. The other three kings have almost made it to their towers. With their regained strength and massive frames, they relinquish Shadows at a quick pace.

On the towers, IC has found the remains of Octoro's spider web stretching over to the next tower. Slowly she crosses the sticky web, stopping every few feet to use her piece of glass to scrape the web from her shoes. At the top of the towers, the wind begins to pick up as the moonlight shines just enough for her to follow the web. Reaching the spade tower, IC slides into the top, just as she did the last one, through the crack between the wall and the light. Having the same setup as the previous tower light did, IC needs to find a way to pull the rope in order to turn on the light. She looks down at the hole; the rope is hanging in the hole just as the last one was. The bottom room has the same kind of trap door as well. IC flies down the hole and searches the nearly empty room. She hears voices coming from outside and figures they must be shadow guards who are guarding the door.

She yells, "Help! Can anyone hear me? I'm trapped in here. Oh, please help."

She pounds her little fists on the door, and the surprised Shadows hurriedly opens it and rush in. They see IC trying to pull the rope but not being very successful at it.

They laugh as one of the Shadows yells, "What are you doing in here?"

IC swiftly replies, "I was walking one of the Jokers' new pets, and they ran in here and up in this hole."

The other shadow asks, "What kind of pet is it? I didn't know the Jokers had any new pets."

"It's some super-fast rabbit. I think they said his name is Clark."

IC makes it sound so believable that the Shadows yell up the hole, "Clark, oh Clark, we've got some juicy carrots down here for you!"

The imaginary Clark doesn't answer, so IC suggests that the Shadows hold the rope so Clark can't go any further. The Shadows grab the rope, in hope that Clark won't get away.

IC tells them, "I'll go up in the hole and lure Clark close to the hole. When I get him close enough, I'll yell and you two pull him through the hole and grab him."

Both Shadows set their feet and prepare to yank. IC enters the hole and immediately stomps around, like she is chasing something. The Shadows become more excited, thinking how much the Jokers will reward them for saving Clark. IC slowly cuts the thick rope halfway through with her piece of glass then begins wiggling it as if she is struggling with Clark.

"Pull guys, pull! He's very strong. You're going to have to pull hard."

Both Shadows begin to pull with every ounce of strength they have.

The light turns on, sending a bolt of energy to Paragon. Feeling the energy, Paragon grows a foot taller, and his quarter of the Horizon lights up and changes to its original form, erasing all Shadows in its reach.

The Shadows continue to pull, thinking that at any time they are going to pull Clark through the hole.

IC finishes cutting the rope and it snaps, sending the Shadows crashing to the floor. IC looks down the hole and yells, "Clark got away! You two wait there. I'll send someone to come and let you out. Then you can help us find Clark. Don't worry. I'll tell the Jokers you tried to help. I'm sure they'll be happy to see you two."

The Shadows collect themselves and wait patiently for someone to come and open the door.

IC promptly climbs back outside and looks for a way to the next tower. There are no more spider webs, and it is too windy for her to chance flying that far. She stops to watch some of the battle, noticing fewer Shadows since the last time she's seen the battle. Paragon and Dayne look much bigger and stronger than Furrow and Truncheon. IC knows they'll win the war if she can get their lights on as well.

With no other option, IC prepares to fly to the diamond tower. Trying to build her confidence, she counts, "Ten...nine...eight..."

Before she reaches seven, the light in the club tower turns on. Immediately, IC looks at Truncheon and watches him regain his total power. She wonders who turns it on...possibly an angel. Either way, the light is on and one less she has to deal with. Watching the club tower for a bit, IC doesn't notice any movement. Now her worry is that whoever turns on the club light might be heading to the next tower as well. What if they're not friendly? Either way, she has to get to the next light and restore the four. If another is there, she'll have to deal with them at that moment.

IC waits for the wind to die down before she attempts to fly to the diamond tower. Since going down to the ground and crossing over is not an option, the battle continues. As soon as the wind calms, IC leaps off the edge and flaps her wings with everything she has.

Down on the battlefield, the Shadows are now pushed back to the base of the towers. They are no match for the mighty kings and warriors who continue to gain strength with every step. Dak and Dayne drop back behind the front line for a quick assessment and a breather. Dak explains his encounter with Jim and the Hangman, telling them how they dragged Spin Doll off with a rope around her neck. He points out a trail from Spin Doll's body being dragged. With things in hand, Dayne orders Dak to take four angels with him and go after Spin Doll.

Quickly retrieving four of his better angels, Dak ventures and hurries off. They exit the kingdom walls and run out into the woods. The path leads them back to Fat Jack's cave. Dak holds his hand up for the angels to stop and remain quiet. Then, with the angels just out of view, he watches Jim, the Hangman, and Spin Doll, standing outside the cave while Jim is trying keys to unlock Jack's front door.

Jim mutters, "All these damn keys. How the hell did my brother know which one is for which door?"

Dak tries to get close to Spin Doll to see if she is okay, but he accidentally steps on a twig, bringing all attention onto himself.

Jim yells, "Who's there? Show yourself."

Dak slowly steps out with his hands up. "Jim, you don't need Spin Doll. You have no more moves. Let her go, and we'll let you be on your way as long as you never return."

Jim laughs. "Who are you talking to, boy? How about this? You and whoever is hiding back there turn your asses around and head back to that perfect kingdom you have. If not, my friend and I'll make it so you never return."

"You know we're not going to let you take her. Please don't make us do this."

Jim scowls. "First of all, you're not letting me do shit. Now you're trying to push my buttons. Hangman, release these kids."

The Hangman drops Spin Doll's rope and turns toward Dak. The four angels who came with Dak reveal themselves as they stand in formation behind Dak, who pulls his sword.

"Listen, buddy, you don't have to do this. If you come closer, we'll have to release you."

The Hangman begins to walk toward them as Jim finds the right key and opens the cave door. He swiftly grabs Spin Doll's rope and tries to pull her barely breathing body through the door. As it becomes hard for Spin Doll to breathe with the rope around her neck, she doesn't put up too much of a fight.

As the Hangman approaches Dak, Dak swings his sword, striking the Hangman in his shoulder. Such a blow leaves the sword lodged in the Hangman's arm, and he backhands Dak, sending him flying to the ground. The Hangman looks at the sword, pulls it from his arm, and drops it beside Dak.

Dak tries shaking his hand to relieve the pain as he reaches for his sword. The Hangman grabs Dak by the hair and strikes him in the face, knocking Dak out cold. The angels charge, flailing their swords. One angel slices Hangman's back, drawing attention to himself. The Hangman grabs the angel by his face and, with a quick twist, snaps the angel's neck and releases him. Jim smiles with pleasure. The next angel charges, and the Hangman grabs him by his neck and crotch, then picks the angel up over his head and drops it down over his knee, breaking the angel's back. The broken angel lies on the ground, unable to move as the Hangman stomps on the angel's face and releases him. One of the last two angels stabs his sword through the Hangman's chest. The Hangman grabs the other angel and pulls him toward him, running the sword through that angel's chest. The Hangman watches the light drain from the helpless angel. The Hangman turns around, grabbing the angel who ran him through. With a hand on each side of the angel's head, the Hangman crushes its skull. With a light chuckle from inside Jack's door, the angel screams while his light rushes from his body.

Finished with the skirmish and still run through by the angel's sword, the Hangman turns toward Jim, who already has Spin Doll in the cave. He slams the door, then locks it, leaving the Hangman outside. The Hangman punches the door to get in, so Jim quickly opens the door and lets the Hangman in before he breaks it down.

After figuring out Jack's key placement, Jim opens the door he wants to enter, along with two more doors. Then Jim pushes Sin Doll through as he and the Hangman follow. Jim figures if they are followed, leaving three doors open, might send his enemies down the wrong path. Little does he know that with the Hangman leaving Jack's front door open, his plan will be abolished. A slight breeze entering Jack's cave door will soon close all three doors.

When Dak comes to, he sees the four swords scattered around with no angels in sight and notices the cave door is left open. Slowly, he enters the cave, only to see twenty or so doors in a line, all locked. Dak has no idea which door they entered or where they are taking Spin Doll. He runs out of the cave and rushes toward the kingdom, knowing he cannot go after Jim alone.

CHAPTER 49

"Chaos turns to calm, as the last one falls." - Hunter

By the time Dak returns to the battle in the kingdom, the Shadows are pushed back into the center of town from all directions. Three of the towers are lit up as they are advancing to the last and final one. With the wind having died down, IC attempts to fly to the diamond tower. With not enough strength yet, she comes up short from her original target. She does, however, grab onto the ledge of a window five floors short of the top floor. Desperately, she tries pulling herself into the window as she clings to the wall. The flight takes more out of her than she thought it would, and she begins to lose her grasp, slowly sliding down the tower wall. Just as she is about to lose her grip completely, a small hand reaches out and grabs hers, pulling her up and back into the window.

IC falls to the floor and looks up to see who her savior is. Standing above her is her smiling sister, Mim. She yells, "Mim! You're alive!"

Mim replies, "You didn't think I'd leave my sister all alone to clean them stars by herself."

The sisters embrace in a hug only sisters can explain. Once the mini celebration is finished, IC says, "We've got to turn that fourth light on and finish this battle."

"Well, then, what are we waiting for? Let's go win a battle."

The two rush out the door and head up the stairs to the top floor. When they get there, they notice the door at the end of the hall is cracked open slightly. Mimic thinks it's a little strange since these doors have switches and locks on them. Cautiously, they approach the open door and peek in. The room looks empty, so they enter. This room seems to be the same setup as the last three, with a hole in the ceiling and a rope hanging down. They have the same problem as before. Even though there are two of them now, they are still not heavy enough to pull the rope. The two fly up into the hole to see if there is something around the light they can use. After finding nothing, they return down the hole to the main room, which seems much darker with door now closed. Mimic tries to push the door open but has no success.

Mim says, "Boy, are we in a pickle. We can't open the door or pull the rope."

IC replies, "And with no light, it makes it hard to see in here."

A different voice joins the conversation. "Kind of ironic, isn't it? You need light to turn on a light."

Another voice joins. "I think it's time for your lights to be put out permanently."

Both Mim and IC feel a large hand wrap around their bodies. Unable to move or see their captors, the two yell for help.

"Shut up, you two bugs, or we'll just end you now," one voice states.

The other voice says, "Now, now, brother, let's not be too hasty. Maybe these two bugs can be useful after all."

Now Mimic remembers where they had heard the voices. It is the Jokers. She tries reasoning. "Yes, we're willing to help. What can we possibly do for you two Jokers?"

Sin hits the switch to the light, revealing the four in the room.

Omin barks, "It's the little bugs who clean stars."

Sin smiles and explains, "Oh, they're more than just star cleaners; they're our ticket out of here. You see, the kings need them to add more cleaners for all the new stars. Someone must teach the new cleaners, and these little bugs are the last two originals. They're very essential to the kings. We'll make a deal. We walk out of here, and they go free from harm. If we don't walk out, neither do they."

IC interrupts. "If we don't turn on this light, then they'll send someone else to do it. That might not turn out so well for you. Just saying."

"You know what? The kings only need one of these bugs to teach the rest. So maybe we get rid of one," Omen threatens.

Sin agrees then stuffs Mim in his pocket and takes IC from his brother. "It's kind of like having a wishbone. You grab one wing, and I'll grab the other. We'll both pull, and whoever gets the bigger piece gets to make a wish."

Omen laughs. "Deal, let's count down from three then pull."

Sin begins. "Three, two..."

The door swings open, interrupting the count and revealing Dayne. The Jokers immediately drop to their knees and begin to beg for their lives.

Dayne points The Releaser at the Jokers and says, "Two clowns, remember when we first met? Well first, let's begin with this."

Dayne punches Omin in the gut, buckling him over. Then she points The Releaser between Sin's eyes and says, "Sin, nice to meet you again. Do you mind apologizing to my friends and pulling that light switch for me?"

Sin quickly mumbles an apology to Mimic and then pulls the rope down, turning the final light on. Furrow feels his energy rise as he regains full strength.

Dayne says, "Now, if you two don't mind, I have three gentlemen downstairs who can't wait to meet you."

Once the fourth light is restored, the Shadows know they lost the war and scatter, every shadow for themselves, into the Horizon.

CHAPTER 50

"All bad things must come to an end… Or do they?" - Jokers

Dayne exits the front door of the diamond tower with the two Jokers shackled behind her. Mim is on her left shoulder, and IC is on the right. Hunter is delighted to see Mim and smirks when she winks at him.

Dayne walks the Jokers over to Hoss and says, "Hey, big boy, can you keep an eye on these two for a minute?"

Hoss grabs each one around the waist and replies, "Sure thing, king." Hunter gives Omin an unseen jab in the ribs with his pool stick, making the Joker cough.

Dayne joins the other three kings in the center of the four towers.

Paragon says, "My kings, it's been a long time since we stood on our grounds."

Furrow adds, "My kings, let's not wait much longer."

Truncheon says, "The sun is almost upon us; we must not linger."

The three kings each approach their respective towers and stand on the crown etched on the front step. Dayne watches, not knowing what is about to happen.

Paragon says, "My king, I would like you to join us on your crown."

Dayne walks to the empty crown and stands on it. The kings raise their hands to the sky as Dayne follows their lead. The sun breaks over the background and everyone watches as the light races across the ground toward the kings. Dayne has no idea what is about to happen, and excitement fills her body.

When the sun reaches the etched crowns, they begin to fill up with light. Once filled, the kings burst into pure white light. Then as the pure light vanishes, it leaves the kings standing in beautiful robes of purple and teal fit for only kings.

Dayne feels enlightened—a feeling she has never felt before. She can see people's faces in the light orbs, and she can hear them speaking to one another.

Paragon says, "It is finished. The Horizon is now right again."

They all step off their crowns, as from out of the ground come thrones where the etched crowns once laid. Truncheon walks over to Dayne saying, "When night falls, the orbs will seek you out for judgment. Since you are the King of Hearts, you will only judge those who lost in love or could never find love. Those who gave up on love or loved too much."

Paragon adds, "I judge those who didn't do their fair share, the lazy or the ones who refused to work and were freeloaders."

Furrow says, "I judge a person's wealth. Not how much wealth they have, but how much of themselves they gave or provided. Whether it is with money, time or compassion."

Truncheon says, "And I judge those from conflict. Those who fought wars and gave themselves for the better of good. For those who stood up for the ones who couldn't; and for those who had a will stronger than any bully."

Furrow announces, "The kings have returned. May the Horizon be forever."

The kings turn to the angels and warriors who remain. Dayne approaches Hunter, Hoss, and Mimic with wide open arms, giving hugs to the group.

She turns to Hunter and says, "Hunter, your will and courage carried us to victory. You will forever be in our hearts.

Your lost friends will be told how much you've loved them."

Hunter bows his head in thanks. Then Dayne gives Hoss the biggest hug she can and speaks with tears in her eyes.

"Hoss, the man with a bigger heart than his body can hold. We thought we had lost you. Kannon told me one night that a big man would win you a war someday—not because of his size but because of his love for protecting people. He charges into danger for everyone who can't. Thank you. I would like to make you guardian of the Horizon."

Hoss smiles. "Aw, little lady, I mean *king*. I accept and will guard the Horizon with every ounce of my light. Kannon is a good man, and you and Dak should be proud to call him family. I know I am."

Dayne holds her hands out and Mim and IC each land in one and says, "My biggest little warriors. I owe my light to you. Tonight, when the moon has company, you will regain your place in the sky. But now you will be our sky generals and will command the new star cleaners. Also, you can come down once a week for some briefing and coffee with pastries." Mimic cheers, as now they will return to their purpose.

Danye turns to the Jokers as she lays judgment. "For the light releasing of Colt, Lakin, Skulk, Dillo, Bug, Cam, and my husband, Kannon, I sentence you for all eternity to the hole in which you placed the kings. No light, windows, or fresh air forever."

The Jokers begin to beg and cry for forgiveness. Sin tries reasoning with a whimpering voice, "My king, we were forced to do all the evil things. Torment and Torture were behind it all. We were scared for our lights. They released our sister right in front of us. You must believe us."

Dayne looks at Hoss. "Take them away, but first…" Dayne punches Sin in the mouth, knocking a tooth out. Then she smiles. "Oh, yeah, one more thing. I need a tattooist."

One of the angels steps out of the celebrating crowd. Dayne whispers in his ear, and the angel nods. Then the angel begins to write into Sin's and Omin's foreheads. When he finishes, the crowd begins to laugh at what has been written on the Jokers' foreheads.

Paragon shouts, "Spot on, Dayne. Spot on!"

Hoss carries the two Jokers off to their forever home, screaming and kicking.

While the celebration continues, Truncheon approaches Hunter and asks, "Since your name is Hunter, I was wondering if you'd like to live up to your name and go hunt down whatever Shadows are left."

Hunter smiles. "Is that an order, sir?"

Truncheon answers, "Yes, sir, it is."

"I was hoping so, sir." Hunter cocks his sticks and walks away.

Dak runs out of the woods and into the reborn kingdom. Out of breath, he explains, "Jim and Hangman took Spin Doll into one of the doors. We tried to stop them but failed."

Dayne hugs him and yells to Hunter, "Hunter, we need you!"

Hunter quickly runs back and asks, "My king, what is it?"

Dayne informs Hunter what has happened to Spin Doll. Hunter holds up the one key that he still possesses, which opens every door. He comforts the newly crowned king by saying, "I'll go through every door till I find her and bring her back. Can someone let the Hangman know that now he's being hunted?"

Paragon speaks up. "If you enter those doors, you may change the outcome of your warriors. But I'll leave you with this. When you find Jim and the Hangman, make them shine!"

Hunter smiles as he walks out of the kingdom.

Dak looks at Hoss and asks, "Well, now, looks like we need to hunt some Shadows."

Hoss smiles. "I thought you'd never ask."

As the two walk away, Hoss says, "Do you mind if I grab some food first and maybe a six-pack of Starletta's?"

Dayne turns toward the kings and smiles, and they look up in the air at all the light orbs. Dayne says, "Thank you, my warriors. In your world, you gave up the fight, but in this world, you brought the fight. If peace had found you sooner than later, you would have brought the beauty of the Horizon to your world. No matter your reason, please never give up the fight."

The crowd of angels erupts with cheers and praise. Dayne leaves the celebration and heads into her new home, the Castle of Hearts. She walks to the top floor and stares out over the entire kingdom. Not knowing how far the Horizon reaches, she speaks to its entirety.

"Love life, even if only for a fleeting minute. Finish your memories so you will last a lifetime."

Why?

A smile, a handshake, a simple gesture of hi,
May make a person realize they don't have to die.
A hug or hand up, jokes so funny you cry,
May make a person realize they don't have to die.
A reason for being, or a friend by their side,
May make a person realize they don't have to die.
An invite to dinner, or a nice country ride,
May make a person realize they don't have to die.
Supportive families and friends all our lives,
May make a person realize they don't have to die.
Yet still we sit and wonder, for just a reason why,
Our family, friends, and loved ones, felt they had to die.

J. L. Schaffer

Acknowledgements

Being my first book, I would like to share my gratitude to all the beautiful people in my life who supported my dream of writing a book.

Thank you to my beautiful family—Kaylynn, Jordan, Jake, Kadi, and Josh. The support and time you've allowed me to finish my book while holding down the fort is amazing.

Thank you to my grandson, Daxton, who makes seeing him every morning and telling him goodnight makes my whole world worth living as long as I possibly can.

Thank you to my mother, Diana, for understanding yet complaining that she never gets to read the book ahead of time.

Thank you to my Aunt Sandi, who proofread, typed, and pointed out my mistakes before sending them to the editors.

Thank you to my friends and family, who didn't know if I was messing with them or not about writing a book.

Thank you to my kids on Bus 8, who listened to all my ideas and supported them.

Thank you to Donna Beauchamp for helping me with a title by telling me my original one sucked.

My memorial page is the names of my family and friends who left us far too soon. They'll be missed every day. Memories crossed my mind the whole time it took me to write this book.

Even though it is a short time, they'll leave the biggest memories. My only regret is not telling them how much they'll be missed and loved.

In Memory...

Russell A. Lazarek
2-3-02 / 5-21-23
Nephew (21)
Russell is one of a kind. Always had a smile on his face and was always hungry. Loved his family, football, and having as much fun as he possibly could. My favorite memory is buying him the most ridiculous gift I could possibly find for Christmas. But nothing could embarrass him; he took everything in stride. Miss him every day.

Charles L. Forbes Jr.
5-14-38 / 8-3-64
Uncle (26)
Uncle Larry, as he was known to me by stories told, was a father and husband who came back from the service a different person. From listening to the stories, he would've made an awesome uncle. I wish I could've met him. Thank you for your service.

Jeff Forbes
8-13-71 / 6-25-17
Distant Cousin (45)
Jeff loved life. In passing, he'd always stop and say hi. We'd catch up in that short time and always suggest meeting up and hanging out. We never made time, and now it's something I truly regret.

Lori Czernecki
3-25-70 / 10-9-17
Distant Cousin (47)
Lori was fun-loving and happy every time we met. I mostly saw her at family reunions and here and there. She always wore a smile like she had just done something cool that most people wouldn't have the balls to do. She had two sons that couldn't be better people. Leaving so soon left a large footprint in our hearts.

Lawrence (Larry) Edward Dingle
4-14-69 / 4-13-2010
Friend/Softball teammate (41)
With his larger-than-life smile, Larry would make you happy just seeing him. Every time I take the field, I think of him being out in the outfield, picturing him catching the ball easily and running in with that huge smile on his face. The world might not know how great a guy he was, but I will never forget. Fly high, my friend. I know you're smiling down at us.
I've been lucky enough to meet so many good people before they left us too soon. Accidents, suicide, alcohol, drugs, mental illness have cost too many people the chance to finish their stories. They will be missed more than they'll ever know. Missing memories are all that we are given with no explanation. It's never too late to help someone—smile, say hi, or even give a small wave. Let them know they're not alone. Hug your friends and family every day, because we are not guaranteed a tomorrow.

***** Special Memory *****

Gordon and Kate Edwards

Thank you for having the front door always open and a place at the table ready. When you were at the farm, you were family. Your first steps inside that farmhouse, you'd hear, "Ahh, sit down and have a drink." "Are you hungry?"

(Fishhooks Forever)